'Cracking thril'er and a g at female protagonist. Swearing, smokin x-music loving (and not neurotic or passive)! My kind oman.' C.J. Tudor, author of *The Chalk Man*

'Totally engaging, fast-paced and edgy . . . completely captivating. *I, Witness* kept me guessing till the very end.'
Elle Croft, author of *The Guilty Wife*

'A humdinger of a thriller debut . . . a maze of lies, deceit and danger.' *Evening Standard*

'As addictive as *Killing Eve*.' *The Lady*

'Tough and uncompromising, *I, Witness* had me totally gripped. I'm looking forward to hearing more from PI Madison Attallee.'
Alex Lake, author of *Killing Kate*

'An absolutely gripping thriller founded on the horror of familial abuse and a great, flawed, female PI. There will be more from Madison Attallee, I hope.' Dame Jenni Murray

'Mackay builds tension to a fever pitch and throws in more twists than a corkscrew. Readers will look forward to Madison's next case.' *Publishers Weekly*

**Niki Mackay** studied Performing Arts at the BRIT School. It turned out she wasn't very good at acting, but quite liked writing scripts. She holds a BA (Hons) in English Literature and Drama, and won a full scholarship for her MA in Journalism.

**By Niki Mackay**

I, Witness
The Lies We Tell

# THE LIES WE TELL

## Niki Mackay

ORION

An Orion paperback

First published in Great Britain in 2019
by Orion Fiction,
This paperback edition published in 2019
by Orion Fiction,
an imprint of The Orion Publishing Group Ltd,
Carmelite House, 50 Victoria Embankment
London EC4Y 0DZ

An Hachette UK company

1 3 5 7 9 10 8 6 4 2

A CIP catalogue record for this book
is available from the British Library.

ISBN 9781409174653

Typeset by Input Data Services Ltd, Somerset

Printed and bound in Great Britain
by Clays Ltd, Elcograf S.p.A.

MIX
Paper from
responsible sources
FSC® C104740

www.orionbooks.co.uk

*To my mum and dad, Kathy and Tom – for being readers.*

# Prologue

## 1994

Everything is blurred. It is as if the world is uneven around the edges. When I try to stand, my legs are wobbly and I fall back down again, laughing to myself as I go. Ben hands me a thin joint and I inhale deeply, feeling it all over. I look at him, he looks even more wonderful than usual. I mumble, 'I love you,' and he says it back, squeezing me gently. I am too overwhelmed to dance. I settle for watching everyone else instead. They all look so beautiful. When Ben leans down and tells me he's going to get us water, I just nod.

Happy, unconcerned, high.

I don't know how much time passes, but he seems to have been gone for ages and I'm beginning to feel unsettled now. Anxious and jittery instead of buzzing and free. The music has changed from bouncy house to a darker, more frantic gabba tune. A distorted voice yells 'this is hell', and the strobe changes into heavily pulsating red and black.

I start to feel sick. I have another go at standing.

I lean against the wall for support, slipping and sliding. My heart is racing. He shouldn't have left me for so long. Underneath the drugs I feel annoyed. I get out into the designated 'chill-out zone' where a long chrome bar glistens and sparkles. My eyes get stuck seeing waves, seeing diamonds. I have to stop again, transfixed. I work on finding my balance, finding my feet – at least here the music is less hectic. The lights twinkle. Fat stars, beautiful and bright. My heart soars again. The dark corners and sharp edges of life recede for now. Held back for another time. I can feel my blood pumping. I take a deep breath in.

People are sitting huddled in groups at tables and in small circles on the floor. They are smoking spliffs and fags, drinking beer and champagne. I'm okay. I feel myself calming down.

Darren runs past, heading into the main arena and I grab his arm. 'Seen Ben?' my voice sounds funny, like it's bouncing off the walls and hurtling back towards me. A force with a physical presence. Then I wonder if I've spoken at all. Darren hasn't responded, he's looking over my shoulder. I try again, shouting louder. He frowns, shakes his head and shrugs, before racing off.

My heart picks up pace. Everyone looks less benevolent, a swarming mass of strangers. I stand still, take a few deep breaths and wander around trying to avoid bumping into people. Finally, I can make out the silhouette of his hair, shoulder length and curly, behind misty white glass. I feel a ball of excitement starting in my belly, working down. Ben.

I've found him. The relief is so palpable it fizzes up within me, forcing a laugh. Joy bursting out. I swing the door open, ready to throw myself into his arms, but he looks up at me, pale faced and ghastly. I'm still smiling until I look down. I see that he's holding Ruby in his arms and something is happening to her. Her limbs are moving, spasmodic and wrong. There is foam coming out of her mouth. I sober up quickly, shock slapping me hard, and I drop to my knees. I grab at her but it does nothing. Then I'm screaming at Ben to get help. Get help. But by the time the ambulance arrives it's too late. Everything is too late.

# 1.

# Miriam Jackson

## *Now*

I finish up at the station. There is a flurry of activity as I try and escape; the phone rings, emails ping in that need attention.

The door is finally in sight when my assistant, Anna, stops me, a big smile on her face. She's telling me about a new bar she's headed to tonight and follows me out to my car, nattering away. She lets out a low whistle and I frown at her, then she adds, 'Look at those shoes.' On the passenger seat of my car. Sparkly Jimmy Choos. Shoes that say, 'Fuck me.' I blush and mutter something about meeting a friend for drinks. 'What friend?' she asks, and I feel unreasonably annoyed, and shrug.

'You don't know them.'

She nods and says, 'Nick's in the States?'

'Yup.' I'm actually getting into my car now and still she goes on.

'No Tabs tonight?'

'She's having a sleepover at Delia's.'

She looks like she might speak again, so I slide myself in and buckle up, blowing a kiss, yelling, 'Bye, darling.' And I'm gone.

She can talk for England, Anna. She's a lovely girl and normally I'm partial to a little natter. But not tonight – tonight I'm in a rush.

A million thoughts press into my mind. Little wispy fragments that contradict each other. Questions, warnings. Unformed things I can't quite catch that I choose to ignore. The satnav tells me to take the next left and I'm startled by the voice. Then I laugh at myself. It's a machine. It doesn't know where I'm going. Or why.

A small inner voice says, 'Neither do you.'

I shush it – putting a lid on my guilt – and I'm there quicker than I thought I'd be.

I sit for a moment in my car. The shoes, sparkly and too high, glare at me from the passenger side. I have on the carefully chosen black dress that I wore to work. Plain and reasonable, but under it I'm all silk and lace.

I kick off my courts and slide on the heels, heart pounding, hands slightly damp. Nick bought me these shoes. For some reason I'd forgotten that. They were a gift from a beautiful store in LA. They cost more than I made in a month at the time. We'd been strolling through Beverley Hills on one of his rare breaks from filming, hand in hand. It was my first visit to America and I'd been star-struck for the entire trip. Gob-smacked at the hotel, the restaurants, the people. At him, and his ease within it.

Everywhere we went everyone knew him and they were keen to have his time. Phones didn't have cameras then, but some of the people did, and he'd stopped and smiled for photos. The man *behind* the camera, not the one in front. But to film buffs he was every bit as recognisable.

There had been lots of women. *They* knew who he was. Desperate blondes with suspiciously high breasts and hungry eyes. 'Nick,' they'd said, 'Nick Jackson.' Women at parties, women waiting tables, the concierge in the bloody hotel. 'I'm an actress, a model . . . a huge fan of your work.'

And I'd sulked. He'd laughed at me for it, taken me in his arms, squeezed me tight. He'd said he only had eyes for me, he only ever would. He'd bought me these shoes to cheer me up. I'd only had to glance at them through the window. Silly shoes, ones I could never have walked in. No one could. I'd worn them to dinner that night and then never again. They were shoes for standing still in. Or for getting all messed up in. They made my legs look never-ending and my arse look amazing. They still do. I checked in the mirror just this morning.

I'd believed him, that he only had eyes for me. And here we are almost twenty years later, and he's been as loyal as he promised. But still I'd pouted because it was a hard thing to have a man like him. *A catch*, my mother said with awe. And he was. He is.

Yet I am here. I blink. Once. Twice. *Send me a sign*, I tell the universe. *If I ought to just turn around and go, send me a sign.*

The door I'm parked in front of swings open. The light makes him just a silhouette. I watch as he steps forward. Now I see him, and our eyes meet. I am a teenager again, full of possibility and things I am yet to become.

I feel an ache between my legs. A shaking. I could still leave. The key is in the ignition.

He is watching. His gaze is still on me. Intense dark eyes. His face has changed, not much, but enough. I noticed it last week. When it was just coffee, nothing I needed to worry about. It still could be. His hair is slightly greying at the temples and not as long. But those eyes are just the same.

I step out of the car onto my ridiculous, glittery stilts and I walk to the door. He pulls me in, too quickly for me to register it or think.

The door shuts behind me and I turn around to say hi, but his lips are hard against mine before I have time. He presses me to the wall and the kisses become deeper, desperate. Mine match his. Everything mingles. Me, him, time. I think fleetingly about my careful plan, to unzip the dress and let it pool by my

5

feet. To step out delicately, at just the right angle for the big reveal. I feel a moment's sadness that I won't get to, and then I don't think at all.

## 2.

# Madison Attallee

It's yet another manic day at the office. After the Reynolds case last year we have been inundated. When Kate Reynolds asked me to clear her name I never thought it would happen. I was pretty certain she'd killed her best friend, though I didn't think she was mentally culpable. Turned out to be a lot more complicated, and I'm pleased to say she's free as a bird and has now received a full pardon. Thanks to me, and my assistant, Emma, of course.

We still get the old bread-and-butter spouse-cheating gigs, and that has recently extended to parents spying on teenagers. Another dubious line which I tread carefully. But, alongside this stuff, we finally have some more-meaty work. I've even been asked to consult on a few cases at the station. I suspect my old colleagues there all thought, as I did, that MA Investigations would be a disaster. Yet here we are, thriving.

Claudia has become a permanent member of our little team and it seems to have done her the world of good – and us. Initially she was going to temp for us after I tied up the case, one that led to her now ex-husband – Kate's brother – being convicted of perverting the course of justice, and Claudia's separation from him. She was meant to be here just long enough to get herself and her young daughter back on their feet. Not an easy thing to do after years of domestic violence. To say she has blossomed is an understatement. She has a law degree, a sharp mind and a way with people that I'll never have.

She's sitting in the outer office at her new desk next to my assistant, Emma. Both of them are tapping away at their keyboards and talking quietly. I tell them I'm nipping out on a pastry run and I walk over to Starbucks. It's not a boss's generosity so much as a way to pack in some nicotine. Both of them are nagging at me to quit. It's my own fault for announcing the date it was going to happen. That bloody date came around way too fast.

My phone rings. It's Peter. My heart jumps a little and I think – not for the first time – how ridiculous this is. I've known Peter my whole life, but us being a proper 'us' is all new. He's taken to calling me every day. Since I'm now queuing, I ignore it.

When I get back, Emma is still typing furiously and Claudia is filing. The radio is on. A talk show, currently discussing stay-at-home mums vs working mums. Claudia fires off that it's good for parents to have a life, Emma makes an agreeable muttering sound. I hand out pastries then head into my office and turn the radio on in here. I missed my daughter Molly's early years by immersing myself in work and she'll be twelve soon. I still don't know if there would have been any other way for me to have survived them, so I can't say I regret it. However, now that our time is limited I do wish I hadn't been quite so absent. My head slips into the dangerous territory of hindsight and I manoeuvre it away.

I listen to the radio over the next hour while I catch up on emails. It's distracting enough to keep my noisy fears away. Fears of failing, of not being good enough. I came closer to death than I care to think about just three short years ago, but I'm on the up again now. I cling to that thought and listen to the show. The presenter is very good. Miriam Jackson, she's a Kingston resident and it's a local station, so most of the town tunes in. I often catch her now as the girls tend to have it on in the office – Claudia likes to keep up an almost constant stream of chatter back to whoever is talking.

There is a clear divide in the callers today. Between the mums who work and the mums who don't. There are no calls from men, as though child rearing is none of their concern. Not for the first time I wonder if the world might be better for the sisterhood if we could just agree that we're not all the same. It ends with a particularly irate caller shouting about a study showing how children with working mums grow up to be almost criminally insane. I switch it off.

The day passes in companionable work mode. No dramas, and by the time five o' clock rolls around, I'm surprised and glad it's Friday. I'm looking forward to the weekend. After the others leave I stay behind for a while. I always do. I read through the day's news. I like to keep up to date with what's going on in the neighbourhood, not least to see if there's work I can poach.

The last 'job' the force gave me was surveillance. There had been a spate of burglaries in the local area. I spent five nights in a row prowling Kingston Hill until I *literally* caught the culprit red-handed. As Peter is always telling me, his team are stretched to the limit and while the budget isn't always there for overtime it often is for 'consultants'. It's probably not right, but it sure as hell suits me. Burglaries are one of those crimes people seem to see as almost victimless. Usually no one gets physically hurt, the occupants are out. But once you've sat with someone whose home has been violated, you get that it's far from victimless. The fear it engenders is real. Everyone needs somewhere safe.

I finish looking over the headlines, most of it shite.

I call Peter.

'Madison.'

'You rang?'

He laughs. I frown into the hand set. He says, 'Always nice to

9

hear from you too.' Boyfriend. I suppose Peter is my boyfriend now, which seems ridiculous and comforting all at once.

I find a smile twitching at the corners of my mouth despite myself. But I still snap, 'I can't see you tonight. I already said.'

He laughs again, 'Yes, I know that. I was calling to say have a lovely weekend and I'm looking forward to seeing you Monday evening.'

He's working Saturday and Sunday. Peter is a DI of the good variety, in that he often shows up for weekend shifts. It's generally the busiest time for the force but plenty of higher up officers ditch out, staying 'in contact' by phone or email. Having time off, effectively. It makes officers on the beat resentful since it's one of the downsides of the job. Peter's not like that, he's a good guy. He's always been a good guy; in the twenty-odd years I've known him I've not met a better one. I soften my voice and say, 'I'm looking forward to seeing you too.'

He says, 'If Sunday's not too hectic I'll pop in and say hi to you guys.' It's my weekend with my daughter, Molly. Thankfully she and Peter get on well, and she'll no doubt ask after him. I say, 'Okay, that would be nice.'

He says goodbye and I pack up for the evening.

I get in the car and turn up Metallica full blast. I arrive at the shitty church hall room ten minutes later. I make polite chit-chat with people that I've come to know and who have come to know me. Martin walks up and asks how giving up smoking is going. I scowl at him and the fucker laughs. Jane comes over and hugs me, despite the fact that I hate being touched and make my feelings pretty obvious. I feel myself stiffen as her arms encircle me. She squeezes before she lets go.

'You're looking well.'

I nod, still scowling, thinking a fourth fag on the way home probably would be nice. I'll start a fresh again tomorrow. That can be day one. I feel an overwhelming relief when proceedings begin. We go around the room and introduce ourselves and I feel my shoulders drop slightly as I hear myself say, 'Hi. My name's Madison and I'm an alcoholic.'

# 3.

# Miriam Jackson

Ben watches everything I do. I have often wondered over the years whether I'd fabricated that, making our romance into something more than it was. His devotion somehow greater. But it turns out I hadn't.

I've never erased him entirely from my mind or my heart, and occasionally I've wondered ... what if? What if I'd gone looking for him then? What if I was his wife instead of Nick's? I feel terrible even playing with the thought, but it would be a lie to say I don't think it. That I haven't thought about it on and off for many years. I have a great life, a better than average life. One that has taken commitment and dedication on my part. I am grateful, I am. But that little niggle has always been there in the background. That maybe something's missing. That I might have been a different person had I made different choices. It's what enabled me to say 'yes' to coffee when my path crossed Ben's two weeks ago. What made me turn up here last night. What is holding the guilt at bay – for now – and keeping thoughts of my husband and my daughter squashed.

What if this is who I was supposed to be all along?

He sits on a long, white sofa and pats at me to sit next to him. I do, still half in and half out of my dress. He pours a large glass of red wine from a bottle on the table and hands it to me. I take a sip. It's nice, expensive. Looking around his place I realise it must have cost a fortune, that Ben must be worth a pretty penny now.

A far cry from the boy from the council estate. He always said he was going places. He used to sell drugs, I know that. He always had bundles of cash wrapped in thick red elastic bands. I'd loved it, the excitement, the danger. Sticking two fingers up at my dad, not that he cared. I'm not certain what he does now. He'd said 'events' when I'd asked. They must be pretty large scale for all this. It doesn't matter. There's no point over-thinking any of this. I don't even know what *this* is – this new 'us' – and I don't know whether honesty is part of the deal. I can't think straight. Certainly not while I'm here.

He runs his fingers over my shoulder, making gentle circles, then he takes the glass from my hand and sips. He says, 'I'll run us a bath,' as I say, 'I should probably get home.'

'Why?'

'Well ...' I actually don't need to rush. Tabitha is sleeping over at Delia's, Nick is away as usual. But staying the night here seems somehow worse than having sex with him. He leans down and whispers close to my ear, 'Let me indulge you, just a little while longer.' And the thought of my empty house, just me and my guilt for company, feels like something I'm willing to put off.

I find I am self-conscious taking my clothes off in front of him. Ridiculous after what we've just done but I'm suddenly aware that the last time he saw me naked I was a teenager. Everything was in the right place and free of cellulite. He sees me trying to pull my dress off slowly, hidden. He frowns and says, 'Stop.' Then he unzips, unfastens, and peels everything away. He runs a hand up the side of my, now bare, body and says, 'You're as magnificent as I remember you to be.' And I suddenly feel emotional, which is ridiculous, isn't it?

Nick isn't a physical man. He's romantic in his own way, and he takes great care of me and Tabitha. But his eyes have never lingered like Ben's are now. Sex with Nick is infrequent – we barely see each other for starters, and the attention is normally on me, so I shouldn't complain, of course I shouldn't. But it's so good to feel the power of Ben's want. Nick is a focused, driven man, and compared to many of his peers, who are like demented rutting monkeys, he's an absolute sweetheart. Which just makes this worse.

I try and push the thoughts away as I sink into the deep tub. Ben has lit candles and brought the wine through. He slides in behind me, his hand rubbing my shoulders again. I lean back and forget about Nick.

I wake with a start. For a moment I have no idea where I am. The room is bare, white. Long curtains blow gently at a slightly open window. Not home. I roll over and my breath catches a little in my throat. For a moment I just stare at him. I am fifteen again, that whirling churn of emotions. I am worn down by my mum, missing my dad, but none of it matters because I'm lying here next to him.

He smells the same. Funny the things you don't forget. Though I've spent many hours reliving moments with Ben, I had never thought it likely that I would be here again.

My parents divorced when I was ten. No one would say it, but my dad had had an affair. With Wendy. My mother was devastated and sank into a deep depression, which terrified me. Initially I went to his house every other weekend. He paid maintenance on time with no complaints, and expensive school fees, but my mum – who already struggled with what I would later learn was depression – never got over it. Our house was dulled after he left in so many ways. All of her sadness, all of her need, was spilled onto me, and a child is no substitute for a partner.

When I was twelve Dad and Wendy decided to sell up and move to Spain. Even now I've not truly forgiven him. For leaving me, not once, but twice. For letting my mother down, for making her sadder and less than I'd thought she was. For leaving me to try and heal her. It was an overnight lesson that grown-ups were not infallible, that they could not be expected to cope but that I somehow had to.

To my dad I felt I became something to be paid for and inconveniently slotted in to his new life at designated, pre-arranged times. I was a leftover link to my mum, a woman who could suck you dry with her need. Her silent, teary recriminations. Even before he went to Spain, he never rang, he never came to a parents' evening.

I didn't stop loving him though, but I wished I had. I couldn't get over it, even if Mum bitterly said it was all for the best, fooling no one, least of all herself. He didn't seem to be the one who deserved happiness. I'd always thought he should have ended up miserable and alone. Punishment.

For the affair.

I feel tears tickling the back of my eyelids as the irony of who I've become hits me. I slide out of the bed and walk slowly through to the bathroom. My clothes are piled next to the tub and are slightly damp to touch. I put them on anyway. Splashing water on my face first, I look in the mirror and am surprised to see that I look the same.

I don't know what I expected. Horns and a forked tail? I wonder if this is how Dad felt after the first time. I wonder if it gets any easier.

I head downstairs and check my handbag. My phone. A message from Nick sent at about three a.m.:

*I'm sure you're asleep, darling. Sorry I haven't managed to contact you sooner. It's been manic here. Thinking of you. Speak this afternoon. Your time.*

That's today. Saturday. My stomach churns a little bit. It's nine a.m. That's late for me, ordinarily I don't sleep much past five. On the three days a week I'm on air, I have to be at the station by half seven, so I start early. When I'm not on air I still have things to do. I don't work weekends. I haven't since we had Tabs and I'm firm on it, even though the station pushed for me to keep my Saturday show. I'd been proud of the decision too. That my daughter came first. But since she hit thirteen she's been around less and less, and with Nick almost nearly always somewhere else, I've wondered if I ought to take up the show again. Especially since I know Anna is jostling for my position.

'Hey.' I almost jump. I hadn't heard him come downstairs. I smile at Ben, though I find I can't quite meet his eye. He's naked and stretches up, yawning. I try not to look. Suddenly embarrassed.

I look at my shoes instead, sitting on the floor, the light catching the glitter, and I feel a swell of self-hatred.

I pick them up, sling my bag over my shoulder. As I go to walk past Ben, he wraps me in his arms. I can smell his smell again. Familiar and nostalgic, lemony and fresh. I am suddenly aware of myself. Sweaty, damp, the smell of sex underneath it. I slept but fitfully, as though my mind knew instinctively that my body was somewhere it ought not to be, trying to take rest it didn't deserve. I swallow, and it feels like sucking chalk. My mouth dry, my heart pounding at the mess I've made.

I say, 'I need to get going.'

He releases me. 'Are you okay?'

I stare at him blankly for a moment. Then I force a smile. 'Fine. My daughter will be back soon is all.' She's not due back until this evening actually.

'Okay.'

He goes to kiss me at the door, and I push him away. 'I haven't brushed my teeth.'

'I don't care.'

And it's so sweet, and so soft, I feel as though my heart might break. He says, 'Call me?'

I nod, but as I walk, barefoot across his drive and slip into my car, I think that I won't. I'm not fifteen any more. I'm a grown woman. A grown, married woman with a child. I, of all people, know how much this would hurt her.

Even if she does seem hard and untouchable, she's much more sheltered than I ever was. A baby really. My baby.

# 4.

# Madison Attallee

Molly never stops talking. It's as though she has so much information to transmit at any given moment that even pausing for air might delay her. I love it, her incessant chatter. Maybe because I don't have to listen to it day in day out. I have Molly every other weekend and over some school holidays. Court designated. That's it. It's not how I saw our lives together panning out but it's the way it is. I accept it now. Mostly. I'm currently getting the lowdown on leggings versus jeggings. Jeggings apparently are a horrifying combination of leggings and jeans. They look great on eleven-year-old Molly but I'm pretty appalled to find out they make them for grown-ups too, and she's suggesting a blue pair for me. I have a horrifying image of myself in them. Since I've been trying to quit smoking I've packed on a few extra pounds. Not loads, but enough to make me think of someone trying to squeeze toothpaste back into a tube. I'll spare everyone that.

I try not to dwell on the fact that I'm still bloody smoking and am likely on my way to being fat as well. Progress not perfection. Fuck it, I'm sure Molly and I can find other outfits to match.

It's been a long, hard year. For us both. She'd never say it, but I know she misses me and that she's had to adjust to a lot of changes. Her father is engaged. To his doting, idiotic PA. That fool loves a stereotype. I'd say I'm dealing with it well and on the outside, I am. Which is what matters most. Molly chatters away about dim and doting Janet and I manage to smile and not make snidey comments. I haven't hunted her down and caused a scene. Most importantly I haven't got drunk to make the uncomfortable feelings disappear. I've been sober two and a half years. I work hard at it. Life is improving. Slowly but surely.

We're making milkshakes. Molly wants one for the car journey. I hate the thought of sticky, stinky milk being spilled in my beautiful, flashy car but it's outweighed by Molly's only fortnightly presence. I spoil her on my weekends. I need to keep an eye on it. I have it in my head that at thirteen or so, she'll make the choice herself and come and live with me. I may be making a rod for my own back here. Either way. Today it's milkshakes. I put hers in a portable coffee cup. And keep looking over as we drive off.

'I'm not gonna, like, spill it, Mum!'

I smile and try to look relaxed as though it hadn't crossed my mind. She only started calling me mum again in the past twelve months. She calls Janet, Janet. I can't begin to express the relief I get from this.

We are going to see *my* mother today. A woman even more useless than I. I had always kept her and Molly separate. Something Rob, Molly's dad, and I agreed was best from an early age. But then an emergency came up on one of Molly's weekends and I was forced to take her. Amazingly, they took to one another straight away.

My mother is an ill woman. An alcoholic with years of practice behind her. She is generally unpleasant, belligerent and self-centred. I have memories of her being another way, but they are from long ago. My main aim when I grew up was to not be her. Unfortunately, that's not what came to pass. I left my daughter to make her own breakfast while I nipped around to the shop for vodka.

I passed out on my way home. I came to under flashing blue lights, and with the realisation that I had indeed become my mother. On the outside, my life looked better for sure. Successful career, husband at home. Money in the bank, house, car. None of these things were enough. I still wanted that drink more than I wanted Molly. That's the truth. I'm not proud of it. It's not how I set out to be. But it became my reality.

My childhood was tortured. I hope Molly's isn't so bad, though admittedly it's had its moments. I am watching her now, slyly, as we drive. She is singing along to whatever godawful pop shit is on the radio and I am overwhelmed. And grateful. I try to keep these feelings for when I'm with my mum and she's driving me mad. I try and think that maybe, just maybe, this is how it was for her once. Before the bottle took it all.

When we arrive, I let myself in. She's on the sofa, smoking. Her flat is cleaner than it used to be – there was a time I tried to tidy it, but it was too much and a lot of what I found felt like an invasion of privacy. I have someone sent in twice a week now. I empty a towering ashtray. Inhaling the putrid odour as I do, and still somehow wanting a fag. She's got one in her hand, and with no respect for current thinking, smothers Molly with smoky kisses. Molly takes the frail little woman in her arms and sits right up next to her. The chatter continues and my mum smiles at me over her head. I smile back. I feel something close to happiness and hope I'm not going to burst into tears.

Crying is my latest thing. Something I have been largely incapable of in previous years. Even in early sobriety. Even at the loss of my daughter, the tears never came. These days they often flow. Over fuck all, the little things, the big things. My mother, Charlotte Attallee, who I've spent years hating, smiling at me over the head of the daughter I often didn't want.

20

Shit changes. If you let it.

I put the kettle on, Molly's still drinking her milkshake, but I make tea for mum and me. When I give her a cup, her hand shakes madly and I get there a second too late. She looks up with shock. Molly shrugs, luckily not scalded by the boiling drink, which is what Mum must be thinking too. The liquid is in a puddle on the floor; Molly heads in to the kitchen for clean-up materials.

It is then that I realise Mum hasn't had a drink yet, that she's been waiting for her granddaughter. My heart is hammering and a glimmer of something fresh comes into my heart. Hope. She looks so little and forlorn, her offending hand now tucked neatly under her leg. I want to hug her – there are a hundred things I want to say, but I don't. It's her life. I remind myself that I can show up in it, but I can't fix it. No matter how painful that is. Molly mops up so badly I re-do the job. She's still talking as she swings in and out of the kitchen.

I don't think Molly is oblivious to my mum's problems. She knows that her nan is not well, she just doesn't care why so much. There is something about the two of them. Something I'm not included in. I busy myself in the kitchen and clean another overflowing ashtray, take out some rubbish.

Molly goes to the toilet and I sit next to my mother.

'You haven't had a drink today?'

She shakes her head, looking almost cross.

'Well done, Mum.'

'I'll have one when you go.' I can hear the same defiance in her voice that I feel in my own heart. I nod and risk it – I lean in and hug her. She stiffens for a moment, and then her hand reaches up and pats my arm. I can't remember the last time we did this.

We don't stay for much longer, but I feel better about her than I have for a long time.

That night is pretty average, the kind of night other parents probably have all the time with their children, nights I've missed and for which I am now so grateful. Peter texts to say he's been called out and won't be able to ring. I say no problem. We get pizza, watch some crap on TV. Molly likes all the reality shows, *X Factor* and *The Voice* being the main ones. She sings along tunelessly and dances around the living room. She's all arms and legs. That borderline between childhood and young adulthood. She hasn't crossed it yet, but she will soon. The years have gone fast. People say they do, and yet I remember the early days, weeks, months of her life. They felt like a lifetime. Each twenty-four-hour period being the longest one I'd ever lived through. This twenty-four hours has flown by. Every other weekend always does.

# 5.

# Miriam Jackson

When I get inside my house, the first thing I do is rush upstairs and check her room, just in case. She's not here, and I'm not expecting her, but I have that heart-hammering feeling that I might get caught at any moment.

I look in at the jumble that is her bedroom. Clothes everywhere, photos from her polaroid littering the floor. 'Retro' she and Delia call it, and they love it. What do you buy a girl who has everything? That's all I'd thought on her birthday last month. I'd remembered my own polaroid. The fact that I still had a bundle of photos from it, hidden in a small wooden box in my knicker drawer. Nick had scoffed, 'She's got an iPhone for goodness' sake. Why on earth would she want a camera?'

But she'd been delighted. I'd felt a small and petty victory that I had won for once and had turned to him to be triumphant but he had been grinning at the pleasure on her face every bit as much as I had, and my heart had softened. She'd been lovely that day, that whole weekend. Polite, even-tempered. How she always is when Nick is home. Sometimes I feel she pushes the boundaries with me in a way she wouldn't with him. Things are always so much better when we are all together. As a family.

I put those thoughts aside now as I strip off my clothes, ball them up and shove them into the laundry basket. I stand under the shower, letting scalding hot water pummel my skin, and I scrub. By the time I get out I am so on edge I feel like I'm trying to digest barbed wire. All of the justifications for my actions that my mind conjured up seem paper thin. I am heavy with the night before, and I realise I'm not going to be able to do this. Not a proper affair. Even if it means I have to break Ben's heart all over again. That's better than breaking Nick's or Tabitha's.

I think, for a moment, about calling my mum, but I know I won't. What would I say? 'Hey Mum, guess what, I'm as much of an arsehole as Dad – guess it's genetic, right?'

I won't tell Mum, I won't tell anyone.

No. Sharing this burden would give me more relief than I deserve. I pick up my laundry basket and take it downstairs. The cat is meowing and I realise he must be hungry. I left a pile of dried food yesterday, but knowing Mr Boots he probably wolfed it down and is starving.

I feed him, then go back into Tabitha's room and start sorting out her clothes. I put on load after load, then I start to stack things from her floor into piles. I wipe surfaces, I change her bedding, run a hoover around. I feel slightly better by the time I'm finished and am surprised to see that hours have passed and it's two o'clock. My phone rings. It's the station.

'Hi.'

'I'm so sorry to call you on your day off.'

'It's okay, Anna, what's up?'

'Um . . . you double booked. I've been trying to deal with it.' It takes me a minute to catch up with her. Today's guests. I try and think who is in, it's interview day. We book local celebs, usually b-list who have something to peddle, a new show, a book. It's an easy slot, un-demanding. Anna takes care of these shows now, but I put everything in place.

'Today was supposed to be Martine Joyce?' A local soap actress.

'Yes, that's what I thought but we've also got an Eileen Baxter here.' Another soap actress. Bad form, and horrible for Anna to have to deal with.

I try and get my brain into action, shocked that I could have done this. I say, 'Okay, run with Martine and tell Eileen I'm on my way.' I quickly make up my face and switch from jeans and jumper to black trousers and a loose red silk blouse. I've been so distracted this past week. I know why, of course I do. But this is a huge mistake to make.

I find I'm shaking as I step out of the car at work. Professional. That's how people think of me, and it's something I've earned. Things like this will damage my reputation. My head is racing – the more I think about it, the more I'm certain Eileen was in the diary for next week.

When I get there Anna is standing outside the studio waiting for me. I say, 'How bad is it?'

She tells me, 'They've both shouted a fair bit. Eileen has threatened to speak to her agent.'

God. I say to Anna, 'I was sure I said Eileen next week?'

She shrugs. 'In your text you said today, I can show you if you like?' She gets out her phone and starts scrolling but I brush her off. I can't remember exactly. My mind has been caught up with Ben, all consuming. Not focused on work like I would usually be.

Poor Anna, having to pick up the pieces. I touch her arm lightly. 'Don't worry.' And I smile, letting her know it's okay.

I plaster a shit-eating grin onto my face, take a deep breath and go into the green room. 'Eileen, darling, so lovely to see you and you look wonderful.' This isn't entirely true, she looks odd as a lot of the women 'in the biz' tend to these days, those past forty at any rate, and I'd say that day was long gone for Eileen. Her face is suspiciously devoid of movement. It's the latest thing, of course, and commonplace now. I do wonder, especially for the actresses who need expression, whether a few wrinkles would be preferable. Most of them are natural beauties who would have aged well anyway. Not that I don't understand it, that pressure.

She is huffy and irritated, but I talk her down. I also put out the offer of a better slot on one of my shows rather than Anna's (it's no secret that I'm preferred), and then I dangle the possibility of a dinner invite at mine. I am not the lure here though, Nick is. He won't consider it, an ageing soap actress isn't even on his radar for work, but Eileen doesn't know this and goes away suitably placated.

I feel a pressure at the back of my eyes, pushing forward. I close them and am assaulted by images of Ben, naked – I'm sure I can almost smell him.

'Miriam, everything okay?'

Jesus. I stare at Anna, uncomfortable with Ben in my head and her right there. I rub my hand across my brow. She squints, tilts her head. 'Migraine?'

I nod.

'I'll get you some pills.'

'And a coffee.'

My phone pings: Nick asking if it's a good time to call. It must be late there. I say no, I've had to come into the station and it'll have to be tomorrow. He sends a sad face and 'I love you'. That chalky feeling is back in my throat, the headache pushing at my eyes.

But there is relief too that I don't have to hear his voice. That he doesn't have to hear mine, laced with betrayal.

Anna is back. I gratefully reach for my coffee, it's scalding, and vile like everything from the bloody vending machine. I say, 'Thanks.'

Anna did some running for a British film that Nick made some years ago now. She'd been fourteen and won the 'prize'

26

of work experience at his studios over the summer. She went on to take a media and drama degree at Kingston University, and she'd emailed Nick asking if he had any work. I'd been in a bit of a flap at the station, trying very hard to stay on top of everything and manage Tabitha's diary as well. Our Saturday host had left at the worst possible time. Tabitha had been twelve then. I'd always thought it would get easier when they got older, but she got busy. It was all drop-offs and pick-ups and netball practice.

One night, at an events dinner of all places, I'd had a few too many and complained to a colleague of Nick's about how much he was away, how my career seemed not to matter, how I was struggling to manage Tabitha and all of her drop-offs. The colleague, of course, had reported back to Nick and he'd been fuming. After a rare, and particularly bitter, argument between us, I was honest about how often he was away and how hard I was finding it to cope. He'd pointed out that his work was what afforded our lifestyle. I couldn't argue, though I'd wanted to. It wasn't his career that bought our lifestyle. Not really. Nick was born rich. There's never going to be a day when he can't make ends meet.

To him though, his work is what defines him. I love my career and I'm proud of what I've achieved but I've never been under the illusion that his didn't take precedence. I knew it when we started out and it wasn't going to change now. He'd suggested a nanny and I almost lost it. We had one when Tabitha was small, and I'd hated it. He'd suggested an assistant then, at work, someone to take over some of the more administrative stuff, to train for the Saturday shows, and I had agreed it wasn't an awful idea.

The station hadn't had the budget for it then though. Luckily for me, Nick isn't the kind of man to leave a problem unsolved. Even the problem of an overstressed wife, and a radio station struggling to keep up when adverts on the internet were practically free. He mentioned an old runner of his who was looking for a foot in somewhere.

Initially, he set Anna up as his employee, but 'lent' her out to the station as a trainee.

From that seed was born a charitable trust for getting people into media who can't afford to work for free. He now runs a series of traineeships within various media groups. Not just us, but a couple of fashion mags in London, a few more running gigs on his production team, and others, all now paid. It's a 'social enterprise' that's done his reputation no harm either. All via his production company.

So, Anna came in for a few hours a week while she studied and when she'd finished, the station had been able to take her on full-time. This past year of having her as my right-hand woman has meant my transitioning out of needing to manage absolutely everything. I've never been able to trust anyone else here to approach my work with complete competence, but Anna is bright, and hungry for it.

She's very good, terribly ambitious, and although we've become friendly, I'm sure she has her eye firmly set on my job.

And one day I'll be happy to let her take it – but not today. I might not be a film director and of the magnitude of Nick, but I'm a big deal here and I need it, especially on the days my daughter is stropping, and my husband is absent.

I rub at my poor aching head and thank Anna for keeping everyone calm. I say, 'Send Eileen some flowers and a spa voucher. Okay?'

Anna nods. She doesn't look much older than Tabitha some days.

I say, 'Thanks for the tablets.'

She smiles. 'Sorry you had to come in at the weekend.'

I shrug. 'It's my own fault, isn't it?'

'I should have looked more closely at the diary.'

'You do a great job here, and I was only cleaning Tabitha's room.'

Anna says, 'Lucky her.' Then she asks, 'Oh, how were drinks last night, did your shoes hold up?'

I stare blankly and then manage, 'Fine, thanks. Anyway, you're on air in less than five, and I ought to get back, she'll be home soon . . .'

Anna smiles brightly, 'Of course.'

I get home and switch back into my jeans and jumper. Half five – I'd been expecting Tabitha by now. I ring her phone and it goes straight to voicemail. I bet she's forgotten her charger. I sigh. Then decide I'll make macaroni cheese for when she gets in, that we'll have a girly night.

I'll speak to Ben in the week, explain how it is, no matter what, and I'll get on with my life.

The life I've chosen.

# 6.

# Ruby Williams

## *1994*

My door hammers. Again. I roll my eyes seconds before my mum pokes her head around and yells, 'Bloody well turn it down.'

I grin and say, 'Sorry, Mum.'

She frowns again, but I can see her trying not to laugh. It's always been this way with us. It's how I 'get away with fucking murder', according to Eric. Thing is, Mum knows she ought to tell me off, but she often finds the same things funny. She had me at fifteen, so sometimes we're more like sisters.

Eric will likely smash my bloody stereo to bits if he gets in and it's blasting though, so I *do* turn it down, still singing along to the Prodigy. When I grow up I'll marry some fella like one of them. A man who can dance like Keith. With a bit of attitude and a skill for beats.

Mum says that's fine, but just don't be having any little chivvies too young.

It's not that she regrets having me, but she reckons I've got a brighter future than she did. I'm singing along full blast now – I've got a good voice. Mum says I get it from my dad – he was a musician. She tells me he was a useless lump of a man, but he could play any instrument he picked up. That's where I get it from, music. As Mum's always saying, great voice and

30

good looks. I can rule the world, she says. She doesn't even mind when I bunk school and stuff, as long as the social aren't knocking on the door.

I don't need that sort of book learning. I'm going to be a singer. And Mum's right, kids can come later, once I've made my name and bagged me a star all of my own.

Mum yells up that she's nipping out. I holler back, that's fine. I wait until I hear the door slam then I switch the music up again. I open up a large blue rizla, sprinkle a fag in, and then a load of weed. I push down the roach, roll, lick and light. The music sounds even better after a few puffs and I'm well away when there's another knock at the door.

Crap, I didn't hear her come back in. It might be the smell. Mum and Eric both smoke, mind – it's their bloody puff I'm on, so they can't be having a go at me, surely. I lower the volume and yell, 'I turned it down yeah.'

A head pokes around the door and a deep voice says, 'Hi to you too.'

My step-brother Ben. I grin. 'What you doing here?'

He shrugs. 'Got some business on the estate to sort out, thought I may as well pop in and see you at the same time. I saw Donna leave, figured he won't be home for a while yet.'

I nod. Ben's banned from here. I'm not one hundred per cent sure why. He and Eric don't get along and I'm under strict instruction to stay away from him. Which is stupid. I like Ben and I love seeing him out and about around the estate and that. He's become a bit of a face, and I know my mates are impressed when I say hello to him.

Ben sniffs. 'Who do you buy that shit off?'

I blush, and he pushes. 'Come on, fess up.'

'Found it in their room.' I lean my head to indicate Mum and Eric.

Ben laughs at that. He sits down on the bed next to me and

31

I go to hand him the joint. He says, 'No thanks.'

I roll my eyes at him and he looks at me seriously. 'I told you, I'm going places. I'm not going to be sitting on my backside smoking that shit all day long like my da.'

I shrug, but honestly, I do feel a bit defensive. Not just of myself, but Mum and Eric too. He might be a bit of a dick sometimes, and he gives me the odd wallop when I step out of line, but he brings home a wedge and he's the first man Mum ever had that did that.

Ben tolerates his dad, but he's always saying he's a wasteman. It's odd because his mum, Reeva, walked out when Ben was only five. But he proper loves her still, says she's a go-getter. He's older and knows more than me for definite, but Eric's a lot better than my old man ever was, and most others too. How many men would keep a kid without a woman around to help out?

I don't say that though.

# 7.

# Miriam Jackson

Six thirty. I've made the sauce, softened the pasta and added a load of garlic. I finish it with a layer of cheese and leave it on top of the oven. It's not going to take long to cook. I'll put it in as soon as she gets home.

I try her mobile again. Still switched off. I feel a wave of irritation and go through mine. I find her best friend Delia's number and use the landline.

I make my voice breezy. Light. 'Hi, Delia.'

'Hi, Mrs Jackson.'

'How are you?'

'I'm fine, thanks.'

Then an awkward pause. 'Can I speak to Tabitha?'

'She's not here.'

My heart skips a momentary beat, 'Oh good, is she on her way home? I was expecting her about an hour ago.'

A pause. 'She left here this morning. About ten?'

Ten. When I was arriving home, in sticky knickers, messed-up clothes and hooker's shoes.

I say, 'Her phone's off.'

Delia manages, 'Oh.'

I swallow thickly, a little red panic alarm is lighting in the back of my mind. I try and quell it. 'Can I speak to your mum?'

It's not that I think she's lying, but I have to check.

Sue comes on the line. 'Miriam, hi, Delia says Tabitha's not back yet?'

'No. Haha.' It's not a laugh, but some sort of cheap imitation of one.

'She left here early, about ten, I think. She got a call, I'd assumed it was you.'

So she did have her phone.

I force another chuckle, 'She must have got waylaid, or forgotten her charger.'

Sue says, 'I guess.' But doesn't sound convinced.

I suddenly mumble, 'Brett, maybe she's with Brett.'

'Ah yes,' I hear relief in Sue's voice that matches the feeling in me. Her boyfriend. Of course.

She and Brett have been soft on each other since junior school. I have actually seen a little less of him recently, but then Tabitha's been out far more than I'd have liked this past year. I've complained to her many times that she practically lives there. Not over night, of course, but most days after school. That's likely where she'll be.

He picks up on the first ring, his happy voice saying, 'Tabs,' and I wonder why he's calling me that, then realise I'm on the landline.

I say, 'It's Miriam, sorry, she's not with you then?'

His voice seems to deflate as he says, 'No.'

'Okay. Have you seen her?'

'Not lately.'

'If she contacts you, will you let me know?'

He sighs. 'She won't – we broke up.'

I don't know what to say to that.

I manage, 'When?'

He sighs. 'Months ago.' I should have known this, why didn't I know? It injects a new dose into what is now a building panic.

34

They broke up, that's a big deal. She hadn't told me, she hasn't been at his house when she said she was. She left Delia's at ten. She's still not home. I catch myself short of bursting into tears. I mumble sorry as he sounds so forlorn, and then say goodbye. I hang up and feel it work its way through me.

Fear.

My sixteen-year-old daughter hasn't come home. The evening is creeping into night-time. She has been keeping things from me. The dread percolates in my bowels, tugging at the sides. Adrenaline fires through my blood. I stand and go to the window, twitching at the curtains, looking out. I check my phone to see how long has passed since I spoke to Brett. Two measly minutes. It feels like hours. I wander across my kitchen and get a glass. I fill it with water from my fridge door and drink. My mouth is dry, like I've been eating sand.

Children. They come along and add another layer to your life in so many ways. If they are not okay, neither are you. How can you be? I take a deep breath, try and calm my nerves.

I think about calling Nick, but I know I won't. He's too far away to do anything. That's what I tell myself. But there's also that little nagging voice that is my conscience – I've messed up. With the most precious of precious things. Tabitha. And look where I was, this morning. The last time anyone saw her.

Last year she stayed out overnight. Just disappeared. She'd been out with Delia and Brett and hadn't come home. I'd been so terrified I called the police. Then she'd turned up at Delia's the following morning, reprimanding me for making a fuss. Claimed she'd bumped into some girls from school, gone back to one of their houses, forgotten to ring.

The story was leaked and it made the front pages. 'Nick and Miriam Jackson's wayward daughter', a picture of her outside the club. Our reputations were tarnished. We are wholesome, respectable. I didn't care. I was just glad that she was home. Nick had been furious at me for causing a scene, and at her, too – God he'd been mad at her. Drinking in public, out hours after her curfew and in a skirt that could have been a belt. She'd been sullen and rude on the phone to me. But her attitude changed when Nick went to collect her. Once she saw that she had gone too far, she'd cried real tears and promised to never do it again.

This doesn't feel the same though. She left Delia's, she's not with Brett. She broke up with Brett. But still. I won't worry Nick with it. Not until I have to, and hopefully by then she'll be home.

I've never felt worthy of my husband. That's the truth. We've been married for almost eighteen years and still I feel less than him. As though at any minute he will realise the terrible mistake he made in choosing me.

I studied Journalism at university, starting my degree at nineteen instead of eighteen. I was fifteen, younger than Tabs, when I'd had a sort of nervous breakdown and been sent to my dad's in Spain to 'recuperate'. That was after him. After Ben.

I'm sure it all but destroyed my poor mother – already in the tight grip of depression – all that trouble with her daughter and after what had happened with Dad. It was more than she could manage. It was my fault. Tears prick at the backs of my eyes just thinking about it.

I came back and resat exams I'd missed, but I could feel the weight of her sadness. I knew I'd let her down. I'd been selfish when I met Ben for the first time. I'd wanted something and just gone for it.

Selfish . . . I think about last night and push it from my mind.

Back then, I'd started A Levels, cut myself off from all reminders of what had been before, and I'd soldiered on. At my mother's insistence I attended the local university and stayed with her while I studied. I graduated with first class honours.

I'd met Nick during my apprenticeship on the local paper at the end of my second year. I knew he lived in Kingston and I'd received word that he was opening a restaurant in town. An interview with him would be a fabulous feather in my cap and I was desperate to progress. To make my mum feel that she hadn't wasted her entire life bringing up a failure. To make her smile again.

The throng of people trying to get near him had been ridiculous and there were reporters from the big boys there with far better methods than me. But he'd refused to comment anyway, posing for a few photos, which I'd snapped from the back of the crowd. The restaurant had shut its doors. The one thing I'd had going in my favour was that I'd eaten here before and knew that the kitchens opened onto a small alley.

While everyone else hovered out the front, I'd waited there and, sure enough, Nick Jackson, director, and handsome, accomplished man – and he was a man, well into his thirties by then – had eventually come out. I'd pounced with no game plan but armed with a pen and paper. He'd looked at me openmouthed when I asked for an interview and, at first, I'd thought he might flee back inside, perhaps have me escorted away. But he'd thrown back his head and laughed instead.

I'd got my interview and I'd also been swept off my feet. I was so in awe of him. So enthralled by his stories, his life, his family. He was polite, kind, interested. When he had asked me questions about myself, though, I'd been ashamed to tell him about my family. I'd just said Mum and I got along well, with it being just the two of us, and that my dad lived abroad. He'd said that must have been hard. I'd shrugged, breezy – that's how I had decided to be for Nick, for life. The opposite to Mum. I'd smiled, shrugged and said it was fine. He'd either bought it or been too polite to press.

When Nick had asked me back then if I'd ever been in love

before I lied and said, 'No.' I hadn't wanted him to know. About Ben, a kid from the local council estate. I didn't want him to know I'd practically lived with another man, or that I'd taken drugs. I'd sensed these things might be deal breakers for Nick. He'd grinned that beautiful grin at me and said it was probably time that changed.

My mother still shares her surprise that such a man would have any interest in me, when he could have had his pick. While I resent her for saying it – she's a woman who happily accepted that life would batter her, that she was undeserving of success and happiness, and therefore so was I – I secretly agree.

The only time I have felt almost worthy was the day Tabitha was born. My perfect, beautiful daughter. I'd laboured for eight hours, appalled at the agony my body could withstand and still survive. Then the magic had happened. The moment I'd held her, the pain seemed to fade away. Nick had sat by my side, tears in his eyes. He said I'd made him the happiest man on earth. I'd believed him because, looking down at that bundle, knowing it was his, mine, ours, it was impossible not to be happy.

And now she's missing.

I sit at my kitchen table. I don't know what to do next. My mobile rings and I scramble for it.

'Hey, hey, beautiful.' And I shut my eyes. Feeling annoyed at myself for the jolt of inappropriate pleasure the sound of his voice brings. It's not just the usual glint of guilt this time either, it's layered with worry for my daughter. I say, 'Ben, can I call you back?'

He reads something in my voice and says, 'What's the matter?'

I laugh though it doesn't sound jolly, even to me. 'It's, um, my daughter.' I cringe a bit at the fact that I can't speak her name to him. The odd ways I have of trying to keep this new aspect of my life separate from my real one. 'She's late home is all.'

He laughs, and says, 'Teenagers, eh? Like mother like daughter.' And I cringe a bit more thinking about *my* teenage years, and how heavily he featured in them. I agree and say I'll text when she gets home. I hang up and feel the same way I always do when I speak to Ben. Absolutely wretched and excited in equal measure.

I bumped into him, two weeks ago now, in Kingston. Literally. I'd been walking head down, reading a text on my phone and I'd felt something slam into me. I'd almost fallen, and my phone had dropped. A voice had said sorry. My heart felt as though it had stopped the second I heard it – a ghost from twenty years ago – and when I'd looked up I'd felt exactly like that girl again. Ben. My first love.

I had tried hard not to make comparisons between Nick and Ben. The only two men I had been in relationships with. But I couldn't always help it. And certainly, since Ben has re-appeared it's all my brain has done. Picking away at my marriage. My husband. I felt annoyed he wasn't home more, wasn't more passionate. I shouldn't mind. It wasn't abnormal for partners' sex drives to differ. And over the years I'd told myself I *didn't* mind. But I had always missed that feeling Ben gave me. Of being wanted.

I shouldn't have given him my number. I knew it at the time. Last night shouldn't have happened, and I certainly shouldn't be speaking to him now.

My phone beeps and I scramble to pick it up. Nick. A WhatsApp. 'Okay, it's the middle of the night here, or early in the morning! I've lost track. I must try and sleep. Missing you both. Speak tomorrow.' I had been hoping it was Tabitha.

Another call. Delia. 'Dee, is she there?'

'Miriam, it's Sue, I'm on Delia's phone. She's not back then?'

'No.' I look at the clock. Eight p.m. Ten hours since she's last been seen. Dinner is congealing on the side. A gloopy mess promising comfort and togetherness, mocking me.

'Delia tried a few of the other girls but no one's seen her, I thought I ought to let you know.'

I manage, 'Thanks, that's very kind of you.'

'To be honest we were quite surprised to see her last night.'

I frown. 'But it was arranged ages ago.'

'Yes, I know, and I was glad she was feeling better.'

'Better from what?'

'Her chest infection.'

I frown. 'What?'

Sue pauses, then says something to Delia, her hand must be over the receiver. Then she's back, 'Yes, that's what Delia said, it's why she's been off school.'

'Off school?' The fear is working up again, getting worse, which I hadn't realised was possible. I wonder how many more levels of panic there are. 'What days?'

She asks Delia.

'Since Wednesday. Sorry, Miriam, didn't you know?'

I go for another laugh, but I don't have the heart. Sue makes me promise to call if I need anything. I say I will and ring off.

Tabitha hadn't been at school Wednesday, Thursday or Friday and yet . . . I'd seen her, in her uniform, at home, lying about her day without even a tremor.

I try her again. Voicemail.

My hand is shaking as I dial 999.

# 8.

# Ruby Williams

## *1994*

Ben works a lot of rave nights and I've been on at him to let me sing at one. Another thing everyone says I'm too young for. I'm nagging at him now, he's rolling his eyes, but I'm making him laugh.

He says, 'Eric and Donna aren't going to let you come out raving with me, are they?'

I sigh, 'We don't have to tell them.'

He's thinking about it. I can see him weighing it up. He'd be hard pushed to find anyone with a voice as good as mine and I say so. He laughs and I think maybe I'm getting him on side. I'm fantasising about standing by a DJ next to a set of decks, singing my heart out. I'm also thinking about bragging about it to everyone I know.

It sucks that my parents are so strict. Not that Eric is even my parent. And you'd think they'd be happy me and Ben get along. Whatever crap he and Eric have fallen out over now should be resolved. Mum's always saying to me, life's too short for upset.

Ben's firing off texts on his phone. The thing is always buzzing.

He says, 'I need to go.'

'Please, Ben, can't you at least think about it?'

He pauses and looks at me, narrow eyed. I bat my eyelashes and he laughs.

I smile. He pauses. 'I'll have a copy of that tape of yours, might get you in to do a night when you're a bit older.'

I roll my eyes. 'I'm plenty old enough now.'

He laughs. 'Whatever. I'll pop over in the week, see what my boys think of you doing a few live tracks.' The thought of performing live at one of his big events literally gives me shivers. I hug him goodbye.

We've always got on well, Ben and I. Eric raised him but by the time Eric came to us, Ben had pretty much moved back in with his mum. Reeva did a bunk when he was really little, married a bloke she used to strip for. You can see why Eric has the hump, that and Ben seems to prefer her even though she left.

They'd stayed in contact at first, and Ben used to come over and hang out with us all, but they've fallen out over something and haven't been speaking for ages. As usual no one tells me anything, but I'm under strict instruction to stay away from him.

The front door goes, and feet up the stairs. 'Turn that shit down.'

I roll my eyes but I do it. I also empty the joint butt out of my window and spray perfume about.

I head downstairs, slob out on the sofa and watch MTV. My mum starts cooking and I realise I've got the munchies really badly. We eat dinner, Mum natters about the haircuts she's done today, I nod along, so does Eric. She can talk for England. Pauses only to take the odd breath in. Eric catches my eye and we swap a smile. She's oblivious as usual. She'd talk to herself in an empty room, to be honest.

I go back to the telly and Eric carries on having his ear yakked off. He murmurs the odd non-committal 'yep' and 'mmmhmm'.

At about one, I say, 'I'm going up then.'

'Night, love.' I smile at my mum. Eric nods.

I shut the door and put Oasis on my walkman so no one can moan about the volume. I lie back, puffing away and thinking if Ben weren't my brother, he'd probably be a right sort, and then I'm wondering if it's a sin or something to even think that.

# 9.

# Miriam Jackson

The police only take thirty-five minutes to arrive. I assume this is a reasonably good result but to me each minute feels like ages. I keep hearing Sue. 'I hope Tabitha feels better.' We're not exactly friends but we have a good mum-to-mum relationship on account of our daughters. I've known Sue for over a decade I suppose – I trust her with Tabitha and we chat. It's never been something I've had a great deal of time for, friendship. Since I married Nick and became part of my own little unit, it hasn't mattered much. I have lots of colleagues, I have Anna, and I guess I prefer that sort of balance where I feel like the one in charge. I'm respected at work, I help out at school, no one would have anything bad to say about me. But I'm also aware that I am married to Nick Jackson, a man in the public eye. My behaviour reflects on him.

There have only been two times I betrayed that, and betray is probably too strong a word. The time I was loose lipped around Nick's colleague. That's when he suggested a nanny and we set-tled on Anna instead. Actually, having her around has been more of a boost than I expected it to be. I'd felt vaguely resentful to start with, at her youth, her drive, her entire story yet to be told. There I was, maybe a little bit lonely, bored. My career, which I'd been so proud of to begin with, always paled in comparison to Nick's. I'd often find myself relegated to 'Nick's wife'. But to her I am so much more than that. I am a successful host of a popular radio show. I found I enjoyed mentoring her. I started to focus on my life as she saw it, rather than dining out on self-pity.

The other time was when Tabitha stayed out, mobile off.

Then there is the third betrayal, of course. The most recent one. That no one must ever find out about.

My heart is hammering when I think of this, as I answer the door to a kind-looking man in a suit, and a frumpy short woman in uniform.

The policeman, a tall fellow, with gentle eyes and a reassuring gaze, is now sitting on my sofa. They've both turned down a drink, and I'm glad. He is asking me to start at the beginning. I blurt out, 'My husband's Nick Jackson, you know.'

He nods. Most local people know who we are. I blush at the clumsiness of this; I wouldn't usually use his profile to try and pull favours. But it's not every day my most precious thing goes missing. I'll do anything for Tabitha, pride is irrelevant.

He asks, 'Will he be home this evening?'

'No, he's away. In LA. He spends a lot of the year there.'

The woman sitting next to him, DS Ockham, or something, has a pen and pad out. She is poised, waiting to take notes. She hasn't written anything yet. I suppose I haven't really told them anything. I look stupidly from one to the other.

The man, Branning he said his name was, I can't remember the title, says, 'Why don't you tell us why you're worried about . . . Tabitha, is it?'

I nod, swallow, and start speaking. I tell him more about my working day than he needs to know – I have a tendency to waffle under pressure. Something I've worked hard to overcome over the years, back like a nervous tic. He kindly manoeuvres me to the point where I get home and she's not here. I tell him about Delia and what looks to be Tabitha's truanting. The woman next to him is now writing at least. He says, 'Tabitha is a teenager?'

'Yes, she's just turned sixteen.' He exchanges a look with the woman. I say, 'What?'

He smiles. 'Mrs Jackson.'

'Miriam.'

'Miriam. Has Tabitha done this sort of thing before?'

'What, gone missing?'

He smiles again. 'Come home late, or not been where she's supposed to be?'

I feel tears well up and blink. He adds, 'I know you called the station last year and filed a report that she hadn't come in.'

I lick my lips; my mouth feels suddenly very dry. Of course, this would come up.

I answer, 'She has been late before, yes. That night she was out with a friend. It was a misunderstanding. A reporter found out I'd rung, blew the whole thing out of proportion.' I sound more defensive than I need to. I lower my rising voice. 'This isn't the same, is it? She missed school.'

He's still smiling, and says, 'Let's go have a little look at her things, shall we?'

I take him upstairs and the female officer pokes around her room. She asks, 'Is anything gone?' I pause as she opens cupboards, drawers, and I nod, hesitant. 'Yes, she's taken her trainers, some clothes, pyjamas.'

The woman smiles kindly, but I can see where this is going. She pulls out her underwear drawer. I nod and half whisper, 'Yes, a few pairs seem to be gone, but she was having a sleepover.'

She's still smiling kindly and is gentle when she says, 'Sounds like she probably has enough for a couple of days though.'

I swallow again. I open my mouth, but she's right. She sits with me and makes a list of what I can't account for. Some jumpers, two pairs of jeans, trainers and the boots she was wearing, the pyjamas, a few pairs of pants, I can't be precise, maybe five. Some bras. Her toothbrush.

We head back downstairs and the man, a detective it turns out, smiles, but it looks strained as he glances over the list, tearing it from the pad, popping it into a slim file.

I sense he's going to say something I don't like. 'Mrs Jackson. In these sorts of instances, we usually find that the teenager is home within twenty-four hours.'

My heart sinks as I say, 'But she's been gone nearly that long.' My voice is high, rising, 'Delia said she's missed three days of school.'

'But you saw her on those days? She came home?'

'Yes, but . . .' And I trail off because there's not much to say, is there?

He says, 'I realise this must be very worrying for you. But she's only been gone a day.'

He sounds like Nick, reasonable and calm, and it annoys me, which isn't his fault. I still snap, 'Do you have children?'

He smiles again but doesn't answer. I pull my cardigan around myself.

'If she's not back by this time tomorrow, call me.' He hands me a card with his mobile number on it.

They stand, and I do too. I walk them to the door, but I am dazed and fuzzy. I can't believe they are going. When they haven't found her. When she's not here. He pauses at the door and says, 'We'll have teams out searching on foot, and we'll check CCTV, I'll keep you updated.' But I can tell he is just following procedure. That he doesn't believe she is in danger. That she is not an emergency.

He goes on, 'You should call a friend. Someone to wait with you until she's home. Or perhaps get your husband to come back?'

47

I nod. Friend. Call a friend. Call your husband. Nick would come straight home if I told him. I've only done it once before. I called him in tears, about a week after the 'clubbing' incident. She'd been on best behaviour while Nick was there, then he went back to film. I'd rung, devastated by a fight we'd had. It had started with me asking her to tidy her room. It ended with her storming out, slamming the door and returning an hour later, refusing to speak to me. But he'd only been in Scotland then. He'd come back. Nick is a pilot, he owns a plane and any short flights he takes himself. He'd flown back that morning, taken her out for a meal and a chat. She'd apologised when she got home. He'd gone back the same evening, hugging me first, saying it would be all right. I hadn't had the heart to tell him nothing was all right. I'd failed at being a mother. He'd have told me I was being dramatic. I'd have said he was probably right. She'd actually been better since. Less rude at least, though she wouldn't let me close. That's the awful truth.

I go upstairs and open the door to her room. Closing the cupboard, the drawers where a stranger had just been. I slip into her bed, under the covers. It smells faintly of her perfume. Sweet and cloying. Worn more for the celebrity who endorsed it than the smell. It comes in a ridiculous pink bottle. She and Delia love it.

I expect to cry, but I don't.

I think about Nick and how disappointed he'd looked that time I'd called him home. He hadn't really seen a problem. He'd laughed and said all teenagers were rude.

Sue had said Delia could be a little madam when I'd tentatively approached her about hormonal mood swings, and she had two older ones who'd also been difficult at the same age. They probably all cut school. I'm sure they all lie.

God knows I did.

# 10.

## Ruby Williams

*1994*

I'm in trouble. It sucks. I got caught by Eric snogging a boy at the playground. It was so embarrassing. He grabbed me and smacked poor Terry right in the face. He looked so shocked I'd almost laughed – I do that when I'm nervous. Eric marched me home. His hand was hurting, digging into my arm. I've got marks there now. He almost threw me through the front door. Then Mum was there all, 'What's she done?' asking him before she asked me. Which pissed me off.

He started shouting and I ran up to my room. I put a mix tape on in my headphones because I didn't want to hear them.

Now Mum is knocking on my door. She doesn't look angry, but I am. I start crying, properly. She sighs, hugs me and says, 'He's trying to protect you is all.'

I tell her, 'I'm practically a bloody grown-up. Why can't he just leave me alone.'

'He doesn't want you getting a reputation.'

I laugh at that and say, 'What, like you had?'

I feel the sting before I register what's happened. My hand shooting up to touch my cheek. Mum's hand hovering just by my face. She looks almost as shocked as I do.

I yell at her, 'I hate you.'

'One day you'll thank us, you know.'

I bloody doubt that, but after she's left I do feel a bit bad.

Eric yells up that they are going to the pub and I'm to stay in because I'm grounded. I don't feel bad then, just more pissed off. As soon as they are gone, I slip downstairs and call Ben.

He listens, sighs and says, 'He's so controlling, isn't he?'

I say, 'He's not even my dad.' Even though the words make me feel bad cause he's the closest thing I've ever had.

He says, 'Yeah, I know.'

Then he pauses for a minute. I say, 'You still there?'

'I have an idea.' And, as he starts to talk, I think it sounds better than being here every weekend where nothing bloody happens, with the world's strictest man watching my every bloody move.

I start to feel excited and I don't feel bad either. Mum and Eric are too strict, and I'm only going to be young once, after all.

# 11.

## Miriam Jackson

I am surprised when I come to. Mainly I am surprised that I slept. What sort of a mother does that make me? When I think back, I've always done it. Slept at odd times. I learned it from Mum, I suppose. Her complete willingness to ignore any problems via sleep. The ultimate opting out often with chemical assistance. I've since read, in my quest to understand Mum, to not be Mum, that lethargy is a symptom of depression. Maybe so, but to me it seems a response to stress as well. After Dad left, I got really sleepy. Relishing the long hours lying in bed, of nothingness. That window of time where the thinking stopped. Where I didn't feel angry, worried for Mum, or demented with missing him. All these thoughts would spin around and around in my head. Unspoken. Reverberating like a washing machine on its final, manic cycle. A build-up so great, so overwhelming, that eventually I would just shut down, and switch off, my muscles would turn to jelly, my eyelids would get heavier, and I could drift away.

Not that I slept well last night. I woke up fitfully what felt like every few minutes and checked my phone, the door. Nothing. Mr Boots is curled up at my feet and I'm grateful for his company, as I often am when Tabitha and Nick are out, which seems to be more and more often. Tabitha has been such a nightmare this past year that I'm wondering if she's toying with me now. Or perhaps she's just off doing something I might have said no to. I run through scenarios in my head. Nick is constantly laughing at what he deems my overactive imagination, but I find if I cover every scenario, good, bad and in between, I feel better prepared.

I was a careless teenager. My mum had been more fragile than I am now, and I took advantage of that. Not intentionally, not knowingly, but I used her fear of upsetting me to do what I wanted. And what I wanted to do was be with Ben.

The police aren't worried. I can't work out if this is a good or a bad thing.

I roll over. I am still in Tabitha's bed. Sleeping in here is something I haven't done for years. Not since she was little and wanted me to stay with her every night. To read another story, to rearrange her teddy bears. It's almost laughable to think of that now. She flinches if I go near her and rolls her eyes if I tell her I love her.

I feel tears threatening to fall. When did that stop? The wanting me. When did she start hating me instead? Nick had been certain that this happened to every mother and daughter. He'd told me not to worry. Said it would blow over once puberty was out of the way. He'd brought up the topic of boarding school again, but I'd put my foot down, it's one of the few things I've stood firm on. Nick went to one of the best schools in the country, then on to Oxford, as was expected. I often think if Tabitha was a boy I wouldn't have won the argument. My family may have been firmly middle-class, but Nick's are a different league altogether – old money.

The truth is I'm totally intimidated by them and their wealth. I always wonder if I wasn't a bit of a disappointment to his parents. He's an only child too. They've never been anything but friendly, but they aren't what I'd describe as warm either, and they took little interest in Tabitha when she was a baby. I think they were vaguely amused at how much of the 'child-rearing' I tried to do myself.

Nick always says how close they all are, but they've never seemed that way to me. I suppose it has something to do with packing up a child at seven and sending them away to strangers. It crosses my mind to call them, they are Tabitha's grandparents after all. But then I'd have to tell my husband, and I at least want to try and resolve it all first. I think about calling my mum, but I know I won't. I hate worrying her, I did enough of that in my youth. I hate the way it makes me feel when she's anxious. Her panic over the smallest things has always felt contagious.

My phone pings and I grapple around searching for it. Nick. Checking in. He's made it through the day, very busy, he says. He asks how I am and I say fine with a smiley and a heart. God.

I head downstairs and check the landline, though I'd have heard it ring. I call Delia's house again. Sue answers.

'Hello.'

I pause, 'Hi Sue, it's Miriam.'

'Hi, is she home?'

I don't even try for a chuckle, there's no point trying to minimise the horror, I say, 'Nope, still out there giving me heart attacks.'

She says, 'Bloody hell, have you called the police?'

I sigh, dropping the pretence at being breezy. I'm sure Sue would feel the same way as I do. 'Yes, they came by yesterday. They didn't seem to take it that seriously.'

'Bloody hell.' My heart starts racing. As though someone else's outrage at my missing daughter, apparently no longer a child in the eyes of the law, gives me licence to panic.

I say, 'We haven't been getting on,' before I can stop myself. I wince once it's out there but Sue's voice is soft when she says, 'They can all be little blighters, can't they? Doesn't stop us loving them.'

I'm close to tears again, at her understanding if nothing else. I know Nick dismisses my worries to try and calm me, but actually being acknowledged helps. I half whisper, 'I wish she'd just come home.'

Sue says, 'She will.' And she sounds firm and sure and I so want to believe her.

I say, 'I guess Delia hasn't heard from her then?'

'She's not even up yet, hang on. I'll wake her.'

I start to say she doesn't have to, but she's already gone. Delia's voice is thick with sleep, so like Tabitha's if I interrupt her precious hours of rest. It makes my heart throb for my daughter. My girl.

I say, 'Hi, Dee, sorry to have woken you. I don't suppose she's contacted you?'

'No.' She pauses. 'Sorry.'

'It's okay, it's not your fault.'

Sue comes back on the line and tells me she'll check in with me later. I say thanks and I'm sure Tabitha will be home by then.

I suddenly decide to dial my mum. It rings once and I hang up. Too late though, and so she rings back almost immediately.

'Hi, Mum.'

'Did you call?' and I can hear it in her voice – worry.

'I dialled by accident.'

'Okay.'

I should tell her. She might be able to help. Instead I ask, 'How are you?'

'I'm fine, love, are you?'

She'd be here in a shot. But then I think about Ben and being with him, how upsetting this would be for my mum. How awful she would feel if she knew what I'd done, how I wouldn't be able to meet her eye. I say, 'Yes, fine.'

'Nick okay?'

'He's away at the moment.'

She says, 'Oh again? Not for too long, I hope?'

And I feel defensive as I always do. 'Well, the bills won't pay themselves, Mum.'

She pauses as though she might say something else, but changes tack. 'Tabitha?'

I run a hand over my forehead where a slow ache is building along with the day. 'Everyone's fine, Mum.'

I hang up the phone and promptly burst into tears, which isn't going to help anything.

I head to the bathroom and run cold water over my face. Then I go downstairs and pick up the policeman's card. I dial his mobile number.

'Peter Branning.'

I say, 'It's Miriam Jackson.'

'Hello, Mrs Jackson, has Tabitha come home yet?'

'No, and you need to look for her.'

He pauses then says, 'We have been looking, and we certainly will continue to do so, though the most likely scenario is that she will turn up of her own accord. Your daughter is over sixteen.'

'She's a child.'

He sighs, 'Not legally, though, and as I said we are looking for her. I will be sending an officer to take a statement from her friend today.' He pauses, and I can hear paper rattling. 'Delia Munroe?'

'Yes, but it's no good, she's not heard from her.'

'Is there anyone else you can try?'

I say, 'I don't have numbers, just Dee's. Oh, and Brett, her boyfriend – well ex-boyfriend apparently.'

'I'm sure she'll come back.'

'You said that yesterday, she's not here.' I'm shouting and force myself to calm. 'Please.'

'Like I said, we'll make a few enquiries, but at the moment, from our point of view, she might just be out.'

I take a deep breath and say, 'There must be something I can do? Or someone I can pay, to help me . . . I have money if that's what you need to get working, my husband is very wealthy . . .'

'Mrs Jackson, we are looking, I assure you, but we don't do private investigative work.'

I'm close to tears again when I say, 'Do you know anyone that does?'

He pauses for so long I wonder if he's hung up. 'Detective?'

'I do actually. Though I know she's pretty busy . . .'

'Please.'

'Can you wait while I make a phone call?'

## 12.

# Madison Attallee

It's Rob's mum's birthday today. My ex-mother-in-law will be seventy. Edging a little bit closer to death. The thought brings a smile to my face and then Molly says, 'What, Mummy?' and I feel a moment of repentance. She's still Molly's grandmother after all. And hey, at least I don't have to deal with her any more. Every cloud has a silver lining. Actually, in the cloud that was my divorce there are plenty of silver linings, the only kicker is not being with Molly properly. It's a pretty big kicker.

'Nothing, Mol, just cheerful. Aren't I allowed to be?'

I glance away from the road and at her. She's frowning and says, 'It's just not like you is all.'

I laugh. 'To be cheerful?'

'Yes.'

Jesus. 'Well, I'm cheerful when I'm with you.'

I glance again, she rolls her eyes but she's smiling at least.

I pull up at the house that used to be mine and marvel at the fact it never did feel like home. I honk the horn and the door opens a second later. I wonder if they were waiting behind it. And it is *they*. My ex-husband and Janet. A unit, and very much looking to send this message to me loud and clear. His arm is firmly clamped around her shoulders. Molly leans over,

57

squeezes me and yells, 'Bye,' as she opens the door, slides out, and slams it so hard I flinch. My beautiful car.

Janet sort of waves at me. I sort of wave back and then I pull away, switching the radio off, Marilyn Manson on and the volume up. I hum along to 'The Dope Show'.

When I get into my flat, my phone rings almost immediately. Peter.

'Aren't you supposed to be working?'

'Hello to you too.'

I wince a bit at my own rudeness, 'Sorry, yes, hello. Aren't you working though?' He'd said as much and that he wouldn't make it before Molly left. They'd spoken on the phone briefly.

'Well, yes, actually the call is work related.'

I perk up a bit. I had been thinking of heading into my office, but the truth is the girls can take care of most of what we have going on at the moment so I'm not even that busy on a weekday, let alone a Sunday.

I say, 'What do you need?' and make it sound like a drag.

'I've got a missing kid. Well, she's sixteen.'

Ah, that awful grey area. A legal adult, but rarely in reality. I say, 'Girl?'

He sighs, 'Of course.'

'She's probably done a bunk.'

'Most likely.'

I'm scouring for a pen and paper anyway, 'Parents worried?'

'Only spoken to Mum and yes, very. She's pretty high profile as well.'

A Post-it note with a shopping list on one side is the best I can do. I turn it over, 'Go on.'

'Miriam Jackson.'

'Oh, the radio woman?'

'Yes.'

I sigh. 'Claudia and Emma love her.'

He says, 'She's quite good apparently. Married to Nick Jackson.'

'Makes those tear jerkers?'

He laughs. 'Bet you've never seen one?'

'Nope, chick flicks, more your cup of tea, right?' I'm smiling.

He laughs again, and says, 'You got me. He's in LA at the moment, filming.'

I make a note of their names though I'm unlikely to forget them in a hurry. 'Well, I'm sure he can stop filming for his kid.'

'I don't think she's called him.'

I pause. 'That's odd.'

'Maybe, people get irrational under stress. Like I said, she's pretty worried.'

'So where are you at?'

'Deanie's at her friend's house, Delia Munroe. Girl mentioned the kid hasn't been where she's supposed to, bunked school Wednesday, Thursday and Friday. But Mum saw her in her uniform after school on all of those days.'

That's not good but probably means she's run away, which is the less sinister scenario. I ask, 'Boyfriend?'

'Nope, did have but they broke up. Apparently, Mum didn't suspect a thing about the bunking and didn't know about the break-up either. Miriam said money's no object.'

I am doodling and realise I've almost run out of space on the Post-it. Damn it. 'Gimme her number.'

He does and I say, 'Okay, thanks.'

'Call you later.'

I dial and am stupidly surprised when it turns out she sounds exactly the same as on the radio.

'Hello, Mrs Jackson.'

'Yes?' And there's that tinge to her voice. I've heard it from many a parent before her. Thinly veiled worry, desperation. Sixteen isn't that much older than Molly. Legal adult or not.

I say, 'DI Branning gave me your number. My name's Madison Attallee, I'm an investigator.'

'Oh, thank God.'

An hour later, I'm pulling up to my office to meet Miriam. There's a sleek white Porsche sitting out the front, which I assume is hers. As soon as I step out of my car – my little TT looking less fancy next to this newer, shinier vehicle – she's out as well.

The first thing I notice is that she's pretty but not insanely beautiful, though I don't know what I was expecting – showbiz good looks? She's a radio star, I guess, not film, and I'm sure most actresses look better on screen than in real life anyway.

She is hovering by her car. Arms wrapped around herself. Sunglasses on. As I head towards her she slips them up, revealing puffy red eyes, but they are a lovely deep green. She's been crying. And who can blame her? I've sobbed many times over Molly's absence and I've always known where she was. This must be hell on earth. I stick out a hand and say, 'Madison.'

We shake. I open up the office, and we head in. I apologise for the fact that it's freezing, slipping the heating up to full blast and putting the kettle on simultaneously.

She says, 'Thank you so much for seeing me.'

I shrug. 'It's my job.'

'But it's Sunday.'

I smile. 'That's okay, to be honest I wasn't up to much else.'

She says, 'You don't have a family?'

The grin slips and I say, 'One daughter, but I dropped her home an hour ago, it's her grandmother's birthday party this afternoon.' I add, 'She doesn't live with me.'

'Oh. Sorry.'

I shrug. Wishing it was a Monday and that Claudia and Emma were here. I'm useless at small talk and now I've got the hump over having to mention Molly. Which isn't Miriam Jackson's fault. I ask what she'd like to drink and then I fuss about making her a tea, and myself an instant coffee since I still can't work out the blasted machine, and Claudia keeps moaning when I 'mess up the settings'. I take a deep breath and try and focus my mind on not behaving like an arsehole.

This woman's daughter is missing, after all.

I sit, usher Miriam into a seat opposite me, then I say to her, 'Let's see where we are. I'll tell you what I can do, and we can go from there, okay?'

She nods.

'What led to you calling the police?'

She does. I make notes. Peter has already messaged me the transcript of Deanie's conversation with Delia. She said the girl was nervous but that's to be expected.

I say to Miriam, 'What's your relationship like with Tabitha?'

She smiles. 'Well, she's a teenager.'

'I've heard they're hard work.'

'Like you wouldn't believe.'

'Has she done this before?'

She pauses, and I push. 'Miriam?'

'She's been late. Not picked up her phone, especially when we've had an argument.' She blushes. 'We've had a fair few over the past year. There was one time about . . . I don't know, nine months ago where she went clubbing. I panicked, called the police. It turned out she went back to another girl's house, I thought she was going to be staying with Delia.'

'Oh dear.'

She smiles faintly. 'Yes.'

I say, 'Misunderstandings happen.'

She nods, but tells me, 'They need not to when you're the Jacksons though. Unfortunately, the papers got hold of the fact I'd called the police. Someone got a shot of her outside the club with her boyfriend.' She winces. 'She looked a bit tipsy.'

61

I murmur, 'I'm sure that's normal.'

She nods but looks forlorn. 'I love my daughter.'

'Of course you do.'

'I'm wondering if she's doing this to punish me.' She scrunches up her face and massages her temples.

'What for?'

Her hands drop, she looks out of the window and back to me with a shrug, 'Who knows? She's always a bit cross these days.'

'Any particular reason?'

She pauses just long enough for me to wonder if she's being entirely truthful when she says, 'Not that I know of.'

# 13.

# Miriam Jackson

I wonder if I am supposed to spill at this point. I wonder if holding back information matters. I wonder if, like so many things, when it comes to parenting, my needs are secondary or in fact just null and void.

I can't.

I'm not ready yet to relinquish secrets that don't seem to matter. I think about talking to Ben last night, being with him the night before. The fact that I want to phone him even now. He isn't relevant to this. She doesn't need the ins and outs of *my* life. Or Nick's, even. My heart races at the thought of it all, the tricky past that I have invited in. It's got nothing to do with Tabitha though.

I write down my daughter's phone number, her Twitter handle, Instagram name, Facebook name (though she never uses it), YouTube channel where she discusses make-up, running tutorials that I can barely keep up with. I write the name of her school, Delia's name, her mum and dad, their phone number, Brett Carmichael. Poor heartbroken Brett. It seems it's not just me that my daughter has turned on.

I don't have any other numbers. I apologise to Madison for this several times, she shrugs and says, 'I don't think we're supposed to know everything about our teenagers, are we? I'm sure sometimes they mess up and I guess we're there to pick up the pieces.' And it's just what I needed to hear, and I could hug her, but I don't. She doesn't seem like the type. I ask about money, she gives me a rough idea and tells me someone called Emma will contact me first thing tomorrow. She's going to go and speak to Delia and she'll call me later.

I ask her what I should do and she says, 'I know it's tough but go home, try to stay busy and wait.'

I blurt out, 'Do you think she's okay?'

She looks me levelly in the eye and tilts her head to the side, a mane of waist-length hair jumps around her, dirty blonde and impressive, almost as if it has a life of its own. 'I don't know yet.'

It's an honest answer but not the one I wanted. She must see the look of panic because she adds, 'I can tell you that ninety-nine per cent of kids that go missing at this age have done a runner, and are either found or come back of their own accord.'

I swallow and nod. 'Okay.'

'She also packed so she was intending to be somewhere else, that suggests that she's gone of her own free will, which is good. We just need to find out where.' She adds, 'You should speak to your husband.'

I nod, but I'm not going to. Not yet. I can almost feel his disappointment mingling with my own. I thank Madison and get into the car on autopilot. Heading back to my empty house.

My mother always claimed she loved me the minute I was born. But that love never seemed to make her happy. She was always volatile, but after Dad left it got a lot worse. I suspect she was depressed for a while before she was diagnosed – looking back I think she had problems before he went, but then they didn't seem to be my problem. They were things for her and Dad to figure out. All I knew was our home, which had felt so solid and secure, stopped being that way, and felt like quicksand under my feet. Before Dad left, things were just provided – clean washing, dinner, a packed lunch. Afterwards, I would constantly be asking, needing, reminding. My dad must have either done those things or he had made sure Mum did. Either way I was unaware that there was anything that needed doing. After he left I realised that seeing to my needs was a lot of work, work Mum couldn't always manage. I felt like a burden.

She described their relationship as a whirlwind. They hadn't known each other long and were quite young. By the time I was eighteen months old, she said, they'd pretty much had separate lives, but carried on living together for my sake.

Until Wendy, that is, when my dad decided that my sake wasn't so important any more. Like all kids I guess I didn't really care why they stayed together, I just wanted that to happen.

My mother never complained exactly, but she cried a lot, or was vacant, sitting on the sofa, whiskey in hand after a long day at work.

She never slagged him off. She never outright said that he had ruined her life, but the slope of her shoulders, the 'at least he's fair financially' said it all. She loved him, I think, and he didn't love her.

Initially I'd go to his house every other weekend. On weekdays, I went to a breakfast club and an afterschool club, and I'd usually be the last one there. At first, my mum coped with the break-up by throwing herself into work, and not complaining. Then she became very down and retreated into herself. I'd wished she would complain. Yell, rage, call him every name under the sun. So I could join in, so we could grieve together.

By the time I started secondary school, I didn't have to go to afterschool clubs any more. I had a house key and I'd let myself out in the morning and back in in the afternoon.

I wasn't great academically, but I wasn't bad either. I wasn't bullied, but I didn't make friends easily. I still don't.

One day, a girl at school, Sarah, announced she had a spare ticket to a gig in Twickenham and no one to take at the weekend. We sat next to each other in maths and she offered it to me. I'd been nervous before the gig. Deciding what to wear, wondering if more girls from school would be there. I'd met her at the bus stop in Kingston. A few others had come and by the time we arrived at the venue it was clear that, actually, she'd just needed the money for the ticket. She wasn't rude, none of them were, I just wasn't included, and I didn't help myself by not being able to find any words to add to their easy, jokey conversation.

I don't remember the bands but by ten o'clock I'd had enough of standing around looking awkward and I left to go home. The bus had been empty, and I made my way to the top, sitting at the front and trying desperately not to cry. I was fifteen. Other girls my age were having a blast, everyone seemed to be having a blast. I wasn't. I spent most of the time missing my dad and hating him in equal measure, and trying not to worry about my mum, who worked too hard, looked too thin, spent weekends in bed, and could only smile weakly when there was nothing to be happy about.

I'd jumped out of my skin when a deep voice had said, 'What would make a pretty girl so sad?' Even though the voice had come from next to me, I'd still looked around to see who it was meant for. It had been a few seconds before my eyes had settled on its owner and when they did my heart had jumped up and stuck in my throat.

It was Ben.

I get in and I'm jittery. Madison has said to hold tight, keep my phone to hand, don't panic. I don't often drink but I find myself opening the fridge, getting out a chilled bottle of white and pouring a glass. It is cold going in but starts to warm me once I

66

swallow. I find myself dialling a number on my phone, kind of hoping he doesn't pick up. But he does, on the second ring, and I find I'm holding my breath.

His voice rumbles, 'Hello.' And I feel almost like the little girl on the bus again. Awash in my own loneliness, desperate for someone else.

I should hang up. I should press disconnect and then block his number. I don't though, I say, 'It's me, Miriam.'

'I'm so glad you called.' And suddenly so am I. Even if I try and trick my brain into thinking that I'd called to end it.

He says, 'Is she home yet?'

'No.' I start to cry then, properly sob.

'Shit. I'm coming over.'

'No.'

'I wasn't asking.' He hangs up before I can say anything else. What had I been expecting? What should I do?

Crisis. Ben and I find ourselves locked in a drama again. When things ended between us nearly two decades ago it had been in another crisis. His step-sister Ruby had taken an overdose and I had found her convulsing on the floor in the middle of a rave. Ben held her in his arms, his terrified eyes met mine. We acted as fast as we could. But it was too late. I waited with him as he sat devastated when the doctor told us and asked for her mother's name. I felt the horror of it deep within my stomach, but it must have been worse for Ben. His face. He had cried openly as he was told that she was gone. News we'd already known made real with the words. I'd watched this young man who I loved. So different to me, with his rough voice, street-smarts and wads of cash.

His shoulders shook, and I'd wrapped my arms around him and held on. I'd wanted to take his pain, make it better, the way he'd done for me. The lonely little girl at the front of the bus. Falling in love with Ben had been a first in so many ways. It had been like waking up from a dark and fitful sleep. I'd felt less of a misfit, less unappealing. It didn't matter that my dad didn't love me, because Ben did, and with a ferocity I never understood, and never questioned.

He was taken off by the police for questioning, and I told him I'd be waiting.

My mother turned up while he was gone.

She and a social worker led me away, into her car, despite my protestations that I had to see him. To make sure he was okay. Knowing that of course he wasn't, but that my absence would only make it worse. I loved him, he loved me. I felt he was the only good thing I had, but my mother was adamant that I wouldn't see him. She felt she'd failed when she found out where I'd been staying overnight. That she'd never checked, that she worked too much. The police advised her to keep me away from him. Said he had a record already. I didn't care. But I was fifteen and social services were involved. When I snuck out of the house in the middle of the night, Mum called the police. Feeling, I realise tonight with an awful irony, much as I do now. She'd shipped me off to Spain.

Ben called, I know that because I heard her telling him no, and once I managed to scream out his name before she hung up. I hoped he had heard. Poor Ben. He'd lost his step-sister and by the time he came looking for me, and I don't doubt that he did, I had left the country, and I'd never had a chance to explain, or say sorry.

I'd never gone looking for him. Though I'd wondered all the time.

My doorbell goes. I can send him away. I can say it has all been a mistake. But I swing the door open and he is there, face concerned, arms reaching out, and I break again. He pulls me in. Memory making the outline of his shoulders, the feel of his hands familiar and untouched by time. Thoughts of my daughter evaporate just for a moment. I feel a stirring in the pit of my stomach and then I catch sight of a photo of us, me and my family, on the opposite wall. I gently push him back.

He follows me through to our huge kitchen. I take down another glass and go to pour him one from the open bottle. I sit at the breakfast bar and he sits opposite, leaning forward and catching a lock of my highlighted hair. He twists a bit around his finger. 'I preferred it dark.'

I must look sad or something because he's quick to add, 'You're just as beautiful though. Shit, have I upset you?'

'No. Sorry. It's just . . .' I think of all the time I spend trying to look nice, how much it matters because I'm married to Nick who is surrounded by beauty. How even though I'm not onscreen I mix with people for whom looks are the most important thing. Not that it is important right now.

I realise suddenly that it is an awful thing for him to be here. In my house. My husband's house. Yet I can't ask him to leave. Not yet. He looks totally at ease. I inhale.

I should say something, anything. I ask, 'So what sort of events do you do, weddings and stuff?'

'Not exactly. Corporate parties and what-not.'

I say, 'It must pay well.'

He grins. 'It does. We put on events for people who don't want them invaded by the press. A lot of celebrities actually, who like their privacy protected. We get paid a lot as we're known to be discreet.' He frowns. 'We don't need to talk about work though, do we? It's boring.'

I suddenly realise that I'm probably a little bit pissed. He asks me what it's like being a parent and I talk for ages about Tabitha, welling up again.

He says, 'You sound like a great mum.'

I snort. 'Shame I'm not a better wife.'

He doesn't say anything to that, but our eyes meet and all

the unspoken words seem to be there in his. They look at me like they always have. With hunger and intensity. I feel suddenly uncomfortable. Like he's looking inside me. I pull my cardigan up to my chin. I wonder briefly if I've caught a chill.

I blurt out, 'Do you think about her?'

'Ruby?'

I nod.

He pauses, still looking at me. He takes a small sip from his glass. Mine is empty. He never used to drink much, I remember that now. Even then, when we were young. And though he sold drugs, and certainly supplied me with everything I wanted, I don't think I ever saw him take even a drag on a spliff. I'm holding my breath. I shouldn't have asked.

But then he says, 'Of course I do. I think about it over and over, if I could have done something quicker. If only I hadn't frozen.'

I lean over the bar and rest a hand on his face. I say, 'You couldn't have done any more than you did.'

He nods but his eyes are damp. I tell him, 'My mum made me go. Away.'

He meets my eyes and says, 'I know. I came looking for you. She told me you were in Spain and that you weren't coming back.'

I find I'm tearful now, so many emotions bubbling upwards, memories tumbling in. Lying in a strange room, in a strange country, wondering how he was managing. Thinking over and over that I didn't say goodbye. I tell him, 'I'm so sorry.'

He shakes his head. 'It wasn't your fault. And your mum, she was only looking out for you.' I nod because it's easier than trying to explain that it almost killed me. The heartbreak. That when I got back I knew I wouldn't look for him because I could only recover from that loss once.

So where does that leave me now?

The thought sobers me slightly. I think of Tabitha and find in my heart that she matters more than this man. That I have found *real* love in her. That I may have failed as a wife, but I *am* a good mother.

That is my identity now. The thing that defines me most. And yet here I am confiding in a man who isn't her father. A man I think I still love. When I met Ben, it was all consuming but it was also easy. I felt like the focus of his world. With Nick it was overwhelming but in a different way. He was older than me, he had a life, he was things. I had to shape myself to fit in with him. I had to work at it and be things too. With Ben I just was. God. I go through my phone again. It's the fourth or fifth time I've scrolled.

He says, 'You're worried about her.'

'Of course.'

He shrugs. 'She'll be out having fun.'

I smile but it doesn't feel real. She's never been gone this long. 'I hope so.'

He says, 'Can I stay?' I'm tempted, even in the midst of all this, with guilt weighing heavily in my heart. The guilt of yesteryear and a whole new load that hasn't kicked in yet. The thought of crawling into bed, pressing my back against his stomach, is tempting.

He says, 'You can't stay here by yourself.'

'I can, I'll be fine.'

He's frowning, and I think he's going to argue. Eventually he says, 'Okay.' But I feel his reluctance.

After he leaves, I sit for an hour, knowing I won't sleep. My mind churning with all sorts of things. Ben, me, Ruby. Tabitha as a little girl. My husband, larger than life, but never here.

My phone rings, a landline number I don't recognise.

'Tabitha?'

He laughs. 'No, silly.'

'Ben?'

'I just wanted to say I never stopped thinking about you.'

I don't know what to say to that. 'Mim.' No one's called me that for years. He asks, 'Did you think about me?'

I swallow, my mouth feels paper dry, my head hurts. I whisper, 'All the time.'

'Goodnight, Mim.'

'Goodnight, Ben.'

I slump at my kitchen table. My eyes come to rest on a picture of Nick and me on our wedding day. I burst into tears.

# 14.

# Madison Attallee

I call Deanie and she goes over what Delia told her, then I call Delia's mum, Sue Munroe, and arrange to go around tomorrow after school. I would have preferred today but she is insistent that Delia has had enough. Deanie is going to email me the transcript now. I look over the list and draw up a plan for Monday. I call Emma. I know I should leave her alone at the weekends but I want to share the news of a new case.

She arrives and flings open windows, looking at me accusingly. 'Were you smoking in here?'

Jesus. I frown, don't answer, and busy myself making coffee. I'm sure I hear her snigger. For fuck's sake.

I say, 'I hope you weren't busy?'

She smiles. 'Elaine's sister is visiting actually.' Elaine is Emma's partner.

I say, 'Sorry to have interrupted you.'

She says, 'Not at all, it gives them a chance to have a natter without me being in the way.'

I nod, glad I haven't messed up her weekend, and curious as always about Emma's partner, who Claudia and I have yet to meet.

We start going through articles that relate to the Jacksons. I get the transcript from Deanie outlining again her brief and largely unproductive conversation with Delia. I make notes about the last time Tabitha went wandering, and that it had seemed to be a case of Tabitha selfishly forgetting to update her mum and Miriam overreacting before ringing around. She said she was at a girl called Stacy's house. Stacy's mother confirmed a gang of them had been there but she couldn't say who exactly as the nanny had been left in charge. She did say Tabitha was a frequent enough visitor. She couldn't confirm who was there exactly, but said Tabitha was a frequent enough visitor. I add Stacy's name to my list. I am thinking about Molly as I go. She will be a teenager before I know it. I have no doubt there will be nights out and slamming doors. I don't want to be a paranoid parent, some of my clients track literally everything their children do. It's not right, an invasion of privacy, but you can understand it. Or I can.

Emma says, 'Well, these things happen.' As though calling the police to report a non-missing child missing is an everyday occurrence. I suppress a smile. Emma is always so understanding and non-judgemental.

I shrug. 'But when you're famous you need to be careful. Miriam should have had all the facts sorted. She caused a right old fuss by phoning the station. Someone blabbed it to the papers.'

Emma looks shocked. 'Why would an officer do that?'

I laugh. 'Money, Emma, why else.'

She sounds huffy as she says, 'A policeman no less.'

I'm scrolling through backdated *Comet* articles and bingo. I say to Emma, 'Look.'

Emma wheels her chair over and looks at the online version of the *Comet*'s front page. Directors under-age daughter, out on the town. Parents report her missing screams the headline. And accompanying it is a shot of Tabitha Jackson, scantily clad and leaning against a wall, laughing. She looks worse for wear, but it might just be a bad angle. There haven't been any pictures since. But, of course, the nationals coined in on it too, and a magazine ran a feature about the 'poor' neglected children of the rich and famous being left to run wild. I roll my eyes. Emma laughs. 'Kids, eh?' I smile, but I'm in two minds. Either Miriam is a natural overreactor and often cries wolf, or it took a lot of guts to call the police this time. My instinct says it's the latter. Though she didn't strike me as laidback, I wouldn't have penned her for hysterical either.

We start a file.

Peter had said he might come over, but by the time he messages me it's nearly half ten. I message back saying I'm on my way to bed and I'll see him tomorrow anyway. He sends a smiley face and a kiss. I'm actually nowhere near being ready for bed though. I'm up, smoking, full of coffee, and scrolling through the Instagram accounts of kids with lifestyles most adults can't even begin to dream of. Tabitha and her friends use various hashtags when posting. #nomnom and pictures of milkshakes, cakes, and elaborate salads. #lifestyle groups of elegant long-legged girls, gazelles in labelled goods, in beautiful settings. #fitspo girls in crop tops and leggings lifting weights, on a treadmill, but somehow still smiling, as though their perfect teenage bodies already need beating into shape and submission. #fashion, shoes, bags, #goals involving movie stars. Some of whom Tabitha may even know. And, finally, the nauseating #instarichkids. Typed, seemingly, with pride and without a hint of irony.

It's a whole different world out there. Tabitha has a lot of followers, and her posts seem to attract reams of comments. Plenty from #actors, #writers. I roll my eyes at the blatant sucking up because of who her father is, I guess. Her Facebook page is pretty unused. Twitter is mainly pictures of things, shoes, handbags, #wantthatdress. Instagram seems to be where she lives out her life.

She's stunning in that way that only money can make you. It can take average attractive and ramp it up to a ten. Her make-up is perfect, her clothes are perfect, her friends all look perfect. And yet . . . she's not home, she's bunking school.

The hours tick by. I eventually fall into bed somewhere around two and my eyes ping open to my alarm at six. I slap it, get up, feed the cat who looks suitably ungrateful, and shower. Listen to Mötley Crue sing '*Girls, Girl, Girls*' while I brew coffee and put on my slap. I light a cigarette and think about whether or not to phone her school first. I end up dialling Miriam.

She picks up halfway through the first ring and my heart goes out to her at the speed. I picture her, robbed of sleep, one eye on the clock, one eye on the phone. Maybe wandering around the house, seeing if anyone's come back.

'Hello.'

'Miriam, it's Madison.' I quickly add, 'No news yet.' Not wanting to build fake and shakeable hope. She needs some, but not too much.

Her voice drops an octave. 'Okay.'

'I'm going to go into her school this morning, but I think it might be best if you give them a quick ring, let them know that's what's happening?'

She pauses. I say, 'Are you comfortable doing that?'

'Yes, sorry. I was just thinking who'd be best to contact. Mrs Marriott, I suppose. She's the headmistress.'

'Okay, then.'

I hang up, turn the music back up, email Claudia and Emma regarding billing and contracts, and carry on making a list of who I need to speak to.

# 15.

# Miriam Jackson

When I started at university I was hard from all that had happened. A brittle shell of my former self. The soft, sad, but ultimately hopeful child I still was when I'd first met Ben had slipped away and been replaced by something else entirely.

For the initial days following Ruby's death, I'd wake, startled in the night, a thin film of sweat lying over me. My mother was terrified by what she deemed my delinquency. She'd look at me sideways and I saw all that worry. I'd lied to her often before. That was true. I'd invented a friendship with a 'Sarah' that didn't exist. After the gig and the bus ride when I met Ben, I fabricated a blossoming alliance between Sarah and me. Enough to fool my mum. Enough to have somewhere to say I was going when I was with Ben. Mum had been tentatively relieved, that I was happy, that I'd made a friend.

She'd thrown herself into her work, armed with a prescription for anti-depressants and a child whose needs were becoming less, or so it had seemed.

Her sadness after the truth was out was refreshed, revamped, ramped up. Her anxiety found new ways to come out. Constant checking, time off work. A return to her long stays in bed, face blank, eyes shiny. That was my fault.

Her daughter, friends now with the type of people who sold

drugs. Not at Sarah's house around the corner studying, but in London. In a house that, it turns out, was known to the police though no one specified why. When I asked questions, no one answered, they just fired more my way. I was not the 'good girl' she had thought I was, the daughter who could be relied upon to not cause any trouble. I was someone disappointing. Someone she didn't know, another person who had let her down.

She did what she thought was best, poor Mum, sending me to Dad's. I think if I'd stayed home it would have been her who wouldn't have coped. Now I think she was right to do it, because at that time I would have disobeyed her without a second thought. So addictive and powerful was the pull of him that I didn't worry about her at all. For the first time I could remember.

The distance did what it was supposed to. When I arrived back, I'd thought about finding him. Ben. But then I'd remember his devastated face holding Ruby in his arms. My screaming. His tears at the hospital and the last thing I'd said to him: 'I'll be here when you get back.' Only I wasn't. I hadn't been there. I'd gone. Abandoning him when he needed me most.

Then, worse still, there was my mother, pale-faced, tearful, shocked. Her voice when I called from my dad's had been wary and flat. She'd had to up her medication. Her nerves, said my dad, and he'd looked at me accusingly. Here I was making her his problem again just by being here. The guilt of it all had been overwhelming. Made worse because, secretly, I'd still wanted Ben. Secretly, I wasn't sorry for the nights in his bed, the drugs, the feeling of being alive.

By the time I came back to England, I was given enough space to somehow morph into a believable enough version of the girl I'd been before. Looking him up wasn't going to happen. Mum's nerves wouldn't survive it. Dad said this more than once, and I believed him. I was amazed her nerves survived anything at all. I made a firm determination with myself not to be the same. To be stronger, tougher, more resilient than she had been, but also not to let her down again.

I'd got on with studying and slowly, slowly, she started to trust me again. Forgave me, even, and stopped mentioning it. We got on far better, I stopped resenting her, or at least I stopped showing it. I'd meet her on her lunchbreak from work, we'd go for a coffee in town, or a lunch by the river. The one time I tried to raise the topic of Ben, to apologise, her eyes dampened and she looked away – I knew it was out of bounds, like discussing my selfish adulterous dad. It cemented in my head that staying away from Ben was right, for him, for her. Even if my heart broke. I trained my mind to look away when the thoughts came in.

And then there was Nick. Wonderful, loving Nick.

After Dad left, Mum sank low. An initial period of manic busyness, followed by lying listlessly in bed. Eventually I persuaded her to see the doctor. I sat next to her, holding her limp, pale hand while he mentioned a period of post-natal depression and other reoccurrences over the years. He gave her pills which made her not very much of anything, though I could always sense it under the chemical layer. Sadness. And the words of the doctor had haunted me – 'post-natal depression'. After me, when I arrived. My fault.

I started university at nineteen and I put on a good show to tutors, and later bosses, to my mother and then to my husband.

I had never told Nick, about Mum and her 'nerves', but as soon as I became pregnant, I felt frightened. Sometimes I felt a quiet, desperate panic. I remembered the doctor muttering 'post-natal depression'. What if this child growing in me set off the same reaction? What if it was genetic?

I wasn't honest with my 'pregnancy team' either, I kept my family's history to myself. Not wanting to tell anyone that I was scared. That it might be in my blood, a false, foreboding poison. I didn't want to have to take those little white pills, I didn't want to miss my life.

As soon as Tabitha was born though, and I saw her face, I knew I would be fine, that my little family would be fine. I threw myself into her life, I threw myself into work. And I was okay. I believed I was, if not exactly happy then at least content. Waiting by the gates at the end of the day, feeling a swell of love as Tabs bounced out of her classroom. And I'd wonder, not without bitterness, why my mother hadn't done the same, and if Wendy might not have looked quite so tempting to my dad if she had.

I wanted another child, but Nick wasn't keen. It didn't matter, life was good, I had enough blessings. There I was with my delightful daughter, a glamorous job, a loving husband. I felt as if I'd somehow cheated.

I'd loved Tabitha's early years, I loved my family and my husband. But sometimes I had a sense of not fitting in. I'd accompany Nick to events, I found them to be a tiring whirlwind of humble bragging and a pretence of warmth. I mostly gave those up after a few social functions, where I'd felt like a leper and run out of words. Standing awkwardly while conversation turned to universities, and they all smiled sympathetically when they found out I'd attended an ex-polytechnic and was raised by a single parent. Even the fact that I was successful in my own right rather than through connections seemed a cause of disdain. Or perhaps, as Nick suggested, I imagined it; had a paranoid chip on my shoulder. He'd pointed out that my childhood was hardly deprived. And he was right. But it wasn't like his, or his friends' either.

My phone rings – Ben. Again. A whole fresh wave of guilt hits me. My head and heart are still full of fond memories of Tabitha. The glory years of my marriage where I'd felt invincible and hadn't thought about Ben at all. What was I thinking now? What was I risking? My head pounds, my mouth is dry. I send the call to voicemail, unable to deal with him at the moment. I call Mrs Marriot instead. My heart beating awkwardly under my rib cage. She is sympathetic as I outline the ways I've failed that most basic of things: knowing where your child is. She says of course she'll see the PI. Of course, and perhaps I ought to come in too.

I hang up and my phone beeps, another missed call from Ben and a voicemail. 'Mim, hi. I just wanted to see how you were. Any news? I've called a couple of times. Let me know you're okay.' I feel a wave of annoyance now.

I dial Madison and tell her she can go in and see Mrs Marriot and that I will go in later.

My phone rings as soon as I hang up. For goodness' sake.

'Ben.'

'Mim, thank God. You've not been picking up.'

'I was speaking to Tabitha's school.'

'Is she back?' My voice had sounded cross and tight. He's either ignoring it or hasn't noticed. I feel bad when I hear his concern. I think again of him, waving at me as he walked into that awful little hospital room. Of how he must have felt when he came out.

I close my eyes. 'No.'

'Oh, I'm so sorry.'

My heart softens again. I slept with this man recently. This man who has shown me nothing but care. I walked out on him once.

He says, 'Sorry, Mim. I was worried. I overreacted, right?' He laughs again.

I sigh. 'It's okay. Don't worry about it.' But *I'm* worrying about it. I've given myself a whole new set of worries. There's now Ben to consider. It means I can't ignore his calls as he'll just keep trying, and I don't think I can handle the terrible conversation I know we need to have. The one where I tell him 'we' can't be. My focus is Tabitha.

And Nick. Of course, there is Nick.

'Can I see you today?'

I shut my eyes. I have to go into Madison's office, to sign some paperwork. I need to ring Nick, he's messaged to ask when's good and I surely can't put it off any longer. It's been a whole day and that's not even including the ones off school. Where was she then? I can't fit Ben in, not now. I should probably accept that I shouldn't see him at all. No matter the pain that brings. 'Today's not good.'

'I don't want you to be alone.' I feel another wave of annoyance. Then I suppress it. I also realise that actually, I *have* changed. The me that Ben knew wouldn't have wanted to be alone. Now I'm on my own fairly often and I'm okay with it.

'I'll be fine.'

I hang up with a growing sense of unease. I'm uncomfortable that he called so many times, that he would drop everything and come to my house, and come to think of it, I don't remember giving him my address, though it's not hard to find out where I live.

Intense. That's how I would have described Ben. Intelligent, handsome. Loving – really, really loving. Like nothing I'd ever experienced before. Or since. But it occurs to me now that I don't *really* know him. And how will he react when I break his heart all over again? Because that is what I will have to do. Tabitha is everything. Ben was once but no love can compare to what I feel for her. Nothing can be worth that. I'll find her. Nick and Tabitha must never, ever find out about Ben. It was a stupid dalliance. Seeing him filled me with a bittersweet nostalgia, but it's not my life.

My daughter is my life, my marriage is my life, and my job.

I've jeopardised those things. Like a lovesick, foolish teenager. A wave of shame hits me. Tabitha went missing while I was at Ben's. I'll never forgive myself for that, but I won't put this burden on them either.

Ben was my first boyfriend, true, but he was probably the first thing I ever had that resembled a real friend as well. *Of course* seeing him now has brought it all up again. I knew we shouldn't have been talking. I tried to tell myself it was fine, meaningless. I never meant it to go any further.

Am I still in love with him now? Yes, I think so. The intensity of it all can't be anything less than that, and it's never gone away. Not really. He's always been there, stored in a little box in my mind. I've mostly kept it locked but thoughts of him have bled through. But I don't really know him that well.

I *do* love Nick. Not in quite the same way, but I love what we've built. Nick engenders the same feelings that Ben used to, in a way, though they are very different sorts of men. Awe, an overwhelming desire to impress. With Nick there's also a sense that at any moment he'll look at me properly, wonder why he's wasted all this time and flee. If he finds out about Ben, no doubt he will.

Tears spring into my eyes. I put on my coat, a hat, a scarf. I wrap myself in wool, do my buttons up to my chin. I put my phone in my handbag, clutching it to my side so if she contacts me I'll feel her. Just like I used to when I was pregnant. First a fluttering, and then arms, knees, elbows, feet. Mine.

I look at the car and decide to walk, pulling our heavy front door shut behind me, but not double locking. In case she comes back. She won't want to fuss with keys. She's always whining when I double lock. *Why bother, Mum? No one ever comes down here.* She manages to say it with disdain as though living on a long, secluded road is somehow a burden rather than a blessing. We've been able to provide things for Tabitha that I never had. Two parents, love, stability and not just financial security, but a dream lifestyle – even if she does often take it for granted. The cold bites at the small sliver of my face between hat and collar, but I start to warm as I go, one foot in front of the other.

I get into a rhythm and my mind starts to clear. Then a black thought patterns it again. I am like my dad. I've cheated on my husband. My perfect husband. I am an adulterer. The word fizzes in my head – adulterer. My brain sees the letters, dark and wispy like little grey clouds. I haven't phoned him yet. I messaged with an excuse: work. Wondering why he didn't immediately call, seeing through its flimsiness, spotting deceit. But why would he? I don't lie. I never lie to him. I am completely and utterly trustworthy. Sometimes, when I'm trying to guess why loves me, I think that might be it.

I'm not an actress, or a fan, or a writer trying to gain footing, wanting a trade-off. I am loyal, and grateful and I love him quietly. I don't demand time, or money, though he is generous with both when he can be. I don't question him, I don't have to be away with him wherever he goes. Some wives do. Especially the wives of the cheats. The serial chasers. LA is full of them. Like an awful goldfish bowl of hormones that never matured. I've never worried about that with Nick. He's not a 'rutting monkey' type of man, as he always puts it. And it's true. His head has never turned. He doesn't demand much of me in that respect, either. There's been times I wish he would. I wonder if that's why I've strayed, not that it's an excuse. Besides, as Nick always says, most married people don't have a lot of sex. I try and think of the last time we did. Our last anniversary? Our next one is due in a month. Is that normal?

None of these things matter, of course. It's startling how when something that has true meaning is threatened you realise how unimportant your other worries are. Tabitha is what counts. Tabitha is everything. I won't see Ben again. My broken heart is inconsequential. I'll tell him. I'll carry on being Nick Jackson's wife, and put this all behind me.

# 16.

# Ruby Williams

## *1994*

I'm shivering. It's the sort of cold that feels like it will never end. My whole body shudders with it and I think maybe it's not just the weather. I'm in my Nikes and they feel flimsy tonight. Eric had said as much when I managed to get Mum to buy them. They were seventy-five quid. He'd said they were rubbish for that price. I'd rolled my eyes and told him they were better than his Adidas, which may as well be in a museum. We'd laughed. Eric. I blink back tears. I'm shaking again. I sing to myself. Stevie Wonder, Mum's favourite.

I look at my watch. It's a cheap silver-faced one that she bought me from Argos for my tenth birthday. It has a little dangly heart on a chain on the clasp. My eyes fill with tears. Ben's been gone for almost two hours now and I'm sitting at Kingston train station, trying to be inconspicuous. Clutching the backpack that I'd already packed, but with nothing useful, I now realise. My Walkman, some tapes, some knickers, a tiny black dress and heels. That's what I was going to wear tonight. While I sang. My first gig. One of Ben's raves. I'd been so excited.

Mum and Eric came home early, or I'd still be excited.

We need to leave here sooner rather than later. I wonder if I'll feel better once we have. I don't think so, I don't think I'll ever feel okay again. I start to cry in earnest, no longer able to keep it in. The tears become icy almost instantly and make me even colder. There is a thin sliver of ankle between my trainers and my jeans that is almost numb now. I wipe at my face and pull my hood down as low as it will go. I shut my eyes, trying to block everything out, but it's no good. I can still see Eric falling to the floor.

They'd been arguing about me. He'd been livid, crazy, proper angry. I'd seen men lose it like that before. Not Eric, not normally. He shouts, he's way too strict, and he'll dole out the odd slap, same as Mum, a swipe around the face, but he'd never beat us, or punch properly.

He did tonight though, I'll have a shiner by the morning to prove it. I'd thought he was different.

He's always said I'm not to hang around with Ben, which is stupid. He should be glad we get along, shouldn't he?

That's why we'd arranged to get going while they were at the pub. They don't usually get back till well after closing. Gav, the landlord there, is always fine for a lock-in and he's a mate of Mum's from way back.

They came home early tonight though, of all the bloody nights. Eric went mad when he saw us at the door. I'd rolled my eyes and gone to shove past him. He grabbed me, hard, on the top of my arm. Dragging me back through to the living room, yelling that Ben shouldn't be here, his own son and my step-brother in close pursuit. Ben called him a fucking loser. I'd shouted that I should be able to go where I wanted, and Eric shouted that I didn't understand. He'd looked deranged. He'd reminded me of Mum's last fella and it occurred to me that Ben was right. He was a fucking loser. But I'd been scared once Eric hit me and I thought he'd do it again. I'd shrunk backwards and down into a ball. Then there was an awful sound like a crack. At first, I'd thought he'd clumped me again, and hard, but he hadn't.

His body dropped onto me. I squeeze my eyes shut now, humming the song I was going to open with tonight. 'Universal Love'.

But it's no good, the thoughts keep coming and I can almost feel it. The terrible weight of him. On top of me, horribly, horribly still. I'd looked up, and there was Ben, holding the poker from the fireplace that we never used. It had been dark and wet. Black, rusting metal, dripping. Blood. Eric's blood. I'd scrambled out from under him and looked down. He was just lying there. Then there was a sound. Terrible and high-pitched. Me screaming. My mum clambering into the room and dropping down next to him. Shouting, *What have you done? What have you done?*

Eric wasn't moving. He'd hit me. Ben was protecting me. I keep that thought in my head. He'd been protecting *me*.

The station's busy and I keep my eyes down. Even at this time of night there's a flow of people in and out every fifteen minutes. But it's where Ben told me to wait. I rest my head into my hands, curling myself up.

I almost jump out of my skin when he finally gets back, laying a big hand on my shaky shoulder. He waves keys at me and says, 'Come on.' I wobble when I stand. My feet have got pins and needles in them all the way up my legs and into my knees. There is a damp patch on my black sweatshirt. My chippie jumper, my favourite. It's blood. It's starting to dry out and become brittle. The thought makes me feel sick, and I think I'll probably never wear this again. Walking is difficult, I feel too panicky to move, but it's made easier by Ben holding me up. Helping me with each careful step. And that he's whispering things. Telling me it will be okay.

He's been home to see his mum. I don't know what he's told her, but now he says he has some money. I know he's been taking care of her business for her, which she runs from a house in London. Ben tells me that is where we are going now, though her and her husband live out here, in the house where Ben has been staying.

He's having to leave because of me. He brushes this aside and says he was planning on going to the London gaff anyway, a few days early won't hurt.

He sounds proud as he tells me about the business though, like he always does when he talks about his mum. My mum says she's a bitch but never really expands on that. The journey passes in a blur. The whole time Ben keeps his arm firmly around me, he's making calls and I zone in and out, listening to him talk about rigs, and decks, and who's playing what and where to meet. The night that was going to be my best ever. I lean into him on the train and am surprised that I fall asleep. He wakes me as we pull into Waterloo and then it's easy enough. The Tube, a short walk.

I whisper, 'Ben, we killed him.'

He sighs. 'Don't think about it.'

I stop then and turn to look up at him and I say, 'Ben.'

He looks away from me, and I feel sorry for him. Because even if it was my fault, it was his hand that held that poker and struck it down upon his dad's head. I want to ask if he's all right, which is a stupid question, of course he's not. I say instead, 'We're killers.'

He looks up now, holds my eye and doesn't answer. Instead he takes my arm gently and says, 'Come on.'

The house is really four flats. Ben tells me his mother owns them all and laughs when my eyes widen. I've never met anyone who owned more than one house, or who owned any, actually. Most of the people I know live on our estate, in rented council flats. My mum's lucky with a house, two up, two down. I feel a stab of longing for that place now but I push it aside. I wonder if this is far enough from home. I suppose I need to start trying to accept that I can't go back. My heart does that sinking thing again. But then I see Ben standing, shocked, with a poker in his hand – a murderer now. *My fault.* Trying to defend *me*.

He leads me in and up two flights of stairs. It's almost as cold inside as it is out but there is heating, which he switches on. I stand, staring at the flat, unable to take in anything that's happened. Unable to work out all the ways things have changed, though my churning stomach speaks of it and a voice in my head whispers that things will never be the same again. He puts an arm around my shoulders and nudges me into a bedroom. He helps me out of my jeans, and hoodie until I'm just in my bra, vest, and pants, covering me up and then getting in too. I finally cry properly. Big, shaky, shuddering sobs that I've needed to be rid of since we left. He holds me as I weep, telling me it will be okay now. The tears become relief and I start to believe him. He doesn't blame me. I'm so, so grateful that he doesn't blame me, even though it's all my fault.

# 17.

## Madison Attallee

I feel faint and wonder what the hell the matter is. Then I realise that I've still got a nicotine patch attached to my upper arm from yesterday. Likely drip-feeding the stuff to me, and about to cause a bloody overdose in light of the cigarette I'm currently puffing on. My third of the morning. Bollocks. I peel it off and it takes little hairs with it. I shout, 'Fuck,' and the stupid cat jumps and looks haughtily at me. Everyone's a critic.

I've got the windows open. I should be out on the balcony, but Molly isn't due for days and I'll air the place before then. It's freezing as well. I'm practically a maternal saint. The coffee pot is empty, which means I've done five cups. I rub at my wounded upper arm and my hand comes away tacky. What do they put on these bloody things, superglue?

I switch on the stereo and sing poorly to the Levellers, hoping the jolly folk music might help me spring into action. Restart my day on a more even, less irritated footing. By the time I'm out the shower I realise it's probably not to be though, the rebel tunes have simply given me a background annoyance about social injustice. Marvellous. My phone beeps. It's Peter. 'Morning, beautiful. Day one nicotine free!'

Great.

I send back a smiley face and an 'x' because it seems too early to lie. My neighbour, Mrs Dodson, is hovering in the hall. I swear she waits for me. I smile politely and say, 'Good morning, Mrs Dodson.'

She beams. 'Good morning, dear, don't you look glamorous and smart as always.' She says this every morning. I'm quite sure it's a polite way of telling me I look like I'm trying too hard, and some mornings that would be the truth, but I don't feel ready without a load of slap and decent shoes. It's like armour – if I'm dressed well I feel like no one can see the mess underneath. I'm sure it harks back to my mum wandering around our estate in pyjamas, or worse, underwear. The embarrassment I used to feel. Even when my drinking reached its peak, I still did my lippy, still laid out an outfit the night before. I keep wondering if my clothes are still age appropriate and thinking I ought to tone it down – not today though. I nod and say thank you and she follows me along the hallway towards the door at the front of our building.

'Are you working another big case?' I see the glint in her eye and feel a wave of fondness towards my nosy neighbour.

'I've just started a new one.'

She nods as though she understands what I mean. 'Pop in with Molly at the weekend, won't you?'

'We'll try.'

'Have a good day, love.'

It's pretty much the same conversation every morning and actually, I quite like it, despite myself. I get in the car and switch on the stereo. Nirvana hits me and I hum along and find that the melancholy tunes start to pick me up.

Mrs Marriott has one of those wide, friendly faces; it looks like she's smiling even when she's not. It's like the opposite of my own small, sharp, pointed, and almost constantly frowning one. I have wandered past this place, but always thought it was a house. It's much nicer than the area's other private, Warrene. I had to deal with the headmistress there on a past case – she did not exude the warmth I'm getting from Mrs Marriott. It's a girls' school, and she tells me they only have thirty students per year, split into two classes. I imagine how much attention each one must get and find it easy to be impressed. The place has a nice, homely feel to it.

Her office is full to the brim with books. Each bit of space is stuffed and she waves a hand around saying, 'I just can't ever bring myself to throw them away.'

I nod. In my house, most of the books are true crime, or textbooks about abnormal psychology. I usually have to do a sweep and shove a few under the bed before Molly arrives at weekends.

I don't beat around the bush. 'You know Tabitha Jackson is missing?'

She sighs. 'Yes, poor Miriam sounded dreadful on the phone. Well, you would, wouldn't you?'

'Miriam tells me Tabitha was absent last week on Wednesday, Thursday and Friday, but that she was unaware of this.'

Mrs Marriott nods, frowning. 'Yes, there was a message on the absent student hotline, honestly it sounded like Miriam, not that we were listening for it to be someone else, if you see what I mean.'

'Do you have the recording?'

She shakes her head. 'I'm afraid not. They delete at the end of each day. Sorry.'

I shrug, it probably doesn't matter, though I'm starting to build a picture of Tabitha. A girl who has gone 'missing' before, made the front pages of the papers. Likes the hashtag #instarichkids and phones in sick to play truant. I ask Mrs Marriott, 'Is it like Tabitha to play hookey?'

She shakes her head again. 'No, or it would have rung alarm bells sooner.'

'What's she like? Personality wise.'

She smiles. 'Lovely.' I'm surprised after #instarichkids – my initial picture starts to be contradicted.

'In what way?'

'Just a nice girl – she and Delia are very helpful, active on the student council. Probably the most popular children in the year, if not the school, and you know sometimes that can bring out spite.'

I nod, wondering at the disconnect between the version I'd come up with and the one Mrs Marriott is telling me about. Having said that, Tabitha could easily have laid in to a lot of the 'sucking-up' social media. Or made fun of them, and she hadn't. I make a note to get Emma and Claudia's opinions on her posts. I can't say I understand Instagram or any other form of social media for that matter. I think back to my drinking, extremely glad that the worst thing I ever did was drunk dial or text. Imagine if I had had Facebook or Twitter or whatever. No. I cannot see the point in broadcasting your every bloody move. Claudia on the other hand loves all that nonsense, and thanks to her, MA Investigations now has accounts everywhere.

I say, 'Miriam says they've had quite a troubled relationship over the past year or so.'

She frowns. 'Well. She and Nick mentioned it when they came in after . . . the newspaper thing.'

'Because it made the papers?'

She nods, 'It was all a misunderstanding between the parents, but even the best behaved teenage girls can be problematic, Ms Attallee, as I'm sure you're aware. It's a strange time of testing boundaries and learning our place. It turned out she'd been at Stacy's house.'

I think about my own teenage years, a lot of them were spent mopping up my mother's sick, taking trips to A&E. Hiding out at Peter's. I don't know when I did my growing up. A lot of the time I feel like I'm just starting to do it now.

I ask, 'What's Stacy like?'

'Also nice – our year groups tend to be quite tight knit, on account of the small number of pupils, I'm sure.'

'But Delia is Tabitha's closest friend?'

She smiles. 'To my knowledge, yes.'

I say, 'Miriam tells me Tabitha can be excruciatingly rude, is that normal?' I was an absolute nightmare of course, but I understand my normal was way off other people's.

'Yes, sometimes. Often girls turn on their mums, but they generally become their closest confidante in later years. She's not rude here. We wouldn't encourage it, and she certainly wouldn't be head girl.'

'So, she's not like that at school?'

'No, she's wonderful. Kind, mild mannered. As I said, very bright but also always willing to help out younger girls.'

I nod. Poor Miriam. I wonder if that makes it worse, that she's good at school and awful at home. It must be very stressful. I wonder if Molly will get like that. Wouldn't that be a kicker, if she turned into a little diva and decided to come and live with me then.

'I'd like to speak to Stacy as well, if possible?'

She says, 'She's at an away game today – netball – won't be back for the rest of the day. You'd need to ask her parents, of course.'

'Maybe I could call them?'

She says, 'You're concerned for Tabitha?'

I don't sugar coat it, largely because I want that number.

'I am, yes, very. So, anything you can do to help . . .'

She nods, turns to her computer and in a few short clicks finds me their details.

I say, 'Miriam also mentioned a boy . . . Brett Carmichael?'

Mrs Marriott smiles. 'Ah, yes, he attends our brother school, they occupy the house next door, so we're more connected than you might think. We also combine sometimes for trips and what have you. Brett's had his eye on Tabitha since they were practically babies. I'm sure many of the boys have.'

We talk for a few more minutes but Mrs Marriott doesn't have much to add. She does call through to the boys' school who say Brett has a free period coming up and that I can nip in after I speak to Delia.

Golden. That's the word that keeps popping into my head the more I learn about Tabitha Jackson. I wonder how much effort it takes to maintain, and if you might sometimes just need a break from it.

I've arranged to see Delia in the school's form room. Mrs Marriott explains it's like a common room. When we get into it I realise it's nothing like the common room at my school. This one is full of plush sofas and tables with educational magazines fanned out. There's a drinks machine that seems to offer herbal teas. What kind of teenagers are these?

Delia arrives and Mrs Marriott 'leaves us to it'. She is a small, dark-haired girl. Very pretty with a round, wide-eyed baby-face. Delia appears very on edge – she chews her lower lip, her eyes dart around the room, looking everywhere but at me.

I say, 'Are you all right, Delia?' before I ask her anything.

And her panicked, 'What?' tells me something's up.

I say, 'Where's Tabitha?'

Her eyes widen and close, a scowl pinches up her features. She shrugs. 'I dunno.' The contraction doesn't work with her voice. I wonder if mockney is as trendy here as it seems to be on the TV. I wait, one beat, two. She fidgets but is forced to look at me. I smile, she doesn't smile back. 'Are you sure about that, Delia?'

She nods, but her eyes look everywhere but at mine.

'Tabitha was with you Friday night?'

Another nod.

'Why was she off school last week?'

The wide eyes again – she carries on with her furtive glances around the room. 'How should I know?'

'She didn't mention it?'

Two small, pink dots appear on either side of her face. 'Chest infection, I think she said.'

'So you did know.'

She shrugs.

I smile, trying to get her to relax. 'You've been friends for a long time?'

She nods.

'Is Brett her boyfriend?'

She sighs so I prod, 'Delia?'

'They broke up.'

I say, 'Who dumped who?'

'She dumped him.'

There's an edge to her voice. But it could mean anything. Teenage girls are often frenemies. I'm almost glad I didn't have any mates at that age. 'Was Brett upset?'

She nods. 'Of course. He loves her.'

I smile. 'Poor Brett.'

'I know.'

'Why did she dump him?'

She shrugs but answers more assertively than she has before. 'I'm not sure. Maybe she was bored?'

'Ah, she's like that, is she?' I smile again, a confidante. I see a flash of a smile so brief I may have misread it. She looks genuinely worried when she shrugs and says, 'I hope Tabs is okay.'

I smile and dig out a card, sliding it across the table to her. I'm

97

not going to get much more from her now, I don't think, but I reckon we'll need to speak again. 'If you hear from her . . . my mobile number's on there.'

She takes the card without looking at it, sliding it into her bag. I wait for her to look at me and I catch her eye. 'Or if *you* ever need to chat or anything.'

She looks away again, nibbling her lower lip and nods. I may be imagining it, but Delia was more uncomfortable than I'd expect her to be. No one wants to be interviewed, of course. But I'd be mighty surprised if Tabitha's best friend didn't know about her bunking at least.

I thank Delia, and Mrs Marriott, and walk over to the boys' school.

Brett is waiting in the headmaster's office. The head makes himself scarce once Brett says it's okay. He is Justin Bieber pretty and my guess is he'll go on to break a few hearts in the future, but right now he looks like it's his that has been smashed to pieces.

I say hello and tell him who I am, and he rushes in with, 'Sir said Tabs is missing?' and I see real, naked concern on his face.

I say, 'She is, yes. Her mother's very worried.'

He nods.

I say, 'Delia tells me Tabitha broke up with you?'

He nods again and looks like he's fighting back tears. I ask gently, 'Had you been together a long time?' trying to remember how serious things feel at sixteen. He sighs and says, 'I've known her since we were little. We've always been best friends. And with Delia too, I guess, though they'd sort of drifted apart since year eight.'

'Drifted apart how?'

He shrugs. 'I don't know exactly but Tabs was moaning that Delia was less fun.'

'Had you noticed this?'

'Nah, not really, but we are at different schools and I mainly hung out with Tabitha.'

'When did she become your girlfriend?'

He blushes and mutters, 'Year eight, I guess.'

I nod. 'And you were pretty serious about each other.'

He visibly squirms and says, 'I know it sounds stupid, but I've always known Tabitha is the one for me.'

I think about Peter who had the same thoughts at the same age. I say to Brett, 'It doesn't sound stupid. Sometimes it's just how things are.'

He smiles at me. 'She felt the same. We'd planned our whole lives, you know. Different unis – she's cleverer than me, I think. So maybe I'd stay home with our kids.' He sighs. Bless him. I can see they had everything planned. I wonder what changed Tabitha's mind.

I say, 'So what happened?'

He meets my eyes, his are wide and shiny, 'I don't know. It was so strange.'

'Strange how?'

His face turns beet red again and I assure him, 'Whatever you say will stay between us.'

He nods, takes a breath and says, 'Okay. Well. I'm a year older.' He checks to see I'm listening and I nod. 'So, I got my licence and we decided to go to this club, loads of kids from school were going. It's not really my thing, and Tabitha doesn't usually drink, but she had a fake ID and was knocking them back. Delia and I both told her to slow down, you know.'

'And she wasn't usually like that?'

He shakes his head. I ask, 'Was something upsetting her?'

He nods. 'I guess. I asked but she said she was fine and I was being boring, it was something with her and Delia, I'm pretty sure of it, and then . . .'

So, the girls had argued. I'd thought as much.

He pauses, seeming to have trouble carrying on, and I say, 'You can tell me, it might help.'

He nods. 'We hadn't . . . you know?'

'You hadn't slept together?'

He shakes his head. 'Not that I didn't want to, but we wanted it to be right. Special, you know?'

I nod. He says, 'She tried, that night, in my car. In front of Delia.' His face is screwed up at the memory.

I say, 'You didn't want to?'

He shakes his head, 'Not like that and she was drunk and being rude. She was so angry, and it wasn't like her. Tabitha is a sweetheart, that's why everyone loves her.'

'So, you said no, then what happened?'

'She got out the car, and I went to chase her, Delia helped look but we didn't find her.' His eyes rise again. 'She dumped me the next day. By text.'

Poor sod. I say, 'It sounds like maybe she was going through something.'

He nods. 'I know. I've tried to talk to her.' He adds, 'Then there was this awful article in the paper, a picture of her drunk, from that night. They were trying to make out she's like some posh party girl. But Tabs isn't like that.'

I can't help myself – I say, 'She uses the Instagram hashtag #instarichkids.'

He grins. 'Yeah, I told her that was pretty knobby, but they all do. It's like some badge-of-honour thing.' He shrugs. 'Girls love Instagram.'

'Boys not so much?'

'I just don't get the point. But the girls all want to be beautiful, they take these pouty pictures and post them. Likes pour in and they seem to love it.'

I say, 'That's odd.'

100

He nods. 'I don't get it. I mean, Tabs is gorgeous and so's Dee, but who cares if strangers think it. Seems creepy to me.' Me too. I make a note to get Emma to investigate Tabitha's social media more closely. Then I thank Brett for his time. He says, 'I hope you find her.' Then adds, 'I miss her.' And I guess he's not just talking about the last few days.

I sing along to Belly in the car and by the time I arrive at the office, my head is thrumming with little lists. Ideas ping around and I'm starting to get a feel for Tabitha in my head. Head girl, golden pupil, mentor, popular. A girl whose best friend frowns at the mention of her name, who has recently started being very rude to her mother, has broken up with her long-term sweetheart, had a disagreement with her BFF that said BFF is not mentioning. Tabitha has developed an attitude problem beyond normal hormone stuff. Miriam is scared of letting her husband down, and maybe scared of her daughter too. Miriam, who sounds so confident on the radio. Also playing out a role. Like mother like daughter? But Tabitha's problems seem quite recent.

Something's gone wrong. And when I find out what, I'll find her.

I get into the office, and everything smells lovely, like fresh coffee and something else, something sugary.

Oh man, donuts. A pile that look like they might have been homemade.

Emma says, 'Claudia has absolutely no respect for our waistlines.'

I smile, Emma is a robust woman. She could starve herself, not that she's the type, and never be thin. Claudia on the other hand is like a leggy gazelle.

Claudia comes in from the kitchen and smiles when she sees me. 'Oh good. I made cinnamon, Bethany and I got through a fair few last night but I saved these. I know they're your favourite.'

She pours me a coffee and I perch on Emma's desk. They are both waiting, ready to take notes. I go over what I know, firing names for them to look up. I tell Emma to call Stacy's parents and tell them I need to speak to her. I ask Claudia to look into the legal ramifications of breaking into Tabitha's social media accounts. I'm humming as I sit down at my desk to make lists on Post-its.

# 18.

# Ruby Williams

## *1994*

Things don't bother Ben the same way they bother me. They never used to. I wasn't a worrier. I think about it now, how carefree I was and realise I never appreciated it. I'd just let Mum take care of me, and Eric. I thought I was all grown up too, but it turns out I didn't have a clue. I'm in the flat, in bed. My heart is hammering, and my palms are sweaty. I roll a joint with a shaky hand.

I feel it now. Grown-up, and it's not good, not at all. I worry. God how I worry. All the time about every, little, thing.

My biggest one is the police. That they will come and find us. Ben will be arrested, and it will all be my fault. I owe him so much. Every time I raise it with him, he is kind, and tells me not to stress. It will all settle down and who's going to care about his dad anyway?

It stings me when he says that, though I know I can't judge. They never got on. I didn't really understand why, but in the five years my mum and Eric have been together, Ben spent most of it with his mum. I suppose that's how I developed a silly crush of sorts on him – he was a visitor and never felt exactly like my brother. Though he does now. And I'm so bloody grateful.

I wonder all the time how my mum is, but Ben has said there's not really any going back. He says I can if I want, but that we'll be in trouble. His face when he says this has that look where he's trying to be calm and fair, I guess. But underneath it I can see he's scared. If it was just me, I think I'd hand myself in. I'm under eighteen after all. I said to Ben I could take the blame, but he shook his head and laughed. 'How would you knock a grown man down dead?' It's all such a mess.

He comes back later that afternoon with someone else – he tells me the boy's going to be doing a bit of work for him and will be moving in here eventually. He's a tall, gangly mixed-race lad. He looks like his arms and legs are too long for his body, they move almost separately of the rest of him. He rolls a lot of joints, one after the other, and he and Ben listen to loud music. I use the stove to make us all dinner and I take hits on the joints as I'm passed them. It stops the worrying at least. The boy, Darren, smiles at me but I ignore him. I'm too stressed out to even think about boys right now.

Apart from Ben, and not in that way. I need to make it up to him somehow. So I keep the flats clean, I cook us food. My mum would die if she saw me. At home I never even cleaned my room. I didn't even know how to use the washing machine. And I never said thanks for any of it either. I inhale on a joint, handing it back to Darren, and blink away tears.

I don't sleep too well. I miss home. I miss Mum, though I can't go back. Not now, after what we've done. What I've caused. I get up and find the end of one of the joints in the ashtray. I smoke it quickly. I'm relieved when the image of Eric's stricken face falling towards me disappears up in the air, along with the pungent, fruity smoke. As my head hits the pillow I feel as though the mattress is made of cotton wool and I am sinking down into it. All the other horrible thoughts that are clamouring for attention fade away into the background and I drift blissfully into sleep.

# 19.

# Miriam Jackson

I speak to Nick – I can't really put it off any longer – but I still don't tell him.

I don't tell my husband that our daughter is missing. Because then I'd have to tell him where I was when she disappeared. And I can't do that.

The worry about her is like a physical thing. A gnawing, churning beast that works to conjure up every worst-case scenario and feed them all into my brain on an awful devastating loop. It is eating away at me, sending sharp, throbbing pain into my head and a spinning acidic churn into my gut. I am without my baby. I don't know where she is. It's so acute I could howl and for a moment I sit dumbfounded. My deceit adds an extra layer to it all. More pain. Pain I've made myself.

There are now so many things I'm not saying. I wonder if this is the beginning of the end. If this is how rot starts to erode marriages. A slow trickle of dishonesty. Starting as minor things, the way I don't tell him that sometimes I get sick with fright before I go on air, that my mother was awful to live with, and I am scared of becoming her. That I'm frightened of my own mind, my genes, of being either my mum or my dad. That I worry about him surrounded by gorgeous actresses. That I wonder why he doesn't want me and if it's them he wants instead. Even though his reputation is solid; there are no rumours. I should be grateful. Nick is a rarity in his business. I am told all of the time I am lucky. Lucky that a man with all that opportunity doesn't cheat. It's taken as a given that I would accept it. I've never felt overly jealous in that way before. But I feel it now. I wonder if this is how insecurity grows, from our own failings.

I've cheated, maybe he would too? I've always trusted him. It's one of the huge comforts of our life. I wonder, have I broken that too? I don't quiz him. I never would.

I don't really tell Nick my inner thoughts.

I don't ever tell him about my past. Not in detail. I don't tell him about being a lonely little girl, scared of my mum and her terrible heavy moods, angry with my dad for leaving me to live with it. I don't tell him that I practically moved in with Ben, I don't tell him about Ben at all. Or Ruby dying in front of me.

Now look where I am. Infidelity. Tabitha. Missing for nearly forty-eight hours.

He chats about LA. Moans about the weather. I murmur that it's cold here, and he says, 'Sorry, darling, I shouldn't complain. I miss you terribly.'

Tears prickle behind my eyes. I squeeze them shut. I miss him too. The pain of it hits me right in the gut. Him pottering around the kitchen, joking with Tabs, helping her learn lines for a school play or attempting to pick up dance steps from her. Ungracefully. He has us in fits of giggles. My family. Where is she?

'Miriam.'

My voice is barely a whisper. 'I miss you too.'

He laughs. 'Miriam, are you all emotional?'

I force a chuckle. 'I guess I am.'

His voice lowers. 'I'll be home soon enough.' And my heart starts to race a little. Not yet. I need to get her back first. As if reading my mind, he asks, 'Is Tabs there?'

'No.' I almost shout.

He laughs again, 'She's got a better social life than the pair of us, eh?'

Everything is always a joke with my husband. Everything is always fine. He's been shielded from life's tougher aspects. He has people he belongs to, does Nick. Not just his family, but his boarding school, his friends and a whole network of contacts. Showbusiness is a lot about who you know and his dad, a banker, made it his business to know everyone. When Nick wanted to get into film, Daddy knew someone they could ask.

Now Nick has come up, made successes of his own. He is sure of his place in the world. Secure. These are the things he has given me. A family, belonging. And look what I've done.

No. I won't tell him yet. I'll find her. *Of course* I'll find her. Anything else isn't an option. The gnawing beast starts up. I push it away, don't entertain it. I don't let the panic take over because it will drown me.

I say goodbye to my husband and tell him I love him. I stare at my phone, I'll call him back now, tell him she's missing. This is bigger than me. Too big. I'm about to press call when there is a knock at the door. I jump and then I'm racing. Her, maybe it's her.

I can almost feel Tabitha in my arms, back where she belongs. But it's not her. I feel sick.

I can see him through the glass and my breathing changes from steady to ragged and uneven. He has been calling, messaging. I sent a curt text saying I couldn't talk and he'd rung again. I'd ignored it. Now he is here, at my house. Mine and my husband's house, again, and this time with no preamble, no invitation. I open the door and he is grinning, a big beaming smile. I manage. 'Ben?'

# 20.

# Ruby Williams

*1994*

Ben and Mim are all loved up. I think she'd be here all the time if she could. She says she has to be around for her mum, though she doesn't say any more. I miss home so badly. For all the moaning I did I was safe there and loved. I thought Ben cared about me, but when Miriam's around him it's like nothing else exists. He waits on her hand and foot.

Ben's hardly ever here, he's got a lot of business to look after, and when he is, he's always with *her*. I know I've got no right to complain and I try really, really hard not to. If anything, I go out of my way to be super nice to Mim. But inside, I kind of hate her. I hate that she's just here for fun, that she could change her mind and go home at any minute.

I find it hard not to compare us. We are both roughly the same age but we're like a different species. Everything about her is shiny, and polished. Her hair shimmers, her eyes sparkle. Her skin is lightly tanned and she talks about trips to Spain to see her dad. I've never been anywhere outside England and I have no memory of my dad. All I know is Mum says he's a prick, and I believe her. She seems to have perfected that little girl lost act and Ben has fallen for it hook, line, and sinker. I am burning with envy. It's hard not to feel excluded when you find yourself stuck in a room with them. They share soft, adoring looks, and he's always touching her. A hand on her shoulder, her arm. His eyes follow her everywhere she goes. I swear he'd go to the lav with her if he could.

Darren has moved in properly now, so the third wheel thing has got a bit better. He's turned out to be okay as well. He's harmless, he just likes to smoke a lot of weed, which I reckon he sells. He spends the daytime in the flat below and I can hear his phone buzzing, people coming and going. Ben's down there a lot too. They are up to something, but I don't know what. Darren likes to make music. Or *chooons*, as he says. I smile thinking about him. He's got me singing again now.

We've recorded some songs together and he's called me into his room to listen back. I sound pretty good, but the production is excellent too.

I tell him he's well talented and he shakes his head. 'Nah, man, I'm determined and I like to learn things. *You've* got talent. Born with a voice like that. I could listen to you for the rest of my life.' I blush when he says this. I like hanging out with him, a lot. He asks me about my mum and whether she can sing. It makes me laugh. I tell him she's tone deaf but loves to give it a go anyway. He tells me about his nan and says she sang real old-fashioned stuff. He says she was a proper cockney and sang in a funny accent. His impression makes me laugh and when I laugh he smiles back.

Darren says I'm going to be a superstar which is silly, but maybe I'll be able to sing full-time – he wants us to form a band, and I think I'd like that. Who knows? So things aren't too bad. Not really.

Even if I do miss Mum.

# 21.

# Miriam Jackson

I am so stunned to see him standing on my doorstep that for a few seconds I don't even speak. My cat wanders out, traitorously, worming its way between his legs, purring. He leans down and scoops her up in broad arms. I think about those arms holding me, feeling safe. Then I think about my husband, who comes through this door all the time. Ben grins and says, 'What's his name?'

'What?' I hear the crossness in my voice, though Ben seems oblivious.

'The cat.'

Everything feels surreal, and wrong, a little off kilter. 'Mr Boots.'

He's still grinning, that wide and gorgeous grin. 'Cute.' And he wanders in, uninvited, whooshing past me. Mr Boots still clutched to his chest. I shut the door and follow. 'What are you doing here?'

He stops in the kitchen and leans down, plonking the cat onto the floor. Mr Boots makes a disgruntled mewling sound. Ben comes over to me and folds me in his arms. I feel his breath hot on my hair and I want to pull away but it's soothing. So soothing, and he's the only person I can tell about Tabitha. He says, 'I wanted to make sure you were all right.'

I feel odd, sick, disjointed from myself, but I should be grateful, shouldn't I? That he's checking. That I'm not alone. Standing in the kitchen wrapped in the arms of a man who is not my husband. A man I've been with recently. I see Nick's reading glasses resting on the side. I push Ben away and somehow find my voice. 'You shouldn't be here.'

He says, 'I know. I'm sorry. I wanted to check you were okay. You didn't pick up your phone.' It sounds accusatory and I feel a stab of annoyance. He is the only one who knows what's going on. My child is missing, yet he suggests I ought to prioritise him.

I don't say anything. He smiles. I feel a stab of pity for him. And also for Nick and for me too. What a mess.

He says, 'You haven't heard from her?' but it's not really a question. I feel tears well up in my eyes. He's there, again, and I'm in his embrace but it is uncomfortable now. I want him to go, I am thinking about my little girl, not him, not us.

I realise I'm crying. He pushes me back, heads to the kitchen side and pulls off some kitchen roll. We never use cloths to wipe the sides, Nick says they spread germs, so we always have an abundance of kitchen roll. I shake my head. I don't like having it full of my husband while my eyes are full of Ben. I take the proffered tissue and wipe my face. I must look wretched. I ask him, 'Shouldn't you be at work?'

He shrugs, 'Will you be okay?'

His head tilts to the side and he places a firm, warm hand on my shoulder. I resist the urge to tell him it's none of his business, to go away. Instead I nod.

He smiles, drops his hand and we start to walk out. He stops at the mantelpiece, fingers a photo in a silver frame. Nick and me.

He says, 'He'll be disappointed, I suppose.'

'What?'

'Will you wait for him to get home?'

I shake my head. Had I told Ben I hadn't mentioned Tabitha to Nick? I say, 'I'm hoping she'll come back before then.'

He says, 'God, of course. Tabitha. That's got to be sorted first, hasn't it.'

He reaches out and rubs my shoulder again. We are standing by the doorway to my kitchen, the picture of Nick and I is askew from where he touched it. His arm drops, and I put my hand where his just was, and ask, 'What did you mean? Will I wait for him to get home?'

'To tell him. About us.'

'Tell . . . Nick about us?'

He nods. I sound like a stuttering idiot. My phone rings. Madison. Tabitha, I immediately think Tabitha. I pick up on the second ring. I answer in small disjointed sentences. But I am grateful for the distraction. Grateful not to have to answer Ben. But she hasn't found her.

I tell him, 'A colleague. She's going to head over. We have some stuff to do.'

He smiles and says, 'No problem, Mim, my superstar.'

I say, 'I'm not.' An automatic reaction to any praise.

He pauses and says, 'Tabitha will be back before you know it.'

I nod, I wish I could believe him. When he tells me, 'I'm here for you,' I feel a mixture of relief and fear. When he's gone, I wish he was back. It's an odd cocktail of contradictory emotions. Is this how adultery always is? How do people do it. At the moment I'm pumped full of adrenaline, high on the crisis in hand. But I can feel the guilt. The guilt that is always there, now accompanied by nervous panic at the thought of Nick finding out.

The doorbell rings and I nearly fall off my seat. I answer and Madison is there. She looks at me and takes me by the elbow, walking me back into my kitchen where I burst into tears.

# 22.

# Madison Attallee

Emma is showing Claudia and me around the new website. It looks really good. I'm so pleased I've left her to get on with it. It has lots of links to the articles commending us for our work on the Reynolds case, and a key interview with Kate Reynolds, whom Claudia is still in touch with. Kate has kept her up to date on her travels. Claudia and Emma are now debating which pictures to use in our bios. I couldn't care less – I tend to look like I've just left an asylum in every single one – so excuse myself and stand out in the cold, smoking. I sent Molly a text via Rob wishing her luck with her play tonight. I check my phone, still no response but hopefully he's shown her the message. I'll be there anyway. The thought causes a spike of anxiety, which I push away. I'll be going with Peter, thank goodness. But I'm nervous as hell. It will be one of the few times I've seen Rob anywhere but at his front door, and at a distance, for a while. No point thinking about it now. It's not happening just yet.

Claudia managed to get hold of Stacy's parents and though they are reluctant they have agreed that I can go and speak to her.

I get in my car and drive back through Norbiton and up onto Kingston Hill.

I ring a doorbell which plays 'Für Elise' at a dreadful pitch and the door is answered by a tall thin woman with a kind face. She says, 'Hi, I'm Lindsay Adams Riley. I'm Stacy's mother.'

She holds out a hand, which I shake. Then she gestures for me to follow her down the hall. She says, 'I hope you don't mind but I told Stacy you wanted to talk to her about Tabitha staying here.'

I do mind actually but it's too late now. I mutter, 'No problem.'

Mrs Adams Riley sighs as we get into the kitchen, 'To be honest, myself and Mr Riley were both away on business and Stacy was here with our old nanny. I'm ashamed to say it but the nanny let Stacy have rather too much free reign.'

I say, 'It's tough if you're both working.'

She nods, 'It is, yes, but bills don't pay themselves.' She goes on, 'Mrs Marriott seemed to think Tabitha was perhaps in some kind of trouble . . .'

I smile, 'I'm sure you can appreciate that confidence is of the utmost importance, particularly in light of who her parents are.'

She nods. 'Of course.' Though she looks a little bit disappointed. 'Hang on.' She wanders into the hallway and calls her daughter's name. A tall teenager appears and Mrs Adams Riley ushers her into a seat on the breakfast bar opposite mine. She slumps down with that closed slouch I am starting to associate with youths. Mrs Adams Riley says, 'I've told Stacy that the truth in this situation is vital.' Looking pointedly at Stacy.

Stacy frowns but she looks nervous too. Mrs Adams Riley says to me, 'We had a little chat before you arrived, as I said.'

I say, 'Hello, Stacy.'

She mumbles, 'Hi.'

Her mother says, 'Tell the investigator what you told me, then.'

She still doesn't speak but I can guess what she's about to say, I ask her, 'Tabitha didn't stay with you that night, did she?'

She shakes her head and says, 'I didn't think it was a big deal.'

I say, 'It's okay, Stacy, you're not in any trouble. Okay?'

She looks at her mother who sighs, 'Nor with me.'

She tells me that they had all been at the club and that she had walked in on Delia and Tabitha arguing in the toilets. They'd all drunk too much and she'd been with her friends. Tabitha had gone home with Delia and Brett, or so Stacy had thought. She said Tabitha rang her at about four a.m.

I ask, 'You were awake?'

She looks sideways at her mum again, 'Um, some people came back, I'd invited Tabs and Dee but they said they were going home.'

Mrs Riley Adams mutters, 'The nanny spent most of that week at her boyfriend's, apparently.'

I say to Stacy, 'So she called?'

'Yes, said she was going to be in loads of trouble, that she'd forgotten to call home, and could I say she was here.'

'Do you know where she was?'

She shakes her head, 'I'd assumed with her new fella somewhere.'

New fella, not Brett. Brett had gone home heartbroken, and she hadn't gone back to Delia's either.

I say, 'What new fella, Stacy?'

She looks from her mum to me. Her mother scowls, Stacy says, 'Some guy, older. I saw them together.'

'How old?'

She shrugs. 'I don't know, old like you two.'

I suppress a smile. I'm thirty-nine. I must be ancient to Stacy. 'What did he look like?'

She shrugs again. 'I didn't see him close up. I saw Tabitha getting out of his car.'

'How did you know he was old?'

'Well, he was driving, and also some of his hair was grey.'

'What colour was the rest of it?'

'Mostly brown. Kind of long.'

'He didn't get out of the car?'

'No, just dropped her and drove off.'

'What type of car was it?'

She shrugs. 'I'm not sure, black, I think.'

'Did you ask Tabitha who he was?'

She nods, 'I remember saying "that's not your dad?" and she laughed and said definitely not. I kind of figured she meant . . .' She blushes, looks at her mum. 'You know.'

'A boyfriend?'

She nods. 'It was just before she broke up with Brett. She told me not to tell anyone about it. I figured so as not to hurt his feelings. I was surprised, Tabitha and Brett always seemed made for each other, you know, and cheating wasn't something I'd have thought she would do.'

'Tabitha's not that kind of girl?'

'No, she's really nice. Considerate.'

'Did you tell anyone?'

She says, 'No, I forgot about it, to be honest.' A shrug.

I thank Stacy and her mother and leave. I dial Delia's mobile number, 'Hello.'

'Delia, it's Madison Attallee.'

'Yes?'

'I need to speak to you again, could we meet?'

She pauses then, 'What about?'

I'd rather be able to see her face but I don't want to spook her. 'Stacy mentioned seeing Tabitha with an older man.'

'Oh.'

'I wondered if you might know who it could have been?'

'I don't know.'

I don't entirely believe her, but Tabitha had told Stacy to keep it to herself, so maybe it wasn't common knowledge. 'Delia, it might be important.'

116

'Honestly, I don't know, maybe it was her dad?' She sounds annoyed.

I say, 'Maybe.' But I don't think it was. I thank her and hang up.

I head back to my office. Where are you, Tabitha? Who is the man in the car? As soon as I find that out I'll find her.

I dial Miriam to tell her as soon as I'm back. She picks up on the second ring.

'Hello.' Her voice is stiff.

'Miriam, hi, it's Madison.'

'Hello.'

'Miriam, are you okay?'

She pauses and then says, 'Yes, fine.'

But she doesn't sound it. 'Miriam?'

She says, 'I'm still here.'

I ask her, 'Can you talk?'

She says, 'Not really.' My radar picks up. Something is wrong.

'Are you okay?' I ask again.

'Not really, no.'

'I'm on my way.'

'That's fine.'

She hangs up. I grab my coat, tell the girls something's not right, and I'm gone.

I get to Miriam's quickly, traffic is light and I say a little thanks to the traffic gods because I can just about fit this in. I can't be late tonight.

When she opens the door, I'm glad I trusted my instinct. Her face is ashen and there is something more there than just worry for her kid. I lead her into the kitchen, towards one of the breakfast stools. She is pale, that deathly grey colour we get before we throw up. I say, 'Miriam, what's happened?'

And she promptly bursts into tears.

I sit opposite her. Glad that I got in the car. Glad that I knew something was off. I ask her, 'What do you need to tell me, Miriam?'

She makes a sound like a small moan and says, 'I've done something very stupid.'

I say, 'You need to tell me about it.'

She shakes her head. I wait, she shakes it again and I snap, 'Miriam.'

She turns big, tearful eyes on me, and reiterates, 'It's got nothing to do with Tabitha.'

'Let me decide that.' Full pictures. That is what we need when we investigate. Even at the end of cases when things are tied up and done, not everything will be known, but knowledge is power. Knowledge is what equips us. I wait. One second, two.

I say, 'You need to tell me.' Softly now. People never realise what, in fact, might help. What is linked and what isn't.

She sighs, but eventually she starts talking.

She starts telling me about her first love, Ben, about a drug dealer called Darren and a girl called Ruby. She swallows a lot. We pause, and I get her a glass of water. She tells me about bumping into Ben recently. I confirm that Tabitha went missing two weeks later. She nods but is quick to add, 'It's got nothing to do with Tabitha.' But I'm not so sure and I make a note of Ben's name, and Darren's and Ruby's, though she's unsure of Darren's surname. She says Ruby was Ben's step-sister.

I ask her what Ben looks like now and when she tells me my heart starts to beat a little bit faster.

I call in to the office and give the list of names to Claudia, I tell her to contact Deanie at the station and have her run them. I ask her to send Emma over and to tell her she'll be needed to stay with Miriam this evening. I send an email from my phone to Emma and Claudia outlining what Stacy said, what Miriam has told me, and my discomfort about Ben.

I ask Miriam if she has anyone she can stay with and she whispers, 'No.' I tell her she should call Nick, tell him to come back, but she shakes her head.

The doorbell rings. I let Emma in. I rest a hand on Miriam's shoulder and I say, 'My kid's in a play tonight. I have to go.'

'Of course.'

Tabitha has been gone for over two days.

# 23.

# Madison Attallee

Once I would never, ever have taken time out from a case. Even if I wasn't being paid overtime. Even if Molly was sick. I'm not comfortable doing it now, but I have that running list in my head of things that are important. Things that matter. My sobriety, for example. Everything hinges on that. I know that now. I get it on a deep level. If I drink, I'm fucked. It's game over. Molly will be gone. MA Investigations will be gone. And I'll be consigned to death, whether it's quick and pathetic or long and arduous. Like my mum's. The living hell of her daily life could be mine, I have no illusions about that. So that comes first. When I discussed amends with a woman who has been sober a lot longer than me, when I said I could never make it up to Molly, she said you will, if you choose to. I've told Molly I'll be there tonight and I'm going to be.

I have a bad feeling about Ben. I'm not a fan of coincidences and I suspect Deanie will turn up something. I'm trying not to panic Miriam but I also need her to be careful. Emma will stay with her this evening, so I know she'll be safe. Tabitha isn't going to show up any quicker whether I hunt tonight or first thing in the morning. Usually when a child has been missing this long, they're dead, with teenagers they are likely runaways, which is where I'd firmly placed Tabitha. But the fresh information about Miriam's lover makes me think there's a pretty good chance Tabitha is not *just* a runaway but in danger from whoever she's run to or with.

I let the thoughts rush around my head and then I push them aside. Just for a few hours, while I'm a mum.

Everything in my wardrobe is ridiculous. I can't find a single outfit that says 'mother watching school play'. I try on about nine different things and eventually put on the black trouser suit I started with. I add a pair of sling-backs and a grey silk shirt. Peter picks me up, and we discuss the case briefly. I'm assured that Deanie will relay any information they have that might help and that the force will step in if and when we need them to.

Then he stretches an arm across to my side of the car and says, 'Are you all right?'

I sigh, 'I think so, yes.'

He says, 'You're her mother and you've every right to be there tonight.'

I'm almost cross at him for knowing my thoughts and am about to snap at him when he says, 'At least you have a super-hot date on your arm, eh?'

I roll my eyes, but I'm smiling, 'This is a date to you? A school play?'

He shrugs, 'Time with you is always special wherever it's spent.'

Tears spring into my eyes, for God's sake. I blink them away. 'The rate you drive at we'll be lucky to make the start, Branning.'

He laughs, 'But at least we'll get there alive.'

When Peter and I do finally arrive at the school I notice that most of the other mums are in jeans and chunky ankle boots. Fucking great. I have a nicotine patch slapped on my arm and

121

it's itching the hell out of me. I try to resist rubbing it. It's not even reducing the cravings and, as a result, I feel a winning combination of rage, anxiety and fear. By the time we park I wish I'd just had a fag. I feel my annoyance levels raising. We do the ticket line, the awkward mum and dad bar where I go for a lemonade for me and a bottled beer for Peter, and now we're looking for our seats. Everything is taking ages of course, and there are people everywhere. I mutter an expletive and Peter shushes me. I frown, then mutter 'sorry', probably insincerely. He smiles at me as though I'm terribly amusing. It makes me want to hit him in his understanding, patient face. But I don't. I smile back.

I hear a voice behind me say, 'Hello, Madison.' And I spin around and come face to face with Rob and Janet. I sigh heavily before I can help it, then plaster a too bright smile on, remembering to at least try not to be a bitch. Even if I am here in awful ex-husband hell. I manage to say, 'Hi,' without vomiting.

Janet looks as awkward as I feel. She's in jeans and ankle boots. Great. I itch at the patch on my arm. Peter shakes Rob's hand despite the fact that the last time they saw each other Rob was confronting Peter at the station. Peter looks relaxed and comfortable as always. He leans down to kiss Janet on the cheek. I see Rob look at him, eyes narrowed, after taking his hand stiffly. I hover behind Peter. I'm no good at genuine displays but fake ones are way beyond me. I'm reminded, not for the first time and certainly not the last, that I'm socially awkward and uncomfortable with physical contact. It's a relief when Janet nods at me. Peter smiles at everyone as though we're all great mates and says, 'Looking forward to seeing Molly do her thing?'

Rob's eyes get even smaller. 'Yes, I am looking forward to seeing my daughter perform.'

He emphasises the word 'my' and catches sight of me as I roll my eyes. He looks me up and down. 'Come straight from work, Madison?'

I shrug and say, 'Sure.' But inside I'm fuming. He knows me well enough to know I will have agonised over what to wear, he witnessed it before many a parents' evening. He also knows that I will have got it wrong. Peter places a hand on the small of my back and says, 'God knows how she always manages to look so bloody gorgeous at the end of the day.' I smile at him gratefully. Janet looks at her shoes. Rob carries on scowling and sort of grabs her by the arm, indicating it's time for them to go. Peter keeps smiling and says goodbye. We find our seats and sit. Peter leans over and whispers in my ear, 'You do look beautiful, by the way.'

I hiss back, 'I don't pull it off like the other mums.'

He runs a hand up my thigh. 'Why would you want to?' And he waggles his eyebrows at me. I feel a flush build up despite myself and move his hand. He grins. Shit.

We sit through half an hour that feels like days of groups of really little kids singing badly. Then the play begins and that drags too. Molly only has a couple of lines but she shouts them out with gusto and I feel immensely proud of her, especially when she flicks a glance at us and smiles. It makes the rest of it bearable. We all wait afterwards. Rob says several times that there's no need for us to hang around. I smile sweetly and say I want to congratulate Molly. Resisting saying 'MY daughter'. Peter smiles benignly, a hand making small circles on my lower back. I feel hugely grateful that he is here.

Molly finally arrives, and waves as though us all gathered here in our awful, awkward circle is the most normal thing in the world. She launches into a running dialogue of the evening and I say she did brilliantly. She asks if Peter and I are coming to dinner with them and there is a terrible, long pause. I should say something, but I can't think what. Finally, Peter ruffles her

123

hair and says not tonight as we have an early start, but we'll definitely do Five Guys at the weekend. She nods, gives us both hugs and heads off with Rob and Janet.

We get in the car. Peter offers to drive, and I say yes because I'm desperate for a fag. He pulls out of the car park gently. I struggle out of my jacket, rip off the patch and fumble around in the glove compartment for my Marlboro Lights. I catch him smirking at me and frown. He tells me I did well with Molly, Janet and Rob. I don't want to talk about it. I whack up the volume on Sabbath and look out of the window. When we get to mine, I expect him to get into his own car, but he follows me up the stairs and into my flat. I turn around to ask if he wants a drink and he leans in and kisses me before I can speak.

It's long and slow, and gets me in all the right places. He pulls back, head tilted to one side. In answer to his question I take his hand and lead him into my bedroom.

We lie in bed, Peter making circles on my back with his fingers. I sigh. He says, 'You're thinking about the case, aren't you?'

'Sorry.'

He laughs. 'Hopefully I distracted you for a few minutes at least?'

I smile. 'Of course.'

He sighs, 'Madison, call Emma, for God's sake.'

Emma assures me that Miriam is okay. Though I know she probably isn't, but she is at least coping. She said her colleague Anna came by to discuss some work stuff and that Emma had advised Miriam to go in to the station tomorrow. I say that's probably a good idea. Though there's really no way of keeping things normal for Miriam right now I don't need her panicking and getting in my way.

I have an email from Claudia. She's found Ruby's mother

who lives on my old estate, and Ben Hedges has a limited company and a website 'All that glitters'.

I update Peter, who nods, but looks sleepy. I say, 'I'm just going to look up a few bits then . . .' He rolls his eyes but doesn't protest.

## 24.

## Ruby Williams

## *1994*

Ben has asked me to put on something nice. I don't have much really. He gave me money for new stuff but I'd bought a couple of pairs of Levis and two tracksuits, nothing 'nice'. Most of my clothes are at home, I think with a sharp pang. I have one black dress with me. The one I was going to wear to sing at the rave. To start my new life. Mum bought it for me, even though Eric said it was too short and too low cut. It had been for my fourteenth birthday party. It's a bit small now but I get in it, thinking I'll just have to sit carefully. I blink back tears thinking about that shopping trip. It was a good day. Mum was never consistent, and she didn't act like a grown-up, but she could be lovely sometimes. Eric had given in over the dress and taken us both out to dinner, saying a hundred times over how lucky he was to be out with two beauts. Eric.

It's too cold for the dress today. Ben said he'd be here to pick me up at lunchtime. I slip into the heels I had to go with it, a shock to my feet after months of my Nikes. I sit nervously by the front door waiting. He hadn't come home last night and Mim's not here either. This isn't that unusual, he does a lot of his 'work' at night. I don't delve too much into what it is exactly. I feel bad that we can't go home and he has to duck and dive. He has a car now so at least that makes things easier.

I don't really mind that Ben is out a lot. Darren is in most of the time and I like hanging out with him, getting stoned and making music. Darren is respectful, not like boys I've fooled around with before, all hands and slobber.

I haven't had a joint yet this morning. Ben had gently asked me not to. I'd shrugged like it was no problem, but normally by now I'd have smoked a few and I'm starting to feel edgy without it. I find that if I go too long, sitting in my own head, bad thoughts start to clamour in, each one vying for attention. Usually it's Eric, falling backwards, lying in a pool of his own blood. And Mum, screaming at me, 'What have you done?' I shut my eyes. Aware that I'm starting to sweat. I dab at my top lip with my hand and try to think of other things.

I sing softly to myself. The song I've been working on with Darren and the next few lines fall into place in my head. I think about Darren and I get that swell in my stomach. Butterflies, I guess you'd call it. He looks at me like I'm the best thing in the world. I often think that Mum would like him and when I'm lying around, stoned and daydreaming, I let myself imagine. Eric, alive and well, Mum, me and Darren. Maybe even a wedding one day. Silly, I know. I don't suppose I can ever take him home, and so far we haven't even kissed, but I'm sure he likes me. I feel it in my guts. I'm about to go and write the lyrics down when the door opens, and Ben is there.

He smiles broadly, 'Hey, kiddo.'

I grin back, accepting now that our relationship is always going to be siblings and nothing more. To be honest I'm kind of pleased with how it's turned out. I'm even trying to make more of an effort with Mim. Especially since Darren joked that I was jealous of her. I don't want him thinking I'm soft on anyone else.

Ben tells me I look nice, and I say thanks. We get into his car, a rickety old BMW, but a BMW nonetheless, as he points out often enough, and we're off.

I'm itching to smoke and ask Ben if I can have a fag. He hands me an unopened box, smiles and says to keep them. I don't smoke cigarettes, not really. But it'll do until I can skin-up. I light it out of the window. Glad of the cool air coming in, aware that my armpits are damp and hoping I don't start to smell.

We head out of London, into the suburbs and back to Kingston. I say, 'Ben should we be here?'

He smiles at me, 'Don't worry.' But I *am* worried. What if we get pulled? What if we get arrested? And then a fleeting thought, would it be so bad? I could go home. My heart aches for my mum, my house. My old life. I get thoughts again of bringing Darren here. Of going home. I push them away, sure that's not where Ben is taking me.

Eventually we pull up outside a large house. Nicer than anything I've ever seen before. Ben sees me looking in awe and smiles. I ask, 'Who lives here?'

'My mum.'

'I'm here to meet her?'

He smiles and nods. 'You're practically my sister, aren't you?' I beam at that. He shrugs. 'See, you're family.'

He helps me out of the car. The door swings open before we have a chance to knock and a tall, smiling woman answers. The woman says, 'I'm Reeva, Ben has told me so much about you.' She's not exactly beautiful but she's really glamorous and I immediately feel a mess, with my painful shoes that are a size too small, and my tiny dress. The woman doesn't seem to mind though and takes me into an embrace, wafting a nice smell as she does, and leading me down a long corridor. She leaves an arm draped over my shoulders.

The house is fancy. I've never been anywhere like it – it even makes our nice flat look a bit rubbish – and everything is so clean. I sneak glances about as we go and reckon there must be at least four rooms just coming off this corridor alone. We end up in a large living room. I try to perch on one of the sofas with Ben next to me. It's so soft though that I sink right in, struggling to stay upright.

Reeva is smiling and I find myself blushing. She's not at all like Donna, though I think Mum is probably prettier, but she doesn't have all the class. Donna looks like what she is. Cheap and tatty, like I'll be one day. I reckon Reeva never looks tatty.

'Can I get you a drink, Ruby?'

I say sure and that I don't mind what. Ben asks for a whiskey and Coke. I watch her pour them from the bar in the corner of the room. She hands it to me and I take a large gulp, immediately scared of spilling it. I don't really drink but find the alcohol soothes my nerves a bit.

I knew that Ben's mum had done well after leaving Ben and Eric. My mum said she was a stripper, but she doesn't look like it. She looks posh. I drain my drink. Reeva takes it and refills it for me, saying, 'Ben tells me you sing?'

I nod. 'What a wonderful talent to have. And you're so pretty.' She's looking at Ben as she says it and I see him nod out of the corner of my eye. I feel my face blushing. I take a swig from the new drink.

Ben says, 'She is, isn't she?'

I wish the sofa would open up and swallow me. I smile, awkward, and slush back more drink.

Reeva says, 'I bet the boys love you, don't they?'

I don't know what to say to that. I laugh nervously. Truth is I've never been with a boy properly, not that I'd ever let on to it, and I give the impression of being experienced. But I always think of Mum, pushing me in a buggy at fifteen. I've messed around but never gone the whole way.

I've decided it'll be with Darren.

The door opens and a fat, dark-haired man comes in. Reeva immediately stands and smiles at him, working her way to the bar, pouring a drink and passing it to him. She introduces us. 'This is Mr Walker. He's my husband.' She beams proudly. My first thought is that Eric is much better-looking. I mean, he's old and everything but this man is huge, he has a friendly face though, like the fat controller in *Thomas*. I stand up to shake his hand and stagger a little bit on the heels. The booze catching up with me. He runs a hand down my side and I jump back, looking to Ben who smiles at me as though it's okay.

The man, Mr Walker, steps back, looking me up and down. I feel uncomfortable being scrutinised and I look from Reeva to Ben for reassurance. They are both smiling.

He says, 'Ben tells me you two have had to leave home?'

Now my heart is pounding faster. Has he called the police? Will I be arrested? Will Ben? If he is, I'll tell them the truth. That it's my fault. That I'm sorrier than I could ever say.

Ben says, 'Yes. We're on the run, I suppose.' And then he laughs like it's no big deal.

Mr Walker nods. 'Eric likely got what he deserved. Useless man.' I feel disloyal when he says that. Eric and Ben had their problems, but he'd been pretty nice to me. I realise now in this moment that I loved Eric. Tears sting the back of my eyes. I don't like the way Mr Walker is looking at me.

I swallow, the big man slides up next to me again, so close I can feel his breath on my cheek. Mr Walker says, 'You'll need some money. Pretty girl like you, and talented, too, Ben says. I think I'll have some work for you.'

# 25.

# Miriam Jackson

I haven't really slept and I feel terrible. When I look in the mirror my face confirms the hours of restless, fitful tossing and turning. My eyes are red-rimmed, inside and out, no amount of concealer can hide it. I try eye drops, a trick I picked up when I'd had to go back to work before Tabitha had slept through. Even though we'd had the nanny. We shouldn't have bothered. I'd hear her anyway, crying in the night, and I could never not get up, could never not comfort her. I feel that awful panic rise up again. My mouth gets chalky. I want to comfort her now.

By the time I get downstairs, I look awake enough.

Emma is already up, having spent the night in the spare room, for which I'm grateful despite my protestations. She makes me add her mobile number to my phone and tells me to call if ever I can't get Madison. She says they are there for me if I need anything, no matter how minor, and that Madison will call me at some point this morning. I thank her, smile and tell her, for probably the fourth or fifth time, that they are overreacting. She squeezes my arm and says goodbye. My heart hammers.

My phone pings. Ben. 'Morning, gorgeous.'

The instructions from Madison are to not engage, do not under any circumstances mention Tabitha. Just in case they are linked – she says 'just in case' but I am certain this is what she thinks, and that me playing my hand could jeopardise her safety.

Last night Emma had done her best to keep me calm and actually the panic is only just now setting in, so it must have worked. She made me tea and thick white toast, slathered in butter. I realised I was starving and wolfed it down. This morning I am disgusted that I managed to eat at all.

At about nine, my doorbell had rung and I had jumped out of my skin, but it was just Anna. Poor Anna who I hadn't even considered in all of this. I hadn't checked my emails, or been in to work at all yesterday, and I usually pop in even on the days I'm not on air. I introduced Emma as a friend. Anna looked at me curiously, the same way she had when she'd asked who I was meeting in my glittery shoes.

It's one of the things about working together so closely. Anna and I know the ins and outs of each other's lives, I suppose. But she didn't quiz me. She had a stack of notes and I'd faltered. Anna took my pause as me being annoyed, but I wasn't. She said, 'Sorry, I thought it would be useful, I know you prefer hard copies and when you didn't come in I thought I ought to drop these off.' Then still in an apologetic tone, 'Eileen said you hadn't responded to her messages.'

I'd frowned. 'What messages?'

'In your inbox. I went and checked, they were opened, I figured you must have forgotten . . .' She was blushing, having to point out my mistake.

I'd shook my head. 'I don't remember reading anything new.'

She didn't say anything just stared awkwardly at her feet. She told me, 'I did email.'

Anna is really good and usually so am I. She must have been wondering what the hell I've been playing at, though she'd never be rude enough to ask. She'd looked worried, like she always does if she thinks I'm cross. I forget sometimes that I'm her boss, not her mother.

I was the one who'd recommended she be taken on permanently. She's been wonderful ever since, keen to tell me she's grateful for the opportunity. She'd been able to move out of home and tells me she has plans for her future. The work climate makes these opportunities, especially in media, pretty scarce. To be fair to Anna, she won the week with Nick and worked her socks off by all accounts, and she'd been almost reduced to tears when he set up his trainee scheme with her in mind.

I'm not used to keeping secrets from her, I'm not used to keeping secrets full stop these days. I'd stood there last night at my front door, aware that I should invite her in. I normally would, and have poured us both a glass of wine. Nick would have joined us if he was there. My behaviour was abnormal and she's not stupid.

Instead, I'd looked from Emma to Anna and Emma seemed to snap to action. Smiling, taking the notes, looking at her watch and saying to me, 'We'll be late.' Anna took the hint and left.

I'd checked my inbox after she left and she was right. I must have opened the emails on automatic, not registered it. Hardly surprising, though of course Anna doesn't know what's happening.

I'd looked at Emma and said, 'I can't go to work this week.'

She'd just smiled. 'Let us find Tabitha. You should carry on as normal.'

So that's what I am supposed to do today. Carry on as normal, though I don't see how I can. I sit nursing a cup of coffee.

Madison rings. Ben's company All That Glitters is an escort service. The words are said but they don't seem to penetrate my mind properly. I don't say anything, she says, 'Miriam?'

'He texted me. This morning.'

She sighs, 'Don't answer, don't engage, whatever happens don't ask him about Tabitha. I'm going to see someone who might be able to give us some more information this morning.'

I drive to work, not really thinking. Not really able to focus. People. Ben sells people. All those years ago. All those bundles of cash. What if he wasn't just dealing in drugs even then? What if he has Tabitha? What does it mean?

# 26.

# Madison Attallee

This estate hasn't changed since I grew up here. The same little ghetto, probably housing the same sort of people, with the same sort of stories. I pass a man with no teeth and dubious personal hygiene. He leers at me as though I might stop and take him up on his vile offer of giving him one.

I flip him the finger and he shouts, 'Lezzer.'

I pass a small group of bored-looking children. The youngest of whom really ought to be indoors. They kick a half-deflated football around under a sign that reads 'No Ball Games'. They glare at me as I go by and I smile back, feeling nothing but empathy, especially for the little ones, remembering my own days of wandering around this concrete jungle. Preferring the dangerous, grey outdoors to my own home. Estates like this get a bad rep, and for good reason, but actually communities are formed here, often amongst the kids, and there will be plenty of good adults keeping an eye on the roving mass of children. I remember a few who knew Mum and who made up for her neglect in little ways – a meal here, a fiver there. Someone asking how I was. When I lived on Kingston Hill, what I considered the epitome of having 'made it', one of the first things I noticed was that people in the neighbourhood rarely talked to each other.

But still, at least there wasn't the poverty.

I get to a worn brown front door. Like all council homes its proportions are pretty generous and it's definitely a step-up from the high-rises that surround this little row. A two up, two down house would have been quite sought after back in the day. I assume a lot of them are private lets now. Landlords caught on that they could buy cheap on the estates and rent to students as the university expanded. 'Social mobility' in action: being abused by those quick to make a buck.

This one is dilapidated. Unloved and unkempt. I ring the doorbell and wait. Listening to a hacking cough from inside and heavy footsteps. That's the cough of my smoking future. I still tap the packet in my bag for comfort, though.

An overweight, red-faced woman answers with a scowl. A large slobbery dog barks at me from her ankles. I smile as charmingly as I can and ask her, 'Are you Donna Williams?'

Her eyes narrow, 'Who wants to know?'

I get out a card and watch her read it with deep suspicion. She asks, 'You a pig?'

I shake my head. 'No. I'm an investigator. Nothing to do with the officials.'

She's still scowling but she swings the door open a bit more. 'What do you want?'

'I'd like to talk to you about Ruby.'

She seems to change right then and there. A cloud comes over her face, tugging the corners of her mouth downwards. She mumbles, 'She's dead.'

I nod and say softly, 'I know.'

I follow her down a dingy hallway, watching her considerable girth sway as she goes and marvelling at the fact she manages to pack it all down into super-tight leggings. She lights a fag in the kitchen and gestures at me to sit at a dirty table. I do so, and she sits opposite, dog flopping at her feet. Her stomach is pressed against the table's edge, rolling over the top slightly. I resist the urge to stare at it. She inhales, coughs, inhales again and repeats, regarding me through narrowed eyes.

She pushes her chair back, stands, reaches into her fridge and pulls out a beer. She waves the can at me and I shake my head. She sits again, cracking it open. It makes that fresh fizzing sound and I watch her glug at it. It was never my drink of choice, but I can smell the alcohol and I know that it will be calming her, salving the memory of a daughter gone too soon.

She asks, 'What do you want to know then?'

I tell her, 'I'd like to know a bit about the time she ran away, and her step-brother, Ben.'

She sucks in her mouth at that, inhaling deeply on her cigarette. 'He was a little shit.'

'Ben?'

She nods. 'Ruby was a handful but . . .' Her eyes well up, she blinks the tears away. 'She was a nice kid.'

'Was she your only one?'

She nods, 'Yep. Had problems when I was pregnant with her.' She meets my eyes levelly. 'Hep C.'

I nod. She takes a swig of her beer and carries on. 'I was relieved, to be honest. I mean I'd always figured I'd have loads of little chavvies but it was harder than I thought.'

I say, 'You must have been quite young?' Despite this woman's extraordinarily worn exterior, I don't place her as being too far from fifty. Either side.

She nods. 'Yep. Fifteen. Normal around here though.'

I nod again. Thinking of all my peers who'd been pushing prams before they'd sat their GCSEs.

I say, 'The police thought she'd run away?'

She nods, I add, 'So, you did report her missing?'

'Course I bloody did,' she snaps, frowning at me. 'Look I wasn't gonna win mother of the fucking year or anything and

137

like I said, she could be mouthy. She was a teenager after all, and Eric was a bit strict, but she was a nice kid.' Her voice softens, 'She was my kid.'

I say, 'Eric was your husband?'

She shakes her head, 'We weren't married. Treated Ruby like his own though. We were all right. A little family, you know?'

'And Ben was Eric's son?'

'Yes.'

'What happened?'

The doughy, pale woman shrugs. 'Had an argument. Ruby, she sung. Beautiful voice. She wanted to go and sing for Ben at one of his rave nights.'

I say, 'You thought she was too young?'

She sighs. 'It weren't just that, though I *was* always scared of her getting up the duff too early like me. Pretty little thing she was, and like I said she had talent, so I figured she'd have some options.'

She pauses to light another fag, and I think about that. To Donna, singing and good looks gave Ruby 'options'. It hadn't occurred to her that education might have helped. But why would it? If it hadn't been for my old headmistress, it wouldn't have occurred to me either and I could be sitting where Donna is now.

She goes on, 'Ben had been hanging around Ruby. Eric didn't like it.' She shrugs. 'Neither did I, to be honest. And from what Eric told me I didn't want them involved. It weren't singing he wanted from her, and she was too young to understand.'

And here we are at the hub of it. All That Glitters is an escort service. High end for sure and it seems to work within legal boundaries, but they make an absolute fortune, looking at their accounts I'd guessed it might be hiding a bit more than 'after date' action.

'Why didn't you want Ruby hanging out with Ben?'

138

She sighs again. 'We should have told her, might have been better. Boy like Ben, Mum like his.' She shakes her head.

I say, 'What was wrong with his mum?'

'Reeva?'

I nod. Donna stamps out her fag. 'Fucking whore. In the literal sense, married her pimp though, so she weren't put out to pasture, started making money off other girls.' Donna adds, 'And I do mean girls.'

Ruby was fifteen at the time of her death.

'Tell me about the fight. The night Ruby left.'

'We came home from the pub a bit early. Eric wasn't feeling too clever. Ruby was sneaking out with Ben.' She swallows. 'Eric lost it, went for him. Silly mare got in the middle of it. Someone bashed her, Eric I guess. Not on purpose, he'd give us a slap if we stepped out of line, but not properly like.' I don't even bother to point out that any violence is wrong. Donna Williams was born and bred in a world where there are varying degrees of it and the odd slap barely even registers. Tough.

I bet Ruby was pretty tough too. But not tough enough.

She says, 'Ben got the right hump. Not 'cause he gave a shit about Rube, mind, it was any excuse to get at Eric. Taking Ruby would have been a fucking joke to him.'

'Why did he want to get at his dad?'

She laughs again, it's a horrible sound. 'I dunno.'

I say, 'Was he an unlikeable man?'

She looks blank for a moment and then says, 'My Eric?'

I nod.

She sighs, 'He was nice. I mean, if you pissed him off he'd tell ya, don't get me wrong, and he was heavy handed with that son of his and he had all of these rules for Ruby, which she hated. But she probably needed them.' She sniffs and wipes a hand across her nose, which is leaking. 'The boy was a little git, though, he'd been banned from our house for over a year by then. Was always hanging around Ruby despite the fact that Eric had told him not to. No one could tell Ben what to do, you see, and he was full of ideas above himself.'

'Like what?'

'Money. All he wanted was money. Like his mother. And didn't give a shit how he got it. Eric was a scaffolder, brought in a good wedge as well. Thought his son would join him eventually, but not Ben. His dad's life wasn't up to scratch for Ben. He wanted more, didn't much care how he got it. No, he wasn't anything like Eric.'

I tell her, 'It looks like Ben's done quite well for himself. I think he still works with his mother now.'

Her face is screwed up in annoyance. She shrugs. 'So I've heard, but so what? Eric might not have been fancy but plenty of men would have dumped that boy on the social, no one bats an eye if men can't cope, do they? He didn't though, he looked after him. Reeva slid in and out as it suited her. Didn't get interested until he was grown and of fucking use, cash-wise. Least Ben could have done was humour his old man. Maybe help him out, know what I mean?'

I nod. I think I do. She goes on, 'That woman dumped Ben without a second thought. Worked as a stripper, met up with her dirty husband at the club. They run girls for noncing pervs, pair of 'em, they're pimps.'

I say, 'You think they are still doing this now?'

She nods.

I say, 'Ben's company – All That Glitters – Reeva's named as a director.'

She laughs, 'I'll bet she is.'

I say, 'The women working there are adults.'

She shrugs, 'It's a cover, they're not stupid. Her husband, he ran the room out the back of the pub that she stripped. That's

140

how they started. Loads of little girls strumping about with their tits out.'

'Do you know Reeva's married name?'

She nods and coughs. 'Walker. Reeva Walker. His name's Colm.' I make a note.

She leans sideways and grabs a picture off the fridge, held in place with a magnet advertising an Indian takeaway, and hands it to me. I study it. A beautiful young woman holding a pretty, dark-haired baby.

I say, 'This is you and Ruby?'

She nods. I could be looking at someone else entirely.

'I loved her. Didn't realise how much until she was gone.'

A fat tear rolls down her cheek. She swipes at it. 'I told the police back then that Reeva was involved, they went looking for her at their place and a London property they had, said there was no sign.' She shrugs. 'Reeva claimed the properties were vacant. Said they were doing them up to let out.' She sighs. 'I figured she'd come home eventually and just hoped it would be in one piece.'

I say, 'I'm sorry.' And I am. I'm never going to win mother of the year either but my heart would break if anything happened to Molly. She nods.

I ask, 'You think that's why Ben was hanging around? To get to Ruby?'

She shrugs. 'Eric thought it, hence the fucking row.' She sighs. 'She was young, beautiful. Sung like a flippin' angel. Like I said, rumour had it that Reeva and her fella were into the young trade by then. Jail bait. They certainly went up in the world quickly. More than a couple of strip clubs would warrant. If you know what I mean.'

I nod and say, 'All That Glitters certainly looks very profitable.'

She laughs. 'Bet it is, and with Ben's brains it'll probably look legit enough as well, like you said. But it'll be hiding something else. There'll be more girls like Ruby. You mark my words.'

I rub a hand over my eyes, an image of Tabitha grinning from her Instagram account hits me. Beautiful, tanned, young, teetering on that edge between childhood and adulthood. It makes me think of Molly again. I push the thought away.

She looks me in the eye and says, 'Men can always make money out of a pretty face, can't they? Then when we're not pretty any more they'll dump us for the next one.'

Donna is the sum of her experiences and I can't blame her for the way she thinks. I can imagine her at fifteen. I could have been her if it hadn't been for the kindness of Jessica Mason, headteacher at my school and mentor for years to come.

I say softly, 'No one made her go.'

She looks at me then and I can see tears shining in her eyes. Unshed and undealt with. 'She didn't know what she was going to though, did she?'

'I'm sure she knew you loved her and she could have come back.'

She shakes her head, swigs from the can, draining the last of it. 'I wouldn't bank on it. Last thing I said to her was, what have you done you silly bitch. Eric was lying on the floor in a pool of blood. Ben thumped him bloody hard. With a poker from the fire.' She lights a cigarette, inhales. 'Look on her face. All her usual cheek was gone, she was absolutely bloody stricken and all I did was shout at her. Told her she could fuck off and not bother coming back.' She shrugs.

'We all make mistakes.'

She doesn't say anything.

The dog makes a sighing sound and Donna pats his head. She says, 'I didn't even get a chance to say I loved her.'

The silence stretches and I let it, then Donna finally says, 'Why you raking this shit up anyway?'

I pause, wondering what to tell her and say, 'I've got a case and Ben's name's come up.'

She nods. 'Involving kids?'

I say, 'A teenage girl.'

'Like my Rube.'

'Yes.'

She sighs. 'You should speak to Michelle Roberts.'

'Who?'

She says, 'A girl on the estate, her mum went to see you lot.'

I don't bother pointing out again that I'm not the police, I say, 'Michelle was caught up with Ben?'

Donna nods, 'Yup. Recently too. People like him and Reeva don't change.'

I make a note of the name and say, 'Thanks.'

She sighs, 'I wish I could help more. No one likes a grass but that lot deserve some comeuppance.'

I tell her, 'You *have* helped.' She smiles faintly. I leave her my card and she says if I find out anything about the last year of Ruby's life to call her. I agree and leave, feeling sad and sorry.

Donna was born into her path. Like she'd just arrived and started playing a tragic role in a B-rated movie. The lines were there waiting for her to say them. The stage directions almost pre-determined. The disasters. The teenage pregnancy. A string of useless blokes. The tins of beer and fags.

I drive off the estate listening to Hole, smoking and silently thanking Jessica Mason for saving me from that kind of life.

# 27.

# Ruby Williams

## *1994*

Though the Walkers' house is gorgeous and like a magazine I don't feel at ease here. And I feel like I'm missing something in the conversation. Reeva is still talking about my talent and my good looks and finding me some work. I see Ben nodding in the background. It would be great if I could earn my keep, I guess. Ben is standing now, and he and Reeva are making their way towards the door. He turns to me and says, 'Mr Walker would like you to . . . audition. For the work. I'm going to leave you with him for a moment, but I'll be waiting to take you home. Okay?'

But something doesn't feel right, I don't want to be on my own with this man I don't know. I say, 'Ben?'

He frowns, 'What?'

I make to follow him out of the room. He takes me by my arm, gripping so hard it shocks me. He moves me back to Mr Walker.

I look at him, frightened now and confused. I'm trying to say things with my eyes and I whisper, 'Ben, can we go?'

'Don't be rude. I've helped you out, Ruby. Now it's your turn to help me.' And his face, usually kind, usually smiling, looks hard and his hand is hurting my arm.

My heart is pounding so hard now that I think I might be

sick, but I can't say no, can I? I nod, he lets go and I almost fall, then Ben and Reeva are gone.

Time stops then. Everything changes in what must only be a few minutes but feels like forever. I hear sounds, horrible awful sounds. They are coming from me, and from the man labouring over me, but I don't recognise my own voice. I feel lots of things. Mainly pain, physical at first and then spreading into something else. Something far worse. Then it's over and Mr Walker is getting dressed and walking out of the room.

I lie still for a moment on the floor, unsure I could stand even if I wanted to. Then Reeva is there, with a cool, firm hand, pressing it to my face. She helps me to pull down my dress and get back onto the sofa. It is torn in different places. I look at it sadly, the dress Mum got me. My shoes lie abandoned on the floor. Reeva lights a cigarette and passes it to me, she pours another drink, which I take without thinking. Then I burst into tears. She wipes at my face with her hand and makes shushing sounds. 'That's the worst of it over with now.' She is stroking my hair. I down the drink, smoke the cigarette and sob until I can cry no more. Reeva opens a small purse and gives me a fifty-pound note. She says I should have a warm bath when I get in and not think about it too much.

Ben appears with a big smile on his face. He puts a hand on my elbow and helps me out to the car, carrying me in the end. I am too ashamed to speak. He hands me a large, ready-rolled joint and chats away about what colour to paint the walls in the living room at our flat. I smoke; inhaling, exhaling, but I still don't have any words. When we pull up outside our place, he turns to me and says, 'I'm glad that you're helping me. I didn't mind helping you with Eric, and I've never complained, have I?'

I feel tears start up again. He is sitting waiting for an answer to his question. He stretches out a hand and pinches my arm. It hurts, and I squeak. 'Have I, Ruby?'

'No.'

My voice is a whisper. And he says, 'What?'

I try again, louder, 'N-no.'

He nods. Smiling again now, his hand still on my arm but gentle. Reassuring. 'I'll look after you. You know that, don't you?'

I can't think of anything to say, I am bewildered, disjointed, separate from myself. I feel like nothing is real. I just nod. When we get into the house he gives me a bag of weed and a couple of little white pills, saying, 'Go on up, kiddo, have a sleep. These'll help.' I nod, taking them, and head up to my room on shaky legs. I shut the door, pop the pills and roll a joint. Then I lie in my bed crying and wishing my mum was here.

When Darren gets home late, well after midnight, he knocks on my door. He says my name and when I don't answer he comes in. I pretend to be asleep. He lifts the covers on my bed over my shoulders. When he is gone, I cry, silently. I wonder if I'll ever be able to look him in the eye again.

# 28.

# Miriam Jackson

I pull into my space and get out of my car, gathering up my papers in a daze. My brain is fuzzy, with worry and fatigue. Which is probably why I don't notice he's there until I hear, 'Mim.'

I scream, a stupid little sound. He laughs and says, 'Sorry, did I make you jump?'

I look at him open mouthed. I try to push past but he holds me and I realise that I am scared. A proper primal fear. I am frightened for my daughter. Frightened for myself. This man is not who he seems. He squeezes me and something gives. The paralysing helplessness gives way to anger. I don't sink into his arms, I don't stand frozen. I push him back and glare.

He says, 'Mim?'

I hiss, 'Leave me alone,' before I can help it.

He looks so confused, I find myself checking in my own mind for a moment. I think of what Madison has just told me. This man is a pimp.

Madison is scared for my daughter.

Oh God. I resist the urge to ask him, but it's an almost physical restraint. Madison was explicit about this, *don't ask him about Tabitha,* though it's torture not to.

I tell him, 'Stay away from me.' My voice comes out sounding small, weak and foolish. Not big and brave like I meant it to.

He makes to reach for me again so I try and run but he grabs me by the tops of my arms. He's smiling but it's not a proper smile, not one that reaches his eyes. There is a suspicion there. I blurt out, 'Where's Tabitha?'

He doesn't bat an eye, but something in his face shifts, and I realise I've messed up. He says, 'Why would I know?'

But there is something dangerous flashing there. A knowledge. That I have given him. I've messed up again.

'You're a pimp.' I spit the words and his hands tighten at the top of my arms. The smile is gone now, the pretence has slipped. He says, 'I'm a businessman.' And I'm surprised at how calm his voice is when his eyes look crazed.

'That's what you were doing . . . even then?'

He pauses. He seems to be battling to retain control. He tries for a smile again. 'Nothing's changed, Mim.'

I say, 'Everything's changed.'

He says, 'Don't you love me any more?'

I'm shaking and I hate myself for it. He says, 'Mim?'

I half shout, half cry, 'I don't know you.'

He says, 'You do. You do know me. Whatever you've found out. It doesn't change who I am. What we are.' And his voice is pleading, laced with that naked need that I have always been so drawn to. I realise the sickness of finding that attractive. The messed-up part of me that isn't right for enjoying it, wanting it. To be needed.

I yell, 'I know what you do.'

His face hardens then. He shrugs, nonchalant and says, 'I work with my mother. I do the same thing I've always done. It doesn't need to change anything.' His voice is some kind of odd medium between wheedling and threatening. I can't think properly.

I tell him, 'Give her back.'

He smiles again, and says, 'I don't know what you're talking about.'

I break then, everything in me unspools. I raise my hands and I go for him, flailing, sobbing, shouting, 'My daughter, my daughter.' And she's all I can see, all I can think about. He grabs me, twists and is holding me tightly from behind, I kick backwards, he waits until I can move no more. Until I am limp, and I say, 'Please.'

His breath is hot in my ear, 'I'm not your enemy, Mim, you know me.' And he turns me around to face him.

I say, 'I don't know you and I don't love you.' And I can see the words hurt. Despite what this monster does, what he is capable of. *My* words hurt him. I feel a dim satisfaction. It's fleeting.

He leans down so close his mouth is almost touching mine and he whispers, 'Are you sure about that?'

I nod. Because I can't speak, because 'yes' would be more than I can manage.

I don't realise I'm not breathing until he turns and walks away. My breath finally escapes in a hot gasp of fear. I wait five seconds, ten. I'd still had doubts, I'd listened to Madison and thought perhaps she'd made a mistake.

Ben was still that sad boy I'd left at the hospital. The man who'd opened his arms up to me as soon as he saw me again. Someone who loved me. Who cared.

My arm still hurts from where he'd just grabbed me. I can almost feel the heat of his angry breath on my face. He has Tabitha. That boy never existed.

My feet finally snap into action. I run up the stairs. Unsure whether he's actually gone. Unsure what to do. I shout his name, because it seems important not to let him get away. Not now he knows I know. And I do. I do know.

I get to the ground floor and find a space in the alcove. I dial Madison with a shaking hand.

## 29.

# Ruby Williams

## *1994*

There are a lot of mornings now where I wake up and wish I hadn't. It starts out as a flutter in my belly, a churning sense of doom, nothing specific. Then memories of my week, day, the night before flood in. I think that it would be a sweet relief not to wake at all. I lean over and reach for the joint that sits constantly in my ashtray and I puff and I puff. I pop one of the little white pills. Reeva recently showed me how to 'chase the dragon'. She told me it would help me feel better afterwards, and she's right. I suspect soon that's how my days will begin. I don't suppose it matters too much.

There is a knock at my bedroom door. I wonder if it's Ben, if I have to go downstairs and work. The thought fills me with dread, but a look at the clock says it's probably too early. The guys who visit me here aren't daylight kinds of people. Or if they are, they are not the same after dark.

I hear Darren call my name and feel my heart break, just a little bit. I call for him to come in, though I don't want him to see me. In bed, unwashed, in flannel pyjamas, my eyes dark ringed, my hair greasy. My body getting thinner all the time as I shrink into something else. Something less.

He's smiling when he comes in though. He sits on the edge of my bed and asks if I want to record today and I say no. He frowns and says, 'How come you don't sing any more?'

I just shrug. I can't explain to him that singing is something I associate with freedom, that perfect feeling of not being yourself, of merging into something better. That now I am tainted, ruined, that when I hear my voice it sounds like nails being run down a blackboard.

'Ruby, are you all right?' He looks so concerned, and he is so nice to me. He never pushes, Darren, but I've moved away from him. I know I have. I feel tears prick at the back of my eyes, and I open my mouth, about to tell him, but then Ben is shouting up the stairs and the moment is gone.

He opens the door without knocking and sees Darren sitting there. He smirks at me and says, 'Giving away freebies now?'

Darren is on his feet and squaring up to Ben in a second. He says, 'What the fuck are you talking about?'

Ben laughs and says, 'She not told you about her new career?'

Darren looks from me to Ben. I look away, pulling the covers up over myself. Lots of things are spinning around inside of me. Horrible, awful things that I can't put into words. Things I need to eradicate.

Darren is leaning down now, touching a gentle hand to my shoulder. He turns me over and says, 'Ruby?'

I stare at him and the tears fall. Darren heads back to Ben and asks, 'What have you done?'

Ben laughs again. 'We've all got to earn our keep, son.'

Darren hits him then, in the face. I scream, then Ben is on Darren, all fists and feet. Darren gives as good as he's getting to start with, but Ben has something else on his side, his tolerance for violence is unbelievable. The pain doesn't seem to affect him, and he punches Darren hard in the kidneys, over and over again. Darren curls up into a ball until Ben is finished. When he's done, the bastard leaves the room, whistling as though nothing has happened. I'm out of my bed and trying to help Darren up.

151

But he pushes me away, staggers out.

The tears have built into awful, wrenching sobs. I feel snot mingle with them on my face. My shoulders heave up and down. I'm sweating, shaking, wretched. Withdrawal mingles with fear, revulsion, impotent and pointless anger ... A cacophony of things I can't take. That I need to silence. I grapple around in the full box Ben has given me. I manage to get the baggy out and I tip powder onto foil and light it, sinking backwards, backwards, backwards into lovely, wonderful nothing.

My fault. Darren is bleeding and battered and it's my fault. Wherever I go, I bring trouble. Awful, violent trouble.

I think I hear him come back in again. Darren. I'm sure I hear him say my name and feel his arms wrap around me. I hear him saying, 'It's all right, Ruby. Everything will be all right.' And I want to laugh but the drugs won't let me. It's funny because it's what Ben said to me. And it's not. It's not all right. Darren's fading, everything's fading, and so am I.

# 30.

# Madison Attallee

I pull up at the station and sit in the car. I'm humming along to PJ Harvey, thinking about the years I spent here. Some happy times, some not so much. I used it as a way to escape Rob, then Rob and Molly, but mostly as a way to escape myself. When my drinking came to a head, and I was carted off to the nuthouse, I'm ashamed to say the loss of my job hit me harder than losing custody of my kid. I've thought about it since – I've had to – and I realised that all of my identity was tied up in being Detective Madison Attallee. So little of it came from being a mum. An area which I knew I'd fail at before I'd even started.

When Molly was little, I used to joke about how lucky I was to have Rob, who was better than any wife could be. It was true too. He far exceeded me in all domestic areas. He was a natural parent. But why wouldn't he be? The precious son of a happily married couple. One sibling, an uneventful childhood. All things provided, everything mapped out. No, Rob's only flaw is that he needs other people to reflect his glory. My inadequacies bolstered his ego. Every time I couldn't settle the baby, or I forgot to sterilise her bottles, he'd sweep in, like a hero. Able, willing, and capable.

The only place he could never, ever be better than me was here, and how he hated my job. He'd have been happier with me at home, doped up on anti-depressants and sobbing my self-worth away on a stream of nappies, and naps, and playgroups where I didn't fit in. Here at work I was someone, the woman everyone turned to. Steely and quick.

I remember having to come back to sign off. The walk of shame through the station. I'd been convinced they all hated me. But then I cracked the Reynolds case when they hadn't, and I learned that most of them still respected me. Despite my decline into the bottom of a bottle. I know now that my last year working with them didn't cancel out the good work I'd done previously. That losing my job wasn't the end of the world, and even if it was it wouldn't be worth picking up a drink over.

I turn off the stereo, get out of the car, take a deep breath and walk towards the door. Deanie is on the front desk as usual – she buzzes me through. I go to shake her hand, but she brings me to her for a hug instead. I roll my eyes, but allow myself to be pulled into her comforting, doughy arms. Pleased despite myself. She pushes me back and tuts, 'Still skinny, I see.'

I grin. 'Hi, Deanie. Thanks for helping out with the case.'

'No problem, child, Peter's waiting for you. He's got that look in his eye.' She wiggles her eyebrows.

'Deanie, I'm here about a missing girl and a pimp.'

She laughs. 'I know that, honey, it's me that sent you the links. But he's still got that look.'

I frown at her and she laughs again. But I find I'm smiling as I head up the stairs. Everyone knows about Peter and me by now. They always suspected. Especially after Rob came in to 'have it out' with Peter, when we first separated.

Peter's office door is open. I head in and close it behind me. He grins. 'Hey, gorgeous.'

I roll my eyes. 'I'm working, Peter.'

'And you look gorgeous while you do it.'

I sit down opposite him and get out my file. I say, 'Deanie updated you on Ben's business?'

He frowns now. 'Yes, nasty bugger. Slippery too. Looks like we've never been able to get anything to stick.'

'Usual kind of set-up?'

He nods. 'They have just enough going on to make it look legit – they hire them out as "dancers". Strippers to you and I, and perfectly legal.' I nod. Escort businesses are all run the same way. Mostly we don't bother to even try and stop them, it's so hard to prosecute. Peter adds, 'Though they'd have to be made of gold for the prices that go through that business.'

I nod. 'Yup. Seems to be about right. Miriam said he had money.'

'What the hell is she doing mixed up with him?'

I sigh. 'Seems she knew him years ago. When she was a kid really. Bumped into him in some sort of chance encounter, he charmed her.'

Peter says, 'She's married to Nick Jackson?'

I nod. 'He's away a lot though. Away now, in fact.'

'So . . . what, bored housewife?'

I think about my answer, think about Miriam. 'She's got her own career.'

'Oh yes, that's right. Radio host. I've never tuned in.'

I shrug. 'I wouldn't, but Claudia likes to have it on all bloody day.'

He laughs. 'I bet she talks to it as well, doesn't she?'

I smile. My funny little team. I look at Peter smiling back – my funny little life.

'She's not a bored housewife though. She's nice but damaged, I'd say, uptight. It's hard to picture her married to some big-deal movie guy. She doesn't seem the type.'

'And the kid?'

'Mixed reports. Teachers like her. Best friend's lying about

155

something, another friend said Tabitha had an older boyfriend who fits Ben's description. I'd be surprised if Delia knew nothing about it.'

'You've pushed her?'

'Called again on my way here to give her another chance. She's adamant she doesn't know who the guy is.'

He says, 'I think teenagers can be like that. One face for the parents, another for everyone else.'

'True, but this one's missing and Mum's ex-boyfriend is a pimp.'

'But if he's in love with Miriam, why take her kid?'

'I don't know exactly.'

'You have an idea though . . . ?'

I play my ace card, 'From what I've found out, Ben's business is hiding more than just run-of-the-mill escorts.'

His eyes narrow. 'Go on.'

I tell him about Donna Williams, what she thinks happened to Ruby and Michelle Roberts.

He says, 'Bloody hell.'

I nod. 'That's where the money's coming from.' And I add, 'Tabitha's just about the right age, or if anything slightly older, but it's too much of a coincidence to not be connected. Maybe he was involved with the kid and found out who her mum was. That's the theory me and the girls are working on at the moment.'

Peter says, 'Tabitha Jackson's profile is pretty high, from what I can tell.'

I scowl at Peter. I had already thought that myself, but I snap, 'I said it was a theory.'

He ignores the sharpness, his work head firmly on. 'And he's still holding a torch for her twenty years later?'

I say, 'More like obsessed. I think Miriam's starting to realise that even back then he was bad news. I haven't spoken to her since I met with Donna. I've only mentioned the escort business so far. I'm not sure she fully believes it even now, and you certainly don't know at fifteen, do you?'

He says, 'Well, God, no, look at the guy you were hanging out with.'

I think about climbing into Peter's bedroom window after running from my own flat, scared, alone. Avoiding Mum's fists, her latest boyfriend. I wish I'd stayed there. Next to him. I was to take a much darker path before I made it back. And I'm still not quite sure where back is.

Peter's smiling, but I don't want to talk about the past.

Getting him on topic gently, we search the database and find Michelle Roberts. Peter mutters, 'She's been brought in twice.'

'Soliciting?'

He nods. It's the kind of job that gets hard to leave behind. I ask, 'Anything about Ben or All That Glitters?'

He shakes his head. 'Nope.' And then, 'Actually, hang on, look, I almost missed this.'

I wheel my chair next to Peter and squint at the screen.

Michelle Roberts' mother had come in about Michelle was just thirteen. She'd been convinced that her daughter had been groomed and gone into prostitution. According to the file, the kid had said her mum was making stuff up. She'd been thin as a rake. Obviously using. Officers went out to see the Walkers, who Michelle's mum said had been keeping her initially. Big house on Kingston Hill. Michelle's mum had claimed that Reeva Bander, now Walker, had befriended the girl and then taken poor Michelle straight to her husband for 'breaking'. But there hadn't been enough to make anything stick. Mrs Roberts came back again; the visit was recorded but not followed up. Shit.

'Reeva Walker is Ben's delightful mum?'

He nods. 'Yup. It's just like Donna Williams said.'

'Apple didn't fall far from the tree then.'

Peter frowns. 'It never does, does it?'

He's right. Of course he's right. You only have to do a week in our job to realise it. Poverty breeds poverty, crime breeds crime, violence breeds violence, and addiction breeds addiction. Our behaviours are learned from the people around us.

God, I hope I've broken the cycle for Molly.

I take the file and say I've got to go. Peter says to call if I need help.

As soon as I get into my car and pull out, my phone rings – Miriam.

'Hello.'

But when she responds, my heart sinks a little further.

# 31.

# Miriam Jackson

When Madison picks up, I try and fail to keep my voice even. She mutters something I can't quite hear. An obscenity which doesn't make me feel very confident. Then she's on the line properly.

She says, 'Sorry, I'm struggling with my hands free.'

'It's okay.'

I fill her in on Ben, fear marking each word as I speak it. I have to stop several times, my mouth dry, my heart racing. I speak in short staccato sentences. Inhaling the horror of it all. Eventually, I tell her I mentioned Tabitha and she mutters something I don't quite catch, but the tone confirms I did the wrong thing.

She asks, 'What time are you leaving work?'

'Four. Why?'

'I'll get Emma to come and meet you.'

I say, 'There's no need.' But I do feel scared.

'No, she'll be there. Claudia will drop her, she can come back with you in your car. You need to contact Nick and get him to come home. I've been at the police station.'

Call Nick. Get him home. Tell him the truth. The idea of doing this fills me with dread.

'Are they worried?' My heart is racing. Three days now. My

baby's been gone for three days. To be honest I'd hoped it was just another thoughtless stunt aimed at hurting me. But a bit of me knew. The hard stone of fear in my stomach. Though it hadn't occurred to me that it had anything to do with Ben. The part of me that wants to go easy on myself says, *why would it?* The other part is laughing in my face.

Madison doesn't answer for a moment then repeats, 'Call Nick.'

I agree and hang up. I get my phone, scroll down to his number. But I can't. The thought of hearing his voice is too much. I know I have to, but not yet. It's more than I can bear right now. I'm holding myself together with thinly woven threads and I know that I'm about to unravel. Nick would be the last straw at the moment. My marriage is now damaged, tainted, because of me. It is full of deceit and lies. Even thinking about it makes the panic bigger.

I have no idea how I get through the morning show but I do. I take calls, laugh in the right places and fire out orders to Anna. We settle into our usual rhythm. The fear steps into the background slightly while I function on automatic pilot. I even catch myself smiling at her as she passes me notes and the odd thumbs up. It could be a normal day. But it isn't.

She steps in a few times when I blunder, as though understanding that I'm not quite with it. I suspect that one day Anna will be sitting exactly where I am. In fact, I'd say she'll go further. She's got drive. I remind myself to be pleased for her, to support her. Today I'm too tired to focus properly but it's okay because she is here and has my back as always. When the show is done I'm surprised to find that I do feel glad for the three-hour distraction. Almost as if it has been some much-needed time off from worrying. Which I suppose it has.

The rest of the afternoon I spend absorbed in admin and at three fifty-five I'm getting ready to go when Anna knocks at my door. She is ashen-faced. I wonder if I've messed something up again, I think back to the double booking a few days ago.

I try for a smile, and say, 'You look worried.'

'Um.'

I frown. 'Anna, spit it out.'

She jumps, and I immediately feel bad, 'Sorry, I didn't mean to snap – what's the matter?'

'We, um, got sent something.'

I smile. 'Okay, well, how bad can it be?'

She says, 'I think you'd better come and see for yourself.'

I text Emma as I walk to say I've been held up but will be down shortly. I head into Anna's office, which she shares with some other juniors who aren't here at the moment. She opens her work email, which is also our studio address, and clicks on a video link. I watch the grainy images and at first I can't quite work out what I'm seeing. It's too surreal to make sense of. I feel in a peculiar state of disconnection as I watch the scene unfold. Then I think I might laugh. Which is ridiculous because this must be one of the least amusing things that has ever happened to me. Then I wonder if I'm going to throw up. My phone beeps – I look down expecting a response from Emma, but it's not.

It's Ben.

*I bet you're sorry now.*

Then I do laugh – an awful, inappropriate, belly rumbling chortle washes up from me and bursts out. Anna is staring at me like I'm mad, and I wonder if I am. If I've come this far along in my life to be struck down by insanity now. I stop, pick up my phone, dial, and say to Emma, 'I think you'd better come in.'

# 32.

# Madison Attallee

I call Ben's office and am told by the receptionist that her boss won't be in today. When I ask when he will be, she says she doesn't know, he's mainly mobile.

Claudia gets me the address for Mr and Mrs Walker, and I get in my car. Kingston is busy as hell today. It seems every lunatic who ought not to have a licence has decided on a bloody day trip. I blast Green Day, smoke and only scream obscenities out of the window once or twice.

I go first to Ben's house, luckily Miriam's satnav saved the address and it turns out he's just seconds away from his dear mum. I'm unsurprised to find the slippery bugger's not there either. I leave my car and walk around to his parents' place.

The Walkers' house is big, ostentatious and tacky. I ring an overly loud bell and the door is answered by one of the most bizarre-looking human beings I've ever seen. A woman, with enormous lips. They protrude ludicrously from her face. Her cheeks are equally as big, giving the overall impression of a plumped-up pillow with slitty, cat eyes. Her mouth seems to be trying to curl upwards and it takes me a few seconds to work out that she's trying to smile at me. Fuck. I try and arrange my own face into a less horrified expression and smile back. 'Mrs Walker?'

'Yes?'

I hand her a card. 'My name's Madison Attallee, I'm looking into a matter involving your son.'

She nods. 'Well, he doesn't live here.'

'No, I know that.'

I think she's trying to frown now but nothing on her face changes other than her eyes.

She's about to shut the door, saying, 'I'm afraid I can't help you then.'

I put my foot in and pretend that the pressure she's applying isn't hurting me one bit. I smile and say, 'No problem. I'll come back with the police. See if you might prefer a chat with them?'

That stills her. She sighs and says, 'Fine, I don't want my day disrupted twice.'

I ask her, 'Are you busy then?'

She laughs and says, 'Darling, we're always busy.'

I smile politely and follow her inside. 'What do you do?' I ask, although I know what the answer will be.

'We run an agency, events.' I look at the pictures in the hallway. Pictures of her and a tall, dark-haired, morbidly obese man with various celebs and, I'm saddened to see, a couple of politicians. I try and memorise the ones I recognise. Certain that they will all be guilty in this vile pantomime. All That Glitters is a cover, and when your cover is an escort agency ... well. I imagine they actually do have a couple of legit 'performers' on their books. From what the police found out, they probably do a few stag dos a year or something. These people aren't stupid. Disgusting, but not stupid.

I say, 'Strippers?'

She makes that pained smile again and shrugs.

The sausage-lipped monster, *call me Reeva, darling*, asks if I'd like a drink. I say no and watch her pour herself a large G&T.

We sit in a kind of living room. Everything looks expensive and gaudy.

I say, 'You re-married?'

She laughs. 'Oh, I wasn't married to Eric.' She tuts. 'Loser of a man. No ambition.'

I nod, 'And you wanted better things?'

She smiles and shrugs, 'Not a crime, is it?' I can hear the rougher vowels peeking through her almost comical imitation of a posh accent.

I smile back, 'Not in and of itself.' The smile wavers.

I say, 'Did you know Ruby Williams?'

She licks the fat mouth and says, 'Pardon me?' But I'm quite sure she knows who I mean. I say, 'Ben's step-sister.'

She looks out of the window, taking a large glug from her glass, 'I think he brought her over. Once or twice.'

My heart sinks a little as I think about Ruby's mum, Donna. Waiting to hear from her precious daughter. I can all too readily imagine what would have happened to her here after reading the report from Michelle's mum. I add, 'She had a nice singing voice.'

Reeva clicks her fingers then, a large jewelled ring slides around her bony middle digit, 'That's right, she did some parties for us, I think.'

'She would have been under sixteen.'

She looks at me blankly. I say, 'She was only fifteen when she died.'

She waves a hand, 'I can't recall. I'm sure we went through the proper channels. I doubt we'd have a record of it though. Not everything was computerised back then. She probably had a fake ID.' I don't point out that Ben would have known her age.

'You'd forgotten that, the parties?'

She says, 'It was a long time ago. I'm getting on, despite my looks.' Jesus, she actually thinks she's winning some sort of battle with ageing. I have no doubt that she'd look far better if she just let nature take its course.

I say, 'What's your secret?' More for fun than anything else.

She shrugs, pretending to be embarrassed, 'Good genes, that's all.'

I resist the urge to guffaw. Fucking hell. I say, 'The um, talent business . . . Mr Walker was running it when you met?'

She smiles, 'Yes, actually I did some work for him. It's how we met.'

I say, 'What was your talent?'

She laughs. 'Dancing.' She seems to be trying to waggle her eyebrows. I suppose she probably had a nice body once. Maybe even a nice face too. It's hard to tell.

I say, 'And how did you get the work? I mean, how did you find out about it?'

Her eyes narrow, I think, if that's possible. We both know what I'm getting at. She drops the smile and says, 'A girlfriend of mine was working with him, and moaning about it. Despite getting paid handsomely. I was seventeen, stuck indoors with a toddler and bloody Eric all day. I saw a way out.'

I nod, 'And you've done pretty well.'

She shrugs, 'I wanted more, as you said. I saw an opportunity and I seized it.'

'Like you help children seize it too?'

The smile is completely gone. Her voice has an edge now. 'We run a business, men want youth, legal youth, I might add. I was young, though I lied and said I was eighteen. You couldn't check so easily then. We do now, and we have a bustling clientele. The girls who come here with sense adjust to their life and make the most of it. It's not a long-term career, admittedly.'

I am sarcastic when I say, 'Talent has an age limit, does it?'

She glares at me. 'Everything has an age limit for women. If

165

you've any sense you use what you have, while you have it.'

I can't help it, I say, 'Ruby was a child.' She sips at her drink looking at me over the rim. I tell her, 'Michelle Roberts was a child.' Thinking of the picture of the stick thin girl in Peter's file.

She sort of chuckles, 'Michelle was a slaggy little cow, willing to do whatever Ben said for a bag of smack.'

I say, 'I reckon Ben groomed her, poor kid probably thought she was in love with him.' Reeva shrugs. I continue, 'She probably didn't know he was planning on being her pimp.'

She puts down the glass, 'I don't think you've got any proof of that. I'd be very careful making allegations about my son. I don't think he'd like it.'

'Are you threatening me?'

She laughs, 'Don't be daft. Though I do think our time is up.'

'I was hoping to speak to your husband.'

She's standing now. 'Well, he's not in.'

'I'll come back another time then.'

She hurries me out of her front door and says, 'You do that, love.' Before she slams it in my face.

A million hours under a scalding hot shower wouldn't rinse the disgusting after effects of that woman away. I sit in my car and light a cigarette with a shaking hand. I blast Red Hot Chili Peppers and drive.

166

# 33.

# Ruby Williams

*1994*

Darren is away. Ben said he has some business elsewhere and Darren has gone to see to it. I hate that he is 'working' with him now. He's doing it for me as well. I know this because *I* haven't had to 'work' since Darren started. No more parties, no more Mr Walker. I wish I was brave enough to tell him to leave me to it.

I hate it in the flats without Darren. Ben leaves Mim here sometimes. I have no idea how to talk to her, so we tend to do our own thing. From what I can tell, Mim knows nothing about Ben's business affairs. Ben knows well enough that I'm not about to mention it. She's out now at least.

I'm lying in bed, smoking a joint and thinking about all of these things, when my door swings open. Ben is standing there. I keep puffing on my joint, looking at him and thinking how funny it is that I ever had a crush on this man, hero worshipped him even. I sort of hate him now, but get that I wouldn't manage without him, and that prison would be my other option. I miss Mum, and I miss Eric. I try not to dwell on it because thinking about Eric really upsets me.

Ben's smiling and says, 'I need you to come down to number two.' I freeze for a moment my mind racing. Number two is the party flat. He promised Darren.

I follow him downstairs on shaky legs anyway, not saying anything. It's never a good idea to argue. We head in and a strong smell hits me. It's incense and skunk, booze and something else. Something bodily. Something that, in this place, never goes. No matter how much it's cleaned and scrubbed.

I hear voices coming from the living room. More than one. I bump into Ben and I half shout, 'You promised Darren.'

His eyes narrow, and he is horribly, scarily still. Then he goes and pulls the living room door shut. He comes so close to me that I can feel his breath on my cheek. 'You fucking shouting at me?'

I try and push him, Ben's hand lashes out so fast I don't see it coming. But I feel it. The appalling sting across my cheek. He says, 'You need to settle your shit down, love.' He goes into the living room then and I hear him make his voice soft and soothing. I am sitting still on the floor in the hallway. My face is burning now, the joint I had been holding fell from my hand as I went down. I go to reach for it, but Ben is back before I even realise and his foot stamps it out before I can get there. He leans down, his face close to mine again, and says, 'You might want something a bit stronger. There's a glass in the bedroom and something for you to change into.' And he stands up, pulling me along by the scruff of my sweatshirt.

Fuck it. I shake him off, and head into the bedroom. I grab the glass and down it. I strip out of my tracksuit and see the 'outfit'; school uniform, pretty standard for these fuckers. More than one. I try not to think about it. I'm feeling smashed quite quickly. For some bizarre reason the uniform now seems funny and I'm giggling as I pull it on. I'm giggling even though I know there's nothing to laugh about. I wonder what he put in the drink. But I don't care, not really, because it's taken the edge off and when he comes in and hands me a refilled glass I take it gratefully.

He lets me lean on him while we make our way into the other room. There are two men grinning at me. They are old. Really old. I recognise one of them. He presents something on the TV, a kids' show. I used to watch it after school. That feels like a different lifetime now. He has thick grey hair and squinty eyes. He smiles at me and I watch him from behind my glass. Ben sits me down next to him and takes the glass from my hand as he does so.

The old guy from the telly puts a hand on my arm, and he says, 'Do you know who I am?' I say that I think so. The words come out all slurry and blurred and he laughs, saying, 'You got started without us.'

The other man slides a hand up my leg. I whimper but it seems to come from somewhere else. Ben smiles at everyone, shoving a wad of cash into his pocket. He says, 'Right then. I'll be back in about three hours, fellas?'

The men nod, but their attention is on me. I shut my eyes, trying to escape. Three hours. Three hours. I try and hum the song I wrote with Darren, but it's no good, I was a different person then, it doesn't feel like my song any more. I can hear a girl screaming. I wish she'd just shut up.

# 34.

# Miriam Jackson

Emma and Anna talk in another room. I am left alone, in my office. I have no idea what she is telling her and find I don't much care. This is a place where I am top dog usually, but now I'm feeling little more than a foolish girl. Emma comes back in and takes me gently by the elbow. She says we are going to nip back to mine. I tell her she doesn't have to come and she looks at me sternly. I nod, a reprimanded child. Any semblance of authority, esteem and adulthood has been stripped away from me this afternoon.

I can't tell Nick about the video. Not yet. Emma says that I should, but I insist I need to do it face to face, I owe him that much at least. It's not just his pride and his feelings, if that video gets leaked the impact on his career will be phenomenal. Family man. He is one of the trusted, well-loved family men in his business. A rarity in LA. A rarity in his industry. I think if Ben was going to send it to him he would have done by now. Though Emma sighs and says gently, 'You're still thinking of him as rational and sane.'

I stare at her stupidly. But I still don't pick up the phone. Not that I can be sure it's the right thing to do. I am especially unsure of myself now. My assumptions are more skewed than even I realised. I never understood Ben, the only person I thought got me. Unwanted child, quiet student, diligent host, amenable girl-friend, wife, mother. Even what I had perceived as my rebellion, a stand almost against my mother's misery, had just been a move from one keeper to another. I'm not sure who I am — I think of myself picking up awards for my drivetime show, a first-class degree. Standing brazen on glittery heels. But none of these things are what they seem. Not spirited and daring but desperate, risky, unable to control impulses I thought I'd left behind. I am still the little girl who adamantly refuses to be her mother, running from the black dog that chases nonetheless.

That video. So shocking. Nothing can compare to the awfulness of watching myself, back pressed to Ben's wall. Ben leaning in against me. Even more of a stranger to myself than usual. A middle-aged woman, so desperate for a bit of attention that I had slipped right in with this bad, bad man. Not different, at all, from teenage me. That shaky, stupid girl I thought I'd left behind. Grown beyond, with my education, my success at work. My husband.

I thought I'd been so clever, I thought I'd won the race, but actually I am insubstantial. A person built on weak foundations. I have grown up to inhabit a blank space. Waiting to see what others expect and adjusting myself accordingly. Like a chameleon, subject to change on someone else's whim. Anyone else's whim.

I have grown up to be worse than my mother. At least she was real, her moods and personality so very flawed, but too strong to hide, and she'd never bothered to try anyway. Or so I thought.

My mother loved me, but she didn't always get it right. But do any parents? I think of all the times at home recently. Tabitha banging around, moody, unreachable. How I backed away, gave her space. The last thing she needed, just as it was the last thing I had needed back then. It took Ruby's death and my absence for Mum to realise it, to understand that she was vital even if she wasn't wanted. I think about the times I'd compared my daughter, obviously caught up in her own struggle, with Anna; so easy to talk to, so diligent and eager to please. Easy. I always want ease and things worth having aren't made that way, are they? I feel a moment's sadness that a few times I've even said to Anna I wish Tabs was more like her. Disloyal.

I blink back tears and I swear to God that if she comes home, I'll be different.

The shame of misunderstanding her hurts, and I am awash with guilt.

I'd not known about Ben, not then and not now. Not even suspected. And there is more. Madison is to meet us at my house to tell me what. I know what it will be though. Because like my mother back then, I am awake now, and once you open your eyes I'm not sure you can ever shut them again.

It was a surreal and disgusting moment. In my office, looking at me, but not just me – Ben. Beautiful, glorious, but dangerous and awful. Anna had stepped back, looked intently out of the window. She'd seemed even more embarrassed than I felt, which wasn't possible, of course. The burden of shame was all mine.

That was me on my computer. Selfish, awful me, out for what I could get.

Claudia and Madison are waiting at mine. Parked on my drive, in her little black car. Madison smiles, but it's not a happy face, and I grimace back. She tells me to go in with Claudia and that she and Emma will follow shortly.

Claudia could be one of Nick's filmstars. She's stunning, but has a lovely down-to-earth quality that I'd always found to be in short supply in LA. She makes tea, and passes the time complimenting me on my show, she says she enjoys it a lot. She mentions that during her married years, when her daughter was small, she'd found it a bit of a lifeline.

I look at her surprised and say, 'You're no longer married?'

'Nope.'

'I'm so sorry.'

She smiles at me though and says, 'Don't be. Divorce was the best thing that ever happened to me.' She pulls herself upwards as she says it. This beautiful, confident, carefree and considerate woman, who perhaps wasn't always this way. She rests a hand on my arm then, meets my eye and says, 'Life can be terrible, but it often improves even when we've lost hope.' A moment passes, one where I am overwhelmed by this small kindness. It's broken by her phone ringing and I'm glad.

I think about Nick and me. Our marriage. This life we have built. So much more than I ever dared hope for. And yet I happily took it for granted once I had it.

Madison comes in and Claudia puts drinks in front of everyone. I see that she's found my cafétière and rustled up coffee, which Madison takes and drinks almost in one. Then the three women, so very different, sit down at my breakfast bar.

I look at them and feel again like a small lost child. It's jarring.

Madison tells me they think Ben's business wasn't just covering an escort agency but also trade in underage girls. Girls around Tabitha's age and younger. I feel my heart sink and then I feel disbelief. I shake my head at her when she starts to tell me about Ruby, because she is wrong. She must be wrong. I had been jealous of Ruby. Ruby who was cool, and sexy. She could roll joints, drink spirits, sing. Madison tells me when she was autopsied she had injuries conducive with prolonged sexual abuse. She tells me running an escort agency with grown-up consenting women is a far cry from what she now suspects. If Ruby is anything to go by, the 'girls' he has working for him are not willing participants.

She tells me that Ben's mother, Reeva, had been a stripper

until she'd taken up with the man who became her pimp, and later, husband. He'd been known to the police, and had been involved in suspected kidnappings and trafficking, back when it was thought to be a rarity. He had actually served a short sentence for pimping but had stayed out of trouble since.

The flats where we lived had been under surveillance on and off for that year during the 1990s. Madison tells me it is entirely likely that some of it occurred while I was living there. They had suspected Ben of dealing drugs, but actually the flats underneath ours were used as a brothel.

A woman whose daughter had been preyed upon by Ben recently had been to the police. But nothing has happened because nothing could be proved.

I say to Madison, 'You think he has Tabitha?' But it's not a question. Not really. I know he does. I saw it in his face when I confronted him.

She looks me levelly in the eye and says, 'He and his family deal in beautiful young women. Tabitha is about the right age. He's suddenly back in your life and now she's missing. It's a hell of a coincidence.'

My stomach drops. I ask her, 'Is Ben a paedophile?'

She says, 'I don't know for sure, but I don't think so. Not in the strict sense of the word.'

I feel something close to relief until she adds, 'That doesn't make him any less dangerous, he's involved in the grooming and the sale of these girls. It may not be a preference for him, but he's not above doing whatever it takes to turn them into cash sales.' I wince and Madison looks like she realises how her words might have landed on my ears. She says, 'Sorry.'

Claudia leans over the bar and takes my hand in hers.

'What happened with the girl's mother?' She'd said Ben had been reported before, not long ago.

'Nothing. She tried to press charges, claims that an older man had started a relationship with her daughter when the girl was just thirteen.' Madison shrugs. 'By the time she reported it, Michelle was of legal age.'

Like my Tabitha. Of legal age. God.

Madison says, 'I'm going to see the girl now, and I'm hoping she might have some information that will help.'

I stare at her blankly. Claudia squeezes my hand. 'I know this is all awful for you to take in, but it will help us find Tabitha.'

I nod. 'Did the girl get . . . rescued then?'

Madison looks away, not meeting my eye. 'Like I said she was over sixteen by the time it came to our attention. No charges were brought, when she was questioned she said Ben was her boyfriend. Claimed they hadn't had sex, therefore nothing illegal was happening.'

I make a sound like a whimper. 'This is all my fault.'

Emma is by my side and puts a firm arm across my shoulder. 'Now now. The only people at fault here are the criminals.'

I say to her, 'I'm her mother.'

Emma beams as though this is in any way good news. 'Well, now she has people looking who care. We'll do everything we can to find her for you. Nothing more can be done right now. I'll bring tea.'

The thought of her being in danger makes me shake inside, but the alternative, sitting here alone, worrying, doesn't seem much better either. In the end I nod.

Claudia says, 'It might be time to speak to your husband.'

I nod, I know I have to. It's out now. I've no way of hiding it anymore, from myself or anyone else. It's not right to keep him in the dark, but it's too awful to even contemplate.

## 35.

## Madison Attallee

As I leave Miriam's house, an angry voice is whispering in my head that the world is a terrible place. When I pull up on the estate I grew up on, where my wasting mother still lives, the sense of despair grows. Day is turning into night, but it's not yet dark enough to hide the degradation that is on display here. Poverty, neglect.

Now is not the time. Now I need to speak to Michelle, face to face. I phoned to say I was coming, she sounded out of it. I knock on the door and a skeletal, worn person answers. She looks terrible, but when I ask her, 'Are you Michelle Roberts?' she frowns and says who the fuck wants to know. And the knotted feeling in my stomach tightens. Nineteen years old. This girl is just nineteen. I tell her I'm the investigator who called earlier.

She says, 'I don't remember,' and she goes to shut the door in my face. I push an arm out to prop it open. 'Michelle, I'm not with the police, honestly. I want to ask you some questions about Ben Hedges.'

She still looks pissed, but she stops trying to close the door on me. 'You can make it quick.'

I follow her down a filthy hallway into an open-plan kitchen diner. The layout of the flat is exactly the same as Mum's, but it's disgusting in here. There's a bare fluorescent bulb throwing a putrid yellow onto everything, and there's nowhere to sit. Michelle slumps onto the floor and I watch her skirt ride up pale, bruised legs. She swats some stuff out of the way revealing a sort of bean bag thing and gestures for me to plonk arse. I do. Trying not to look as grossed out as I feel.

I say, 'Hi, Michelle.'

She says, 'Hi.' Her voice is so young. Not in-keeping with the rest of her at all.

I ask, 'How old are you?' Just to be sure, and because I can't quite believe it.

'Nineteen.' Jesus.

'Like I said – I'm an investigator.'

She frowns, 'But not old bill?'

I shake my head. 'No, I'm not. I do similar sort of work, but I'm nothing to do with the law.'

She seems to relax a bit. I say, 'I told you I'm looking for some information on Ben Hedges.' Her shoulders stiffen anew. 'And Mr and Mrs Walker.'

She looks down at her hands. They are clasped in a little ball on her lap. I say gently, 'Michelle.'

She looks at me, and as her eyes widen, I can see the kid she really is, the one she didn't get to be. She says, 'Why?'

'I know that Ben is a bad man and that he's hurting other girls, ones like you.' I pause as my words take effect. A necessary cruelty. I see her face fall. I go on, 'A woman I'm working for, her daughter's missing. We think she might be with Ben. Or maybe his mother.' I let it sink in and see a myriad of things cross her face.

I add, 'I think he hurt you?'

She laughs, it's like a bark. She's wearing a thin T-shirt. It's cold in this room. I can see her shivering slightly.

I say, 'Michelle?'

177

She shakes her head. 'It's all my fault.'

'What was your fault?'

She shrugs. 'This shit. Where I've ended up.' Another shrug. 'My mum's a nice woman.'

'I spoke to an officer your mum visited at the police station a while ago, he said the same thing, about your mum, I mean.' I know Michelle's mum is different to many others who live around here. My own included. If I'd gone missing I doubt Charlotte Attallee would even have noticed.

She nods, a thin line of snot escapes her nose. She wipes it away. 'She didn't raise me to be . . . this.'

'To be what, Michelle?'

'A whore.'

I shut my eyes momentarily. Trying to take a breather from her broken voice, and her broken body. Her awful surroundings, and the drug paraphernalia that she doesn't even bother to hide. Trying to push Miriam's sad and panicked face from my mind. I am livid that Ben has still managed to attack her, and under my watch.

I ask, 'What happened, Michelle?'

She starts making a roll-up, and I hand her a packet of ciga-rettes out of my bag. She takes one, lights it, hands them back. I empty half the pack out and put them on the floor. She nods, 'Thanks.'

'I'm trying to quit.'

She sighs, 'Fags are the least of my problems.'

'They don't have to be.'

She looks at the cigarettes lined up. 'That's what my mum says.'

'Your mum's right.'

She smiles but it's not a happy look. 'What do you want to know about Ben?'

'How did you meet?'

'He chatted me up. I was walking Mitzi, my mum's dog, to the shops.'

'How old were you?'

'I don't know. Thirteen maybe. Just.' For fuck's sake.

I say, 'He's pretty good-looking.' Miriam's told me as much though I'm yet to catch sight of him.

She inhales and nods. 'Yup. He really is. All my mates were getting chatted up by then. Me not so much. I looked younger than them all.' She laughs again. 'Hard to believe now, ain't it?'

I shrug but she has a point. 'So, he chatted you up?'

She nods. I ask, 'Did you have a relationship with him?'

She nods again and says, 'Yeah. I guess. We didn't have sex though. I thought he was being respectful. I thought we were in love. Isn't that pathetic?'

I feel anger rising and that black cloud at the back of my mind. *Look at the shitty world*, it whispers, *what's the fucking point*. I tell Michelle, 'You were a kid. He was a grown man. It's what he wanted you to think.'

She nods again. 'I fell out with Mum. Moved into Ben's for a bit, he said he'd find me somewhere of my own.'

'Did he?'

She tips ash from her fag onto the floor. 'Yup. His mum's for a couple of days, then he moved me into a brothel.'

I play a longshot and ask, 'Will you give me the address?'

She shakes her head. I expected as much. I nod, not ready to push it now. 'Were there lots of girls there?'

She nods. 'About ten of us. Only two English.'

'Where were the others from?'

She shrugs, 'Poland some, an African girl. The foreign ones had kids or siblings, families that needed money, you know. That's how he'd got them. Said they'd be able to send cash back for them.'

Fuck. I ask her, 'And did they?'

179

She laughs that barking laugh again, 'Doubt it. I didn't get to keep any. Just drugs. Weed, then sleeping tablets, then skag. They gave us shit loads of that. The other girls, they weren't the types who'd have got into it on their own. Know what I mean?' I nod, not pointing out that she wouldn't have been either. That no one makes a conscious choice to part with their soul.

She goes on, 'Thing is. It makes it easier. The parties would be bloody awful sober.'

'You attended parties?'

'Yup. At the flats. That was most of the work. Sounds fun, doesn't it?'

'Not really.' She smiles. I say, 'Were all the girls as young as you?'

She nods. 'Yes. Or they looked young. He has some older ones. The ones on the books. They do stripping and shit as well. Mostly they weren't at the flats though. I only met a few occasionally.'

My stomach turns. 'But you reckon the girls you shared a flat with were underage?'

She meets my eyes levelly and her voice is barely a whisper. 'Yeah, we were kids, thirteen was the average age, I reckon. The older ones came by sometimes, like checking up if Ben wasn't around, but they were a different line to us.'

The legitimate arm of All That Glitters, if you could call it that. Michelle stamps out her cigarette and says, 'We were for a certain set of Ben's customers, not ones who'd make an online booking for a real party – stag dos and all that. Not the ones I got anyway, the proper monied ones.'

She pauses, lights another cigarette. 'What they want is us when we're in that in-between stage. Not girls any more, but not women yet either. Know what I mean?'

I nod, unfortunately I do. An image of Molly springs to mind, Tabitha smiling from her Instagram page, the image merges terrifyingly. I push it away but my heart is pounding. 'So, you all got sent to these parties.'

She shakes her head, 'Not sent, they happen at the flats. We live in the top one and the ones underneath.' She shrugs. 'They theme the rooms and stuff. For rich blokes, most of them wore wedding rings.' She says this like it is a normal thing. Married men, raping children. Girls two, three years older than my daughter. She adds, 'Sometimes we'd do private jobs too. In other places. Not often, Ben preferred it to be there.'

I shut my eyes and when I open them again she's staring at me. Her face blank. Immune to the horror of her words. She says. 'He filmed it all.'

I say, 'What?'

And she looks at me and smiles that awful skeletal grin. One of her front teeth is yellow and thin. It'll fall out soon. She nods, 'Yeah, that's why it was better at the flats. For Ben. Cameras everywhere. That's where the proper cash is. I overheard him bartering with a guy once, after I'd done a job with him. They talked like I wasn't even in the room. I was a bit out of it, to be fair, but I remembered. Ben showed him footage. The guy was pretty pissed. I remember being shocked at how much Ben wanted for it.' She shrugs. 'These men don't want their wives to know. Or their fans.'

I say, 'What fans?'

And she's still smiling that horrible smile, 'Oh yeah, he had some guys you'd know come to parties, come to the house. Like I said, proper money.'

I feel sick. I ignore it and ask her, 'You're not still . . . working?' Not really wanting the answer.

She laughs again, 'Not for Ben or his evil fucking mother, look at the state of me. His clients are fucking minted, like I said, high profile, he called them. You'll have seen some of them in the papers and on telly and that.' I'm sure my blood chills a few degrees. She says, 'Looking a wreck has done me a favour really.'

God. 'How're you paying for what you're using?'

She shrugs, 'I cater to the cheaper end of the market.'

For fuck's sake. 'Why don't you go home, Michelle?'

She looks at me wet-eyed. 'To my mum?' I nod. 'She wants me clean. She let me back. I kept robbing off her.' She shrugs, eyes downcast. 'I never meant to.'

I say gently, 'You should take her help, clean up.'

She sighs, 'What for?'

I take her hand and hold it in mine. 'Michelle, you're young. You're obviously bright. You have someone who cares about you.'

She looks at me and nods but as I leave I hold out little hope that she'll go home. Her poor, poor mother.

I call Emma, she picks up on the second ring.

'How did it go?'

'Are you at Miriam's?'

'Yes.'

'Step outside.'

'I already have. Claudia's with her.'

I say to her, 'We're looking at a very organised ring. What he did to Miriam is how he extracts cash from his customers. It's what I suspected. Well, not the filming, that's a whole different league. The young ones. We can add blackmail on top of the rest of it.' I tell her about Michelle and her mum's earlier reports.

She says, 'But the police had been warned?' Incredulous.

I tell her, 'I know it seems shocking, but they don't have the time or the resources to investigate without evidence.'

She's frowning, 'They had the girl's poor mother, she came in and told them what she suspected.'

'The police had Michelle's mum, but not the girl herself. There are videos, they are the hard evidence. We need to get to them.'

She sighs. 'What a mess.' Then adds, 'Miriam still doesn't want to call her husband.'

I say, 'She's better doing it before he's sent that footage. That's for damn sure.'

Emma says, 'I know that. Poor woman's terrified, for herself and her child.'

I say, 'Unfortunately she's right to be. Deanie's sending a list over of all known brothels and missing local teenagers.' I swallow thickly. 'Those reported by parents and as truants by schools. We're going to need to sift through them all.'

She says, 'Okay.'

I pause and say, 'This case . . .'

'Isn't pleasant. I get that.'

I say, 'Are you going to be okay?'

'Of course. We're on the good side, right?'

'Yes.'

Emma is a genius when it comes to computers. She says she'll go in to work, start digging, and she'll meet me at the office. I try Ben's house again, no answer there. I ring into All That Glitters and am given the same spiel. I message Peter telling him to send officers out. He agrees when I update him.

When I get to the office Emma is there as promised, even though it's past eight and her partner, Elaine, must be waiting for her. I'm immensely grateful. She cross references information we've got from the police with various searches of her own. Her research is fast, efficient and what she finds is disturbing. There are plenty of shared videos but she tells me it'll take a while to get into them.

The worst bit of the police reports are the kids reported by the schools, and the kids in care. A lot of times when their parents were questioned they didn't give a shit. In England, in 2018. No responsibility taken by social services. I look over Ruby's autopsy report. Deanie has scanned a copy. Her body was covered in bruises and other injuries. Not unusual for a junkie, but knowing what we know now . . . God.

Claudia calls in and tells us she's stepped out, that Miriam is going to Skype Nick. I rub a hand over my face and go outside to light a cigarette with a shaky hand. I keep thinking of Michelle and her sunken face and dark ringed eyes. I think of the pictures of Tabitha, healthy, smiling. But for how long?

# 36.

# Miriam Jackson

We couldn't get a strong enough connection for Skype. I'm glad I at least didn't have to look him in the eye. Though the phone call was no better. Claudia stepped out to give me some privacy.

He'd been chatty, normal, pleasant. He'd apologised for us not being able to connect sooner. I'd butted in with, 'Tabitha's missing.'

He'd sounded amused and said, 'She's gallivanting with that Delia, or Brett.'

'She's been gone three days.'

A pause and then, 'Why didn't you tell me?'

'I thought the same and that she'd be home.' It's not true though. I think back to the first day, crawling into her bed, waiting for the police. I'd known. Something in the pit of my stomach had told me all wasn't right. I've always doubted my own instincts and look at what it might cost me now. I should have done more, I should have spoken to Nick sooner. I was so busy burying my head in the sand. The story of my life.

He says, 'Try Delia.'

'I have.'

'Sorry. Of course you have. God, where would she be for three days?'

I shut my eyes. 'Someone I used to know has been . . .' I paused here, unsure how to put it. Not at all certain that there could be a good way, 'back in contact, the police believe he is a criminal.'

'What do you mean "someone you used to know"?' His voice at this point was still light, still jovial, still kind.

I blurted out, 'He's an ex-boyfriend.' My voice was barely a whisper.

Nick said, 'Miriam?'

And I hadn't wanted to tell him, even as I knew I must. But not everything. Not detail; that we'd been flirting, that Ben had made me feel all kinds of things that Nick never did. That I was lonely in my life, that I'd always been this way except for that brief time with this man who'd been a boy then. Who had come back.

I do tell Nick that Ben comforted me when I was worrying about Tabitha, and I'd let him. That I'd gone to his house, he'd come here, to ours. That I didn't know what it meant for my marriage, or what it said about me, that this is all it took.

Nick stayed silent while I said some of this and then all I could say was, 'I'm sorry.' Knowing it was too small.

I let him fill in the rest. Which judging by the steel in his voice, he did.

'What the fuck, Miriam?' And then I had to make it worse. I'd told him what Ben did, to girls. Girls who are just our daughter's age and some younger. My mild-mannered, easy-going husband had asked for the man's name. I'd given it. Each syllable sticking at the roof of my mouth. My husband had sworn then and hung up.

Now I'm just sitting staring at my phone. Replaying the conversation. Numb.

Claudia comes in and I smile though it takes effort. She asks, 'That bad?'

186

I nod. She sighs, sitting next to me, an arm around my shoulders, and says, 'Emma's going to come over. I need to get back for Bethany.'

I say, 'No, please. I could do with some time to myself.'

She shakes her head at that. I snap, 'Claudia, please. I need to think.' And I do. I need to think about my marriage, my daughter. I need to prepare for when Nick gets back, because knowing my husband he'll pull out all the stops and be here in no time.

She says, 'Madison has us under strict instruction—'

'I don't care.'

She sighs and sends a message from her phone. She squeezes me and goes.

My phone pings. Nick is at the airport waiting for a standby flight. My phone rings, it's not him, and it's not Tabitha. My family, my entire world, so perfect just three days ago, now out of my reach. They should have been enough. I should have called Nick straight away. Not Ben. I feel sick with it, with what I have brought upon us all.

It's Madison.

I assure her, again, that I'm fine and don't need company. She doesn't sound convinced, and she definitely sounds annoyed. A woman used to having her orders obeyed. It reminds me of myself at work and almost makes me smile. We are many things to many people. She says this is against her advice and I say, 'I understand.'

She doesn't push. The girl she went to see, Michelle, seems to think the flats I practically lived in are still where Ben works out of. She'd described a block of flats. Madison tells me they think that his mother owns the block, not just the one we had lived in on the top floor, but the two underneath as well. She asks if I remember the address, I don't, though I could probably find it walking from the station. She says they are having

187

trouble knowing which property. It turns out Reeva has gone on to buy several in south London, quite a few of which are converted houses.

Their family business. Flats in various prime locations in London would have brought in enough in rentals. Why that line of work? It's not work though, is it? It's abuse. And the answer is greed, of course. Pure greed. A man like Ben can never have enough, it sounds like an inherited trait from his mother.

I say goodbye and hang up. I look at all the pictures on my wall. My little family, now in tatters. Because of me.

I rack my brains trying to find clues, moments from my past with Ben that should have warned me that something wasn't right, that he wasn't. I want to find fault to lay blame. But I only recall that time as golden. A sense of being loved, having fun, which I desperately craved. A time of smoking weed, taking ecstasy, doing much cooler things than those girls at school, and Ben. Busy being Ben while I waited in the shadows. Never questioning, never asking anything of him, just grateful for his attention, his love.

Darren was in love with Ruby. I knew that much. She and Ben had a connection before I came along. I knew they shared secrets I wasn't privy to. I'd never questioned Ben about it. Not about any of it. Habits I've taken into my marriage.

I am upstairs now, I'd been thinking about getting into bed. I'm still in my jeans, standing at the sink staring at my face. Surprised and uncomfortable at my reflection. The woman looking back is one I no longer trust. She looks tired.

I dig my phone from my back pocket, go to the top of the stairs where the signal works, and dial Madison. When she picks up and says, 'Everything okay?'

'Darren,' I say stupidly. She doesn't speak. I look at the clock: almost ten. Where has the evening gone?

She says, 'What?'

'The other guy who lived with us. Ben and he worked together, but I'm pretty sure Darren never liked him. Ben, I mean.'

'Surname?'

That I do remember and I give it to Madison. Pleased to be
of some use after all.

I should at least try and get some sleep. I'm sitting on my land-
ing, phone still in hand. I gather myself up. My body is weary,
spent and shattered, I don't know if my busy mind will oblige
me with any rest, but I ought to try. My phone pings, I pause
and check it. Nick has a flight. He'll be back by mid morning
tomorrow. My heart sinks a little at the thought of facing him.
I text back, 'Okay.'

Then I send an 'X'. He doesn't respond. Who can blame him,
I suppose. I get into my room and scrape my T-shirt over my
head, tugging at my trousers and am about to sink into my bed
when I see something nestled on my pillow.

It's a long-eared stuffed bunny. One that I have watched
Tabitha drag absolutely everywhere over the years, that she
hasn't had out for ages. The last time was about a year ago
when she had the flu. One of the only times lately where I'd
seen a flash of the sweet little girl she once was. She'd burned
with fever. Laying in bed crying and calling me Mummy. I'd sat
with her, stroking her hair. I'd brought her soup and herbal teas
and she'd clutched this very rabbit. I'd looked at her make-up-
free face and thought how young she still was really. Bubbles,
she called him. Bubbles the bunny. I can almost picture her fat,
chubby toddler hands working away at his ears, rubbing them
softly against her face. My girl.

Last time I'd seen him was shortly after one of our morning
fights. She'd been grumping around, getting ready for school,
rolling her eyes at me and generally being rude. I'd told her to
buck up and she'd stormed out. As I often did when we fought,

I cleaned her room, a peace offering she was usually grateful for. Bubbles had been in her desk drawer. I'd wiped under him and placed him softly back, thinking about Tabitha.

I run from my bedroom into hers. Mr Boots is purring on her bed. Everything else is exactly as I left it. I open her desk drawer. Empty. Because Bubbles is on my bed. That's when my heart starts to beat a little faster and I become aware that I am standing here, vulnerable, in just my underwear and a thin white vest. That someone is or has been in my house, messing with my head via bloody Bubbles of all things. My chest tightens, I can hardly breathe. I realise my extra stupidity in that my phone is two rooms away and that I told Emma not to come.

I hear a click behind me. The sound of a handle being turned, my bedroom? I shove a hand over my mouth to stop the scream escaping. I can't seem to think quickly enough and by the time I snap into action my legs feel like rubber. I move anyway, grabbing at things as I go, the edge of the desk, the wall.

I make it back into my room, empty. It's empty. I dive over my bed, lunging, and grab at my phone. Madison, Claudia, Emma. But my message screen is flashing: a video from Ben and the image is Tabitha. I click on it and everything stops. Seconds, minutes, hours. Time doesn't matter any more. I feel sick, but distant from it. As though the nausea isn't mine but another woman's. Some poor cow watching this video. My daughter. Crying. Telling me she's sorry. To do what Ben says and she can come home. Oh God.

He says, 'Sorry I had to do this.' And I look up at him. Standing in my bedroom doorway, silhouetted but recognisable. I stare, he walks nearer, sits himself on the edge of my bed and takes my forlorn hand in his. My phone rests just by it.

I say, 'Please let her come home.'

He nods. 'I will.' Then casually adds, 'She's been going on about that bunny.' Rolling his eyes like it's some big joke.

'What do you want?' But it's only a formality of a question. I think know what his answer will be.

He smiles softly, that smile that could shatter my heart, and says, 'You, Mim. The only thing I've ever wanted.' I know as he speaks that this is true. My heart is heavy with that truth.

The only person who ever wanted me is a complete nutcase. But he's persistent. I'll give him that. I look at him blankly. He says, 'Come on, get dressed. I packed a few bits.' I reach for my phone, but he gets there first, sliding it into his pocket.

I run then, something primal rises up in me and I go, managing to be fast enough to get around him, to try and get to the front door. I half slide, half fall down my stairs and land in a heap at the bottom. I am up and stretching for the lock when I feel a shove and my face slams into it. He spins me around. Pressing my back against it, an arm raised and held across my throat. I whimper.

He says, 'You're coming with me. Make it easy, she'll be back here by the morning. Make it difficult and my patience will wear thin.' I look into his eyes and see the truth there. He means it.

'How will I know?' My voice is strangled. The air is being blocked by his arm, and he's not even pressing hard. The strength of him.

'What?'

'That she's home?'

He smiles and relaxes, dropping his arm but catching both of mine in his hands. 'Oh, I see. You can speak to her, and Nick if you need to.'

'Where are we going?'

He releases me fully now, sensing my surrender, but he still holds me in a parody of intimacy, one hand resting on my shoulder, one hand on the small of my back. I wouldn't get very far before he got me anyway. I now realise the game he has set, the one he needs me to play along with.

'Eventually we'll go far away.' He shrugs, like this is meaningless. 'I have people who can run things here.'

I let out a small cry then, and he looks at me concerned. 'You won't be homesick for long.' He follows me upstairs. I am sore. All of the places I banged feel red and throbbing. My face hurts, my throat. I swallow and it's painful. I half hobble into my room, he stands while I dress and pack a few more bits. I stroke Bubbles. Then he sees me down the stairs, hand on my elbow, to the front door and out. It closes behind me with a terrible foreboding and I have to physically resist the urge to run again. He pushes me gently into his car. It's not only the thought of being far away that is filling me with dread, it's the thought of him continuing 'things' here. Of how, to him, all of these girls' and women's shattered lives are nothing more than business. He carries on, 'Unfortunately I've got a fair bit of sorting out to do first. We won't be off for a while.' I allow myself to hope, but not too much.

'Where will we go now? Yours?'

He shakes his head and sighs. 'No, that bloody bitch you employed will have my address, won't she?' I feel a small amount of misguided triumph.

He turns on the engine and grins, 'It'll be a surprise.' And we're off.

# 37.

# Madison Attallee

When I open the door Peter pops his head out of my kitchen and I jump out of my skin, shouting, 'Fuck,' and preparing to smack him in the face. He starts laughing but I keep frowning. I say, 'Emergencies, Peter. You've got that key for emergencies.' Mimi is sitting in traitorous fashion by his feet. Usually her instant leg winding, purring and attention-seeking gets on my last nerve. Today I feel annoyed without it. Betrayed.

He shrugs. 'I thought your day would have been pretty stressful, and that you probably needed to eat, that is an emergency, and I couldn't wait to see you.' He takes my reluctant hand and leads me through to the kitchen. There are two plates on my table with steaks on and he fusses around piling on chips and green beans. He grins, says, 'Voila.' And before I can stop myself I've grabbed my plate and emptied it into the food bin. He stares at me, open-mouthed. He looks from me to the bin.

I realise what a shit I've just been. What a shit I am, and I burst into tears. For fuck's sake.

Instead of telling me off, which would be the appropriate response in light of my crappy behaviour, he folds me into his arms and strokes my hair. I blub onto his chest. When I finally pull back he's still smiling and says, 'Not hungry then?' I laugh, despite my sorry self. He sits me down. 'Come on, you'll have to share mine. Lucky I did too many chips.' I shake my head but as he cuts food and passes it to me I do start to feel a little bit better. He asks, 'What's the matter?'

I sigh. 'Everything. The world's a horrible shitty place full of arsehole people and desperate people. I'd be better off fucking pissed than having to deal with this shit.' I push the plate back to him and light a cigarette, sighing. Marred in the blackness of the world. Weighted down by Michelle's awful young-old face and her skinny arms. Thinking about privileged men who can pay for women as though they are nothing more than knickknacks, and girls, if that's their thing. I think about Ruby and Michelle, a block of flats where lives are ruined, and the 'well-known' people who paid to visit. I'm heavy with thoughts of Tabitha, and where she might be, and Miriam; a lonely young girl, a lonely wife.

I think about my mum, Charlotte, who used to be fun and full of life, sitting in her gross armchair shrivelling away. I start crying again.

Peter says gently, 'I think you ought to get to one of your meetings.'

For fuck's sake. I'm about to tell him where to shove his fucking meetings and then I see his face: kind, soft, concerned, helpless. I remember him when we were kids and he accidentally discovered the horror I was living through at home. He helped me many times to sort my mum out. He helped me to pick myself up and he never mentioned it unless I did. Peter has been one of the few constants in a life afflicted with uncertainty.

He is too good for me. I think this often and I think it now.

There's a meeting within walking distance. I reluctantly pick up my keys and fags and head for the door. He calls, 'I'll wait for you, but if you want me to leave when you get back that's fine.'

I nod. Unsure what I want right this second let alone what I'll want in an hour, or two. I think I want a drink. Even when I try and picture Molly, a small child, scared because no one was there – left alone by me because vodka took priority – even then, I can't help thinking how soothing that vodka might be. I walk around the corner anyway, trying to let my feet do the thinking, since my head's clearly not up to it. I wipe at my tear-stained face and smoke.

I take a deep breath and head in. Jane is making teas and she waves at me as though she hasn't got a care in the world. I raise a half-hearted hand and go and ask for a coffee. She's grinning like an idiot. Every bloody meeting I go to, she's there. Smiling, waving, trying to fucking hug me. She asks how I am and I scowl, annoyed when she smiles and moves on to the person behind me. I settle into a seat at the back, ready to make a quick exit if I can't bear it. And then I realise that Jane is going to be chairing and I wonder if I ought to leave right then and there. What the hell do I want to hear from an overly cheerful, dumpy middle-aged chick with pink hair, for fuck's sake? Oh well, I'm here now.

She starts speaking. 'My name's Jane and I'm an alcoholic.' And I feel the fag packet in my pocket, I'll nip for one as soon as she's not looking. Then she starts to tell her story and I'm suddenly glued to my seat. Listening to Jane describe growing up in an alcoholic home. Leaving before she was of age. It resonates with my own experience and my heart goes out to the kid who'd come in and find the grown-ups completely out of it. She talks about picking up a drink then a drug. Sleeping with men for money. Two suicide attempts.

I feel my heart break even harder, not sure I can take much more of this shit, and then she smiles and starts talking about her son. The day he was born, how she held him, looked at him and vowed never to mess up. How she drank the day after she got home. Confused as to why she would when she loved him so much, when she had made a decision to do better by him than her parents had done by her. She says at some point in his early years she realised she couldn't stop and that no one was going to do it for her. She saw her doctor, who didn't have many suggestions but said some people went to this sort of self-help group. He gave her a phone number and she came to a meeting. She said what she'd been hoping was that someone would offer to take care of her son and teach her how to drink properly, but what she got was a whole lot better.

Her face is beaming as she tells us about the kind of man her boy grew into. The kind of mother she became. How she learned to be, not just a parent, but a human being. One who thought it was worth getting up in the morning. Who saw bad things and knew that good happened too and that it was up to her to be that good. She says she's convinced that goodness ripples out and we get to touch the people we care about, the people we meet. And I want to believe her. I so want to believe her.

Other people share about their own families and I realise I'm not the only one. Hell, I'm not even the worst one. Someone mentions the key to avoiding the craving for a drink is trying not to be an arsehole, and I think about throwing Peter's food in the bin. Shit. I see Jane waving for me to hang around as the meeting packs up. I point at my watch and shrug, not ready for a heart to heart, but I leave the shitty church hall and I feel a little bit lighter, a little bit more hopeful.

My work is good, I'm doing the right thing. It's not too late to save Tabitha, I have to believe that and I have to do my job.

I have some humble pie to eat right now.

I take a deep breath at my front door, saying to myself, 'Try not to be an arsehole.'

When I get into my flat, I go and put my arms around Peter, say sorry and mean it when I ask him to stay.

# 38.

# Ruby Williams

## *1994*

I think that Mrs Walker, Reeva, is scarier than her husband. I tried to explain this to Darren but all he could understand was the physical danger. I couldn't articulate it properly. But I've thought about it, and it *is* worse because she, Reeva, pretends to be on your side.

It's very confusing.

I'd been pretty messed up after the two posh blokes. I must have looked bad because Ben was even nice and he sounded sorry for me.

He rang her, Reeva, and she came to the flat. The bitch hugged me, and I was so damn grateful I hugged her back. I hadn't known I could hate myself any more than I have since Mr Walker, but it went up a notch then. With my stupid arms wrapped around my enemy.

I've thought about it a lot, and it's because I miss Mum, and that's what Reeva seems like when she's being like that. You can forget for a minute that she's bad.

My mum probably hasn't been the best mum, she's mouthy and stuff, but she loves me. The shit Ben and Reeva are putting me through isn't worth this.

The following morning, I wake up and look at myself naked in the mirror. Inspecting the damage. Nothing on my face.

Everything is below the neck. But my face doesn't look like it did a few months ago. I look harder, rougher.

I hear Ben come in, whistling, and he yells that he's going to have a shower and I'm pulling on clothes, my trainers, and opening the front door before I can think about where I'm going. I don't have any money bar a few useless coins in my pocket. I think of the wedge that Ben took in last night, or this morning it would have been. The dark awful hours where bad things happen. I run a hand over a tender bruise coming up on my arm.

My wounds are the cash in his pocket. I feel a surge of anger.

I cover my arm, yanking the sleeve down. It'll be sore, but I ache all over anyway, there's not a bit of me they didn't grab or paw at. I pull my hood up and go and sit in the waiting room at the train station. A woman sitting opposite glares at me like I'm shit, and I suppose that's how I look. I ignore her. My mind wanders to the men who've turned me into this. Suited, booted, with their silky voices and mean hands. This woman wouldn't look at them the way she's looking at me. No one would. I have a brief thought about going to the police. I'd get done for Eric, but honestly even that doesn't seem such a big deal now. It might save me from worse things, it might save other girls. Because I'm sure I'm not the first and that I won't be the last. I catch the woman's eye again, see her glaring.

No, there'd be no point. Who would believe me? The men who use Ben's services have money, power and respect. I get up and leave.

As I walk back, I'm thinking about Mum. Whether she'd be pleased to see me. Whether she blames me or Ben for Eric's death. I have even started to wonder who was really responsible. I've seen Ben in action now. I have a gut-level understanding that he's not right, not in any way. My mum's not far away. She's in Kingston, and although I've only been back to the Walkers' in

Ben's car, I know I could be there in an hour by train. Maybe I could take Darren. Maybe I wouldn't get arrested. Even if I did, maybe Mum would have me after prison. Maybe Mum would be all right to have us both, me and Darren, just until I can sort something else out.

Maybe prison would be better than this anyway.

It's all these thoughts that make it possible for me to get out a twenty pence piece from my pocket, exactly half of all the money I have in the world, and put it in the first call-box I come to.

I dial, and stand, waiting. Waiting to hear Mum, waiting to find out if I have the guts to face up to it all. If I can throw myself on her mercy, on the police's mercy.

It rings twice and a voice says, 'Hello.' And I can't breathe but I have to speak. The voice says, 'Hello?' again. Annoyed this time. Likely seconds away from hanging up and before they can, I ask, 'Eric?' And he says, 'Ruby, love, is that you, my God, it's her.' He's yelling now, calling Mum's name. My money runs out and the call dies.

I could call back. I could reverse the charges. But I can't think properly, my head feels like it's scrambling and I slam the phone down. I march back to the flats. So many things are rushing through my mind. Eric falling backwards, blood everywhere. My mother, screaming. My gratitude at Ben's rescue. For having a roof over my head. For not being left to rot on the streets. Ben saying that we were wanted. That he'd get sent down, and it would be my fault. Then the Walkers' house, and that awful man. Other men. Ones who get to swan around being heroes in the world while people like me are smashed to pieces.

Me, doing what I needed to do. To pay him back. Because I was sorry. Because I thought I'd made him a murderer. Ben. And it suddenly clicks into my brain with chilling certainty. He knew. Ben knew that Eric was alive. He told me he'd read about the murder in the papers and he'd banned me from reading them. I'd been grateful. I'd been bloody grateful. For his protection.

The anger starts up then, sizzling and raucous.

When I get in Darren is back and on the decks. Mim is there, sitting on the sofa smoking a joint and looking adoringly at Ben. Ben grins and ruffles my hair when I walk into the living room. I smile at him though it's a strain. This isn't a conversation I want to have in front of Mim. Telling her, or at least the threat of it, I reckon, will be what buys me my freedom, and Darren's.

I don't think that Ben will do to her what he's done to me, what I'm certain he does to other girls. I know he views her differently to us. We are little business opportunities, sweet money-makers but ultimately disposable. I suppose eventually Mim will get over whatever drama she thinks is happening in her life and move on, leave all this behind. At least that's what I hope. To be honest, I'm at a point where I'm willing to take the risk. I want out, I want Darren to be free of whatever Ben's got him tied to as well and Mim is really the only thing the psycho cares about.

Ben's singing along badly to Soul II Soul. Darren rolls his eyes and passes the mic to me. I almost don't take it, I hardly ever sing any more. Yet another thing Ben has unwittingly taken from me. Anger courses through me. I lift the mic, and when I open my mouth I find a peace in it that's been missing for ages. Ben shuts up when I start singing. They all do. By the time I'm finished Darren is looking at me in that soft way he does, even Ben looks pleased. Mim is glaring. Her jealousy would be funny if it wasn't so completely ill-placed. If only she knew. She'd be glad of her own life. I smile at her and she blushes, smiling awkwardly back. She's a kid really. Like I was just a short while ago. I thought I knew everything, had the whole world sussed, but I was naïve and young. *I envy her.*

I understand in my bones that even if – no, when, *when* I manage to escape this, I'll still be damaged. The things I've felt, the things I've seen. I make a decision then and there. I'll go to the police. I won't tell Ben that. But that's what I'll do. Because his 'business' is growing. These men think they are untouchable. And that means more girls' lives will be shattered.

Ben announces to us all that he'll be working a rave later. Says he has a few cash-flow problems that need solving. That means we'll be there selling drugs. Darren specifically, but me too. It's always the same answer to cash-flow problems. Mim's eyes widen and she says she's never been to a rave. I'm almost sympathetic, for the stupid shit she thinks she's missing out on. But I put it aside. Sympathy isn't something I can afford right now. I have to stay focused. I count out ecstasy tablets into bags, and comfort myself with the thought that this will be the last time I have to break the law for him, or anyone else.

We all get our stuff together. Miriam looks so excited that I *do* feel sorry for her. I'm tempted to tell her everything before I go to Ben. It would be the right thing. It would free her. I could tell her to run a mile, to not look back. He says he loves her. She believes him. Maybe he even believes it himself. But men like Ben don't love. Not really.

My mum had this boyfriend – Colin – for a while. Years, actually. He started out just like Ben is with Mim. Donna was over the moon, thrilled. I was only little; eight, maybe nine. The first time he battered her was because she'd gone to the shops with make-up on. I'd gone running in and he'd swatted me against the wall. He'd been sorry, and Mum had apologised. To him. To me. She stopped wearing make-up, but it got worse anyway. Soon he even had to come on the school run. My larger-than-life, loud-mouthed mother became quiet, subdued.

He got hit by a car on a Friday night. Drunk, unsteady. Dead in an instant. I'd been relieved. Mum had cheered up. Stayed on her own for a while. I don't think we'd ever have escaped him if not for that car and his drunk stupidity.

We went to his funeral and I saw Mum trying to hide a smile, but I felt it too. The day after, Donna put the red lippy back on and whacked up the tunes. It felt like life had started again. Eric isn't a saint; he's got a temper, he likes a brawl, and he'll dole out a slap, but he wouldn't batter a woman. Not like his son. That's who Ben is. He's Colin. But cleverer, better looking. Mim isn't as streetwise as Mum either. Mim is just stupid, easy prey. I watch her now, staring at the man who will ruin her life in admiration as he chatters away about nothing in particular. Nothing bloody important.

I felt that way about him too. Impressed with his confidence, his looks, his keen desire to own the finer things in life. That's what Mim is to him. One of the finer things. I felt a lot of things just a year ago that I don't now. Now I reckon I can tell which men you can trust and which you can't.

I leave the room, head up to Darren and help him measure out pills and powders. He's definitely a man you can. Trust. And I'm going to. I'm not going to be ruined by the others and their disgusting pawing hands. By Mr Walker, or Reeva, or Ben. I'll be like Mum. When this is all over, I'll put on my red lippy. We work with music in the background in companionable silence. Tonight, I will confront Ben. I will tell him that Darren and I will be leaving, with no hassle, or I'll tell Mim.

I'll sacrifice her for us. Because I have no other choice.

# 39.

# Madison Attallee

I ask Emma what she's found on the name Miriam gave us: Darren Lewis. She comes up trumps, and it turns out that he's known to the police already. For both good and bad reasons. The bad ones are historical. She's found his work and home address, which are the same. I call the number listed on the website, and am told by a receptionist, 'Suzie', apparently, that he's in meetings for the next forty-five minutes but then is free until lunch. I tell her what it's regarding, and that I'd like to come in and speak to him. She says she'll let him know, and to go right ahead and come in, they have a very open-door policy. She pauses then adds, 'The kids don't like uniforms though.' I assure her I'm not an investigator for the police and she says fine.

Darren works in Battersea. At a charity that he set up called 'Youfscape'. I drive into London with my usual sense of trepidation. Both Claudia and Emma had suggested I take the train, but I prefer to be able to listen to music, and smoke, while I go. Even if it does mean having to deal with halfwits who haven't learned to drive properly.

Finally, I pull up outside a dilapidated-looking warehouse, though I reckon that's probably the intention. The large sliding doors are half open and covered in various bits of graffiti.

I stop to admire some of it, and I'm still doing that when a dreadlocked man comes out and grins. I see a flash of gold as he smiles.

'Good stuff, isn't it?' He gestures at the wall.

I nod, it is. It's one of the offences I hardly ever bothered to arrest people for. I used to love the big mural pieces on my bleak grey estate. Most of this stuff is done by kids looking to brighten up an otherwise desolate landscape. I know that these pictures, and their meanings, are like roses growing in between paving stones.

He comes and stands next to me, looking at a particularly fine piece showing Snow White and seven demented and stoned-looking dwarves surrounded by trippy colour bursts. He's tall, probably has almost a whole foot on me. I pull myself upwards on my heels. He says, 'A kid called Noah did this. He'd been in and out of gangs, and prison. We got him to start decorating here, his last piece was paid, and for Benetton.'

I say, 'You're doing good work.' Peter knows of this place and has told me as much. Praise from him doesn't come lightly.

He nods, dreads shaking around. 'We're trying. Madison, right?'

'How did you guess?'

'Suzie said you were coming, and what you did. Investigator, cop, can smell you lot a mile off.'

I shrug.

He laughs. 'You both walk the same.'

I relent with a smile. He's not wrong, and I find I quite like him.

'You here to talk about Hedges?'

'I am.'

He sighs. 'What's that mother fucker done now?'

I say, 'That's where I'm hoping you can help.'

'Let's get inside then, eh?'

I follow him. There's a pool table, sofas, a TV, an Xbox, a PlayStation, and a row of computers in a large open-space room full of kids – young adults, I suppose. I guess it's my age that makes them look like children. Just off to the side is a kitchen where we head now. He puts the kettle on to boil and asks what I want. I say coffee and I'm relieved when he gets out a cafétière and the proper stuff. I'll take instant for the caffeine hit, but it's a poor imitation. He waves a tea bag at me and says, 'Green tea, you should try it.'

I frown. 'Have, tastes like hell.'

He laughs that low booming laugh again and I find myself suppressing a smile. 'Well hey, you get used to it and it flushes out the toxins.'

This man served a five-year stretch for dealing class A drugs. Not the fluffy kind either. The big, life-stealing H. He is one of the few people connected to Ben who did any time for anything, not that I'd have made the connection if Miriam hadn't given me his name. He was twenty when he went down. Two years after Ruby's death. Peter and I think now, looking over the files with new knowledge, that he might have been directly supplying Ben's 'girls'. He was never registered as living at the flats and at the time of his arrest 'no fixed abode' was noted.

When he came out, and still on probation, he volunteered as a youth worker. Within three years he'd set up this place. His reputation is good. Youfscape offers, among other things, counselling, advice, employment and training help, but perhaps most importantly it's a place where kids, those under twenty-one, can 'drop in'. As if to punctuate this point there are plenty of them milling about now. Even from the kitchen, and with the door closed, we can hear raucous laughter, the pool cue hitting balls and the beeps of computer consoles.

I say to Darren, 'This is some place.'

He grins. 'It's home for me these days. I've got a flat above it.'

'You're a reformed character.'

He tilts his head to one side. 'Met a man, on the inside. Helped me learn a lot of things.'

'About green tea?'

He laughs. 'Among other stuff. Showed me there was another way.'

I nod. I think about the child I was, first reformed by my old head teacher, later moulded by the police. Taken out, beaten for a while by the same affliction that got my mum. One I thought I'd escaped. Brought back to life via a rehab and kept sane sitting in meetings with other nutters. Darren's watching me, and he says, 'I read about you. Reckon you get me.' He's talking about my own brush with the wrong side of the law. I was drunk on duty, sent home. The following morning I left my daughter, a minor, at home unattended. I could have served time for it. Luckily I got sent to a rehab instead. The papers made a meal out of it at the time, mind.

I nod. A moment passes. I let it, and then I say, 'Ben Hedges?'

Darren's face darkens. He pulls out his wallet and fumbles for a minute then he produces a set of photos, the kind you get in booths, ones I'm sure kids wouldn't bother with today now they've all got iPhones. He hands them to me. It's him, young him, shorter dreads, chubbier face, and a girl, just on the cusp of adulthood, dark hair, dark eyes, kohl ringed. He says, 'That's Ruby.' And I feel a wave of sadness for the child staring back at me. One who never made adulthood.

I say, 'She was very pretty.'

He shrugs, 'Inside and out. Know what I mean?'

I think I do. He sighs. 'He took her to that freak of a mother of his, and her husband.' He shudders.

I ask, 'Ben?' just to clarify.

He nods. I tell him, 'They all still work together, you know.'

He kisses his teeth then, a darkness washes over his face. I see the man he could have been, dangerous if left unchecked. Perhaps the man he once was. 'I know that.'

I wait, one beat, two, then I say, 'Do you remember Miriam Jackson? Would have been Sheefer then?'

He nods, 'I remember Mim. Poor kid. Ben was bloody obsessed with her. I saw her wedding pictures in *Hello!* magazine. Glad she went on to do all right.'

I say, 'Not so much today.'

He takes a sip of his tea, I can smell it from here. Musky and hippyish. 'That so?'

'Seems like Ben still had her on his mind.'

He says, 'Then she should run a mile.'

I say, 'Too late, and her daughter's missing.'

He stills at that. 'How old?'

'Sixteen.'

'Shit.'

I nod. 'Not great news, in light of the family "business". But you say he loved Miriam?'

He shakes his head, his hair takes a second to catch up. 'Nah, man, said he was obsessed with her. Guy like Ben loves nothing.' My heart quick-steps, I feel a foreboding hit my stomach.

'How did you meet him?'

He runs a hand over his face. 'I was a kid still really. I lived with my nan, till I was sixteen.' Miriam had said he was a couple of years younger than Ben.

'What happened?'

He smiles. 'She died.'

'I'm sorry.'

He shrugs. 'She made old bones. Despite a pretty hard life. I like to think I made it better.' He takes another sip of his tea. 'She had a thing about gangs did Nan. Made me swear down to her that I wouldn't join one.'

I nod. He goes on, 'Thing is, gangs were one of my limited

choices. And I didn't fancy abject poverty, which was one of the others. I knew Ben, he was on and off my estate often enough, though he came from the suburbs. Knew that his mum and her husband ran girls. Didn't know they also catered in *actual* girls, mind.' He looks at me sharply. I nod to say I believe him and I do.

He says, 'They had this block of flats. Where the work was done. Ben was living in the top one. He knew I served up, but like I said I wasn't affiliated with any one set of people in particular but I also didn't piss anyone off.'

He wouldn't have been able to stay on his estate and do that for long. 'I didn't nick customers 'cause I valued my health.' He laughs, but the reality of his life without his nan sounds as harsh as mine and plenty of others. Like he said, there are limited options in the English ghettos. And limited aspirations too. He shrugs, 'Ben asked me to serve for his girls. Offered me a room in the flat. I didn't want to deal forever, but my mum was a sad arse crack addict and I didn't want to be her.' He shrugs.

I say, 'Sounds like an easy choice.'

He nods, 'It was, but it was the wrong one. College, man, education that would have been a better way out. Dealing was the same thing, even if I convinced myself it was some kind of step-up.'

I tell him, 'Seems to have come good.'

He smiles. 'Shit, I know that. And, hell, I wouldn't change it. My experience has led me here. Now I can save others the same lessons. If they're listening.'

I say, 'Ruby was living with him?'

He smiles and everything on his face softens. 'The only woman I ever loved.' That statement is so bittersweet I don't know how to respond.

He turns to me then, anger now on his face. 'She thought they'd killed her step-dad, Ben's dad. He let her believe that.

Took her from her home to his mother's clutches. Put her on the game. She wasn't an angel, she was mouthy and smoked way too much dope, but she was a sweet kid under it, talented too.'

I nod and say, 'She took an overdose,' and he kisses his teeth at me again.

'With Ben standing over her holding the needle.'

I pause. Thinking back to the autopsy report. She'd been found in a little room at a rave. Ben had found her. Miriam had stumbled in on them.

There'd be no way of proving it, I say to Darren, 'You think Ben killed her?'

He nods. 'I didn't then. But afterwards.'

'Why?' Pimping out kids is dark, but the girls were border-line. Ben also ran older women, and latterly a fair few parties for posh blokes with 'hostesses' in attendance. I'm sure they'd have been paid well enough and as far as we could work out, the ones on the books were of legal age, and signed contracts with All That Glitters.

I know people can convince themselves of all kinds of things when money's at stake. Murder is an entirely different beast though. Ben had been arrested, initially after Ruby's death. He was charged with supplying the drugs that killed her, but ulti-mately the case couldn't be proved.

Darren sighs and says, 'I didn't go to her funeral. I just couldn't, but a few years later, I went to see her mum, and I remembered Ruby saying over and over that Eric had died and it ate her up. I found out he hadn't.'

That's not it though, or not entirely. I can see him struggling. To find the words, or deal with the memories. I give him space. His voice is lower.

'Ruby had been in a good mood, the day of the rave. She'd been ... hopeful, and it had been a while since I'd seen her like that.' I nod. 'She was dead just a few hours after. I think she'd found out, about Eric. Night she died she'd said she had something to tell me. She'd seemed happy.' He swallows, looks at his feet. I look away.

He goes on, 'I carried on working for Ben, didn't know what else to do, truth be told, but I started to get real uncomfortable. Saw girls treated in ways they shouldn't be. Saw there was like a two-tier aspect to it all and one tier, well, they were younger than they ought to be. Then some of the girls saw the light. Fucked off back to where they came from. Home for these kids is usually bad, but what Ben had going on . . .'

'Far worse.'

'Not always, you wouldn't believe some of the stories I hear here.'

I'm sorry to say I would, but I don't comment.

He looks me in the eye. 'Ben found out about another source.'

I think about what Michelle had told me and say, 'Trafficked girls?'

He nods. 'Cheap, un-documented.'

'Much harder for them to leave.'

He sighs. 'The last six months I was with Ben, before I got sent down, two went missing.'

'They left?'

'That's what Ben said.'

'You didn't believe him?'

He shakes his head. 'No. Nice girls, both of them, Eastern European. One of them, Margot, she had a kid back home to feed, hated what she was doing but she wasn't a quitter. Used to check in with people back there. She'd use my phone. One day one of them rang me. She hadn't been in touch.'

My stomach feels weighted, heavy, I say, 'You think Ben killed her?'

He nods. 'People aren't people to Ben. The girls are commodities, and when they're used up he'll chuck 'em out.'

211

Jesus. I drain my coffee, put down the cup. Darren says, 'Back then it was the occasional girl from overseas, now the problem here is rife. All those people, no documents.' He shakes his head. 'It's only going to get worse.'

'Why haven't you told the police?'

He almost growls, 'I did, when I was in prison. When I started to get well, decided to take a different path.' He shrugs. 'They didn't believe me.'

Jesus. I ask him, 'What do you know about his business now?'

He says, 'I get some girls in here, not often, but sometimes they know someone who's been with Ben's lot. I know he's got a wealthier client list.' He looks at me then, levelly. 'And I also know that he's branched out.'

'Into what?'

'Blackmail.' And I think about the video he sent to Miriam, about the devices we all carry, how much easier this must be today. Michelle has told me as much, but this lets me know that Ben's secret isn't as well kept as he thinks. Which is good. And this is information that *I've* found. That the police have missed. And this stuff is big. Bigger than just Tabitha now.

Darren says, 'He has a rich list. Powerful names in his pocket. That's what the young ones are for.'

I wince at that.

Darren nods. 'Yeah, now I've only heard it second hand but sometimes the customers get a bit nasty and the problem of where to put the girls goes away. Ben encourages this, then uses that too.'

Shit. 'Darren, he has Tabitha.'

'And who knows how many other kids. Ones that aren't being looked for.'

I take that on board and make a decision right then. I'll bring home who I can. Wherever home is.

Darren goes on, 'My guess is he'll be pretty organised about it. Always was methodical.'

'Videos will be how he's blackmailing.' Darren nods. I say, 'They'll be filed somewhere.'

He says, 'Find them and you can topple the fucker.' He pauses, and I wait while I watch him weigh something up.

He narrows his eyes at me and says, 'You strike me as all right. Despite being ex roz.'

I laugh at that and shrug, 'I think I'm okay, might be biased though.'

'I know a girl that you spoke to recently.'

I frown and think, 'Michelle Roberts?'

He nods.

I ask him, 'How would you know that?'

He says, 'Like I say, I take a personal interest in Hedges. If something official happens, I tend to find out.' He has policemen he speaks to, I'd got the information about her from the station. But he'll have better information too, straight from the street, things they can't access.

I say, 'She won't talk to me. Not on the record.'

He says, 'You can't blame her, she's likely scared. Like I said, some girls gone, never seen again. She's not stupid by all accounts.' Then adds, 'If you might be able to give her some assurances . . .'

I say, 'She needs help, she's a drug addict.'

He tells me, 'I've got programmes that can help.'

I nod. Michelle will need not only a detox but also some future protection if she's to act as a witness. All of these things will cost. I say to Darren, 'If you can get her on the record I'll make sure steps are taken.' I'll speak to Peter later.

He says, 'Okay.'

I say, 'Who did you ask, about her?'

He sighs. 'Couple of ex-gang boys. They won't go on the

record, but one of them was in with her cousin. They actually tried to help her, believe it or not.'

I say, 'I'm surprised there was nothing they could do.'

He shakes his head, 'Don't think you get the scale of Ben's operation. People they're involved with have more power than a few hood rats.'

I pause, 'You're telling me the gang was too scared of Ben?'

He nods. I let that sink in. We are talking about people who use knives, sometimes guns, now acid, people who don't usually think twice about fear.

He says, 'Michelle was underage when she was with Ben.' He adds, 'She's also English.' Shouldn't matter but it will be easier to use an English girl to testify.

I smile sadly to show I follow his thinking and say, 'Yes.'

He says, 'Maybe I could help, get some of my contacts to speak to her, see if we can't all work something out.'

I grab it. 'I can speak to the police.'

'You do that. I'll get in contact with her, let's speak tomorrow.'

I tell him I need the address of the flats too. He writes it down and I leave.

I know that this is beyond what I've been employed for, but I can't leave it. I won't. This could be huge for us right now, and in many ways not being tied by red tape makes this job easier. I nod, we shake hands and I leave with a whole mix of feelings.

I get into my car and call Peter. I update him on everything I've found out and the fact that I might be able to get Michelle Roberts on the record. I tell him I'll need police help, which he agrees to immediately, then I remind him it's my coup and he mutters of course. His tone is serious. Which is appropriate, this is some serious, messed-up shit.

I blast Nine Inch Nails, light up and head back to Kingston. When I get to the office, Emma must hear me pull up because she's out and rushing down the steps before I even get out of the car.

I grin, 'You running some kind of greeting service?'

She doesn't smile. 'Nick Jackson is here.'

I glance at my watch. 'Straight from LA?'

She shakes her head. 'He's been home. Miriam's not there.'

Shit.

## 40.

# Miriam Jackson

I open my eyes and a wave of pain hurtles in behind them. Headache. Pounding relentlessly. I blink, once, twice. There is a strong white light washing over my face. I think I must have forgotten to close the curtains. Then I remember the night before and the days before that. I sit bolt upright. My heart starts racing and I feel a spike of adrenaline. Useless and unhelpful. We drove for about an hour, and we are inside a large converted house. I am in a small room. It has several beds in it. Cots really. It's crowded, like there are too many people who live here.

Tabitha's toy had been on my bed, but she hadn't been home. Ben had been in my house. Again. Uninvited this time.

He'd shown me a short and awful clip on his phone. Tabitha, teary eyed, frightened. 'Sorry, Mummy, I just want to come home.' *Mummy*. 'Ben says you'll know what to do, what he wants and I can leave. I . . . I shouldn't have come.'

Her hair was messy, pulled back, her face, devoid of make-up and the usual sneering frown, looked so young. My little baby girl.

Now I'm here. Doing what Ben wants. In the hopes that by now, she'll be home. Or at least on her way.

I rub my eyes, run a hand under the cover and up and down my body, checking again. Pants, vest, bra, tracksuit bottoms. I even have my socks on. Though actually any sort of obvious taking advantage probably isn't Ben's style. He's definitely the type of man who likes to believe it's all on his own merit. As though manipulation and fact twisting doesn't count.

He'd had to go to work, he'd said. Ben. When we arrived here in the middle of the night. Probably his busiest hours. I shut my eyes, rub harder at my temples. I'd smiled and nodded like a kind of dutiful wife. The fight had left me. I was relieved that he'd gone, but still no better off. Just delaying the inevitable. He'd locked the door behind him. I sit up now, ignoring the pounding, and swing my legs out of the bed. I go to it anyway, the door, and turn the handle, knowing it's pointless.

My phone, he took my phone. Of course he did. I *am* stupid. I should have let Emma come around. My stupidity knows no bounds. But then I'd not have got her message. My girl's message. Ben has Tabitha. Now Ben has me. Nick will arrive home to an empty house. He will likely speak to Madison since he knows now that she is investigating. At some point he will realise I am missing too, but by then Tabitha will be home.

Will he care? Nick. He is probably picturing life without me anyway, his adulteress wife.

Just he and Tabs. They'll think I've left with Ben. That I have chosen a maniac over them. I crawl back into the bed and pull the cover up over my shoulders. My heart rate is slowing down. I am defeated, weakened. As usual I am prey to my own foolishness. My own ineptitude.

But while I lie there, still and pathetic, a new steel enters into my heart. I am alive. I am still in the game. I can still act. When Ben comes, I will do whatever it takes to make sure Tabitha gets to go home. That is the decision I made after all. When I saw her tear-stained face. 'Mummy, I did a bad thing and I'm sorry. Ben didn't make me come here, he actually told me not to. I'm so sorry. Ben says I can only come back if I tell you that and also

217

to do what he wants. He says he just wants it to be like it was, that you'll know what he means, Mummy.'

I will make sure she and Nick get their happily ever after. Even if I'm not in it. Even if she hates me forever.

When she was a newborn, neither me or Nick had really known what to do. We'd had help. Nick had found a wonderful nanny who came in, looked after me, Tabitha. She did the cooking and housework as though it were no problem at all. I let her make all the decisions. Even when I hadn't wanted to wean Tabitha off the breast. The nanny had sighed, told me I'd needed rest, and not to be a martyr.

That's not what I'd been doing though. I liked feeding her. I didn't mind being tired. But then Nick had said he needed me to attend a few things, work things that required his adoring wife by his side. Making chit chat with the other wives about my radio show, the new baby, and my excellent husband. Those wives all quietly glared at me. The only one whose husband probably didn't have his mistress somewhere at the same event.

The good one.

I'd relented, even though I'd sobbed in private as my breasts swelled and I expressed it away into the bathroom sink. I'd looked at my small daughter's scrunchy red face crying out for me. I leaked every time she did. The milk had flooded in, and in the night I'd go running to her, but there was the nanny, reminding me not to get too close, lest my daughter smelled me and her appetite be whet. I'd left the nursery. Watching a stranger plug my daughter's little face with a plastic bottle.

I took advice, and direction. I did what I was told. Like I always do, and I let my heart break quietly and without fuss. Sobbing in private while my milk dried up. I returned to work, supported Nick and nodded along with people who said how lucky I was to have help. What did I know about mothering, after all? What did I know about families, other than the need to keep mine together. Whatever the cost, and the price didn't seem high. Just little things that added up to bigger things over the years. I slipped back into my expected role without hesitation, and without complaint. That bond between my daughter and I lessened the busier I got.

I remember moaning once to my mother. She was busily boinging Tabitha about on her knee. She was well into middle age by then, still attractive when she dropped her worried frown. But also working too hard, still not pursuing a relationship, or even dating, as though after Dad there was no point. Or perhaps she was frightened of her illness. She lives a life so finely balanced that nothing could be allowed to upset it. No risks at all, no travel, no companion. No close friends. She went far at work but turned down a big promotion in case it 'was too much'.

I had said to her that day, tentatively, that sometimes I felt a little left out of my family.

She'd stopped, turned to me, taking my hands in hers and said, 'All the stuff when you were a girl . . .' Which is how we referred to Ben. To Ruby's death. 'I was so worried for you, that Dad and I had failed you so badly, that my . . . nerves may have got into you, you know, and yet, you bounced back. Look what you've achieved.'

I wonder if I have done all that much better really, though if you'd have asked me a week ago I'd have said yes without pause.

I hadn't been able to meet her eyes then, my own clouding over with un-shed tears.

'Nick loves you,' she'd said, 'he loves Tabitha, and he doesn't resent you your career.'

I'd nodded, knowing she was right. But I'd felt an awful maelstrom of emotions. I hadn't wanted to tell her I knew I was lucky, but somehow I *wasn't* grateful. I felt lonely. I missed Ben and had never been able to tell her or anyone else. What they all saw as my greatest achievement – moving on, bucking up my ideas – had broken my heart. It felt to me he was the first person who loved me when he didn't have to. Or so I thought.

I don't suppose this is love, is it? It's some sort of sick, and twisted obsession.

I hadn't raised it again, with her or anyone else. I'd remembered what she'd said, recalled feeling abandoned by my dad, thought about the other wives of movie men. The ones who didn't call, didn't come home, who went on many trips, not work-related. Men only, nudge nudge, wink wink.

I hear a click and the door swings open. I scuttle up into a sitting position and find I can hardly breathe, a heady combination of fear and panic, the adrenaline rushing straight back in. He's grinning and holding a large steaming takeaway cup in one hand and a small paper bag in the other. He heads over to the bed, sits heavily, putting the stuff on the bedside cabinet. He peels back the covers and takes me in his arms. I whimper a bit and he looks at me, cocking his head to one side. 'Are you okay, Mim?' As though nothing is wrong, and this is all normal.

All fine.

I look at him, appalled but trying to hide it. Thinking about the clip, of my tearful daughter. He's smiling. 'Mim . . . ?' Then he reaches for the cup. 'Oh look, I got you a latte, and there's a pastry in the bag. You've been sleeping for ages.' And it starts to sink in fully, what is expected. The role that I am to play here, and I almost laugh, because I've had a lifetime of preparation. Put the feelings to one side, don't let despair take over. I think about grabbing the coffee and throwing it at his face, but that would risk her safety so instead I force myself to smile back. When his grin widens, I understand this is the right thing to do and that if I play this game, he will not hurt me, and hopefully by extension, he will keep his word and he will not hurt her. Today, he'd said she could go home today. My stomach churns with nausea, grossed out and raging. But my priority is not me, not my feelings. I need to get Tabitha back to her dad. I reach for the coffee and smile again, 'Thanks.'

He says, 'Do you recognise it?' and waves a hand around. I look unsure why I should and then I realise why the street seemed familiar, even in the dark – the path, the door. How could I forget. I am at the flat. This is our old room. Differently furnished, but, yes, our old room. I say, 'Oh, it's the flat.' And try and inject delight into my words.

He nods like an eager puppy and tells me, 'I've done it up, the whole block, actually, a few times. Do you like it?'

I nod, not pointing out that we are sitting in a room with four beds in it. I sip my drink. He hands me the bag. 'You should eat.' I open it, and get a greasy pain au chocolat out. I take a bite and chew and chew. He says, 'Unfortunately we won't be able to stay here. I figured you wouldn't want to do a long drive overnight and I wanted to show you the place quickly, remind you where we started out, Mim.'

I look at him and realise he's serious. He goes on, 'I hate to hurry you, but we need to get going. I'm going to nip out for about fifteen minutes.' He glances at his watch. 'You've probably got enough time to shower. Then I'll be back to collect you.'

My heart starts racing I say, 'Where are you going?'

'To switch cars.'

Oh no, no. I need to find things out, I need him to talk. Madison will get this address. I know she will. I need to be here. I make my face sad and say, 'You've just got here.' Wondering how far I'll go to get him to stay.

He smiles, leans over, ruffles my hair. I'm taken back to the same action, years ago. He used to do it to Ruby too. It would send butterflies racing round my tummy. Now it shoves bile from my guts to my throat, but I keep smiling. I shuffle towards him and against every instinct, wrap my hands around his neck, 'Surely you can stay?'

221

He leans into me, the feel of his body pressed to mine is awful, but I don't show it. ''Fraid not.'

'Please?' and I lean harder.

He pulls my hands off, 'Later.'

I say again, 'You've only just got here?' My voice is high.

He looks at me. It's not an overtly menacing look but he's getting annoyed, 'I said I needed to nip out.' He's firm there's no room for argument. I remember the violence at my house when I tried to run. That the bruises are starting to swell and blossom. I make myself smile, 'You won't be long?'

He tells me, 'Fifteen minutes tops, so be quick.'

I kind of pout. 'Promise?'

He looks me intently in the eyes. I keep his gaze, he says, 'I promise. Be ready to go yeah?'

He kisses me then, and I force myself to kiss back. When he goes, he locks the door behind him. The pretence only goes so far, I see. I stay on the bed and finish the coffee. I put the pastry down, I can't bear to force it in. I get up, stretch and wander around the room. I scour it slyly because my guess is he's watching, or someone is. I don't shower, the thought of being naked is awful. Instead, I head into the small en-suite and wash at the sink. I look around at stuff in the bathroom, at all the things that could do damage and I'm remembering the layout beyond the door.

And also, that Madison has Darren's name and that he will know this address.

# 41.

# Madison Attallee

When I get back to the office Claudia is bustling about in our tiny galley kitchen, Emma is settling back down at her desk, and Nick Jackson, whom I've only seen on the TV and in magazines, is sitting limply in our 'reception' area. This is pretty much just a large cream sofa, a coffee table, and a couple of newspapers shoved into the corner of the front office which Emma and Claudia use. He looks forlorn. A tall man, with long limbs, very handsome, but utterly deflated. His shoulders are drooped, his hands dangle loosely between his legs and his eyes are focused on his feet. He hasn't heard me come in. I nod at Emma and clear my throat. He stands when he sees me, his head almost touching the ceiling. I shake his hand and ask if he'd like to come to my office.

My desk is covered in towering piles of various things. No matter how often Emma and Claudia tidy it, it ends up the same way. I push a few piles to either side and he sits opposite me. Claudia comes in with two coffees. The smell makes me realise I've been desperate for one and I smile my thanks. Nick reaches out for the cup, sort of touches it and then draws his hand back.

He says, 'Where's my daughter?' before I even have a chance to speak.

I sigh and tell him, 'I'm not sure but I have a lead that I'll be following up today.'

He says, 'She didn't even tell me.' And I know he means Miriam.

I pause, take a sip of my coffee and try to choose my words carefully. 'I believe she didn't want to worry you.'

He nods. 'That's very like Miriam.' He takes a sip of his own drink. 'I wish she had though.'

I feel sorry for this man. Called from halfway around the world, told that not only is his teenage daughter missing, but also his wife has cheated on him and the man is likely involved. Poor Nick. I like Miriam, having said that, and I don't get the sense that she is a thoughtless person.

As if reading my mind, he says, 'I'm probably not home enough.' He runs a hand over his eyes, he looks tired. I suppose he's been flying all night, though I suspect it was in business class. Everything about him shouts 'money'. Miriam's clothes are also expensive, but she doesn't wear them with the same ease as her husband.

I nod but don't respond.

He says, 'I'm not happy.'

I tell him, 'That's understandable. If it helps at all I know she's extremely sorry.'

He nods but his face is tight.

He goes on, 'I know she loves me and Tabitha.' I hope this means he is planning to forgive her. I work on a lot of divorce cases and in my experience, women are quicker to forgive. Men see adultery as a matter of pride, almost like an ownership thing. Women will usually work through the pain if they think they have something worth keeping, or if they've invested a lot of time. He seems so unbothered I wonder if it hasn't sunk in yet, in light of Tabitha it probably feels like a lesser problem to him right now.

I say, 'Emma tells me your wife isn't home this morning, do you know where Miriam is?'

He shrugs, 'I don't, no. Maybe she couldn't face me. She's not good with confrontation.'

I feel a ping of worry in my stomach – that doesn't seem right to me. Miriam would be desperate now, I think, to get this conversation out of the way. Setting my concern aside for a moment, I say, 'Well, she did tell you the truth.'

He laughs. 'Only because she had to. I would have come straight home. I love my child more than anything, Miriam knows that.'

I nod, not pointing out that perhaps to someone like Miriam that was even more of a reason not to tell him.

He says, 'So what can you tell me?'

I fill him in on All That Glitters, though I don't give details about Michelle Roberts, she's not on the record yet and I'm also aware that for now at least my client is Miriam not Nick. I tell him that I understand his concern but that I am determined to find Tabitha.

He fires questions at me, mostly about Ben. Why haven't the police cornered him yet? I tell him I have got an address for the flats where Ben and Miriam lived in the 90s and I'll be heading there next. The place we suspect is still a base for a lot of his goings on.

Nick says, 'That's where you think he took Tabitha?'

'Yes.'

'And his home address? Office?'

'The police now have both buildings under surveillance, and his mother's house as well.'

'When will you know if she's at that flat?'

I look at my watch, 'Within the next hour – dependent on traffic.'

'What do I do?'

I tell him, 'Go home and ring me if Miriam's there.'

'You'll let me know . . . if there's any news?'

I nod. 'Of course.'

He goes, making sure we all have his mobile number.

I wait for him to leave and I'm out into the main office, dialling. It goes straight to voicemail. That ping of worry goes again. I hang up and mutter, 'Shit.' I grab my coat. Emma is standing, looking at me.

'Madison?'

'Emma, come with me, Claudia, call Peter and tell him Miriam's missing.'

Her eyes widen but she gets the urgency in my voice. Jumping into action quickly. I grab a Post-it and scroll through my phone where I've made a note of the address Darren gave me. I shove it towards Claudia. 'Here, we're headed here. Tell them these are the flats Michelle was on about, and to send some blue lights. Hopefully they'll get there quicker than we will.'

She nods, and I hear her say hello as Emma and I dash out and into my car. The music blasts, making Emma jump, and I turn it down with a sheepish sorry and a wheelspin. She inhales sharply.

Of course what Emma considers bad is actually a skill. I excelled in advanced driving at the station. I say to her, 'Ben's got Miriam.'

'How do you know?'

'It's the only reason she'd be out of contact right now.'

My phone rings and I go to grab it, Emma gets there first with a frown and mutters, 'Hands-free, Madison.'

I roll my eyes and she puts it on speaker.

It's Deanie. She has officers in the area who've just arrived. Based on my suspicion that Miriam is in immediate danger and Tabitha may be being held in the building, they broke down the door. The flats are empty. I half yell, 'Put Peter on.'

Deanie sighs but transfers me.

'Madison.'

'Peter, you need to search the area.'

He pauses. 'Are you in the car?' For fuck's sake.

Emma pipes up, 'She's not using her hands-free either. Don't worry, I've got the handset.'

'It's a mobile, Emma, not a bloody handset. Do you even remember landlines?' I swear she's not even thirty yet.

Peter says, 'Go back to your office, Madison, there's nothing you can do there right now.'

# 42.

Withheld number: I see Tabitha's been causing trouble.
Delia: I tried to stop her, she won't listen.
Delia: Are you there? Are you cross?
Withheld: Not at you, beautiful.
Delia: I did try.
Withheld: I know, you're a good girl, and I've missed you a lot.
Delia: I've missed you too.
Withheld: I'll come and see you soon.
Delia: I can't wait. XX

# 43.

# Miriam Jackson

I am sitting on the bed; there is no other furniture in this awful locked room from yesteryear. I am thinking about my daughter's face. 'I'm sorry, Mummy. I just want to come home. Ben says if you do what he wants I can come back.'

How? How did this happen to her? How did she become embroiled with Ben? Had he targeted her, seen some weakness, or was it just part of his obsession with me? And why now? I hope he hasn't hurt her. I hope he hasn't touched her. That thought makes me feel sick. The thought of his 'job' nauseates me.

How could I not have known? Why did he not use me in the same way that he obviously did Ruby? But I know the answer really. He thinks he loves me. He actually believes this. And while that is messed up and revolting, it's what makes me think he probably hasn't harmed my daughter. That he'll let her go. As long as I behave.

Tabitha was leverage, I guess. Got me into his car with a minimum of fuss. Got me here. I assume he'd hoped I'd come willingly, and maybe she had been there of her own free will to start with. I have to accept that was probably the case. A mockery of history distorting itself in repetition. Ben can be tempting. I should know, and she's a sixteen-year-old girl after all. She broke up with Brett, she's been out more and not where she said she would be. She's been grumpier. A dalliance with Ben, a seductive older man, goes a long way to making sense of the change in her.

My stomach is like ice. I hate Ben. Really hate him. But I love her. Nick loves her. She will be okay. This is just a hiccup in her life. She'll get over it. Instinct tells me he won't have crossed the line with her physically. In a messed-up way Ben understands me. Enough to know that I love her. That that would be an end to this sick, ridiculous game. Even if she has to live without me. Because I'm quite certain that if he, for a second, thinks I won't comply, my chances of getting away from him alive are slim. So I am to act the part. This part, the one he's written, and hope against hope that at some point the chance to escape will come.

Suddenly, the lock turns, the door swings open and I plaster a smile onto my face.

# 44.

*Withheld: She'll be coming back soon.*
*Delia: She's going to be mad at me.*
*Withheld: Don't you worry about that.*
*Delia: I am worried.*
*Withheld: I'll take care of you. You trust me, don't you?*
*Delia: Of course!!*
*Withheld: I have to see you.*
*Delia: I can't wait XX*

## 45.

## Madison Attallee

I don't go back to the office, of course. Well, I do briefly to drop Emma, who frowns as she gets out of the car. I slot in Blur and hum along to 'Park Life' while I get straight what I want to say at the station. I pull up into my old parking space. It's not mine any more but I use it anyway.

I ring the office to see if they've managed to get hold of Miriam. Emma picks up and puts me on loud speaker. She tells me they've tried to call her with no success, but she's just received a text from Miriam's phone saying she needed some space, couldn't face Nick yet and would be in contact later. They tried ringing again and it's going straight to voicemail.

No. I don't buy that. This isn't good, and I feel a tremor in my stomach as I enter the station, something's not right.

I like Miriam. I expected her to be the way she sounds on air. Confident, in control, light-hearted. She's not really these things in real life, she's smart and thoughtful – though I don't think she realises it – she's also nervous and unsure of herself. After meeting him, I can imagine Nick must be quite overwhelming for her.

I don't think she's okay.

I chat to Deanie briefly, despite saying I'm in a rush – I get the usual diet update, bless her.

I get into Peter's office and say, 'Miriam texted the girls.'

'What did she say?'

I tell him and he narrows his eyes. 'You don't believe her?'

'Fuck no. She's with Ben, against her will. Are your officers still searching the flats?'

'They are, yes.' He goes on, 'The flats are registered in Reeva's name but are being privately rented. Tenants listed as a couple of numnuts we have discovered work for All That Glitters. The Benton brothers.'

I scowl. 'From the Cambridge?' The estate in Kingston where Ben and I both started out. I've heard them mentioned over the years.

Peter clicks at his computer and says, 'Yes, here they are. Underage so no charges but they attacked a girl at their school. They were only thirteen and fourteen respectively. Can't be much more than early twenties now.'

I say, 'Sound like real charmers.' I tell him as gently as I can that I'm having Claudia draw up a contract that updates everything we've worked on so far. I add, 'Not because I don't trust you.'

He smiles and tells me, 'Madison, it's fine. You've done some brilliant work and you should be keen to make sure you're recognised for it.'

I add hastily, 'I'm not covered like I was when I was here either.'

'I know that, honestly. It's fine, and I'm proud of you.'

'Thanks for getting it.'

He shrugs. 'We didn't have proof of anything like this.'

I narrow my eyes at him and point out, 'I'm the one who's found the proof now.'

He laughs, 'You are yes, and you'll have our full resources at your disposal. The trafficking and everything you've discovered is going to help build a solid case. We need to get the videos and we need to get Michelle on the record.'

I say, 'Darren thinks Ben is incredibly organised, almost obsessive about keeping a paper trail, and now he's branched out into blackmail Darren reckons the footage will all be stored methodically.' I swallow. 'The parties are just a front. Bad enough. But Ben's just using the company to find the proper nutters, and separate them from your average entitled perv.'

Peter says, 'Entitled perv?'

I frown. 'You know what I mean. The parties are big functions for rich blokes, on stag dos, men-only events. It's known they offer extras but Ben's on the sniff for the ones he can make a little more off. No one cares about the parties, rich men using hookers. So what?'

Peter mutters, 'Their wives might.'

I shrug. 'Not going to ruin their careers though, is it?'

He sighs. 'And these are businessmen?'

'Mainly, Heads of with titles starting with C, like Chief Operating Officer, a few actors, some MPs. Influencers. I reckon it works like this: Ben gains their trust, isolates them at the parties, then films them up to no good with underage girls, taking things too far.'

I carry on, 'Like I said, girls are missing. Darren reckons at least one girl he knows has family who stopped hearing from her.' I pause. 'Seemingly a lot of it's online now and Ben actually breaks down "services", what girls do what and the like. Based on what he thinks he can sell and use I guess. It's certainly a modern take.' But it's not new news. We know these fuckers form their own little sick networks, but it's still that one area of our work that hurts. No matter what.

I say, 'The parties in themselves make enough, but Ben's a greedy bastard, and an opportunist. I think he found out with Ruby that men were willing to pay a little extra for things they wouldn't normally be allowed. Darren says that sort of clientele will be quality rather than quantity.'

'He's after the sickos.'

I nod. 'Ones with money, and status.'

He sighs. 'Makes some sort of sick business sense, I guess.' He adds, 'For blackmail.' But I know what he meant.

'Right now we need to find Miriam and Tabitha, as soon as we do I'm going to get Michelle on the record.'

'This is going past just bringing Tabitha home.'

My phone rings. Miriam's landline. I feel a wave of relief, 'Miriam, hi.'

'Actually, it's Nick.'

'Sorry, Nick, how can I help?'

And his voice is gushy, pleased, 'Tabs is home.'

'That's wonderful, wonderful news. I'll head over.'

He pauses, 'Look . . . she's not . . .'

'She doesn't want to talk?'

'No.'

I say, 'Other things have come up, I'm afraid she's probably going to have to, and to the police as well.'

He sighs, 'I appreciate that. Look, can you just give us a day?'

He hasn't even asked about his wife, and what he wants is completely unreasonable. This is about more than just Tabitha now. But I don't want him having time to arm himself with lawyers. I make a non-committal noise, but I don't agree.

I hang up, fill in Peter, stressing my concern for Miriam and the fact that we could use Tabitha to back up Michelle. She's been with Ben, I have no doubt about this. He says, 'Call Miriam again.'

I'm surprised when it rings, and more so when she picks up. Her voice is soft and odd, 'Hello.'

'Miriam, Nick just called. Tabitha is back.'

'That's good, really good.' But it doesn't sound like she means it, and she also doesn't sound surprised.

'Miriam, where are you?'

235

'I'll transfer the money I owe straight into your account now.'

'Don't worry about that. Miriam, where are you?'

'Yes, no problem.'

'Miriam?' My heart is starting to race. 'Is someone listening to you?'

'Yes, that's right.'

'Can you tell me where you are?'

'Yes, that's right. Send the paperwork by email.'

'Miriam, we'll find you.'

'Thanks for all your help.' She pauses then says, 'Yes, you too. Bye for now.'

Peter is waiting. I say, 'Miriam's definitely with Ben.'

And he's standing up, grabbing his coat and his phone. I swing open the door.

We get into my car, I turn on the engine and Blur blasts. Peter jumps. I switch it off. 'Sorry.' I wheelspin out of the car park and say to him, 'Miriam's done some kind of deal, that's why Tabitha's back.'

'We need to speak to Tabitha. Now.'

# 46.

# Miriam Jackson

Ben takes a call about twenty minutes after we leave the flat. He's driving, phone perched between shoulder and ear. I have a fleeting thought about the danger of this while driving in London and almost laugh. A car crash is the least of my worries. He mutters, 'Shit,' and pulls over. I am surprised when he takes my phone from the glove compartment and turns it back on. It beeps as messages come in, and rings almost immediately. Madison's name flashes. He says, 'I texted your PI from it, she's still hassling you. Answer, tell her you're fine and you'll settle the bill.'

But of course. Tabitha is back, and he knows that I'm not going to risk anything. So really, he knows that I am doing this for her. That I am with him not because I want to be but as a trade. An awful, necessary trade. He smiles while I speak to Madison, runs a hand across my shoulder. And I wonder, doesn't he understand that I don't want to be here? Is this man – who seems so sane, and so knowing – actually that mad, that delusional? I smile back at him as Madison says, 'Miriam, is someone listening?' And when he looks at me adoringly I realise that, yes. Yes, he is that unhinged. I pause still smiling at him and I tell her, 'Yes,' my heart beating fast, a mad, feathered bird butting against a cage. Too big, too confined, too trapped. My breath catches, my mouth dries out, speaking is an effort, but I finish the conversation. Convincingly enough for Ben to be okay.

He tells me to send her the payment and sits watching my shaky hands do that. Then he reaches out his hand for my phone, which I give back. I don't get to keep it. I guess just in case.

So, not delusional. Not sold on my genuine complicity, still doubtful. What then?

He looks intently at me, one hand on the wheel and the other resting on my arm. 'You loved me once.' I look at him and nod. It's true enough. He waits until I meet his eyes. Then he tells me, 'You'll love me again.'

I don't nod this time, I just stare at him. His hand is making small and gentle circles. Gentleness from the man who took my baby. A man who must have won her trust. As he did mine, I suppose. Tabitha is home. I allow myself for a moment to think only of that. To be happy. There is a ringing sound that makes me jump. Ben smiles and waves another device at me. Not my sensible black android, an overly large, all singing, all dancing iPhone. Like Nick's but not. His. Ben's. He answers.

'Hi.'

We are pulled in in front of a row of shops. I look out of the window. I see London. South. I know that. Battersea, but it could be anywhere this side of the city. I see a tower block in the distance. Just outside the car is a string of cafés, vintage stuff. People hurry by. Men with puffy fisherman's beards and puffy fisherman's jumpers. Women in full skirts with rockabilly hair and snug cardigans. It could be the fifties, I think, like I always do when I'm in town. These are our young people, but they could be middle aged. They are dressed as such. Unlike me. Sitting here in my skinny jeans, and flash overpriced jumper. Clothes bought for my husband. Who I might never see again. And who perhaps doesn't mind that.

Ben is finishing his conversation. I have missed it. I should have been listening. I need to try and work out what to do next. He says, 'Okay, just as well we left, the police have been to the flats.'

I look at him blankly, 'Where are we going?'

He smiles as though I am very stupid. 'We can't stay here, they came for you, I reckon.'

They. My family. The police. But he's not worried about them. He goes on, 'Tabitha won't say too much of course, but I get the feeling that investigator woman has been poking her nose in all over the place.' I blink. Madison. He's worried about Madison. And he's right to be.

I tell him, 'I just transferred her the money, like you said.' The last action before my phone was gone, into his big pocket.

His face flashes. 'She went to see my mother.'

'Well, she was looking for Tabitha. Tabitha's home now.'

He nods, but he's unconvinced. He's humouring me like I'm a silly teenage girl obsessed with him. But I'm not. I'm a woman, a silly woman who was seduced by him, but I'm not now. I *am* a grown-up even if I lapsed. I have my own drive-time show; my lonely life with my unpredictable mum gave me skills I never knew could be useful. I am sensitive to others' tones of voice, moods, I have a radar for picking up signals and responding. I recognise pain. I realise I've learned a lot. In life. Since teenage me, since Ben. I wonder if any of it will ever be of any use again.

He says, 'Look, we need to get away.'

Then it hits me and I can't contain it. I say, 'I'm never going to see her again, am I?'

He smiles but it's a sad smile. One that says it's a terrible pity, isn't it? Rather than, no, and it's all my fault.

He tells me, 'Maybe you will. But not at the moment.' Then his look changes, is sharper. 'Once we're away we'll think about it.'

I look at him and am annoyed when a tear escapes. He sighs,

wipes it away and says, 'I didn't touch her, you know.' He shrugs in a carefree way, certain that his putrid words will offer me some comfort. I keep staring and half smile, focusing on how much I hate him. Awful steaming hate, building by the second, and a thought forms in my mind. I will kill this man. As soon as it is possible. As soon as I can find a way that won't fail.

I say, 'She liked you?' It's half question, half statement.

He sighs and nods. 'She did, yes.' Then he grins. 'I'm old enough to be her dad though, aren't I?' he says this as though it is a safe assumption. As though he doesn't trade in girls her age and younger. As though we are in a different life, reading from a different script. My face must look appalled, and he frowns, 'Look, you'll understand it all soon enough. Right now, we need to go. Okay?'

I force a smile, hiding a scream, and I nod. Come on, Madison. I hope she's been to see Darren. I left my engagement ring back at the flats, and I'm hoping she'll recognise it. It's hard to miss. I stare at the wedding band that is left, a remnant of happier times, of hope, and a life not yet lived. My engagement ring will be there, sparkling, perched on the edge of the drawers, in what turned out to be a south London brothel.

I wonder if it will help.

# 47.

# Ruby Williams

*1994*

People here are off their heads. They wander past, wobbly, ridiculous, eyes like saucers. I'm not partaking for once. I'm not trying to fill myself with the things that take away the feelings. I'm going to stop with the drugs.

I watch them dance, drink, laugh. I see Darren zipping in and out, making deals, slipping bags into sweaty, grasping hands, collecting cash. These middle-class ravers are so lucrative. This is a sideline for Ben, nothing major. He sells flesh, but sometimes he sells drugs too. Or has his lackeys do it. The crowd is unrelenting, colourful, psychedelic. Throwbacks to the era of the hippies that they missed, punks they can't remember. Most of them will go home tomorrow morning, back to Mum and Dad, or rolling it alone with the comfort of their finances.

This is just a bit of fun, a Saturday night. Mim is taken with it all. I watch her sitting quietly at the back of a dance floor, and I feel that pang again. That I can't help her. But I have to help myself. I don't think I can take another one of Ben's parties. Another will break me. My body, my soul. I'm spent and used up. I see Ben and I grab his arm. He looks at my hand and I snap it back.

I'm scared of him, and that fills me with hatred. I say, 'I need to talk to you.'

He shrugs, already looking over my shoulder. I'm not important to him. I never was. He barely even bothers to pretend any more. That's one of the worst things, understanding that he doesn't care about me. He took me because he saw an opportunity, a bit of money to be made, maybe two fingers up to his dad for extra fun. But nothing more. Nothing less. He shrugs, 'Sure.'

We go into a side room. I shut the door. The bass is still booming but it's background enough that we can talk. And I need to be heard. I say to him before I have a chance to back out, 'I phoned home. Eric picked up.' He stares at me blankly. I say, 'You told me he was dead. I thought we'd killed him.'

He's still looking at me, down at me. I'm suddenly aware of the difference in height and strength. Darren should be here. I haven't thought this through, but I have to continue now I've started.

He says, 'So.' And then he smiles. Lips curling up at the sides.

I hate that my voice is almost a whisper when I say to him, 'You ruined my life.'

He looks at me, still smiling, those cold, hard eyes focused on my face. How had I thought once that they were kind? He says, 'I provided you with a roof over your head, food, drugs.'

I shake my head. 'I would never have left home.' Something changes in the room, the atmosphere, the temperature. Something about him changes so drastically that I could be looking at someone else entirely. He is dangerous. At levels I had underestimated. He has hardened me, made me wiser. But the cold, heavy feeling in my stomach tells me I am not wise enough.

He shrugs, 'They told you to stay away from me though didn't they, but your little ego wanted to sing. You assumed, about my old man.' Then he laughs. 'To be honest, it was a bit of a gift. I knew he was still alive, old codger can take a kicking pretty well. I thought I'd have to work a lot harder with you.' He shrugs again. 'You were an easy mark, Ruby. I'm not gonna look a gift horse in the mouth, am I?'

I say, 'You're going to let Darren and me leave.' The words are braver than I am.

He shakes his head, 'Nuh-uh. You can do one, but I need our Daz.'

I make my voice bigger, firmer, and I say, 'No.'

The bass switches into something darker. The red and black strobe seeps out from the main arena into here and I watch Ben's grinning face, the devil with a smile. He says, 'Or what?'

'I'll tell Mim what you do.'

His hand lashes out then, swipes me across the face; I can feel the sting of it. A red mark will be starting up. I'm almost immune to physical pain now. I've hit the sweet spot though, the only one he has. But suddenly it doesn't feel like winning, it feels like fear. I say, 'I don't think she'd like it.'

He pounces then, pushes me to the floor. I'm winded instantly. His face comes down towards me, close, too close, 'I don't think so.'

I wriggle and try and free myself. He uses his knees to hold me by the shoulders and he's reaching into his backpack. Getting out his kit. Not that he uses. Clean. Ben stays clean. Doesn't even drink. I watch him cook a fix, wriggling pointlessly, but a part of me actually wants what he's about to do. A longing breaks through the fear, the certainty that I have misplayed my hand.

I say, 'Please, Ben. Just let us leave.'

'No fucking way.'

'We won't tell.' I add, 'I won't tell her.'

'Course you will.'

He smiles, and I feel a sting on my arm. His hand comes away, and he wipes something, the needle. His fingerprints. He thinks of everything. That's the thing. And I hadn't thought at all. Not properly. A few seconds, minutes, I don't know, but there is

243

a peace as it washes into me. Sweet oblivion. Like a cushion reaching from the ground, enveloping from underneath. And then I start to retch and when I try and roll over he keeps me pinned. Smiling still, 'You're not going anywhere, you junkie bitch.'

I hear the door open. Ben turns, I hear a voice, a girl. Mim. But far away. The vomit seeps back down my throat, I can't breathe, and then my limbs start to move without me. Outside of me. I think about Darren, and Reeva hugging me. My mum dancing, singing badly in our kitchen, and then I think nothing. Nothing at all.

# 48.

# Madison Attallee

The station really isn't that far from Nick and Tabitha's house, but the traffic is terrible. Kingston has always been a bastard on account of its time-stealing one-way system, but it's getting worse as the town becomes more densely populated. We're overrun now with professionals who like the suburban feel and the links to London, and students. But our students are the wealthier kind, ones who can afford not only the sickening fees, but also the sickening royal borough rents. And all of these buggers have cars. Which I'm having trouble pushing my way through now. Peter says, 'What?'

I glance at him, flushing, suddenly aware that I was grumbling out loud. I frown and fling my handbag to him, almost crashing into one of those obnoxious Land Rovers. The woman, blonde, identikit yummy mummy, looks at me aghast. I beep and weave around her. Peter mutters, 'Jesus.'

I frown again and point out, 'I don't get sirens any more.' In a tone sulkier than I meant it to be. I see him suppress a grin. Git. I snap, 'Call Nick. Number's in there.'

'It's going straight to voicemail.'

'Landline, under Miriam's name.'

A few seconds pass, and he says, 'Answering machine.'

'You'd think he'd be expecting Miriam.'

Peter says, 'Perhaps he doesn't want to speak to her.'

'Punishing her, you mean?'

'Maybe. She cheated on him, look where it led. He doesn't know she's in danger.'

I chew the inside of my mouth. I'm finally out of traffic and I put my foot down. 'True. He would if he picked up the bloody phone though.' Nick is probably pretty pissed off and has every right to be, but whatever Miriam has done, she's his wife. The mother of his child. He must know that she wouldn't just go wandering at a time like this. Maybe he's not thinking straight. He's probably in shock of some kind and parental instincts have overridden everything.

I tell Peter, 'He said they were going to lie low for a day or so.'

'Exactly, and Tabitha obviously doesn't want to talk to us.'

I shrug, 'She'll change her mind when she knows where Miriam is, and who with, or Nick will.' These are my priorities right at this moment. I need to get to Tabitha and find Miriam. I will take Ben down, but I will do it properly, and not at Miriam's expense.

We pull up at the house. Miriam's car. Nick's. But when we get to the front door and I look through the glass, it looks empty. I ring the bell. Knock. I look at Peter, he looks back at me. My heart hammers in my chest. Something is off. We each take a side, meeting at the back. Neat rows of flowers. A fence that I get over easily. A beautiful, precise garden. French windows or bi-fold doors or whatever they're called now. Shit loads of expensive-looking glass. Nothing to be seen through any of it, other than pretty house – no people, no evidence of people. Not a coat slung on the back of a chair, no cups or glasses on the side. But both cars here.

I ring again, knock. Knowing it will be pointless. I believe she's in danger so we have just cause and I smash a small window

246

at the back and climb in. I check every room, carefully, just in case. The house is empty.

I leave via the front door and tell Peter. He calls the station and arranges for a beat officer to come and wait. We stand at the end of the drive. I say, 'Fuck.' Miriam needs help. Now. Tabitha has information that I need.

Peter says, 'They'll turn up.'

I say, 'Where have they gone though, and why isn't Nick picking up the bloody phone?'

The officer arrives. He looks about twelve. Peter apologises to him, says it's a dull job, which it is, but he's to call him straight away if he sees Nick, Tabitha, or Miriam go into the house. The kid's eyes widen at the mention of Nick's name. I roll mine. Peter frowns at me. He's still frowning when we get into my car. I say, 'My office,' before he can suggest anything else. Then I fiddle with the CDs, blast ACDC and head down the road.

Peter is tapping his hand against the side of his cup, it's an annoying habit that he's unaware of. He does it when he's thinking. It doesn't usually bother me. But it does now. I've fucked up. Missed something. People are in danger. My bloody client is missing. I've lost two for the price of one. No, that's not right. Tabitha's with her dad. Wherever that is. Emma has called the numbers we have for him and left calm, polite messages saying we have reason to be concerned about Miriam and could he contact the office as soon as possible. She's also sent him a WhatsApp. Peter's officers have been in the flats. Miriam isn't there. No one is. They are spotless, apparently, but the two on the lower floor are quite obviously used for nefarious dealings. In kids. I shut my eyes. Pushing aside the horror. Not now.

No computers, which means no footage, no files. Nothing that can't be explained away. An array of school uniforms, whips and gags is suspicious, but not in itself illegal. Each flat is covered

247

in cameras, and they found a ring on the top floor on the side. They sent Peter a picture. It's Miriam's, I recognised it – diamond that size is hard to forget. She's left it, a message for me.

Claudia comes in and puts a plate of biscuits on the table. She sits down next to Emma, chewing her lower lip. And still that bloody tapping. I snap, 'Peter, stop,' and three sets of eyes turn to me. I say, 'It's annoying.' And I can hear the defensiveness in my voice. My irritation is raised further as I see the fuckers exchange little smiles. I sigh.

Emma says, 'You realise we shouldn't even be keeping the case active. We won't be getting an income from it.' She looks at Peter, who smiles. 'Maybe we should hand it over.' Like she's asking him. About my case!

He opens his mouth to speak and I say, 'It's ours, and it's staying open,' more harshly than I mean to. I scramble to add, 'The police are happy for us to carry on, Peter?'

Peter nods. 'Yes, of course, like you said it's your case. I'm not sure I can find the funds to pay you though.'

I say, 'That's fine. We've got plenty in the bank.' I look to Claudia who nods.

Emma says, 'Okay. Where do we go now?'

I dial Darren, he picks up and I tell him I need Michelle talking as soon as possible. He says she's there now, speaking to one of his counsellors. I feel a wash of relief that he is as good as his word. I tell him the flats were empty. He says word has it that Ben knows we're closing in. I'm about to ask how, but there's no point.

Ben has Miriam. Miriam phoned me; that was a holding call. Ben likely told her to make it. What a bloody mess.

My phone pings, and it's Delia of all people. 'I know where Tabitha has been.' I'd thought there might be something up with that kid, and I was certain she must have known something about Ben despite her denials. I'd assumed though that she wouldn't have had details. Ben relies on secrecy and Tabitha will have been under his spell.

I call her, it rings out, she texts again: 'I can't talk now. Tomorrow morning.'

I type, 'Miriam is missing.'

A pause, I pass the phone around, Claudia and Emma exchange worried looks, Peter frowns at me and then a ping, 'I'm at school. Meet you after?'

My mind is racing at a hundred miles an hour. I tell her, 'My colleague Claudia will be there to meet you.'

I'm starting to wonder if Delia may have somehow been connected to Ben, that Tabitha coming along was just a coincidence that re-ignited the Miriam obsession. Man like Ben would see it as a sign I reckon.

Darren rings to say Michelle is ready to talk and to head over now.

Peter drives. I sit sulkily on the journey. He also has turned off the music and LBC is droning on. My phone beeps – Emma: 'Nick's WhatsApp message has been read!'

For God's sake. I tell Peter, who agrees it's odd. I dial Nick. It rings but he doesn't pick up. I call baby cop and he says no one's been back to the house. I say to Peter, 'What the hell is he playing at?'

I'm still thinking about Delia, something is there. Obvious but out of reach. It'll come. The radio is distracting me. In the end I turn off LBC, that undercover National Front dickhead is droning on and it's giving me rage. I put Metallica on and am instantly soothed. Peter turns it down. I sigh. He says, 'Your phone might ring.' Perfectly reasonable. I roll my eyes anyway.

He mutters, 'Maybe a meeting tonight.' And I'm about to bite his head off, then realise he might be right. I pout and smoke and keep trying to catch that thought.

We are at Youfscape in less than forty-five minutes, but it feels like ages. Useless, impotent minutes. I wonder if I should call Delia's mum. Probably. But she's over sixteen now, and I get the feeling that involving a parent might hinder whatever it is she needs to tell us.

# 49.

# Miriam Jackson

We are in a car, but it's a different one. Ben is driving and keeps glancing over at me, a soft smile on his lips. The words of the social worker who took my case all those years ago echo in my head now. She'd said Ben's behaviour was inappropriate. I nearly laugh at how little then I knew, and how little, it turns out, I've learned.

I wonder if I've passed this blindness on to Tabitha. That she fell for his bullshit as readily as I did. I smile back, though it pains me. I've done call-ins on stalking in recent years. It's been a hot topic and I've blundered my way through them. I had almost longed for such attention. Their stories of 'true love' echoed with my version of it so deeply. They never ended well though, neither will mine.

We see persistent men as romantic creatures, don't we? But I suspect there's a reason they are drawn to women or girls like me. Ones who haven't experienced enough love anywhere else to know what it looks like. Ones let down by other men. Fathers in name only. The every-other-weekend dads who don't call in between, who don't make parents' evenings, or know the names of your friends. Who remind you that you're an inconvenience. A mistake from yesteryear. Who are guilty by their apathy. We should know, shouldn't we? We should be taught that love is gentle and loose. Not cloying and all consuming.

Why Tabitha? I think of Nick. Who loves her so, who worships her even, as I do too. And I wonder if that has been too much in its own way.

Ben says, 'This is quite a new car, it's a spare though really.' He puffs his chest out. 'I've got a few.' And his voice sounds boastful and stupid. The way it must have always sounded, though it rings differently today. As we drive to I don't know where.

I've never dealt with those young years, and I've never really left them. I've never been honest with anyone else about it all, and I've never been honest with myself.

I've gone along with life as it presented itself. I made a go of university and a career because that's what Mum needed me to do. My dad wouldn't fly back for my graduation, so the photos are of Mum and me standing awkwardly, surrounded by families. Proper ones. Mum had wanted to stay for the after party, and then go out for dinner. But the thought of her realising I had no friends was too much. I said I had a shift at the paper, and wasn't my career more important than the party and dinner? Wasn't that the point of the degree?

I hadn't worked though. I'd spent the rest of the day on my own, in my tiny bedsit. I'd pictured all of the others there with their proud parents, mums and dads with shining eyes. Parents who they so often complained about. I didn't come from the sort of people who celebrated things, I didn't know how.

We pull up at a small house. I ask Ben where we are and he says, 'A little cottage, I've hired it for a few days. Until we can fly.' We've left London, driven out towards Sussex, which means Gatwick. I memorised as much of the journey as I could.

I say, 'Fly where?' my heart aching.

He says, 'It doesn't matter, we'll finally be together.'

And I nod. Careful what you wish for.

He knocks on the door and tells me, 'I've got us a bit of help, to keep an eye on you, because I'll need to run a few errands.'

A captor, he has found me a captor. I don't say anything, thoughts of escape slowly disappearing. He rubs my hand which he has been holding since he leaned down and got me out of the car, escorted me to the door.

He says, 'I think you'll be pleased when you find out who.'

The door swings open and my brain scrambles. Not pleased, confused. The person smiling at me has no place being here. In this situation. Linked to this man, this awful bit of my past, now here today, in my present. I can't make sense of why. And then things start to ping and join.

And I know, with absolute certainty that I will have to find a way to get out. Because my baby girl isn't okay after all.

# 50.

# Madison Attallee

Peter scours the outside of Youfscape. Taken in by the same artwork that I was. But there's no time for this now and I snap, 'Come on.'

His lips tighten slightly, but he nods and follows me to the door. Darren answers with a 'Hi,' and a perturbed frown at Peter.

I sigh and say, 'He's police. Real police. If she wants a deal, she'll need him.'

He pauses, weighing it up. I add, 'You said she wanted help. This is help. DI Branning has already spoken to various services that you or I cannot access.'

He says, 'I gave you contacts for drug rehabs.'

I nod, 'Yes, and they've been great, we're close to securing her a place, but Peter has been able to get a safe house and there will be space for her mum to go too. We'll also have them under sporadic surveillance.' I add, 'Until we lock these fuckers up.'

Which seems to be the deciding factor for Darren. He nods, dreds bobbing about, and says to Peter, 'I don't like to have police on the premises, freaks some of the kids out, they haven't all had the best experiences with the law.' I look away. What Darren says is probably true. Runaways are hard to deal with, and often antagonistic. I reckon working in a city like London you eventually get immune to them. Even the best officer probably stops seeing things eventually.

Peter's not like that though, he says, 'I'm sorry to hear that.' And he means it. Darren seems to hear the same thing I do and relents, swinging the wide door open. 'Come through to the kitchen, I'll go fetch her. I have a girl, Penny, who deals with the chicks. She's with her now.'

It's not so busy today and I wonder why and then realise; schools aren't out yet. It cheers me a little to think, or hope maybe, that the kids who 'drop-in' here are going to school. Or maybe they heard we were coming. I go with the first thought. Then I take a deep breath, tell myself internally that the world is not broken, just some of its people. I want to be the solution. Sometimes I have to step into the darkness to do that.

Peter says, 'This is a good set-up.'

I say, 'It is, yeah.' He'll have taken note of the fact that Darren has a female on site. Not every place like this operates so well. He murmurs, 'I'd heard good things.'

There was a really great outfit operating not far from here, but it turned out their accounts were flawed. Lots of money unaccounted for – it undid a lot of good work. I'd dealt with a fair few youth workers from there over the years and had been sad to see it go. I'm pleased that Youfscape seems to be taking over and taking it all so seriously. The key when you're working with youngsters is to be as transparent as possible.

Darren is back with Michelle. And it's not so bad. She looks cleaner than when I saw her. Her hair, washed and no longer greasy, is a beautiful chestnut brown and falls in soft waves around her too-thin face. Her eyes are wide, frightened, like sunken saucers, but today, she looks closer to her age, and closer to being alive. Her face is scrubbed and her body, desperately in need of food, is housed in a soft tracksuit. Her pale, track-marked arms are hidden. I think fleetingly that with the right clothes and some make-up she'll be fine in court. It shouldn't matter but, of course, it does. She sits opposite us and rests her hands on the table. They are hands that could do with a mani-cure, and some moisturiser.

I suspect she nibbles her nails, and around each cuticle are small torn bits and specks of blood.

Darren says, 'Michelle, you know Madison, I believe?'

She looks up at me and I smile. The corners of her mouth turn up slightly, and briefly. I say, 'Hi.'

She nods, raises a small hand to her mouth and nibbles at the corner of her fingernail. Yup. One habit I'm glad I don't have. I look down at my own well-groomed digits. Ignoring a slight yellowing on my right hand.

I say, 'I think Darren has told you that I spoke to the police?'

She nods, looks out of the window. I tell her, 'This is DI Peter Branning.'

She looks at him and her face goes into a proper smile. But it doesn't quite reach her eyes. I suspect she's trained to do that for the boys and I don't take it personally. I've experienced it with working girls a lot over the years. They can switch it on like water and don't even know they're doing it. I guess when your livelihood, and sometimes your life, depends on it, you do what you need to. I think about Michelle, yesterday, sitting in her flat, still at it, and wonder if this might be the start of something better for her. I look at her little worn face and am horrified that that smile might be how she still manages to draw the punters in. What sort of man . . .

I push the thought away. I say to her, 'Darren says you're willing to undergo a rehab?'

She sighs, says, 'My mum . . .' The sentence trails off.

I tell her, 'We think we've found somewhere for you, in Toot-ing. They have a three-month place. Dependent on whether you're willing to take it?' I find I'm holding my breath while I watch her bite the skin on her hands. It's not just the case,

256

though God knows we'll need her, and clean would be better. I also realise, one fucking addict to another, I want her to find a bit of freedom. To be able to take a day off. I feel tears spring to my eyes. For fuck's sake. I blink.

Her small voice says, 'Yes.' And I feel relief on all kinds of levels. It's a first step. The most important one. I pat her hand, the one on the table, awkwardly. Her eyes meet mine, just for a second and she nods. I see something there, something new, a bit of steel. She'll need it. Peter gets out a recorder and shows it to her, she nods agreement and I wait for him to set the tape up.

'Michelle, tell me about the man you were working for.'

Her eyes are trained on the table, just in front of me. She says, 'Ben,' in a voice so tiny I ask her to repeat it. She whispers again, and I say, 'Ben Hedges? Just for the tape if you could speak a bit louder.' It's not a tape though. No one uses tapes now. I can't be arsed to say digital recorder, or whatever it's called.

She nods and then seems to remember what I've said and adds, 'Yes,' too loudly now. I smile encouragingly anyway.

I glance at Peter and nod, he asks, 'How did you meet Ben?'

She looks up at him then back to me, and her voice is small again. 'I was walking my mum's dog. He stopped to stroke her.'

I say, 'You had a relationship with Ben?'

She sighs, 'Of sorts.'

'Did you have sex?'

'You asked me that last time.'

'For the recording.'

She shakes her head, 'Not with him.'

I say, 'But with other men?'

Her eyes fill with tears and she tells us in detail now that Ben took her to his mum's house. That Reeva Walker's husband took her then and there.

I say, 'How old were you, Michelle?'

'Thirteen.'

I ask, 'Were you a virgin?' hating the discomfort of asking this of a girl who was essentially a child.

She nods then remembers the recording and says, 'Yes.'

I say, 'What happened next?'

She tells us the same sort of tale I've heard over and over, but not often about a kid that young. Darren looks carefully out of the window. I think about the strip of photos in his wallet. How he must be thinking of Ruby, the girl who will never get justice. I know I am.

Michelle tells us that eventually, as well as the parties, Ben started sending her out to 'recruit others'.

My heart sinks. It's a usual scenario though. Often the girls in these gangs go on to groom other girls. There's a case at the moment where one such girl, now over eighteen, has been prosecuted. It's something of a grey area, legally speaking.

I ask Michelle how old she was, she tells me she must have been fourteen.

I say, 'What did you do?'

She shrugs, nibbles her finger. Her pupils are wide, dilated. She's high but her body is so used to it you wouldn't know. 'I'd hang around the parks, in London, or outside shelters. Offer them drink, drugs, fags.' She shrugs.

Darren says, 'Tell them about Cyn.'

The tears come then, though her voice remains steady, her eyes blank. She rolls out the words, a description of a young girl who went by the name of Cynderalla, 'Cyn for short.' Michelle sort of smiles.

'How old was Cyn?'

'I don't know. Same as me maybe, thirteen. She was little.'

'And what was she like?'

She sighs, 'Nice. I took her to the flats.' There is a long pause while we all think about the implications. Michelle seems to notice for the first time that she's crying. She wipes a hand

across her face, mingling snot and tears. She says, 'Can I smoke?'
We look to Darren who sighs.

'We're not supposed to,' but he shuts the door and opens a
window. She pulls out a packet of tobacco and some papers, I
take my Marlboro Lights from my bag and hand her the box.
Watching her light one.

'We pulled the usual routine with her.'

I ask, 'Which was?'

'Take her to the top flat, feed her, let her have a bath. A drink
and a sleep. She started to relax. Then Ben came.'

'Was he nice to her?'

Her face falls again but she nods, 'To start with. He always is.'

'Cyn liked him?'

She stares at me like I'm stupid and does the last of the fag
in two long, hard pulls, stubbing it out on a saucer Darren has
placed next to her.

She says, 'These girls, they don't just like him, they think he's
their saviour.'

'Did she have a relationship with him?'

She shakes her head. 'Not exactly.'

I ask, 'Sex?'

'No. He never does, he's not into kids, I don't think. But
for these girls it's part of it. Adds to the trust. She would have
though.' She glances at Peter, her face red. 'We all would.'

I say, 'He's very good looking.' Groomed. Vulnerable girls
groomed by Ben. I bet it hardly took any effort at all on his part.

She nods. 'One day he says he wants to take her out, to put
on something nice. She was all pleased.'

I wait while she pauses, I can see her struggling with tears.
'But I knew what that meant, it was her time. He took her to
his mum's house.'

I wipe a hand over my eyes, I ask, 'Was her husband there?'

She nods, and the tears start in earnest then. Darren walks

to the other side of the kitchen and comes back with a box of tissues. I see him flinch as Michelle tells us again all about Reeva and her husband. She's repeating things she's already said. Things none of us want to hear, but I don't interrupt her.

She tells us in detail about parties she and Cyn attended. She laughs, a mirthless, raspy chuckle as she describes her and Cyn as a 'double act'. Then she adds, 'Cyn understood that I'd brought her in. I wish I never.'

I say gently, 'You were a child, and a victim, Michelle.'

She doesn't say anything for a few seconds, and then, 'Cyn did the same to other girls eventually.' She shrugs, 'It's how it was.'

I say, 'Where's Cyn now?'

'Gone. I think Ben hurt her.'

And when I ask why she thinks that her story goes from bad to worse. Cyn found out that Ben had been blackmailing some of the men, two years ago, just before Michelle was 'let go' with orders to 'keep my mouth shut or they'll kill me, or my mum.' She looks in panic at us both then. Peter says, 'We'll make sure you're both okay.'

Michelle scowls, 'You fucking better.' The smiles are gone now. Probably the reality of it seeping in. A grass is worse than a tart in some quarters. Though even the most hardened criminals draw the line at children. I allow myself a moment of pleasure thinking how uncomfortable prison will be for Ben. Goals. Get him locked up. I also let myself recognise that the chances are that this is a murder investigation now. Ben, the Walkers, they aren't just selling these girls, they are silencing them when they misbehave. And I can't believe Cyn is the only one who has stepped out of line.

Peter nods again, her eyes go back to mine. She tells us about the friendship that developed between her and the other girl.

Full of fear and mistrust, but also a mutual suffering. One of those delicate, intense relationships born of necessity. Michelle says, a week before Cyn went missing, she had apologised to her. She shrugs. 'For bringing her in. She didn't blame me for any of it. Like I said, she did the same.' Her voice is defensive, though it needn't be. I don't blame Michelle, a child at the time, for any of this.

She says, 'Cyn found out that all of the videos were at Reeva's and she was planning to break in and get them. There was one guy in particular who she knew was loaded and wouldn't want anyone to know.' A little ping goes off in my mind, and I'm about to say something when Michelle goes on. I decide not to interrupt her, realising this is likely the first time she's said any of this.

'We never got paid exactly. Ben gave us stuff, clothes, drugs. But Cyn, she wanted some money.'

Michelle looks at me and Peter, her eyes wide, and says, 'Cyn wasn't bad, she just wanted out.'

I can see where the story's headed, and I say to Michelle, 'How did Ben find out?'

She looks at the floor and she's sobbing again. 'I told him.'

Oh God. I close my eyes and when I open them again she's sitting there crying. She tells us, 'He said he knew she was up to something and that if I just said, he'd give me a fix and I wouldn't have to work for a bit.'

Poor kid. She goes on, 'It was after this awful night and this man, this film guy, really hurt me. I just wanted it to stop. I've not seen her since. I didn't get to warn her, and I didn't get to say goodbye.'

She carried on 'working' for Ben for another eighteen months from what I can figure out. Quite sure that he'd killed her friend, that he'd do the same to her. How little value she placed on her life. She's been living from one fix to the next.

Thank God she's got her mum. Someone to love you makes all the difference to a recovering addict, whatever their choice of poison. I don't buy that learn to love yourself crap. For those of us that need to medicate, all we have to give ourselves is hate. It's the people who love us that provide hope. For me it was Molly. Now I let other people love me too. Michelle can get there. She can win.

Darren stays with Michelle, Penny comes in. Peter and I step outside. He calls the station, we need to try and find out who Cyn really was. I check my phone. Claudia is with Delia. She'll call me shortly. I step outside and light a fag with a shaking hand. Ben is a sick fucker. He's not after the girls himself, he really sees them as nothing more than a commodity. I reckon he only got into young ones via Ruby. Merely an opportunity that presented itself and look where it led.

All these ruined lives. And where the hell is Cyn? It won't be anywhere good. Peter comes out. 'Okay, the rehab for Michelle is confirmed and I've found a place up north for her mum. Michelle can join her once she's out. We'll collect her for court, if it gets that far.' I shut my eyes and make a silent vow in my head. It will get that far. This hasn't all been for nothing. The bravery I just witnessed from that ruined girl will get some kind of justice, if I have to spend my life working for it. He adds, 'I've just got a warrant for the Walkers.'

I nod. Put out the cigarette. And that little ping is back. Something Michelle just said, the thing that had been bothering me. Ben turning up now after all these years, and Delia ... My phone rings and I know already what I'm about to hear. I say, 'Claudia,' and I pick it up as Peter goes back in.

I tell Claudia what I'm thinking, still hoping I'm wrong. She sighs and tells me what the girl had to say, even knowing it was coming, it still makes my blood run cold. I hang up telling her to keep Delia there.

I run in and say to Michelle, 'The movie guy . . .'
She nods.
'What was his name?'

# 51.

# Miriam Jackson

Ben doesn't leave me alone with her, which is just as well because I'm currently thinking of ways to rip her limb from limb. I glare quietly, and she focuses on a spot directly over my shoulder. The betrayal is like a sharp, physical pain. My mind is whirring back over the past three years.

Anna.

Young and fresh faced. So eager to help, so keen to work with me. My head speeds up a notch. I fight nausea. The urge to scream, to run at her fists flying and grab handfuls of hair, to spit and rage. Not now. Not yet.

Another man arrives. Anthony Benton. He has that wild look around his eyes, a look that you instinctively know you'd do well to avoid. For a stupid second I'm glad that she is here with me, forgetting that she is one of them. That she has infiltrated my life, my family. I feel sick.

Ben cuddles me to his chest, in front of them both, and looks meaningfully at Anthony as he says, 'Take care of her, okay?'

I'm not at all comforted by the fact that the instruction was necessary. He leaves and for a moment I am bereft, wishing he'd return. Better the devil you know I guess. Anthony lights a cigarette and wanders into another room. I am sitting primly on the edge of a sofa and she is looking at me, a slightly bemused smile on her lips. 'Cat got your tongue, Miriam?'

I look back at her squarely and I feel a swell of hatred rise up. It is a whole-body feeling, internal bile struggling to get out. I clench my fists, hard, then I sit on them. Answers are more important than making her hurt. I say, 'Why are you here?' Thoughts are flitting in and out of my mind. Little painful jabs that I can't quite understand. That I don't want to make sense of. Why *did* Ben show up right now? She doesn't answer me though, just continues to smile that familiar smile. The one that usually says 'team-mates' and 'I've got your back'. The one that now means something else, even if it looks the same. Why matters less all of a sudden and I whisper, 'You knew where she was all along.'

She shakes her head at that. 'Actually, no. No, I didn't. Looks like you've been keeping secrets from me lately, Miriam.' And I feel some relief in my head. If she hadn't been part of Tabitha's downfall, maybe her release was to be trusted.

I say, 'I thought we were friends?'

She rolls her eyes, but there is a moment of wavering, where the bravado slips. She says, 'I was there to keep an eye on you.'

I think about that for a moment, and where we are, with whom, and what he does. I say, 'I always thought you wanted my job.' Pointlessly.

She shrugs, 'I just wanted him, Miriam.'

How long has he been watching me, waiting? 'You were spying for Ben?' She looks confused and my hands suddenly feel unbearably cold. Actually, all of me does. This isn't just something that happened since our paths crossed. Anna has been working for me for a few years now. She was a runner for Nick's production company many years ago. The coldness is everywhere and my teeth start chattering. I wrap my arms around myself. The shaking seems to ramp up. I rest my head down into my chest and focus on making it stop, getting my breathing to even out. It's shock. Trying to kick in. I did a show on it once. It's a physiological reaction to stress. I'm not actually cold, or shivering, and I say this in my mind until I'm okay again. I look up and she looks worried now and she says, 'Are you all right?' The smug smile is gone.

Everything is too surreal, I say again, 'Were you . . . working for Ben?' trying to wrack my brains, to recall her situation when she spent the summer at Nick's. I can't think straight though. I don't recall her being vulnerable, which seems to be a prerequisite for Ben's girls. The ones who are easy to poach. No, of course that wasn't Anna. Her parents helped her enter the competition to run at Nick's place. That would have taken time, input, love. Then why? The awful voice at the back of my mind pitches in, '*Come on, Miriam, you know.*' I force it down like vomit. Unwanted, unnecessary, something to be kept in. But the truth is what's causing the shock. Even as I hide from it. Even as I lie to myself.

She sighs. 'No.' Then adds quickly, 'I knew nothing about him.'

What the hell does that mean? 'Then when did he make you start spying on me?'

For a moment I think she might laugh, and I'm scared that if she does I will hit her, that once I start I won't be able to stop, that the thug outside might not get there before I kill her. I rearrange myself, forcing my hands further under my thighs this time. Forcing my eyes to look at her. I say, 'Well?' and she finally meets my gaze.

She's shaking her head and says, 'I wasn't spying for Ben.'

And there it is rushing in again. Fully now. No longer a small voice on the periphery. Now it's shouting, laughing, mocking me.

266

'Anna?'

She grins that foolish grin, full of bluster that doesn't quite meet her eyes. Eyes that look tired and frightened. 'Miriam, I reported back to your husband. Not your lover.'

# 52.

*Unknown: Why aren't you picking up?* ☹
*Unknown: I'm sorry I got cross. Forgive me?* ☺
*Unknown: I'll be back soon I promise . . .*
*Unknown: Delia . . .*

# 53.

# Miriam Jackson

Everything that was foggy, grasping, pushed to the edges of my mind suddenly moves to the forefront of my consciousness with an awful, startling clarity. My head thumps with the familiar tension headache threatening to build itself into a migraine, propelled by this new knowledge. It is like a knife, sliding through the warm butter that is all my other thoughts.

The knowledge of who Nick is. Of what.

And suddenly I can't sit idly while the world falls to pieces around me and I remain still, even tempered, reasonable.

I'm up, out of my seat, and I'm on her. She falls backwards with the shock and my hands go madly. Slapping, punching, my feet kick.

My brain races, speeding about as my limbs work almost without me. I think of things, mistakes at the station, double bookings, messages mislaid. That since Anna came along I have been so blown over by her efficiency, so reliant on her to cover for me, that I'd never thought for a second that she might be the one causing problems.

Why would I?

Anthony comes in and picks me up as though I am no more than a small child. He sits back heavily in the armchair I leaped from, arms wrapped around me like an immoveable cage. I try to move but I can't. I scream and shout instead. Anna sits up, a mess now. Hair askew, clothes torn, lip bloodied.

I feel a small flicker of triumph.

Anthony squeezes harder. So hard the breath rushes out of me and I feel a primal fear. He could kill me, just by tightening those broad arms. As if to demonstrate it, he pulls them in more and my lungs start to ache, my breath becomes a little more shallow, he whispers, 'Don't make me.'

I can't breathe, or I'd agree.

He loosens me, and it rushes out, whoosh. I slide from his lap to the floor. He looks down amused, then at Anna who flinches backwards. He kneels and says, 'I need to make a call, can you behave?'

I nod. I nod because I have to.

I lie on the floor catching my breath. When I am strong enough to get up Anna reaches out a hand to help me and I slap it away. I face her, glad to see the lip is swelling now. Glad to see her pale and ashen. We sit wordless. My heavy, jagged breath the only sound between us. I wait for it to even out. For the air to become more useful, less strained.

As my breath calms so does my head and the awful grasping out of reach things crystallise in my mind. They add up into a coherence I don't want, and I can't believe that I am so blind.

Blind and foolish.

I ask, 'How old were you, when you worked for Nick?'

She frowns. 'Old enough.' Fourteen, she must have been just fourteen. And only one thing will get this from a woman, this devotion.

I shake my head. 'Anna, you were a child.'

She narrows her eyes at me and says, 'You're just jealous.'

And I laugh, who knew I had it in me, but I do, a proper belly laugh. At my own stupidity, at the monster I loved who holds me captive now. At the monster I've been living with for all these years.

Not me. It wasn't me that brought Ben back into our lives. It would be funny if it wasn't so horrific.

Anna. Anna was a child. My husband had an affair with her – no, that's not it, a grown man can't have an 'affair' with a child, can they?

He sent her to work for me. To keep an eye on his dull, easy-going wife. That offer of help when I lost control, when I bled in public, instead of quietly, tidily. Privately. The way he preferred. Anna was there not to soothe and aid, not to make things better. She was there to befriend me, to make sure I was behaving. Now, Anna is here, taking care of Ben's interests. Ben has let Tabitha go. She has gone back to her dad. Her dad is one of Ben's clients. Oh God.

The shaking threatens to start up again. Anna's looking at me and hisses, 'Stop it.' She looks at the door. Benton. The awful Neanderthal man. She is scared of him. She doesn't want him to come in any more than I do. I nod and focus on catching my breath. I mutter, 'My head hurts.'

With bittersweet familiarity she reaches into her bag and hands me two pink pills. I say thank you, swallow them dry. In time, they should be just about in time.

I wait, a second, two, then I say, 'Why would I be jealous?'

I know the answer, but I want to hear her say it. She puffs herself up then, silly little girl, and here she is at twenty what? Two? Three at the most, and I can see now the child that never grew up. She says, 'Nick loves me.'

Even though I knew it – my brain had made that connection, there could be no other reason – it still wrenches.

My husband. The paedophile. 'How long has it been going on?'

'Since we met. It was love at first sight.' Her face is defiant,

271

stubborn. I don't know who she's trying harder to convince, me or herself.

I shut my eyes and think about Nick. All those years, how lucky I felt that he wasn't chasing after his leading ladies, how undemanding he was of me. Once we'd had Tabitha we were barely together, physically. I'd hosted phone-ins where women complained of being constantly pestered by their husbands, tiring of the physical demands. Wishing to be left alone. I'd thought, Nick's not like that at all. I'd even thought if I didn't go to him, I wonder if we ever would.

I'd only ever been with him and Ben. One extreme to the other. I'd just assumed that Nick had a low sex drive and convinced myself it didn't bother me. I dropped my knickers when a man showed interest though, didn't I? Still desperate for love. Still pathetic.

I say to Anna, 'How's it been lately?' and her frown tells me what I need to know. My husband is not interested in women. He is one of Ben's clients. That's how Tabitha became involved with him, and probably what led Ben back to me.

Nick had no idea of my history. He has never asked many questions about me or my life. I suppose I am an open enough book to someone like him. The main criteria was my gratitude, my compliance. He's never really known me, as it turns out I've never known him. I almost laugh again, but what's the point. Anna's shrill voice breaks in, 'He's going to leave you, you know.'

I shrug. That video. Anna must have sent him the recording of Ben and I before I called him. Jesus. But he didn't know Tabitha was missing before that because I hadn't told Anna. Even though I'd wanted to. He's on the wrong side of the camera, Nick. Who knew what an accomplished actor he is.

He knew. And still pretended to be hurt. He still punished me. He made it possible for me to go as soon as Ben came for me. No questions asked, making sure I did the right thing by her. Tabitha.

Anna. 'He's stayed for Tabitha. That's all.'

I turn sharp eyes on the silly girl now. 'He was . . . Tabitha?'

She frowns at me, looks at me like I'm sick in the head. 'No, she's his daughter, for goodness' sake.' Stupid that I feel some sort of relief. It might not even be true. I think of my daughter now. How I was always jealous of her good behaviour around Nick. How I complained about it to both of them. Now I wonder why that is, and what she must have known, because she left with Ben. Of that I have no doubt.

I say, 'She was with Ben.'

Anna sighs. 'Well, that must be your fault.' She hasn't made the connection that I have. She doesn't know what Ben does, or if she knows she hasn't thought of Nick. She's simply doing what Nick has asked her to do, and not questioning him. We are not so different, Anna and I.

It's all so complicated and grim. There are so many questions, so many things I need to ask, and so many things I need to tell Anna. But I can't see a way out. I slump down, let my eyelids flutter. My headache is dying down and underneath the pain I'm absolutely exhausted. A phone rings. Not mine. Ben has mine. Anthony comes in, heavy footed, like an angry Shrek. Tabitha loved that film. She'd sing her heart out to it. This one, not Shrek, not a benign, friendly green ogre, but a bad man, says, 'Ben, he says you'll be needed here for another few hours.'

She sighs. The awful man leaves the room. She tells me, 'Nick will come to get me. We'll finally be together.' Silly cow thinks when it's all over, Nick and she will swan off into the sunset.

I say to Anna, 'Do you know what Ben does for a living?'

She shrugs, 'Why do I care?'

I say, 'You get that these guys are criminals?'

I gesture out towards bad Shrek.

She says, 'What your boyfriend does doesn't matter to me.'

I say, 'But Nick didn't think twice about leaving you alone with them, did he?'

She says, 'His main priority is Tabitha.' Then adds, 'I offered to help.' But it sounds feeble.

I say, 'So where are you meeting him?'

She says, 'Once he and Tabitha are away, probably France, I'll meet them there.'

Away? He'll be heading for his plane then which will be in Surrey. And taking my child with him.

I don't think so.

The anger tremors inside again, so much better than the fear. The fear is there whispering to me. But I won't let it win. Not this time. Her mobile phone is on the arm of the chair. I stare at it, brain whirring, she coughs and I jump slightly. As though she might be able to read my mind.

I say to Anna, 'Tell me about you and Nick.'

She glares, 'I already have. He loves me, he's going to leave you.'

I nod, and she studies me intently, her hand goes to her fat lip. I'm surprised how much pleasure the injury brings me. It must sting. I need to keep her talking, find out what I can. I'm smarter than Anna. 'You've really been together since you first met?' I ask casually, as though it is a normal thing. Not rotten, and foetid and vile.

I know the answer, of course I do, even if part of me still wants to resist believing it.

She says, 'Since we first met.' When she was fourteen, an intern, a child on her summer holidays. I am surprised that the answer I knew was coming hurts nonetheless.

I am one of those women that you read about, that I might do a show on. The wife of . . . How did she not know? Of course, she knew, was she protecting him? She must have been . . .

274

But I didn't. I didn't know.

I say, 'That's a long time.'

Her face softens for a moment, this poor girl who doesn't even know she's been brainwashed. My anger towards her evaporates a little. The swollen lip, the bruise to be, now just an angry red mark on her cheek, no longer feels victorious. No, it's just more abuse heaped upon this complicated young woman.

I say, 'I'm sorry that I hit you.' And I find I mean it.

I think as I often do around Anna that she reminds me of Tabitha. So young. She says, 'I'm sorry we have to hurt you.' We. She believes in that 'we'.

A child. She was a child. Younger than my baby is now. This isn't the usual mistress scenario. Nothing about this is usual.

I say, 'It's okay.' And in terms of her, it is. I don't need to forgive her, she's a victim. Though I'll take her down if I need to. I'll do anything for Tabitha. That thought fortifies me a little.

She says, 'You have Ben now anyway.'

I nod, because it's vital that I look compliant. Then I ask her, 'So you didn't know Ben then?' but she's saved from answering me as the phone rings again. The man calls from the other room. Anna says, 'Stay there,' as though I can go anywhere.

Her phone is still there, resting on the arm of her chair. Dare I?

I've nothing to lose.

I run, text 'Nick involved taking tabitha, plane at redhill aerodrome not my phone anna don't text'. I think I remember Madison's number and I punch it in as best I can, and then delete the sent message and slide back to the sofa.

She comes into the room, and the screen is still lit on her phone. All she'd have to do is look over. One look. I hope the number was right. If it's gone to a stranger, they might send back a 'who is this?' message.

Anna doesn't look, and I watch it fade to black. She says, 'Ben, on the landline, the signal here's rubbish, couldn't get through.'

I nod, that means the message won't have sent. And my heart sinks.

# 54.

# Madison Attallee

Peter and I are both quiet on the drive back. I put The Specials on, but it's background noise, volume low. My phone might ring, his might. We are nearing the end of the investigation. I feel that. We may be successful, we may not. I need to find Tabitha and Miriam, to reunite them. I need to arrest Ben, Nick and any of the other sick arseholes I can take along with them. I light a cigarette but don't find it soothing. My head is fuzzing, full of images of Michelle. Of Ben's smug face, and Reeva Walker's sausage lips. Fuckers. The lot of them. I think about Cyn and where she might have gone. Michelle is sure she's dead. I think she's probably right, and, if that's the case, I hope to hell that we can at least find some evidence of it.

Emma is currently attempting to unlock various forums on the dark web. She's very skilled technically, more so than I ever will be, and getting better all the time, but Ben has managed to hide his hideous operation well.

When I get back to the office Claudia is sitting with Delia, they are stuffing brochures into envelopes, a task I knew Claudia was keen to get started on. A mail shot to potential business clients. She says, 'Delia was bored, I figured she may as well help out until you and Peter arrived.' She smiles, keeping everything light and airy, as is her way. Good at contracts, dry work that I find too dull, and good with people, who on the whole drive me to distraction.

She says, 'Hello, Peter.'

'Hello, Claudia, Delia.'

Delia keeps stuffing envelopes. Claudia pats her arm. 'You remember Madison and Peter?'

Delia nods and looks up. There are dirty black lines on her cheeks. She's been crying. The anger ups itself a notch as I take her in: cute, curvy-body and her baby face.

Claudia says, 'I said I'd stay with Dee while you all had a little chat. Emma's doing boring IT stuff in your office.'

I sit down. Peter takes a seat off to the side. I say, 'Hello, Delia.'

And she bursts into tears, envelope and brochure discarded. 'I'm so sorry. I knew where Tabitha was. She was so mad at me already.'

I say, 'It's okay, Delia.' Then I pause. 'Would you like your mum to be here?'

She shakes her head. I add, 'I think we'll have to speak to her soon, don't you?'

Claudia moves closer to the girl, and says, 'I've said to Delia that I'll nip by and have a little chat with everyone when she goes home, okay?'

Claudia is smooth and unruffled, though I know she must be feeling as disturbed as the rest of us.

I say to Delia, 'Do you mind if we record this conversation?' She looks at Claudia who smiles and nods. Delia says, 'No. That's fine.' And then, 'Am I going to be in lots of trouble?'

I say, 'No, not at all. We're just glad of your help. We think Tabitha is with her dad?'

She nods. 'He said he'd take *me* with him.' And then she bursts into fresh, new tears.

I say, 'Where was he going to take you?'

She shrugs, 'I don't know, just away somewhere. He said we'd be able to be together. Properly.'

I force the words out and say, 'Were you in a relationship with Nick Jackson?' Careful to use language that isn't going to scare the shit out of her. Even if relationship is totally the wrong word.

She wipes her eyes and nods.

I keep the disgust off my face though I see Claudia wince slightly behind the small girl.

I ask her, 'How did it start?'

She shrugs, 'He's always been . . . nice to me.'

'You've known him a long time?'

'Oh yes, most of my life. I've been Tabitha's friend since infant school.'

I nod and say, 'How has he been kind?'

'Well, when I was little he'd play with me, sometimes after Tabitha went to bed if we were having a sleepover. I was crying one night after I wet the bed, and he got me up and bathed me. The next day he dropped me home, brought me sweets, and he didn't tell Tabitha that I'd wet the bed. He said he'd keep it a secret.' She shrugs. 'Lots of things like that.'

Jesus. Secrets as currency. So easy for someone like Nick, and with the safe cover of not just his fame and fortune, but also his wife. His child. Access. Grooming. I say, 'Was Miriam there?' Because I have to ask, because you never know.

'No, we played together more when she wasn't.'

I nod, again as if this is the most normal thing ever. I say, 'When did you start spending time together on your own?'

'He saw me walking back from school.'

'When was that?'

'Um, year eight, I think, maybe the start of year nine.'

'So you must have been about . . . thirteen?'

She nods. 'I know he's older and stuff, but it just happened.

You can't help who you fall in love with.' And it's his voice I hear talking through this fragile little girl.

I smile and don't answer. She pulls a tissue out of the box Claudia has placed in front of her, wipes at her cheeks.

I smile again though it's a strain. 'So your relationship started then?'

'Yes.'

'Did anyone know?'

She shakes her head, 'Not then. People wouldn't understand.'

For fuck's sake. 'Where did you see him?'

'At his house to start with.'

'And then?'

As she speaks I nod in the right places and images spring into my mind. Ones I don't want, that I'll never be rid of. I remind myself it's worse for her. So much worse. And I vow that I'm going to take Nick Jackson down along with the rest of them.

'But Tabitha was with a man called Ben?'

She nods. I say, 'How does Ben come into this?'

She says, 'Tabitha saw him with her dad sometime last year in London. She went over to say hi, by the time she got through the crowds she said Nick had left but she spoke to Ben.' She shrugs, 'She says they hit it off straight away. They swapped numbers and . . . at first it was just texts and stuff. I figured when she dumped Brett that maybe something more was going on.' She shrugs. 'I said to her it wasn't a good idea.' I don't bother pointing out that it wasn't nearly so bad an idea as sleeping with your friend's dad.

I say, 'So how did you know she was with Ben this week?'

She blushes. Her whole face goes bright red. Claudia rests a hand on hers again and says, 'Go on, Delia.'

'She found out about me and Nick.'

So that's why she ran. I ask her, 'How?'

'She found stuff, on my phone.'

'What was on it?'

She sniffles, 'Pictures, some recordings filmed.'

I say, 'So what happened?'

'Tabitha sent herself the films and threatened to send them to my mum if I told anyone where she was.'

'What were they of?'

She's crying again, but less hysterically. 'They were of me. I made them for Nick. There was one of me and him.' She quickly adds, 'I'd told him I deleted it.'

'He wanted you to?'

She nods, 'I sent clips when he asked, but he usually filmed . . . stuff, he said he liked to be reminded of me.' She smiles fondly. I feel nauseous. 'He had a separate phone for it. But he'd forgotten it that day, so we used mine and I sent it to him. He was cross because I didn't do it right and you could see his face. He was never meant to be identifiable.' She quickly adds, 'Because of who he is, you know?'

I don't say anything or point out how flimsy this is. He was quite happy to film her, and my guess is he was sharing that footage with his internet buddies. There's always a currency needed to get into these sick, secret little gangs. Like fucking promotional videos.

So Tabitha had been involved with Ben. Or thought she was 'involved'. He must have felt like he was getting one over on Nick and also getting closer to Miriam somehow too. Opportunistic sick fuck.

These girls were both dealing with things that were beyond them.

She wipes her face. 'I told her to come home.'

'Why are you telling us now?'

She says, 'Nick called from LA. He said Tabitha was missing and it might be about a man. Did I know anything about it? I broke down and told him everything. He . . .' She pauses, the

281

memory seeming to cause her some pain. 'He went mad. Called me all sorts of things, said I'd betrayed him. That he'd destroy me.'

I say, 'You were shocked?'

She nods, 'Yes. I said I was sorry over and over. He called back, just before he was leaving, he said sorry but . . .'

'But what, Delia?'

'I was scared, and he said he'd come and get me as soon as he was back, but he hasn't. I think he's going to take Tabitha away somewhere.'

I say gently, 'You care about her?'

She nods, 'Of course, she's always been my best friend.' Nick had underestimated this girl, this poor girl he has almost broken. He didn't take into account that her loyalty would extend past him, and to his daughter as well. The sheer arrogance of it, but it will be his undoing.

I say, 'Delia, do you still have the clip, of you and Nick?'

Her eyes widen and her face flushes, I glance at Peter. Bingo!

## 55.

# Nick Jackson

Tabitha is totally unsettled. She's all restless and not quite right. I am so cross at her right now, and her stupid mother. Who'd have thought Miriam had skeletons rattling around in her dull, little closet.

Tabitha should never have found out about Delia. Actually, I am a little sorry about that, I kind of knew it was tricky territory. Though I couldn't have predicted this level of fuckery. Worse thing is I was done with the girl a while ago anyway. If I'd just trusted my instinct, Tabs wouldn't have known a thing.

Delia would never have said anything. They never do.

I sigh and sit on the twin bed. I smile at my daughter. She doesn't smile back, she says, 'I miss Mummy.' And her voice is small and babyish.

I snap, 'I told you Mummy's been very bad.'

She doesn't say anything to that. I'm sorry to badmouth Miriam to her, but really. Fancy Ben being her sodding ex. I hadn't even known she'd had an ex. Not a proper one. Totally inexperienced I'd thought when I'd picked up Miriam. Exactly what I wanted.

Ben didn't mention it either, bastard, and he must have known. Jesus. If I'd dug a bit deeper . . . Ah well.

I rub at my forehead. We'll leave today, in a few hours. I'm busy on my laptop, shunting some capital around. My palms are damp as I type. But I can't let the panic in. Now is not the time. Thank God I've got the plane. Not that I thought it would be used for escape. I start to feel annoyed again. I shouldn't have to bloody escape.

Tabitha seems to sense my disappointment. She looks meek.

Hopefully I'll be able to come back soon enough. I'll let Ben move Miriam, though I'm bloody livid that he took her. It's not that I want her home, particularly, not now she's ruined things. But it's the principle, isn't it?

As for his tricks with Tabitha . . . I push the thought aside for now. Though it makes my heart race and my adrenaline spike.

Ben Hedges. Bloody oik. I've never liked him, jumped-up little chav with ideas well above himself, but I've needed to keep him on side of course.

Anna should have known about it. She's proved herself pointless in all of this. Never mind. We'll jump ship for a while and let all this nonsense blow over, the PI won't be getting paid, so she'll lose interest soon enough. No one has any proof of anything anyway. My mind keeps going over things, checking out the possibilities. The videos of Dee that I'd shared, and Anna, and others. But we're not stupid in our little club, we make sure we're not in them. I start to relax. No, if anything, it's the girls that come off looking bad, not us. Not me.

Tabitha says, 'Can you stop humming?'

I look at her and laugh, 'I didn't know I was, darling.'

She frowns. 'Well, you were.'

I stop, get up off the bed and stretch. I fancy a little snifter, nothing like a whiskey to take the edge off. I head to the mini bar. Ruffling Tabs's hair on the way. She flinches, as well she bloody might. I stick my tongue out at her. Trying to make her smile.

I point out that all this nastiness, and having to do a bunk, is her own damn fault. I would never have left old Miriam, she's been terribly amenable all these years.

Retrospectively, I should have left Delia well alone I suppose, I can see why Tabs is peeved. I couldn't help myself, to be honest, and I'd never have touched Tabs, not like some of the sickos I've met who draw no lines anywhere.

The internet has been a wonderful thing overall, but it does free up some rifraf.

Tabitha has the TV on some godawful programme, I grab the buttons and turn to BBC News. She looks annoyed but picks up a magazine off the side.

She'd usually be buried in her phone, but I've taken it for now. Just in case.

'Daddy, stop humming.' Her voice is shaky.

I think about shouting at her, and I can see fear in her eyes. I take a deep breath instead, then I grin, and say, 'Sorry, darling.'

I'm going to need her on side over all this.

# 56.

# Madison Attallee

I stare over Emma's shoulder at the information she's managed to gather. The dark web looks like early browsers did, and on the surface it's reasonably benign: a lot of paranoid IT geeks who think the government is spying on them; quite a few sites offering drugs. But the more we delve the nearer we get to the bad stuff. And there's plenty of it. The chatroom linked to Ben's office is busy, and sickening. There is indeed a menu on offer and a detailed means of sharing images and footage. These vile men discuss it all avidly.

Ben is clever, his 'profile', which likely isn't him directly, is incredibly well protected and well hidden. But we've traced a server back to All That Glitters. Peter is on the phone. His team will be much quicker than we can be in tracing the rest of these fuckers, though as I'm starting to grasp the sheer scale of it I'm thinking it's going to be a real long investigation. I'll be insisting on keeping my oar in too. These things have a habit of making headlines, being run by fools and petering out into nothing. Not on my bloody watch.

We know which one's Nick, only because he's shared lots of videos of Delia and other girls we are yet to identify. Poor kids. We will need to prove it though, and that's where Peter's specialists will be faster than we can be.

We've got the footage from Delia's phone, which pretty much confirms his guilt, at least in terms of her. Hopefully she will be willing to go on the record too. Claudia spoke to her mum and has arranged for a counsellor to visit them. I'll speak to Sue Munroe myself as soon as I can. I hope they are okay. The devastation from this kind of crime spreads far and wide.

I tear my eyes away from the vile conversations and pictures and I step outside on shaky legs, light a cigarette and dial my old house.

Rob picks up, clears his throat and says hello. I'm amazed every time I have contact with this man that I ever thought marrying him was a good plan, or that I ever thought I liked him. We go through the usual awkwardness of me asking nicely to speak to my daughter and him trying to block it, but eventually she comes on.

'Hi, Mum.' And she's straight into chattering about her day, her friends. What she's watching on telly. I smile as I listen to her and ask a couple of questions, giggling along with her as she tells me about PE and how horrible hockey is. Apparently they have to wear dreadful skirts and large PE knickers with their names sewn on. She describes this as 'shocking' and I giggle. She talks on and on almost without pause for nearly ten minutes. Then Peter is here waving for me to come in and I tell her I have to go. She says, 'Okay, cool, love you.' She hangs up before I can say it back.

I feel a little better for hearing her voice, for letting some light into the darkness. For forcing my head to remember that it's not all bad. I hang up and say, 'Molly.' He smiles.

'How is she?'

'Good, talkative.'

He nods. 'Are you okay?'

I smile. 'I'll be happier once these fuckers are taken out.'

He's watching me closely. This man who knows me, who

287

knows my life. The things I endured as a child. I look away, not meeting his eye. I need to find Miriam and Tabitha, I need to bring them home. But there are other people involved in this who need justice too and I have to make sure we pave the way for that. I've never dealt with the sex abuse cases well. I take it personally if I can't close them, and really, since I can't take away what's happened to these girls, there is no justice as such. My head starts to spiral. No. I take a deep breath. This is work, this is good work, and we'll be making a difference to girls yet to come. And reminding these lowlifes they can't get away with it.

Peter says, 'I've got the warrant for the Walkers. Our team will take over with the forums.'

I nod, glad. Emma's done some fantastic work here, but I'm very pleased that now she can pass on the rest. I go back into the office to collect my bag and she is ashen faced. Claudia looks at me and I can tell she's worried. I say to Peter, 'I'll meet you in the car?'

He nods, leaves, and Claudia disappears into the kitchen.

I look at my PA who has become so much more. She's not okay. I can imagine what she's seen trawling through those sites, and I give her shoulder a squeeze. I have to get going. I want to sit here and tell her what a great thing she's done, how she's finding evidence that will put these people away. That I couldn't have done this without her.

She looks at me and waves me away. 'Go, I'm fine.' A weak smile. 'I deserve a raise, but I'm fine.'

I return her smile and hesitate, but she points at the door, 'Get a move on.'

Claudia comes in with two cups of tea and sits next to her. My team.

Claudia says, 'Peter told us you're taking part in the televised appeal?'

I nod, 'It's our case after all.'

'I'll live stream it on our Twitter account.'

'Good idea.' I head towards the door. 'I'll update you as soon as I know anything.'

I tell Peter what Claudia will be doing and he sighs. I snap, '*We* invited *you* in on this.'

He says, 'We are still the police, Madison. I'll have to let Deanie know about any media interaction.'

He's right, but I still feel annoyed.

It's time for us to go, he calls Deanie as we walk which annoys me. I get in, slam the door and turn the music up.

He turns it off, I drive out of the car park. A moody silence develops.

He looks at my obviously huffy face, and says, 'Madison, we have the same goal, for goodness' sake.'

I say, 'Yes, but you'll get paid no matter what. I want the credit for the solve.'

'I've said I'll make sure you're there. I'll introduce it and do the official bit, you can do the actual press conference, I'll take a back seat, okay?'

I can't argue with that really. I say, 'Okay.' And he's right, we are after the same thing.

But I do need to start taking Claudia and Emma more seriously and I probably do need to pay them more, so my comments regarding marketing stand. I'd hate to lose either of them. I keep my eyes on the road and let my head drift to the task ahead.

We have Delia's phone, the footage of her and Nick. Delia is a couple of months younger than Tabitha, so was fifteen when the film was shot. The footage is proof of crime, this is why we have a warrant, and why we'll be able to put out a search for Tabitha and Nick.

I remind Peter of this now, adding that it was my work.

He's grinning at me, I take my eyes off the road long enough to frown back. He says, 'Madison, I'm not your enemy.'

I sigh. 'I know, and I do appreciate you letting me in.' In fairness to him it's unusual that a non-officer would be allowed such public involvement. I could pipe down and have a bit more grace.

He says, 'Like you said, it's your case. You've always been smarter than the rest of us, my controlling love.' He's still grinning, and I find myself smiling back. I am controlling, and arrogant probably. He also does cut me a lot of slack in official terms. I could probably lighten up a bit. Officers are keeping a lookout now at traffic points and the airports, so Ben and Nick will have a hard time going far, and I don't think they'll hurt either Miriam or Tabitha. This thought staves off some of the worry for now.

I glance at my watch; we have two hours until the conference. Let's hope it's enough time to find something to incriminate the Walkers. I'm almost cheerful as we pull up onto their drive along with a few black and white panda cars. Time's up, shitheads.

# 57.

# Miriam Jackson

I am an inconvenience. Both to Anthony and to Anna. Neither of them wants to be here, on this glorified babysitting job. Also, they don't seem to like each other very much. I play it around in my head and wonder if I can somehow make this useful for myself. Can I play them off against each other? Can I interest them in something else long enough to slip away? Probably not.

The house is dull and dingy. A simple two up, two down, and judging from the view there's nothing much around it either. Which I guess is its appeal. I wonder briefly what horrors this house might have seen, and an image of Tabitha's scared face assaults me. I push it away, it's not going to help. Ben has been gone for about five hours. To do I'm not sure what. He has my passport, I know that much because he waved it in my face like a prize while he explained we'd be jetting off. Just for now, in his words, but I will be his prisoner, and it turns out no one here will mourn me. Except her. Tabitha. I will *not* leave her. I cannot let that happen. Once I'm gone, coming back will be hard. I know that much. Having said that, I will find a way no matter what. I make that resolve to myself now, try it out in my head and am glad to know I mean it. Ben thinks I am that same naïve little girl he knew back then. When I met him this time I was certainly vulnerable again. The increasing arguments with

Tabitha had been wearing me down, more so than I realised.

Anna comes in and slumps down in front of me with a sigh. This girl who has worked for me for years. Eager to please and so efficient. So indispensable. Not unlike me, and I guess even more malleable at fourteen. Perfect for a man like Nick. And suddenly it clicks, after all these years.

Not why me, but of course me.

Unsure, insecure. With only my mother in terms of family – another insecure, unconfident woman. No one who would care or look too closely at my life, my marriage.

Yet I'm reasonably bright, quite successful, okay to introduce to colleagues. But all that insecurity, and the lack of people. I feel a rush of anger. Nick understood me better than I'd thought. Something I'd always wanted from my husband now feels like a slap in the face. Quiet, obedient, unquestioning and grateful. Another woman would have asked questions. About where his time went, about what happened in bed, or didn't. About his past, his personality.

Another woman might have expected something more, a real connection. But not me. I was just grateful to be chosen.

I ask Anna, 'Are you all right?'

And she looks at me surprised. 'What do you care?' I shrug. There is a pause. She says, 'Thanks for asking.'

I smile. 'It's okay.'

'Sorry that you're here.'

I blink back tears. 'Me too.'

She falters for a minute, looking like she wants to speak but is unsure. She says, 'Nick says you love Ben.'

I don't say anything.

She's almost pleading, 'You can be with him now, can't you? You won't have to worry about anything here after all. I saw that footage of you two, remember, I could tell you liked him.'

I can hear the murmur of Anthony's voice in the next room,

but not what he's saying. He must be on the phone. I risk it, I speak quietly, and I say to Anna, 'Like you said, Nick doesn't love me. Ben came along and showed me some attention. If I'd have known what he did, what he was involved with, I would have run a mile. And I would have taken Tabitha with me.'

Anna looks suitably perturbed, which is exactly what I want. She says, 'Well, I'm sure it's not that bad.'

'You don't think what Ben does is that bad?'

She frowns. 'I . . . I don't know.' And I realise with a growing fear that she is telling the truth. She hastily adds, 'And I don't need to.'

I ask then, because I have to, 'The double booking . . . ?'

She looks away from me, her face flushes red.

So those 'mistakes,' the little things that have gone wrong, the things that have not only made me doubt myself, but also think of her as indispensable and reliable.

She says, 'Nick wanted to make sure I earned your trust.'

Earned is totally the wrong word. Nick wanted to make me question myself, to have doubt in my own abilities, to stay compliant. I open my mouth to say all of this and tell Anna what she's dealing with, but I am interrupted. The door swings open and Anthony gestures to her. She scurries out of the room behind him. My heart is thumping. I'm angry at this latest revelation, Anna's little betrayals, though it makes a sick sort of a sense. But I'm also more concerned than ever about Tabitha's safety. I'd assumed Anna knew what Nick was up to, that she knew about Ben.

So what the hell has happened?

# 58.

# Madison Attallee

Peter and I won't stay for the search, but I take great pleasure in issuing the warrant. The big-lipped, plumped-up monster woman looks suitably frightened. Her immovable features seem to sag a little as we head in, team streaming along behind us. She follows us into the living room, floundering on about breaches of justice and unfairness.

I think about the girls she's lured here, the kindness after the brutality, and feel no sympathy for her whatsoever. Mr Walker it turns out is hiding out in the living room. He looks like a jolly un-bearded Santa Claus. His features are plumped out like his wife's, but by natural causes in his case. He has a benign, wide friendly face. I'm not surprised, evil often lurks behind a good disguise. My last nemesis, Dean Hall, was probably the best-looking man I've ever seen, but he still killed his own mother and a teenage girl, and would have gladly taken out his siblings if we hadn't managed to stop him. I stand directly in front of this one, and I repeat everything I've just said to his wife.

She scurries around to his side and rests a small scrawny hand on his arm, he shakes it off and she keeps it hovering close, just by his elbow. She makes a small whimper. He leans forward and says to me, 'None of this is anything to do with me, it's her twisted son you ought to be looking at.'

Her face drops, she looks from her husband to her feet. I tell him, 'I'm pretty sure you've got a stash of footage here, and we're going to find it.'

He puts his hands out in a surrendering gesture and says, 'If there's anything here it'll be hers and Ben's, they own the business, not me.' He's right. In legal terms everything is in her name and Ben's. This man might be a wrongun but he's not stupid. The Walkers have an awful lot of assets, most of those are joint.

I turn to Reeva and say, 'Hey, he's a keeper.'

She is still looking at her feet, but the hand she had rested on her husband's fat arm has fallen forlornly by her side. I think she's crying. Good. Honour among thieves is rarely a reality, but among this type of vermin it's always non-existent. We'll use it to bring them down. Fuckers.

I leave the paperwork, wait while Peter makes sure everyone knows what to look for, and then we're gone.

They will film the news piece at the police station. I make Peter take a pit stop at mine, where I freshen up, i.e. spray a load of YSL all over myself, brush my teeth, touch up my make-up and change into a suit and better shoes. Peter makes calls, getting everything put into place before the conference. Time is of the essence now.

Emma will be kept in the loop. Claudia has gone back to the Munroes'. The poor family are in pieces, and I will get over there as soon as I can. In the car, I place a call to Donna Williams. I tell her we might have new information about Ruby and that we are about to make a statement related to Ben. She thanks me.

When we get to the station everything is chaotic, cameras are being set up, a reporter, Mike, who I've known for years waves

295

at me. I nod, and flush. Last time I saw him I'd been worse for wear. He could have run that story. I remember telling him plenty of things I shouldn't have, though the memories are patchy. He hadn't, and he hadn't taken me down when all the other papers did either. He ran a huge double-paged spread about MA Investigations when we broke the Reynolds case. I emailed him to say thanks and arranged an exclusive interview with Kate Reynolds, but I haven't seen him in person since that wobbly night outside the Oak.

He's heading over. Shit. I really need to be calm before we have to speak. He's smiling and I force myself to at least look relaxed.

'Hey, Madison.'

'Hey, Mike.'

'I heard you'd broken this one, you guys are doing pretty well, huh?'

I shrug. He's still grinning and fiddling with a Dictaphone. I haven't seen one for a while. Most people record on their phones these days. He sees me looking and says, 'Old habits die hard. I don't trust new technology.'

I smile. 'I don't blame you.'

'You going to be able to give me anything the others won't have?'

'Not yet, Mike.' I fumble in my bag for a card and hand him one. 'This has my mobile on it though, be sure to call once we've got the kid back safe.'

He says, 'The Jackson girl, right?'

I nod. He pauses then says, 'I followed her just before the whole "clubbing" story, you know.'

'Oh yeah, where to?'

'The back seat of a car, with her boyfriend. They had an argument, she stormed off.'

'Jesus. You didn't run the story?'

He shakes his head. 'Nope, she's a kid, isn't she?'

This must have been shortly after she met Ben. Tabitha meeting him coincides with her attitude towards her mother deteriorating too. Literally history repeating itself, from what Miriam told me of her own relationship with Ben all those years ago. Poor Miriam, none the wiser.

Mike says, 'I heard your divorce came through?'

I grin. 'Good news travels fast.'

He shrugs, still grinning. 'Maybe we could grab a drink sometime?'

I'm saved from answering by Peter swerving in behind me. 'Showtime. Hi, Mike.' The two men shake hands and Peter and I head to the front of the room. He whispers, 'Did I hear him ask you out?'

I'm saved from answering this time by a woman with a light in her hand, motioning for us to come forward.

Someone counts down, the cameras start rolling and Peter addresses the gathered media. I stand by his side and wait for him to outline my involvement. And then I speak, asking for anyone who sees Nick to contact our hotline immediately. Then I speak directly to Tabitha, and I hope to hell that wherever she is she's listening.

# 59.

# Nick Jackson

Tabitha is sulking since I turned off whatever reality crap it was she was zoning out to. I've done her a favour. It's like brain rot that stuff. Not that I can complain. Similar audiences like my flicks. Rom-coms with happy endings. Bubblegum for the small-minded. People who think within the confines. So easy to read, so easy to cater for. Laughable, really. The industry. The world.

When I was a boy, my dad used to say to me, 'You're white, male and rich. You can do whatever you want.' I didn't believe him. He said, 'Two types of people, son, us and them. Just be glad you're one of us.' School taught me the same. When we all arrived, pasty skinny seven-year-olds, we were weak, crying for our mummies. After a few terms you learn to buck up.

Dad was right, better to be one of us. I look over at Tabs and smile. I'm sorry she has been dragged into the 'them' camp, sorry and mighty cross. I'll let that Ben fucker take Miriam, couldn't care less what happens to her now, but he's got a screw loose if he thinks he can get away with taking my Tabs.

She's had a glimpse at a different sort of world now, one for other types of girls. No real harm done, of course, and she'll get over it.

I'm quite sore about the whole Delia thing. Kicking myself

in hindsight. My palms start to sweat again. I can feel the old adrenaline spike, and not in a good way. Not in a good way at all. I ought to have known better. Shouldn't have got involved in those sites either. All That Bloody Glitters is well known in show-biz circles in the UK. Not for anything too appalling; tits and arse dressed well, willing to host events, happy to do little additionals while being super discreet. Ben found out I liked something a bit extra and offered it, I didn't realise he had a vested interest in my family. I start to feel cross thinking about it. Damn Miriam. This is all her fault really, I'll explain that to Tabs eventually when I think she's ready to understand.

She'll bounce back. He didn't touch her. Not his taste. I'd always known that, so I'm not worried.

Tabs is sheltered, still a child really. Not like the ones who work for Ben. They might *seem* to be the same age, but they aren't innocent. None of them are. All the fuss the papers make about exploitation and whatnot. But most girls like a bit of power and some cash. Even if they don't at first, they adjust. Still. Not all.

An image of Delia's little face comes to mind. I push it away. I've reprimanded myself once. No need to dwell. Besides, it will probably be the most excitement she ever has. Underneath that annoyance though is that awful fight or flight drip drip of cortisol. A terrible feeling of things spiralling away from my control. I take a deep breath. I'll make Ben pay for this. This is my life he's messing with. Some uppity urchin from a council estate thinking he can meddle in my affairs.

I won't be able to sort out Ben myself of course. But I know a man who can. I feel okay again. Tabitha's frowning little face is pissing me off though. I look away, back to the screen, and everything inside me seems to cool by a few degrees as I watch my name scrolling along the bottom of the news. I turn up the volume. A tall dark-haired man comes on. My heart starts to beat harder, faster. Then that fucking PI. All stiletto heels and confidence. Just the sort of woman I hate at the best of times. I hate her even more now. Tabitha whimpers as her picture come onto the screen. I hear the words 'nationwide search' and the fear pushes out past everything else, rude and cruel. Fuck. Fuck.

# 60.

# Madison Attallee

The cameras stop rolling and we are bombarded by questions. I follow Peter, keeping my head up, my eyes ahead, and we walk out. I switch my phone on, it pings, a message from a number I don't recognise. Miriam, but from Anna's phone. Anna. Christ. I recall Miriam saying Anna had been Nick's intern. Shit. I call Emma, ask her to check out when Anna worked for Nick.

Redhill aerodrome. I wave at Peter. He comes over, listens to me intently, then he makes calls, gets officers sent out and tells them to assemble the armed unit. I stress to him not to send uniforms.

Hopefully Nick will have seen the broadcast. Hopefully he'll panic and fuck up. Emma will find out everything she can about Anna. Deanie is heading up the team taking appeal-related calls and is passing on anything she thinks might be useful.

I call Claudia. She is still with the Munroes and steps outside to speak to me. Delia is apparently beside herself. Awash with guilt. Her dad, Maurice, shouted at her until Sue calmed him down. When he realised it had begun three years ago he started crying. She says, 'Her poor parents feel like they've failed.' I hate Nick even more in that moment. She's a kid, for Christ's sake, a kid he's known throughout her entire childhood.

Emma calls. 'Anna did indeed do work experience for Nick Jackson on her summer holidays.'

Shit. I ask her, 'How old was she?'

Her voice is low as she tells me, 'Fourteen.'

'God.'

'I know. There's an article in the paper about the scheme, she's quoted as saying it was the best summer of her life.'

'Is that how she ended up working for Miriam?'

'According to her profile on the radio station's website, yes, she stayed in touch with mentor Nick Jackson who suggested work experience, set up a charitable organisation to run paid internships. She was the first one.' She pauses. 'It stresses that she impressed everyone there and was offered a permanent job.'

'For fuck's sake.'

'Quite.'

My mind is racing. 'She was sent the video, of Miriam.'

'She was.'

My brain clicks. Anna. Nick. Fourteen. His obedient wife, whose every move he seemed to pre-empt. 'She's been spying on Miriam for years. For Nick.'

She sighs, 'Might have been, yes.'

'Nick Jackson isn't stupid, is he?'

'They never are, I suppose. The ones who get away with it.'

'Emma, you've met her, haven't you?'

'Yes, why?'

'Look through the videos in the forum. They'll be old, but see if you recognise her.'

'Blimey, Madison.'

'I can get someone from the station to do it.' Poor Emma's been looking at horrors all morning.

'No. It's fine. I've logged on to the radio station's website too, there's a picture of her on her bio. I'll get back to you.'

'Thanks.'

I drop Peter at work, they are inundated with more calls than they can handle. The world is such a shitty place that all it takes is mention of a celebrity and everyone wants in on the perceived 'action'.

I put Green Day on and hum along to 'Time of Your Life'. The irony isn't wasted as I pull up around the corner from Delia's. I take a moment, walking slowly, and I use the time to smoke a cigarette and try and steel myself for what's about to come. Those things you can't un-hear. Stay calm, the world is not evil. There is plenty of good. But as soon as I see Delia and her parents' stricken faces I get that thundering combination of anger and sadness. I focus on the rage as I sit and talk to her, her poor parents full of questions they shouldn't have to ask, that I answer carefully. The rage builds and I welcome it in, because the rage is what will bring these fuckers in.

# 61.

# Miriam Jackson

Anthony pokes his head around the door and says, 'I'm nipping out, you're in charge,' to Anna. Then he looks at me. 'Won't be long.' I look away. Big Neanderthal freak. He looks like evolution left him behind. It's an unkind thought but he deserves it. I guess he must be hired muscle. Who knew that was an actual thing.

I rub my eyes and say to Anna, 'Have you got any more headache tablets?'

She opens her handbag and produces a packet of Migraleve, popping out two yellows and handing them to me. She seems to realise the oddness of it all at exactly the same moment I do. How many times we've done this before. We've worked side by side for years. I stare at the tablets, then I look at her. She seems to be fighting tears. I don't know what to say. I just want my child back. I swallow the tablets without water. She reaches for the remote and turns on the television. I guess it saves us trying to make some semblance of conversation.

Nick's face stares back at us. I mutter, 'Turn it up.'

She does and we both sit, transfixed for different reasons. Then there is a picture of Tabs. Her last school one, she looks so sweet and so young. My heart lurches. Back to Madison and Peter. Madison says, 'We believe that as well as his long involvement in a paedophile ring, Nick Jackson was conducting an affair with an underage girl. She has supplied us with footage which leads us to believe his guilt. If you see Nick or Tabitha Jackson, do not approach them, call the number running at the bottom of the screen. Thank you.'

Oh my God. This is one of the most surreal moments I've ever experienced. I shut my eyes and massage my temples. Willing the next set of Migraleve to kick in, willing the headache to go and give me enough space to think.

I feel movement next to me; Anna, standing. She's grabbing a set of keys, and she says, 'Let's go.'

I look at her and say stupidly, 'You told the man we'd be here.'

She looks shaken, cross. She tells me, 'Plans have changed.'

I don't argue. I follow her outside. It's grey and raining. We get into her little red VW. She's looking over her shoulder as we go. I'm damp and I'm sure I'll be cold soon, but for now an excitement has kicked in, the shock has abated and the fuzzy tentacles of the migraine snap back. My head has finally stopped pounding and I'm so glad to be out of that house and doing something that I can barely think straight.

We wheel-spin out of a muddy field and head down a long drive. Anthony is coming back up it, on foot, and the look on his face would be priceless if I wasn't so bloody scared. Judging by the swerve in the car so is Anna. I mutter, 'It's okay, he can't run as fast as a car.'

She nods. Regains control. He chases behind us, she speeds up and he becomes a small dot in the background.

I ask her, 'Where are we going?'

'To get your kid.' She glances at me.

I say, 'What changed?'

She smiles but it's not a happy look. 'What Madison said, about his involvement in a ring. The affair with another girl.'

'Did you never suspect?'

305

She looks like she's on the verge of tears and she mutters, 'I thought he loved me.'

'Didn't you wonder what Ben did?'

'Why would I?' Her voice is low and full of shame. 'Miriam, I was just glad you had someone else.'

Jesus wept. I have been married to a terrible human being. Evil. I can't think of any other word. He's manipulated all of us.

I ask her, 'Are we going to Redhill?'

She shakes her head and my voice is a little hysterical whine when I say, 'But the plane, he'll be going for the plane.'

She nods. 'He moved it last week.'

'Where to?' She tells me.

'Give me your phone, Anna.'

She flings it onto my seat and I call Madison.

# 62.

# Nick Jackson

I pull up at Milburn, the estate where I was born, where I spent my early years. I didn't really want to be at Mother and Father's this early but needs bloody must. Luckily for me they're away at the moment. They've got a place in the Caribbean and they, sensibly, spend winters there. Well, why not?

It occurs to me that they may have seen the news by now. They won't be happy about this. They won't understand. No one ever does. And it's so difficult to explain, isn't it?

Society pretends to judge me for it, me and my fellows have discussed this many times. Strippers who look young can strut about in school uniforms and no one bats an eye, but for us, the men brave enough to go for what it is we actually want instead of pretending, we get reprimanded, imprisoned.

It's always been that way, men always want youth, it's a sad fact of life that females peak early, quickly. And then it's gone. Poor women, spend lifetimes wishing for equality, pretending the world is different, God knows I've cashed in on that need. Whenever I'm sent one of those empowering scripts, the ones that feed women false narratives about where they can go in the world, what they can achieve, how finding the right man means they'll be adored forever, I know they'll make a bundle. But they're not true.

I sigh and say to Tabitha, 'This should be yours one day. Shame we'll have to leave it for a bit.' She doesn't look sorry. She looks scared.

I try smiling at her, I've lost my temper with her a couple of times of late and I know she's frightened of me. I say, 'Sorry about all this.'

She doesn't say anything.

# 63.

# Miriam Jackson

I've never liked Milburn, the sprawling estate where Nick was raised and his parents still live. At least some of the time. Right now they are in the Caribbean, they have a team of gardeners and cleaners who keep everything here in order, but currently no one 'living in'. It's not a house really, it's more like a museum. Cold in temperature and cold in atmosphere. Built to make only the very few feel at home and relaxed. Most of us wander in and feel less than them, which I suppose is its intention. I wonder if that's a stupid thing to think, that a building means anything at all. It's not warm though, or comfortable. But it is impressive. Grand. Overwhelming. Like Nick.

Anna and I park up at the end of the lane and get out of the car. I say to her, 'You can go if you like.'

We've arranged to wait for Madison, off the drive. We are well hidden here, this property is surrounded by woodland, places to get lost. I'm itching to go tearing in, get my girl. But last time I disobeyed Madison's direction, I gave it all away to Ben, and look where that's led.

Anna's voice is small when she says, 'It's okay, I'll wait with you.'

I nod. I'm not going to argue. It's getting dark and I'm full of so much fear and anticipation that I'm surprised I don't faint.

Anna says, 'I knew it was wrong.'

I look at her. 'Then why did you do it?'

She shakes her head. 'Not initially. Not to start with. I was stupid and young.'

I say softly, 'You were a child, Anna.' I'm surprised to hear myself offer her anything in the way of comfort. At this moment, when all I can think about is Tabitha, I still have room for empathy.

She nods. 'I realised that. A couple of years ago. Do you re-member that teenage singer we had on the show?'

'Michaela Adams?'

She smiles. 'You remember everyone's name.'

'It's part of the job,' I say automatically, back to our old roles and routines. Mentor, mentee. Wife, mistress. No, not mistress, that's not right, and I won't think of her in those terms. Victim. But one who has made a decision today, to step out of that role. It's a wise choice. I say, 'What about her?'

'She was the same age as when . . .'

'Oh.'

'She looked so young.'

I nod. She said, 'I hadn't thought about it. But Nick and I weren't really physical very often as I got older.'

I say, 'Well, no, you wouldn't be I suppose.'

She says, 'I was kind of relieved, I never really liked . . . that side of things.' She cries then. I go and put my arms around her, imagining it is my daughter I am holding, remembering that she is someone's. Despite what she has done to me.

Even if we can never go back to the way it was, and I don't want to, I can be there for her now. And that's where we are standing as I hear a car drive up towards us, lights off. When Madison steps out I feel – for the first time in what feels like a longtime, but has somehow only been days – hope.

# 64.

# Nick Jackson

I've got the television on, just to keep an eye, though it's probably not good for Tabitha to be listening to. It can't really be helped, I need to know what's happening. I wish they'd stop scrolling my bloody picture though.

My phone pings. My private one. It's one of my fellows. They've seen the news. Brotherhood. That's what it's all about in the end. Us men banding together, it's how we change the world. And how we run it. It's a particularly fine fellow on the phone, he's helped me cover my tracks in the past. Not of the same cut as me, not by birth at least. Man's forged his own way, as some do, and he's a well-known figure now. Admirable.

Ping, another message, this time suggesting I destroy the phone. Bloody cheek, and I realise they are scared too, this little group. I start to feel that panic again. Maybe not the brotherhood I envisaged. None of them will want to be where I am today. I know I wish I wasn't.

I say to Tabitha, 'Get your stuff.'

She doesn't respond and I snap, 'Now.' There's no need for rudeness. Especially not from my own bloody child.

She nods, still looking all sad and forlorn. I say, 'Cheer up, you've got a face like a slapped arse.' She makes a semi sarcastic attempt at a smile. I decide to let it go, for the minute. I've got more pressing things to attend to. I'll need to get her in line though, that's for sure. Especially as we are going to be 'on the run' effectively. My reputation has been smashed to shreds – even if I get away with it in a court of law, which I might, prison is for the plebs after all. Not the likes of us. And it's borne out, isn't it? In history. Men like me don't get locked up. Men like Ben do though. That thought cheers me, but not much.

I wonder what he's doing to my wife. I feel a moment of pity there. She'll be missing Tabs, and actually Tabs will miss her too. I don't dislike Miriam, not really, though I'm bloody annoyed about the Ben connection. What were the chances? Really, I consider this whole unpleasant situation her fault, and if it was anyone else . . . *But* she's Tabs' mum, and she's been good at that.

Tabitha's pissing about, pulling things in and out of her bag. In the end I tear it from her hand, shove everything in, swing it over my shoulder and grab her by the arm, 'Time to go.'

I turn on the outside lights, ah, there she is, my little plane. It's not going to be a particularly comfortable ride, but it should get us to France at least.

# 65.

# Madison Attallee

It's dark. The drive is long enough to be an entire road. We kill the lights as we go, so I'm slowed, driving carefully, watching closely for movement, for anything. Peter is by my side and eventually we find the enclave that Miriam described. We pull over and I flash the lights quickly. Illuminating two women, closed in an embrace. Miriam and Anna. I step out of the car, a small torch shining a path. Peter walks beside me. I say, 'Are you okay?'

Miriam meets my eye over the girl's head and says, 'Nick is a terrible person.' I can't disagree. I don't.

I say to her, 'We're waiting for a van and a small car.' I glance at my watch. 'They should be here soon. They'll take you back and we'll take over from here.'

She shakes her head and I frown though I don't know if she can see me. This is the dark of the English countryside. That sort of pitch black is so heavy you feel like you could reach out and grab it. I say, 'You need to do what you're told.' More sharply than I mean to. We are all silenced by the sound of cars pulling in behind us, the team are here. Including armed response. Miriam told me on the phone that Milburn is full of guns. All licenced, all legal.

There is a flurry of activity and a few low-level torches

illuminate us all. We look odd in the light. Miriam is still clutching the girl who must be Anna, and isn't really a girl. I tell a female officer to get Anna in the car. Then I tell Miriam to do the same.

She takes a step nearer to me, and I can see her face now, make out her expression, strained but determined. She says, 'Madison, please.'

I sigh and go and find Peter. I tell him she wants to come, that she can stay with me behind the team and in the car. 'Tabitha might need her, she might be useful to talk the kid away if need be.'

He mutters, 'It's an insurance nightmare and it's not bloody right.'

I snap, 'I'll take the fall.'

'For God's sake, Madison.' I stand my ground. Hoping like hell that this is the right call. Something on Miriam's face tells me she needs this. And, while I'm hoping it all goes down okay, there's a strong possibility it won't, and she might need closure. To feel like she did what she could. My heart speeds up at the thought. I push it away.

Peter says, 'Time's running out, team are moving in. Vest up.'

I am strapped in and the officer hesitates when I say Miriam too. He glances at Peter and I snap, 'She's with me.'

Peter goes on with the team. I take our small car, following closely, and then we park up again, nearer, and take the rest on foot. We come up to the house. If you can call it that. I'd considered Miriam and Nick's place a mansion, and it's certainly a few million worth. But this, this is another level.

Lights suddenly come on and we all freeze, the six officers ahead, including Peter, and Miriam and me at the back. We seem to be collectively holding our breath. But no one comes.

Miriam whispers that they'll be at the back of the house and we can get in through there without triggering more lights. I nod, relay the information to Peter and we go.

# 66.

## Miriam Jackson

We all panic a little as the light comes on, but it won't be seen at the back. More light floods around from the side of the house and I tell Madison, 'That's the back lights, to the garden. That's where the plane will be. They're leaving.'

She nods and says, 'Right let's go.'

They all surge on ahead. I am kept at a slower pace at the back by a female officer, who seems nice enough. She's built like a large man, which I guess is why Madison has left her in charge of me, any thoughts of trying to outrun her are fleeting. As if to punctuate this, she rests a hand on my elbow; gentle, but one squeeze and I'd be immobile. I smile at her. She doesn't smile back. The police are all annoyed that I'm being allowed to tag along. I get the sense that some of them would prefer for Madison not to be here either. I can understand it I suppose, but I'm not going anywhere.

We are standing at the back of the house now. Hidden behind a large shrub, the officers ahead all in black. Me, trying to still my beating heart and not sweat to death. The arrested, thundering headache makes grabs near my temples.

It's freezing but the bullet-proof vest and adrenaline are keeping me from actually feeling it, though my fingers are complaining somewhere in the background. I touch them to my face and am surprised when they feel like little spindly icicles.

Madison is heading towards the Amazon officer and she leans in, whispers, 'They've opened the back door.'

Which means he's not spotted us, he doesn't know we are here. It feels like a victory, though the only real win will be when I'm holding my daughter. Darling Tabs. And then, all of a sudden, there she is.

# 67.

# Madison Attallee

When Miriam catches sight of her daughter, for a second I think instinct might take over, that she might just run and blow it for all of us. I get ready to grab her. But she doesn't. She seems to regain composure, control. I hiss at her, 'Stay.' And she nods. She learned her lesson after spilling to Ben last time.

It must be torture. I imagine if it was Molly.

I jog on silent feet up to Peter. The armed team are in place. I whisper, 'We need to move, they are heading to the plane.' And they are, in ten seconds, nine, they'll be on and harder to get. Peter gives the signal and they come to life, I hear, 'Nick Jackson, freeze.' And he looks around, panicked, surprised. He must have seen the news but still, getting caught, or stopped, is a shock for this man.

He flounders for a minute, frozen with indecision. Another officer calls out, 'Tabitha Jackson, come to me.' She makes a step to go and then her father stops her, an arm firmly around her neck and he pulls her close into his body. Using her as a shield. Worst-case scenario. Shit.

Another officer will be circling around and hoping to get a clear shot from behind, risky, and hopefully unnecessary – though we know there are guns in the house, there is nothing to say Nick's armed. We'll try to keep him talking. I step forwards, hands up and say, 'Nick, I know you don't want to hurt Tabitha.'

He smiles, but there is panic in his quick jerky movements. He looks wilder than the man who sat in my office. He knows the game is up, and yet he won't relent with ease. People like him never do.

He snarls, 'Ah, you. Still sticking your fucking nose in, eh?'

I repeat, 'I know you don't want to hurt Tabitha.'

He says, 'Then don't make me.' And the poor girl lets out a whimper.

I hear Miriam shout, 'Let her go.'

Bollocks. She should have stayed in the car, but actually Nick relaxes his grip on the girl, just for a moment. He fastens it again, but I make a gesture to Peter behind my back and hope he gets it. Bring Miriam.

He does and Miriam steps forward. Peter on one side, big Georgina on the other, keeping a restraining hand on her shoulder, but Tabitha can see her mother now. She says, 'Mummy. I'm so sorry,' and breaks down in tears.

Miriam smiles, finding that strength somewhere within her. When all is lost we can still be strong for our children. She says, 'It's okay, baby, you've nothing to be sorry for.'

Nick says, 'You should have told me about Ben, this is all your own fault, you know.'

Miriam seems to keep her cool, sensing that she is dealing with madness. Sensing that she needs to keep him talking.

She nods and says, 'You're right and I'm sorry. I didn't realise.'

He seems to relax a little, Tabitha takes a step forward. He still has her upper body but his arm is no longer clenching. He sighs, 'We had a fine system, Miriam, and you broke it.'

She nods though she must feel more sickened by this man's arrogance than I do. Which is saying something. She says, 'You're quite right, and I know you love Tabitha.'

He says, 'I do love her. I do love you, Tabs, you know that, don't you?' She is squirming in his grip and he lets go, just for a second, probably to look her in the eye. She isn't stupid, she takes the chance and runs. Nick waits one second, two, our officers head towards him and he makes his own dash. I almost laugh. Because he's surrounded and there's no way out. As he is brought down by two sergeants I feel a surge of satisfaction, and when I turn around and see Miriam holding her child, stroking her hair, the darkness lifts.

# 68.

# Miriam Jackson

I held my daughter to me that awful evening, when she was almost gone. I held her face against my chest. She's been through things she never should have. And she is the daughter of a monster, just as I was his wife. We must both make our peace with this as best we can. And I have to say, she's doing remarkably well. My girl. My clever, resilient, strong little girl. Who I love so much it shocks me each time I think how close I came to losing her.

My mother has come to stay at mine. I have looked at her through new eyes, as a woman who finally understands her fears for me as a girl. I don't resent now that I made choices partly for her. I'm glad I did. I wish I'd considered her sooner, looked at her not as someone to pity, but as someone who stayed strong and kept going even when she didn't feel like it.

She's grown into someone I don't really remember, she's quick to joke and makes Tabitha giggle madly, they both like the reality TV shows that seem to be on endlessly. I've kept her at arm's length for so long it turns out I don't really know her at all. I've always been so hesitant to tell her my troubles, scared that she might shatter under their weight, or say the wrong thing. Now I know that even if she does, it doesn't matter. She's my mum. She's not going to get it right all the time, just as I don't. Lately she's started telling me things too, that my dad was controlling, that she didn't see it but that by the time he left she was so convinced she wouldn't be able to manage without him it became a self-fulfilling prophecy. It's good to talk, to try and understand. Life, it turns out, is for living, warts and all. Not something to hide from behind a smile.

We seem to be working as a funny little threesome. There is healing in it for us all. My mother has just taken retirement. I have stopped working, and started to pick up some freelance work that I can do from home, more so I don't get bored than anything. I need to be here for Tabitha, and since Nick's incarceration it turns out the assets are mine. I'm the kind of rich that means my family won't have to work for generations to come, unless they choose to.

Tabitha comes down the stairs. She is in black trousers and a white button-down shirt. So are me and Mum. The solicitor suggested this would be the best way to dress. Simple, uncomplicated. All that would matter then would be the words. I smile at her and ask, 'Are you okay?'

She nods. I add, 'It's all right not to be.' And exchange a look with Mum. We have both been worried about how well Tabitha has been coping, which sound ridiculous.

She rolls her eyes and smiles. 'I'm more worried about you guys.' We get in the car and drive. My heart hammering the whole time and my sense of outrage growing again. That she has to go through even more than she has already. We step out the car at the courthouse and my brave daughter takes my hand, looks me in the eye and tells me, 'This is the right thing to do.' And I know in that moment that she is going to be okay. And that I will be too.

# 69.

# Madison Attallee

I overheard them all debating whether or not to buy champagne and in the end, it is me who produces a bottle now. Peter and Claudia look at me wide eyed as I squeeze out the cork and watch it pop and fizz. Emma steps in smoothly, taking it and filling the glasses I've laid out on a tray. She wanders around the office handing them out, with an orange juice for me and Tabitha. Once Peter seems to realise I'm okay he relaxes, and even manages to keep his gob shut as I make a speech thanking everyone and pointing to the kitchen where I have laid out bottles of red and white wine. Claudia circulates with nibbles. Nibbles of course is a word that does not do justice to the tasty and ridiculous morsels she has conjured up and someone says she should be a chef. She laughs graciously and says she has a job she loves, and I smile to myself.

Peter slides a hand over my lower back, nods and goes to speak to the members of his team who were such an integral part of this investigation. It's still making front-page news some six months later and lots and lots of things are still being investigated. It will take years to catch everyone involved, if they are ever caught at all.

Ben, Nick and the Walkers at least will be locked up for an awfully long time to come. We couldn't get them on murder, we couldn't find Cyn, or even work out who she was. It's heart-breaking to think that a girl that age can just disappear and not be missed. The reams and reams of lists that we got through from social services speak of the volume of girls just like her; lost, unloved, unsafe.

Prey to men like Ben and the predators who will pay for their services. We have incriminating footage of lots of people, high-profile 'members' of All That Glitters, who have been taken down and will never work again. Plenty of Nick's colleagues have come forward to say they had suspicions, there seemed to be many open rumours. People sort of knew but didn't have any specifics. As a result, the secret remained safe. Power. That is what people like Nick have. You might suspect something, but if you've no proof and the person you suspect can make or break your career, what are you going to do? Who can you tell?

There were other Annas, it turned out. There was even a pay-out to a set of parents who found out, Nick persuaded them it would never be heard in court. They were baffled, ashamed, unsure who to turn to. His word against their daughter's, a girl who, as Nick pointed out, had a reputation for partying. They have come forward, added their voices, their evidence. There are cases running in America, people at Nick's studio are being questioned. The victims have finally been heard, hopefully that will mean something. Hopefully the culture will start to change.

I see Miriam, chatting animatedly to Donna Williams who is standing next to a tall skinny man, laughing and looking a lot better than the last time I saw her. When I go over she says, 'This is Eric. He wanted to meet you.' She's blushing as we shake hands. He thanks me for looking into things and there are tears in his eyes as he says it. Nothing's really changed for them. We haven't been able to bring any charges on Ruby's behalf but Ben and the Walkers being locked up seems to have brought

Donna some peace. Judging by the way Eric looks at her, he's been missing her, and I hope she can let some happiness in. Even without Ruby around.

Donna and Miriam have become unlikely friends and I know that Miriam has made a huge contribution to Youfscape. Donna has been taken on there, and now works with the parents of runaways.

Darren is here, I see him across the room, he raises a glass to me and I raise one back. I'm glad to see him mingling with everyone. Michelle Roberts gave evidence. It was heart-breaking and brave. She has put on weight, now raises her head when she speaks and is, I think, on her way to a better life. She and her mum are staying up north. They didn't want to come today, which is fair enough. I received a letter from Mrs Roberts that had me in tears. Thanking me. Though I wish I could have done more it's not a bad result.

Tabitha has given evidence and so has Delia Munroe. The girls have spoken and made their peace with each other, though I doubt their friendship will ever be rekindled. Delia is getting some help, the family didn't want to come today, but they sent a thank you card to the office. They needn't have, I just want Delia to recover, move on and keep going. Which is what Tabitha is doing. She was astounding in court. Clear, confident, and articulate and I watch her now, Brett standing a foot or so behind her, and feel in awe of a girl who's been through so much and come so far in such a short space of time. Miriam meets my eye over her head and we smile.

It's a day full of good feelings but for me the party goes on for a few hours more than I would have liked and I sneak outside for a cigarette. Claudia and Emma appear seconds later. Claudia hands me a coat, telling me, 'You'll catch your death.' I roll my eyes but smile. She comes and puts an arm over my shoulders and I allow it, reneging momentarily on my no-touching rule.

Emma comes up next to me on my other side and squeezes my hand. I'm still clutching at my orange juice and Claudia raises her glass and says, 'To MA Investigations.'

Emma and I clink back, and I feel a tingle of excitement. I have a feeling that the best is yet to come.

# Acknowledgements

Thank you to everyone at The Blair Partnership, especially my wonderful agent Jo Hayes, and also to the brilliant Amy Fitzgerald.

Thank you to my editor Francesca Pathak and assistant editor Bethan Jones. This book was very difficult to get just right, and your tireless editorial attention and patience has been hugely appreciated. We got there in the end!

Thank you to everyone at Orion for all of the work it takes to produce an actual book! To Jo Gledhill, who copy-edited the book and left delightful notes in the manuscript. It made that stage a lot less painful!

Thank you to Mark Piper for helping with my police related queries. I hope I've got things right.

Writing is a funny business and I'm immensely pleased to have made some incredibly supportive friends within the industry. Thanks to all of the lovely writers/publishing peeps who've been on the other end of the phone or at a literary bar or two this year, especially Elle Croft, Victoria Selman, Lara Dearman, Robert Scragg, Adam Howe, Clare Empson, Phoebe Morgan, Keshini Naidoo, Kerry Fisher, and Margaret Kirk.

To my non-writer friends who have listened to me blether on about little other than books for ages and who always pretend to be just as fascinated by plot holes and narrative structure as I am. Rachel S., Rachel E., and Rachel C., Kay, Zoe, Gemma, Gillian, Graham, Tracy, Edel, Claire, my baby girl Madison, and Karen. Karen thanks also for all of your sought after and very kind advice. Thanks to all friends of Bill W.; as ever, I'm very happy to be trudging with you.

Thanks to my sons Elliot and Eddie for not moaning too much about rushed meals and my forgetfulness when I get very busy.

Thank you to all of the readers, of course.

And last, but never ever least, my husband and best friend Andrew.

**Don't miss P.I. Madison Attallee's**
**first heart-racing instalment . . .**

NIKI MACKAY

'A cracking thriller'
**CJ Tudor**, author
of *The Chalk Man*

I,
Witness

She isn't a murderer.
So why did she plead guilty?

### They say I'm a murderer.

Six years ago, Kate Reynolds was found holding the body of her best
friend; covered in blood, and clutching the knife that killed her.

### I plead guilty.

Kate has been in prison ever since, but now her sentence is up. She is
being released.

### But the truth is, I didn't do it.

There's only one person who can help: Private Investigator Madison
Attallee, the first officer on the scene all those years ago.
But there's someone out there who doesn't want Kate digging up the
past. Someone who is willing to keep the truth buried at any cost.

'Totally engaging, fast-paced and edgy ... completely captivating. I,
Witness kept me guessing till the very end.'
**Elle Croft, author of *The Guilty Wife***